Angel's Kiss

The Phantom Saga

Jessica Mason

Published by Murmuration Books, 2023.

ANGEL'S KISS

First edition. July 11, 2023.

Copyright © 2023 Jessica Mason.

ISBN: 979-8988421108

Written by Jessica Mason.

Table of Contents

This book is dedicated to the thousands of actors, musicians, creators, crew members and artists who have brought the story of the Phantom of the Opera to life for over a century. Especially the final Broadway cast and crew who took *Phantom* into its final bow at the Majestic îheater in New York. Your art changed my life.

The Music of the Night will never be over, as long as it sings in our souls.

Thank you for everything.

Foreword

B ook Two, ladies and gentlemen, of our story told in pieces. Some of you may already recall the strange affair of *The Phantom of the Opera* and its mysteries which have never been fully explained. My work here is not to undo that legend, nor to restore it, but to fit that old frame with a different tale to bring our ghost's story into a new light. As once again we return to the Opera Ghost and his angel, I ask your indulgence for that which is new and all that has changed.

After all, how else can we enjoy a story that has haunted us for so long, unless we find a new way to tell it? This is the very story that has been inside my mind like a persistent ghost for many years, haunting me with hints of what romance we could find if it were to be reassembled.

Perhaps now we can revive the ghosts of so many years ago with a little...illumination.

Let us begin.

Prelude

J oseph refused to use a stick to walk. Those were for cripples and old men. He was still strong and if every other step had to hurt from heel to balls so he could walk like a real man, so be it. The trip to the tavern on the *Boulevard des Italiens* was just long enough to make him rethink his pride, but soon enough, he was at a table in the back with a sour bottle of wine and an even more disagreeable companion. Franc passed Joseph some of his cheap tobacco and Joseph rolled a cigarette as he glowered around the smoky room.

Joseph and Franc did not speak. The barge of a man never had much to say. Stagehands from below were like that: brutes with no skill beyond turning a crank and pushing a table to the right place. They didn't have to be clever like Joseph's men in the flies. Their job required real skill, balance, and nerve. Up there, you had to move quick and sure, or else you'd end up another story. It was a wonder Joseph got away with only a limp after becoming such a cautionary tale himself. Of course, he hadn't fallen.

"He's here," Franc grunted at last, flicking his eyes to the door of the tavern. LeDoux looked like a poodle tiptoeing through a den of tigers as he made his way to Franc and Joseph. He jumped out of the way of one customer, while trying with all his might not to touch a single surface. Joseph had always wanted to see what would happen if he threw Carlotta's pet in the sewer. Or the Seine.

"You're late," Joseph said as LeDoux reached them. "That means you pay for this round and the next."

"Is that really necessary?" LeDoux asked back, puffing up.

2

"You did the summoning, you'll do the paying," Joseph replied, sneering. Franc grunted in agreement.

"Fine. *After* she speaks with you," LeDoux huffed.

"Where is her ladyship?" Joseph asked. Usually, Joseph never dealt with the bitch herself. She didn't like to get her hands dirty. Maybe something had changed in the months since his accident. The Opera had probably gone straight to hell without him.

"She's outside," LeDoux answered. "She'll speak to you from her carriage."

"She too good to come in?" Franc demanded.

"She is, actually," LeDoux sneered. "And the smoke irritates her instrument."

"I'll give her something to irritate that fancy throat of hers," Joseph said with a sneer and finished the dregs of the wine as Franc chuckled. The men snuffed their cigarettes on the table and followed LeDoux out and around the back to an alley where Carlotta Zambelli's carriage waited, snow gathering on the roof.

"It's fucking freezing. Let's get this over with," Joseph snapped as the diva opened the window and surveyed them. She was wrapped in fur like the empress she fancied herself. Even her hat looked like a weasel taking a nap on her head.

"So, they took you back?" Carlotta asked, rolling her eyes.

"The new management was happy to have me," Joseph replied. "Or so I'm told. Things got messy with the old men leaving so sudden and putting this lot in charge."

"They're idiots," Carlotta snapped. "And I'm going to bring them to heel."

"So you want my eyes?" Most people didn't realize how much you could see from the flies if you were looking. He'd used his position to great advantage for Carlotta in the past.

"We'll pay the same as before, but there will be extra if you can bring me something I can use on them."

"You didn't need to haul us out in the snow to ask that," Joseph said, narrowing his eyes at the woman. She looked even angrier than usual. "This about your new rival?"

"I thought you'd be interested in her, my friend," Carlotta smirked and nodded to LeDoux. "My dear secretary keeps careful track of all the rumors and stories throughout the Opera, even those concerning the so-called ghost."

Joseph gritted his teeth and flexed his hands. "That thing is a demon. Not a ghost. A monster."

"Of course, I almost forgot," Carlotta sneered. "A *monster* threw you off the catwalk. You didn't fall like an idiot."

Joseph drew back his fist, ready to throttle the smug expression off the bitch's face. He'd never forget that night, no matter how drunk he was. He still saw that horrible skull in his dreams. He woke more nights than not in a cold sweat, with the feel of skeleton hands on his throat.

"He tried to fucking kill me!" Buquet spat. "Because I saw the truth!"

"Yes, yes. LeDoux, read me that bit. About poor Joseph's accident," Carlotta sighed.

LeDoux flipped through his notebook. "Ah, yes. Before the accident you claimed a witch called the ghost down on you earlier in the day. A costumer, perhaps?"

"She's friends with that mulatto bitch. Don't know her name."

"Her name is Christine Daaé," Carlotta said. Franc made an expression that passed for interested. "And that same ghost she summoned to torment you has been very generous to her during your absence. She's a singer now. Fancies herself my equal, if you can imagine. She and her ghost poisoned me to keep me from the New Year's gala and then tricked me into letting her take my place in the last *Faust*."

"So, the witch is your rival?" Joseph asked with a dark laugh. "You want to hurt her? And the ghost?" He could almost taste his revenge now.

"He won't like that," Franc muttered.

"Exactly." Carlotta gave a triumphant, smug smile. "We're not just going to hurt them, though I do intend to put that girl through a lot of pain. We are going to wipe this girl and her Phantom from the face of the earth."

"Where do we start?" Joseph asked with a grin.

1. Seen

For the third time in as many days, Christine Daaé found herself following a ghost through the underground reaches of the Paris Opera. And for the hundredth time, she pondered how her unremarkable life had come to be filled with ghosts and fallen angels. The Phantom who held her hand looked exactly as the legends described him: tall, clad in black, his sweeping cape engulfing him in shadow. The only thing to distinguish him from the dark itself was the meager light of his lantern and the answering glow of his white mask. Christine was afraid, of course. Anyone who knew the stories of the Opera Ghost would be. But she felt many other things alongside her fear: Curiosity. Pity. Wonder. And, most strangely, familiarity.

The first time she'd entered the Opera Garnier had been confusing, wondrous, and frightening too.

Three months ago, Christine had arrived in Paris with nothing to her name after her dismissal from the Conservatory of Music in Rouen. She'd had no hope, save for an old, foolish promise. Though her father had not kept up his end of the bargain by sending her an angel to guide her after his death, Christine had been determined to find her way onto the stage of the Opera they had dreamed of together. She had found herself lost and soaking in the stables of said Opera, and a decidedly un-angelic being had taken interest in her instead.

Christine still didn't know why the Phantom who now led with a gloved hand had helped her then. Pity, perhaps? Whatever the reason, he had steered her into a job in the costume workshop and allowed her shelter in his theater. She had repaid that charity by loudly and resolutely not believing the Opera's ghost stories when she heard them. How foolish she must have seemed to him: a vagrant girl with no faith challenging the Opera Ghost aloud to make her believe. She'd been looking for something, anything, to believe in again after years without the angel her father promised. Either through pride, charity, or both, the Phantom had obliged her.

A real ghost had appeared to Christine – or so she had believed – emerging out of nowhere to resurrect her neglected soul. Later that same night, she had snuck to the stage to keep her promise to her father. She had sung and prayed and again, the Ghost had answered. It was on that stage, when she had first heard his inhumanly beautiful voice, that the Phantom had become her Angel of Music.

Now, in the dark far below that stage, it stung for Christine to remember how entirely and instantly she had believed. The drip of water and the scurrying of vermin pierced the blackness around them. The only other noise was the echo of Christine's steps in the shadows, for her guide made no sound as he moved. It was easy, even now, to forget that he was human.

Had she been a fool to believe him? He had been a voice without a body. He'd performed miracles. For months, her supposed Angel had taught her with unparalleled skill, lifting her voice to heights she had never dreamed. And in return, she had given him everything.

Christine's cheeks heated at the memories, even more so when her guide's long, skeletal fingers tightened around hers as they turned a corner. She had loved her strange angel and begged for his touch like a wanton trollop, thinking it was heavenly. Again he had answered her prayers and blessed her with pleasure beyond her imagination. She had laid herself out for him like a whore, and he had not stopped her until it was too late. Until he stole everything from her.

The first time he had led her to his domain had been the night before last, after he had cleared Christine's path to a glorious debut as Marguerite in *Faust*. She had been so overwhelmed and desperate for him that she had not questioned it when he had somehow led her out of her dressing room, engulfed her in the magic of his song, and ferried her to his strange home. Then she had slept in his arms after he had...

No. She refused to think about *that* right now, with her hand in his. Nor was she eager to remember the following morning, when she had learned her angel was just a man. When she had torn off his mask to reveal the horror of his face. The visage of living death.

Her guide looked over his shoulder at her for the first time and Christine caught her breath. Even shadowed by the wide brim of his hat, his eyes appeared to shine, glinting like gold stars in the dark. How could a mere man have eyes like that or the voice of an angel? Had it been some horrible heavenly trade, recompense from fate for giving him the face of a monster?

He turned away from her, his focus returning to their path. But his mask remained in Christine's mind, like the bright disk of the sun seared into her eyes. She remembered him in the moments after she had torn it away, after his fury and her screams had faded. He had wept and sung to himself like a frightened child. He had agreed to let her go but begged her to come back. So he would not be left alone in the dark again.

It had been Raoul de Chagny of all people that had (quite unintentionally) convinced Christine to return. Her first love had found her at the perfect time to remind her that perhaps there was a reason her angel had come in such a form. This bizarre man's fate was bound to hers now. If she wished to keep singing, she had no choice but to return. And so, here she was, following a shade into the underworld, choosing the foolish hope that the man who had used and condemned her might somehow be her salvation too.

"Are we going back to your...home?" Christine asked, shivering. She still wore the long cloak he had placed around her shoulders the day before, but the cold of the cellars was already deep in her bones.

"Yes. Don't worry, we're not far." His words were careful and clipped but it was still the perfect voice of her Angel of Music – dark and soft, but clear and piercing, like silver upon velvet.

"So you do *live* down there?" Christine's voice was unsteady as she considered what kind of person would choose such a home. Her guide nodded without breaking his stride. "But why here?"

"Well, you know how difficult it is to find a decent flat."

Christine nearly tripped. His flippancy annoyed her enough for curiosity to break through. "I still don't understand *where* it is. There was water and a boat. I don't understand how that could be."

"Haven't you heard the legends of the Opera Ghost lurking beyond the lake?" he asked back as they descended yet another flight of stone steps. "Or better yet, rising from the black waters at night to wander the empty halls. I always liked that one."

If he was trying to comfort her, it wasn't working. "I thought that was just another story."

"Every legend grows from a seed of truth," the Ghost replied with a shrug. "My Lake Avernus is very real." He raised his lantern higher, revealing that they had come to a large, open space.

There it was. A lake in the foundations of an opera house. At first, it looked like a cavern, but no, the wide columns were man-made. They simply appeared exceptionally long because they were reflected in the surface of murky water. Faint light came through a single grate above, but it was barely brighter than an oil lamp and served to give the whole space an eerie glow. The water had a smell, like a stagnant stream under a bridge, but it wasn't awful.

"How – why is this here?"

"When Garnier began construction twenty years ago, the builders came across an underground tributary of the Seine right where the foundations were to be laid." His was the voice of a teacher again, formal but familiar. It was strangely reassuring in such a grim, dank place. "Instead of moving the site, they drained and dried out the earth. It took months. But they couldn't change the river's path. So, to keep the water in check, Garnier installed a lake within the foundations. They couldn't just dig a hole, so they made a huge casing to hold the water, like a great bowl. And to make sure nothing would leak they built another one around it. There is a great deal of space between the two casings."

"And that's where you live? In the space between?"

"I never thought of it so poetically," he replied quietly. "I like that better than a tomb beneath the streets. Come," he ordered and turned left before his words could frighten her more. They made their way along the edge of the water, the same way they had followed when he let her go the morning before. He had released her on the condition that she not reveal him, and only hours ago, she had been given the opportunity to do so.

"So no one has ever found you?" Christine asked carefully.

He looked back over his shoulder at her, golden eyes sparking with danger. "Not yet."

"But someone is looking." His shoulders tensed and his grip on her hand tightened. She pushed on, trembling again, but not from the cold. "Your Persian friend."

"So the Daroga did find you."

"That's not the name he gave me." The foreigner who had accosted Christine this morning had called himself Shaya Motlagh and been convinced that the man whose home Christine was about to enter was a monster.

"*Daroga* was his title in Persia when I knew him there. I assume he asked you for information about me." Nothing of the menace in the Phantom's aura abated, even with his aloof tone.

"I didn't tell him anything," Christine blurted out, surprising herself. She had been sure of one thing in the past few days: that whatever resentment or fear she harbored for the man who had been her angel, she would not condemn him to the clutches of the world above.

"Thank you," the Ghost said softly as he stopped and released her hand. Without him holding her, she felt unsteady on the platform; like the dark was alive around her, ready to swallow her whole. "Did he say anything else of particular interest?"

Christine stared up at him and swallowed. He was so tall and so solid, but she could not feel a single hint of warmth from him, as if he truly was death made flesh. "He told me you were dangerous," she confessed tightly. "Are you?"

"Yes," he replied without hesitation. "Are you afraid of me?"

"Yes," Christine answered just as quickly, her breath sticking in her throat as he stared down at her with his shining eyes that were so sad, even in the dark. She waited for him to reply, for some sort of consolation that she was safe in his company. But none came and he turned away from her.

"Look at the water," he ordered instead, and Christine obeyed so swiftly it made her guts churn. Was it habit, to follow a command from that voice without thinking?

"Why do I need to look away?" she forced herself to demand, turning back around to look at the wall. Only there was not simply a wall there. The Ghost stood next to a door that had appeared from nowhere. He swept his arm out and gave a bow, allowing Christine to enter the strangest flat she had ever seen.

"Welcome back," her host said as Christine tentatively stepped across the threshold. The warmth that enveloped her was a head-spinning contrast to the cold of the lake.

"Dear God, I thought I dreamed it," Christine gasped as her eyes fixed on the massive pipe organ that occupied almost the entire wall opposite what could be termed the front door. But there it was, brass pipes shining in the candlelight, bounded on both sides by packed shelves. In the middle of the room, set off to the right, was a fine piano. On the walls, shelves, and tucked into corners were still more instruments – viols, winds, a guitar, a harp. There were even some she did not recognize. It was somehow the exact home she would have imagined for an angel of music.

Set in the wall to the left of the entrance was the fireplace, flanked by more crowded shelves of books. In front of the merrily burning fire were two imposing chairs and a worn couch, none of which matched in style or color. The walls (at least what Christine could see of them past the pictures and papers hung on them) were painted a deep yellow, much – or perhaps exactly – like the walls of the Opera above.

The floor was covered in rugs which, in combination with the fire and well-used furniture, made the strange parlor warm and inviting. Christine looked up to the ceiling, which was oddly dark. Christine gasped when she saw that what she had mistaken for soot on the ceiling was blue-black paint, and upon it, rendered in shining gold and silver, a perfect night sky.

"How?" she breathed in unthinking awe. "How did you do all this?"

"Very slowly."

Christine whipped about to face her host, her heart jumping into her throat when she saw that he had removed his hat, gloves, and cape. It transformed him from the menacing silhouette of the Phantom into *Erik*.

She had seen the Ghost, and her angel was a familiar dream. But Erik? He was a stranger. He was exceptionally tall and thin, but his impeccably tailored jacket fit so that she could tell he was muscular as well, in a wiry, angular way. His limp black hair fell well past his jaw, but at least the mop was better combed than when she had seen it last. His thin hands hung at his side, flexing his long fingers absently. Those hands were almost as pale as his mask.

His mask itself was smooth, with sculpted brows and a narrow nose to conceal that he had no actual nose beneath it. And it was delicately painted. Had he done it himself, just as he had made this strange home? Erik stared back at her as blatantly as she stared at him and it made her remember the first time she had looked into his eyes in this home, drunk on lust and delusion and what he had done then. Christine shuddered.

"What happens now?" Her voice was small as she remembered the pleasure and pain the man before her had caused her. "You asked me to come back and I'm here. But what do you want from me?"

That was the question she could not avoid. She had come to find an angel, but what sort of deal with the devil would that require? Erik looked at her forlornly.

"I have been alone for a very long time," he began and familiar pity shivered through Christine's heart. "And so have you. It is my hope that we can remedy that together. Your company and presence here is all I ask."

After all she and her angel had shared, she found that hard to believe. Still, Christine swallowed her fear and met Erik's plaintive gaze. "How long do you wish for my company?"

He turned away from her, shoulders tense. "You will stay with me for five nights, so that you can know me," he said, formal and stiff. "You will be free to go to rehearsals, of course, but you will return here. And after those nights have passed, you may go wherever you wish. But perhaps by then, you will want to..." His voice faded as he glanced at her.

"Where – where will I sleep?" she asked, her heart thundering at the idea of returning to his bed.

She could not forget what had passed between them only two nights before. He had bound her wrists and blindfolded her, and she knew now it had been so that he could keep his secret. In the dark, he had ravished her with his mouth and hands and she had never experienced such ecstasy. Would he do the same again or use her for his pleasure? If she resisted, would he force her? How had she come here, knowing this might be the price to continue her career?

"You need not fear for your virtue," Erik said, bitter and dark, turning away from her once again with forlorn eyes. "Or worry yourself about my feelings for you. I intend to host you as a gentleman, as your teacher, and, perhaps eventually, your friend."

"Friend?"

"Let me show you to your room," Erik muttered.

"To my – *what*?" In a few long strides, Erik was at a door to the left of the fireplace which he opened to let Christine see inside. Hesitant and wary, Christine stepped inside.

At first, she didn't understand what she saw. It was a fine bedroom, but it was also so undoubtedly *her* bedroom. For months, she had slept in the Opera on a borrowed prop bed beneath a bower of silk flowers, where she had nested and gathered trinkets like a magpie. And now, she was staring at her bed and bower, in Erik's house. There were her brush and baubles; her shawl draped over a chair. There was the clock he had supplied her, and her books arranged carefully on the nightstand. He had even placed a vase she recognized from her dressing room on the mirrorless vanity and supplied it with a few violets.

But it was also like the other room, with inviting but old and mismatched furniture, mostly in the Louis-Philippe style. The floor was piled with soft carpets and the walls were crowded with exquisite paintings. A door to the left of the bed caught her attention and she rushed to it. Her jaw went slack when she saw the comfortable bath chamber, complete with a beautiful copper tub. She turned to Erik in awe.

"The rooms were here before. I just made them yours," he explained with an aloof shrug as he remained at the door. Once again, Christine could do nothing but stare.

Months ago he had revealed himself to her in a darkened hall, and it had been the sadness in his eyes that had made her pity the Opera Ghost. Now those same lonely eyes watched her as silence rose between them like the tide. He was even more of a mystery now than he had been then and it terrified and fascinated Christine.

"How did you find this place—"

"I will leave you to make yourself comfortable," Erik cut off her question, stiff and formal, and retreated without a sound. As he closed the door, Christine suddenly found herself alone in a room beyond all her dreams within the home of a man so many knew to be a living nightmare. She didn't want to make herself comfortable, she wanted the answers he had promised her, but she stood frozen on the spot.

This wasn't right. She was in a windowless room with a dangerous man outside her door, a hideous creature that pretended to be a ghost and yet still wanted to be her teacher and angel despite all his monstrousness. Why? What did he actually want from her? Why had he done this to her in the first place? It was anger that propelled her from her room and back into Erik's parlor with demands for answers ready on her lips. But she found the room empty.

"Erik?" she asked the silent walls, her terror rising until she saw a note on the piano, written in red ink with an angular hand.

I have errands to attend and will be back soon. You have nothing to fear in my home.

Christine's heart fell again, though she knew she should feel relieved. He was gone and she was free for a while. If she wanted, she was sure she could leave and find her way back to the land of the living. Couldn't she? She had come here of her own free will and had agreed to stay. Though, now that she considered it, hadn't she simply been told to stay? And for five days at that.

She pulled her cloak closer around her shoulders as she shivered. If she had come here willingly and had nothing to fear from Erik as he said, then why did she feel like a prisoner?

Shaya Motlagh let out a sigh that turned to a cloud of steam in the frozen night as he trudged down the *Rue de Rivoli*. The Tuileries "gardens" were even less like a garden than usual this time of year: a barren landscape of leafless trees and pale stone. A desert of a different kind in the land of his exile. At home, it would not even be dark yet. At home, he would not have missed the sunset prayer. Even in the depths of winter, Tehran would be hot and crowded and alive, redolent with the scents of cooking meat and sweat, the air full of the shouting of merchants, the whispers of women, and the distant call to prayer. Thinking of home made him remember how and why he could never return. The anger warmed him more than a fire.

"Spare a sou, good sir?" a brittle voice asked from a dark doorway along his route. Shaya did not hesitate to delve into his pockets, pulling out a few small coins that were so chilled from the January air that he could feel the cold of them through his gloves.

The beggar, an old woman wrapped in rags, took the alms with a nod of blessing. "Thank you, sir. God bless you."

"*God is great*," he whispered in his own tongue beneath his breath, so she would not know it had been a Muslim who had given her alms, obeying a prophet she did not know. This cursed country was full of men and women like her, lost souls doing all they could, knowing no better. Shaya wondered, as he pulled his coat tighter for the final push home, if Christine Daaé knew better.

He had been shocked to see the girl alive and in one piece after Erik had stolen her away right out of her dressing room. And yet, somehow, he had not been surprised at all that she refused to reveal the monster's secrets. He was far too familiar with Erik's ability to manipulate the fear and suspicion of others or the strange control the "Ghost" had over the Opera. Therefore if the girl was protecting Erik out of fear, that made sense. She had to be an innocent in all this.

Shaya came at last to the door of his flat, which opened before he could even fumble for the key.

"It's late, sir, I was beginning to worry," Darius chided before Shaya had even stepped through the threshold.

"You know the rules, you have to wait three days before going to the police if I don't come home," Shaya replied as his servant took his coat and stood aside to allow Shaya entry into the humble parlor of the flat they shared. Thank Allah, Darius had stoked the fire.

"I must say, as always, that I disagree with that rule," Darius muttered as Shaya sank into a chair and took the cup of tea that was ready for him.

"Your concerns are, as always, noted, but irrelevant," Shaya replied. "There are innocent people out there that need protection."

"What if they're not innocent?" Darius asked back. He did not need to speak Christine's name.

"The girl will require more convincing of the danger she is in, that is all." Shaya said it as much for himself as for Darius. Perhaps if he could explain better who Erik was – what he had done, how much he had destroyed, what the monster looked like, for heaven's sake – she would see the light. The girl could not possibly have seen Erik. If she had, she would not have protected him. "I will try again. Perhaps tomorrow."

"You think the creature will allow that, if he is as interested in her as you suspect?"

"If he has his sights on corrupting her, then may Allah protect us all," Shaya whispered.

Erik knew the path up from the Opera cellars into the world above by heart, which was a blessing today because he could not have thought of anything but Christine if he tried. He had no lantern now, so he merely saw the shadows with his waking eyes. But in his mind, he saw only her. He saw her expression of awe as she entered his home, he saw her curiosity when he had revealed the secret of the lake, but above all, he saw her fear. He saw the way she had shivered and recoiled from him, the terror in her eyes as she had looked at him and remembered what was beyond his mask.

And so he had run. He had fled his own home and the relentless pressure of Christine's gaze. Back into the cold and the black where a creature such as he belonged, hiding his evil away from the searing light of her goodness. He found himself too soon above ground in the gaslit halls. Even that light stung his eyes after so long in the dark.

He had been such a fool to think she would return to him with anything but horror in her heart. He was a monster, and she was right to fear him, but there had to be some way to earn back her trust. To make her look at him with a fraction of the adoration she had given to her angel. He just had no idea how to accomplish such a thing. Frightening people was what came naturally to him. He didn't know how to comfort someone. Not anymore.

The Opera kitchens were small, compared to the huge building they served. It was a haphazardly added place, adjacent to the grand salons, built when the management had realized that the well-heeled patrons expected a few canapes and pastries between acts as they sipped champagne. Erik usually found the food left there to be stale and uninspiring, not that he minded. But he needed something fresh to feed her, didn't he? He normally waited until much later at night to visit, but it was past dark and a Sunday; surely no one would be there at this hour.

"Who's that? What are you doing here!" A male voice demanded from the hall before Erik could even enter the kitchen proper. Erik sighed and turned to the fireman that had spoken. Of all the Opera employees, it was always these steadfast fools sent to patrol the grand Palais that gave him the most trouble. It was not that he begrudged them their important task of keeping the building from burning down like the old opera on the *Rue Le Peltier* (and a hundred other operas and theaters before it), but he did wish they wouldn't get in his way so often.

"Walk away, young man, I don't wish to do harm tonight," Erik said, raising himself to his full height and staring down the quaking youth. He was ashen with fear, having recognized that he had accosted none other than the Phantom. Would he run or would he be foolish enough to try bravery?

"Get back," the man – a boy, in truth – stammered as he fumbled at his collar to pull out a silver crucifix. Erik rolled his eyes as the idiot began to mutter a prayer. "*Yea, though I walk through the valley of the shadow of death, I will fear no evil: for thou art with me."*

"No one is with you," Erik sighed and sprang on his prey, grabbing the boy by the lapels. In a heartbeat, the poor wretch found himself flung across the hall, crashing into a marble column. The boy gave a groan and shriek, not even bothering to look back as he scrambled up and fled. How unsatisfying.

Erik took his time, waiting to be sure no one else was close before finally stealing into the kitchen to collect his supplies. He was equally careful in his return journey, his pace slowing the closer he came to the lake. How could he face her again? How could he bare himself before her eyes when he had just proven what a despicable creature he was? He could stop it all now, but the thought of letting her go was even worse.

He poled the boat over the glassy waters of the lake, heart heavy and tight with guilt and dread. It was so much easier to love her when he could hide and forget himself. Was there nothing he could conceal himself with now?

He lingered outside his hidden door, leaning against the wall that now separated him from Christine and tried to find some strength or composure. He had begged for this; to simply be close to her, to have the chance to be known. He could not squander it.

He had not expected Christine to be in the parlor when he entered. The strangeness of another person waiting for him in his home was immediately replaced with concern when she spun from where she stood by the organ and looked at him with horror in her face.

"Where were you?" she demanded before Erik had even closed the door.

"As I wrote—"

"'Errands' means nothing," Christine snapped. "You were gone for an hour. I was alone here for *an hour.*"

"I'm sorry," he replied as he doffed his hat and cloak. "I thought you'd want supper." He indicated the pack of food he held.

"I'm not hungry." Christine's face was as cold as her words. "Never leave me here alone again."

Erik turned away from her wrath, skin crawling. "It will not happen again," he muttered. Even without looking, he could still feel her staring. "If you are not hungry, I will not trouble you," he said and made to retreat to his room.

"Do you not want me here?"

He spun at the question and the tone of offense in Christine's voice. "What?"

"You won't talk to me or answer my questions. You claim you want me to know you but how am I to do that if you won't even *look* at me or tell me of your life?"

"My life," Erik scoffed. "That is a story far too ugly for your pretty ears."

"Don't condescend to me. I'll decide what I need to know to trust you." Her tone smarted but the fire in her reminded Erik exactly why he loved this woman. "Please, tell me *something*."

"I..." Erik could not even find the words to explain, and Christine heaved a furious sigh. She cast her gaze about the room until it landed on the great organ. To Erik's horror, she picked up a sheaf of music that she had obviously taken from his shelves.

"This music. It's handwritten and I don't recognize it. It's yours, isn't it? You're a composer. I knew you had to be—" Before she could speak another word, Erik snatched the parchment from her hand, his heart pounding in horror.

"Don't touch that!" he growled and turned his attention to the rest of his work. If she had found his *Don Juan*, she would not still be here. He had been an idiot to leave her alone in his home! Terror rose in him until he saw that the great, red, leather-bound score of his most terrible work remained safely on the highest shelf. He turned back to Christine only to have his relief replaced by guilt as he saw the fresh fear on her face.

"I want to go home. I was a fool to come here," she declared and stalked towards the door.

"No, please stay!" Erik's first impulse was to seize her, but he knew touching her would shatter any hope of winning her back. So instead, he turned to the organ. His hands fell on the ivory keys and a swell of music filled his home, booming through the shadows. He played a fragment of a composition from years ago, when he had first assembled the instrument. It cried out with pain, burning and searing for a terrible moment before he stopped. He listened to Christine's ragged breath as the notes faded, the very walls trembling with memory.

"What are you doing?" she whispered.

Erik could not turn. He could not bear to be seen by her. He never wanted to be seen, or known. But if she wished to, out of some madness, he would try to let her. Or at least let himself be heard.

"Allowing you to know me the best way I know how."

He did not hear her move, only the soft sound of her breath as she waited. Praying she would truly hear, he sat at the organ and began to play in earnest. Without words or vision, he gave her what he could of his story.

The notes blossomed from beneath his fingers and the great pedals beneath his feet, dark as a storm. The harmonies were harsh, discordant and unresolved, the rhythm irregular. It was the sort of music that would never be allowed in the Opera above. It was too modern, too wild and uncomfortable. But it was him, or part of him. It was the dark and the pain that he had been born from, the loneliness and the loss. There were flashes of peace, of promise, but they were deceptive and only led to more suffering. Yet still, there was beauty, hidden beneath and between the roiling darkness. There was hope.

It was small, this hope, this fraction of a melody that fought through the thundering sounds of his life and travails. But it was there, a wisp of beauty that demanded to be followed, even if it led him to new pain. He chased the motif, trying to fit it into the discord and in turn bringing a new harmony to the sound. The melody grew, like a call, begging him to resist the shadows. It was the music and hope that had sustained him amidst all the blood and grief and loneliness. But it still wasn't enough, in the minor key in which the motif settled and it faded away. Just as he had, it died softly, until it was but a ghost.

But then...her. Even though he could not look at the woman behind him, he could imagine her. He could die a hundred times and still hear her voice in his heart and see her smile in the dark of his mind. She had become his hope, somehow, and with the thought of her, the melody returned, in glorious major harmony as rich and beautiful as Christine herself. She was the music, the hope he had held onto for so long in the dark was her. It had to be. She had to hear that. She had to.

The final notes of the organ lingered in the air, echoing as Erik's home returned to silence and he listened once again for her breath behind him. It was rougher now, unsteady. Worried, he turned to Christine to find her standing just a few feet behind him. Her face was wet with tears.

"I'm sorry," she whispered and, for the first time, Erik did not feel the instinct to avoid the pressure of her gaze. She was looking at him differently now. Perhaps it was pity in her expression, he truly could not say. But the fear and anger were gone. For now at least.

"I'm not accustomed to people, as you may have intuited," Erik told her slowly. "It may take me a little while to remember how to be a proper host. I beg your indulgence for that shortcoming."

"You're as afraid as I am, aren't you?"

Erik nodded. "Tomorrow, I will be more forthcoming. I promise."

"And for tonight? Will you play more for me?" Christine asked carefully.

"The organ?"

"What instrument soothes you most when you're afraid?" It was an intimate question, the sort that would have made him turn away an hour ago.

"The harp," he said at last, and her forest eyes widened in interest. It was a relief to retreat to the instrument in the corner as Christine took a seat on the couch by the fire. He chanced a look at her as he began to play. Perhaps she had expected something suited to the Opera or the fine salons of Paris. But she had asked for comfort, and so that was what he provided: an ancient song of Ireland. It was music that sounded like rolling green hills and gray skies, of ocean waves and lost places.

He was not sure how long he played for her, selecting ballads and bard's tunes; even a few airs of his own composition, until the candles around them began to gutter. He played her ancient songs of magic and tragedy and watched her eyes droop and her face fill with peace. He would play for her forever if he had to. As long as there was music for her, even in this dark tomb where he had built a life, she would stay. It was music that had brought him to this place, and music that would keep his only hope in the darkness there with him.

2. Lessons

Christine stared at the door of her room, willing her body to rise and her feet to move. It should be easier today. Erik was just a man; one who was apparently nearly as frightened of her as she was of him. She had nothing to fear in his company. Yet even with that maxim repeating in her head, she could not move.

She could go back to bed, but that would mean more time lying there hearing his music in her memory. It had haunted her the entire anxious night, in and out of her restless dreams. The first composition he had played for her, that incredible wall of sound from the organ that had ensnared her and told her his story. She could never forget it.

It had begun like a cry, a visceral chromatic fall into despair and loneliness. Had she possessed the presence of mind, she could have picked out the harmonic innovations that pushed the sweeping, keening melody to incredible heights. But that had been impossible. Erik's remarkable music was too full of anguish and beauty. She had been swept into a storm, barely able to hold on as the organ filled the strange house on the lake with waves of sound, dark as the catacombs around them.

Then, out of the darkness, a new motif had emerged, thin and delicate as a spring shoot. Under Erik's masterful hands, it had grown and bloomed into a melody of longing and hope that had taken her breath away. She had wept as her angel transported her to heaven with his music once again.

And that was why she could not move. Because she had thought her promised protector was gone, but Raoul had been right. Fate had chained her to an angel of a different kind, but his power remained as great. The music that entranced and enraptured her had not been a dream or a phantom. It had been *Erik*. That music could still wrap her in a spell she could not resist and that was terrifying.

In the quiet, her stomach growled. She had not eaten since the morning before, and the nervousness that had kept her from accepting Erik's food had faded at least. Yet even her hunger could not make her move.

She dug her fingernails into her palms and screwed her eyes shut, screaming at herself in her head to stand, to do *something*. She could not run from her fallen angel forever, nor could she hide. His music would find her, even in the silence. She could hear it now in her heart: the plaintive lilt of a violin played with such mastery it made her shiver.

Christine's eyes opened as she relaxed, that fantastic music encircling her like a fog. It was as dark, strange, and as enthralling as her mysterious teacher. And it called to her because it wasn't a memory. The Romani air was real. Erik was playing for her once again. Alarmingly, she found herself standing at the door, turning the knob, and drifting through the threshold, summoned inexorably by the masked man in black in the windowless parlor.

His eyes were closed, Christine noted as she regarded him from beside the fire, the way Papa's always had been when he played. His long body swayed to the music, like a dance, where the instrument was his partner. She watched his fingers fly over the strings with effortless precision until his eyes opened and he caught sight of her. The bow scratched terribly across the strings as he staggered back.

"I'm sorry!" Christine exclaimed as Erik stared at her like he had never seen her before. She was wearing her white dress with black lining today, and the exposed skin of her décolletage was suddenly very warm, as were her cheeks. "Good morning?"

"Good morning," he replied after too long, and she finally breathed again.

"Did you..." Her words were moving from her brain to her mouth at the speed of molasses on a cold morning. "Did you sleep well?"

"No." Erik cringed he said it. "I don't sleep much anyway." He looked at the instrument and bow still in his hands and set them down hastily.

"I didn't sleep well either." Erik looked up at her in alarm. "It's alright. It's always hard sleeping in a new place," she tried. He simply continued to stare at her, gold eyes offset by the blacks and dark blues of his ensemble. "I am hungry now," she muttered, and Erik startled from his reverie.

"Of course." He moved carefully across the room, avoiding her eyes. "I hope you don't mind fish. A fresh one may take a while – I would have to get the boat." He caught Christine's gaze, the faintest smile on his lips at the edge of the mask.

For the first time in that dark place, Christine found herself laughing. Erik's sly smile broadened at the sound, gentle mischief in his eyes.

"Perhaps you would prefer an apple."

"Yes, please," she said softly. Erik ducked into what she supposed was a storeroom and emerged quickly with the promised food. "Are there really fish in your lake?"

"A few, but they're dreadfully hard to catch," Erik answered with a shrug. "They're not half bad. But you may prefer this."

He offered Christine the apple and retreated as soon as it was in her hand. She could not help but note how careful he was not to touch her. He set the kettle to boil above the fire, back once again steadfastly to her.

"Aren't you going to eat anything?" she asked as he straightened to his full height and turned to her, the white mask catching the glow of the candles and lamps.

"I ate earlier, I apologize. I don't eat a great deal either."

Christine looked down at the apple in her hand, trying not to stare at him and think of how terribly thin he was. But at least he was *telling* her something about himself at last.

"May I ask you a few more questions?"

"If you wish it. I will try to answer as well as I can." His jaw was tight, and his lips pursed. Christine was thankful the mask left at least his mouth visible. Said mouth wasn't quite normal, she could tell that now; the shape and the sickly-pale color of the skin around it hinted at what was hidden and a few dim scars strayed from behind the white material.

"Were you born—" She caught herself as Erik's sad eyes met hers.

"In France?"

Christine looked away. "I'm sorry. I shouldn't have—"

"It's a fair question," Erik said quietly. "The answer is yes. I've always looked...the way I do. Though a life with this face has also left me, shall we say, worse for wear."

"I'm sorry," Christine whispered.

"So am I." He turned from her again to watch the fire.

"Were you?" Christine stammered. "Born in France, I mean? Erik is a northern name and I thought perhaps—"

"That I was one of your countrymen? Alas, no. I was born here, in a small, primitive little village near Rouen. My name came to me by accident." She had no idea what that might mean and was too frightened to pry. She watched the low burning flames in front of them, amazed that somehow, he had contrived a way to keep the smoke from filling the room.

"You built this place, all of it?" Christine gave voice to the question in her mind. To her relief, Erik turned back to her with more warmth in his eyes.

"I did."

"How? How did you find it? How long have you been here?"

"It's a complicated story," Erik replied hesitantly.

"And we are on such a tight schedule today."

Erik's mouth twitched in amusement. "Very well. I came to Paris for the first time a little under eleven years ago," Erik began as he strode to a cupboard and took out a teapot, cups, and tin. "Can you tell me why that was poor timing on my part?"

"That would have been 1870... The war?"

"Very good," Erik said with a nod. "I'd only been in the city for a few months before the Prussian army decided to join me. It was quite an experience. Paris was under siege. German bombs were falling everywhere, and the citizens felt it was their duty as Frenchmen to have another revolution. In the countryside, they were content outing Napoleon III, but here in the city, they declared the commune of Paris. I found the cause just, so I joined them."

Christine's eyes widened. "*You* were a communard?"

"I've been many things," he replied meaningfully. "A builder is one of them, as you have guessed from my home. For the communards, I was a great asset in fortifying their base of operations, which happened to be in the half-finished opera house commissioned by the emperor they so hated, ten years before."

"I heard about that," Christine muttered as Erik spooned a generous portion of tea leaves into a chipped porcelain teapot. "An opera house seems an odd place to headquarter a new order."

"It was big and empty. We used it mainly as an armory, but it's such a maze it was a useful place to hide treasure as well. And prisoners. The building was half-finished, so it was easy to modify."

"Modify?"

"Trap doors, false walls, hidden passages," Erik bent to retrieve the kettle as he hesitated. "Trick mirrors."

"So, that's how you walk through walls?" Christine ventured, more disappointed than betrayed, as he poured the water into the pot and returned the kettle to a hook by the fire. "That's so ordinary."

"I'm sorry to disappoint you," Erik said as he turned to her. He held out an empty hand, then with a flourish, a silver teaspoon appeared between his fingers. Christine gave a crooked smile. With another elegant movement, the spoon was gone. "But most magician's tricks are fairly ordinary and disappointing when you know how they're done." He turned his hand over to show her where the spoon was hidden between his fingers.

"Is that what you are then? A magician?"

"As I said, I've been many things." Erik set the spoon down and sighed. "Thanks to the work I did as a communard, the Paris Opera has an entire architecture that no one knows but me. And now you."

Erik indicated a large, framed cross-section of the Opera hanging above the fire. It was vastly different from regular schematics of the Opera, covered with extra lines and with small notes in his messy, angular hand.

"The communards also kept their prisoners by the lake, in a chamber like this. I claimed this one as my own and I took to spending my time here as things worsened above," Erik continued as Christine's eyes found the lake on the diagram. "The leadership of the commune and I had, shall we say, disagreements, so I left before the siege ended and the commune fell. My modifications were hidden well enough that when the workers returned, they didn't know anything had changed."

"You said that was the first time," Christine ventured as Erik carefully poured them cups of tea. "When did you come back?"

"Six and a half years ago," he answered, far more darkness in his tone and demeanor now. "My second adventure in Paris went even worse than my first. And I was..." He flinched, reaching for his left shoulder, then pulling his hand back into a tense fist. "I was hurt. I needed somewhere to hide. I remembered this place and took refuge here. And I simply stayed. It turned out to be the perfect place: close to music, hidden away, an entire realm of illusion and magic between me and everything else."

Erik took a careful sip of tea. It was odd to see the notorious Phantom do something so human.

"And when did you decide to become a ghost?" Christine asked, as she sipped her tea, which was an earthy sort of mint flavor that she had never had before.

"I don't think you'll believe me when I say I became a ghost rather by accident."

Christine raised an eyebrow. "You're right. I don't."

"There were already stories about ghosts at the Opera before I returned," he said, holding her gaze. "They started when the workers came back after the war, knowing so much suffering had happened here. People saw things, heard things. When I took up residence, well – even with the passages, it's difficult to be completely invisible. People saw a shadow in a mask or eyes in the dark. And the story grew into more. Within a few months, I was a phantom and I have been since."

Christine considered him as he took a seat by the fire, gesturing for her to do the same. The chair was comfortable and well-used. It had to be after so long, didn't it? "Six years down here," she muttered as she took another sip of tea, trying to imagine what such a life would be like and how incredibly lonely it had to be. But maybe that's why he had chosen it. "How old are you?" she asked, the words passing her lips before she could stop herself.

Erik blinked, as if it was a question he had not considered in a long time. It probably wasn't. "Thirty-five," he answered, then frowned. "No. Thirty-six. I know, I look older."

Christine tilted her head, ignoring his dark joke. She was intrigued. "Have I just missed your birthday?"

"By a few weeks, I think."

"You *think*?"

"I know it's in early January, but...it was never marked."

Christine winced at the sadness in his tone. "Mine is in July," she offered hopefully.

"I know. The eleventh, correct?"

Christine nodded. Of course he knew. She took another sip of tea, enjoying the taste and smiling. "This is very good."

"I'm glad you like it, it's my own blend," Erik replied, and Christine nearly laughed.

"Where on earth did you learn to blend tea? I doubt from the communards."

"First in China, then India," he said matter-of-factly, and Christine's jaw dropped.

"You've traveled that far?"

Erik nodded, clearly pleased to have impressed her. "For much of my life, I never stayed for longer than a few months anywhere. I've seen a great deal of the world."

"What's it like – the Orient?"

"Warm," Erik began with a smile as Christine finally began to eat her long-forgotten apple. "The air is heavier there, the sun shines at a different angle. Even the color of the sky is different, like it's been painted with gold. The air smells of sweat and spices in the cities, and at night, in some places, you can hear birds and tigers in the jungle..."

Raoul missed the summer. The snow had stopped in the early hours of the morning, leaving the streets of Paris a mess of puddles and small melting hills of ice, all stained gray and brown from the detritus of the city. Raoul wondered if there was any point in trying to avoid the muck or if he should give into the fact that his poor valet would be stuck scrubbing his trousers and boots for an hour tonight. He had stopped the carriage at the *Place de Notre Dame des Victoires*, for discretion's sake, and now regretted it as he made his way to Christine's door.

He'd barely slept the previous night, going over his strange encounter with Christine again and again. The more he considered the conversation, the less it made sense. She had seemed so happy to see him, yet so sad at the same time. She'd spoken of the angel of music her father had promised and her mysterious teacher. She had assured Raoul that this unnamed benefactor was not his rival, but everything pointed to the conclusion that he was. It was all too mysterious, and he was highly concerned for his old friend. So, he found himself haunting her door again.

The street entrance to access her flat was open, surprisingly, and Raoul marked the draftiness of the foyer as he looked around. How sad that people had to live in places like this.

"—how could you let her go!" a voice above Raoul demanded, and a slightly familiar one at that.

"I'm not her jailer, Julianne!" Raoul did recognize the voice of the reply: it was Adèle Valerius, the singer who shared the flat with Christine. Why was Christine's maid harassing her at this hour? Raoul was torn between wanting to bound up the stairs and interrogate the women and the far less-gentlemanly urge to lurk and listen to what they might say about Christine. He settled for approaching slowly.

"This is different and you know it!" Christine's maid went on. "Something changed the other night."

"Yes, she stopped living in a dream," Adèle snapped back. "I'd say that's a good thing. Now she can get on with her career."

"This isn't about her career. Christine's not like you, she's—" Raoul cleared his throat to interrupt, and the women turned to him.

"Are you being bothered, Madame Valerius?" Raoul asked pointedly, choosing to ignore the indignation in the maid's dark features. He did not like to think of Christine working in the Opera with such an exotic.

"No, we're fine. Julianne is here for the same reason I assume you are, Monsieur le Vicomte, to look in on our dear Christine," Adèle replied, more tired than concerned. Her chestnut hair was barely up and her ample curves. "And as I told her, Christine left earlier this morning."

"To where?" Raoul asked.

"She didn't tell me, but probably the Opera," Adèle said before Raoul's mind could rush too far afield. "She likes to practice in peace when no one else is around, or so she says."

"Oh," Raoul muttered, his attention returning to the maid. "If she's at the Opera, why are *you* so concerned?" he demanded and the girl bit her lip sourly. "Christine is lucky to have such a concerned domestic, though she does need to teach you better as to how to address your superiors."

"I know how to say 'fuck off, you condescending clod' well enough," the mulatto snarled with a final glare to Adèle and Raoul before rushing away.

"She's just worried," Adèle sighed. "And you should know she works for the Opera, not Christine. She's her friend from when they were costumers together."

"Costumers?" Raoul echoed. "Christine didn't begin as a singer?"

"She's risen quite far, quite fast," Adèle replied, looking Raoul over. "One of her many mysteries."

He didn't like the sound of that. "You're sure she's at the Opera? Do you think I'd find her there?"

Adèle looked to the stairs where the maid – no, costumer – had left. "There's a chance. But it's a big place, very easy for someone to hide. And that's to say nothing of—"

"Of what?" Raoul asked, troubled by Adèle's dark look.

"It's nothing, just superstition. The Opera isn't terribly welcoming to intruders who dare to walk the halls alone," Adèle explained with lightness in her expression but darkness in her voice. "Just be careful where you look."

"I will be," Raoul replied. With a quick bow and a tip of his hat he was off again, back into the soggy January chill, a cold fear in his heart to match it.

Christine looked so beautiful today. Erik's mind kept returning to that one incredibly distracting thought over and over as they sat and talked by the fire through the morning. He had tried, many times, to let the observation be made and to move along, but she was there – *right there*! – in his home with no mirror or shadows between them. The candlelight made her skin look golden and warm, and her forest eyes dark and alluring. Even as he spoke to her of his travels from the Punjab to Hong Kong, he could not keep his eyes from the long line of her neck, the delicate lift of her collar bones, the perfect cupid's bow of her lips, and most remarkable of all: her smile.

It was a treasure, that smile, as was her laughter. They were gifts he had not even considered possible to receive when he had asked her to stay, and yet, she gave them. Speaking of India had led him to a passionate diatribe against the British Empire. That had become a discussion of Shakespeare and how his mastery of words to an extent that was nearly musical was the reason the English had so few great composers. Christine had mused on whether it was bold or arrogant for any composer to adapt Shakespeare into opera and whether the same applied to other poets.

"Do the words or story even matter in grand opera if the music is right?" Christine asked, and Erik shot her a scandalized look.

"The music is there for the story," Erik argued. "It can't be gibberish."

"*The Magic Flute* is gibberish," Christine said with a shrug and another precious smile, which unfortunately could not ease Erik's indignation.

"It's allegorical," he replied slowly.

"It's incomprehensible."

Erik could do nothing but sigh and look to the ceiling. "I fear I have taught you nothing."

"It's still wonderful, it just makes no sense," Christine replied. "And that's fine. I don't think something has to be perfect or even sensible to be beautiful." He looked back at her, curious and awed by her once again. "Anyway, you won't let me sing the Queen of the Night yet, so it doesn't matter," she muttered, her head falling back against the back of the old blue couch.

He drank in her beauty like water from an oasis as he watched her look around his home. He reluctantly tore his eyes from her to follow her gaze to the great organ against the back wall. "You can take a closer look, if you wish."

Christine sent him a hesitant look before rising. She looked so small compared to the enormous pipes that went all the way to his high ceilings as she approached the huge instrument. Erik rose as well, attentive to the wonder on Christine's face as she drew close.

"Do you like her?" Erik asked.

"Her?" Christine echoed, turning to him. "Does she have a name?"

"Cecilia. I didn't name her though; she came with it." He watched as Christine oh-so-carefully touched the keys he had played so often and it gave him a strange thrill. "She's over a hundred years old. Her previous home was a church that was damaged in the siege of Paris. She sat in the elements for years before the land was sold to be turned into something new and fresh. I bought her for fifty francs."

"You saved her," Christine corrected, running the back of her knuckles over one burnished brass pipe.

"It took me a week to disassemble her, working at night. Then I had to move her piece by piece down here. Then it was a month to put her back together. But I'm glad I did. An organ is the closest thing I can get to my own orchestra in terms of voices and sound."

Christine smiled wistfully and looked around at the other instruments on the shelves and hung carefully on the walls. "How many instruments do you have?"

Erik laughed softly, amused by Christine's uncanny ability to ask him questions with answers he had to think so hard about. "I don't think I've actually ever counted."

"And you play them all?"

"Some better than others. Most of the instruments I own came to me like Cecilia. I rescued and repaired them, then learned to play as I did." Erik paused, trying to discern Christine's face and the sadness there. "Would you like to see my workshop?"

Christine's eyes lit up and she nodded. He picked up a candelabrum and showed her to the door to the right of the organ, on the same side of the parlor as his bedchamber.

"You call this a *workshop*?" Christine asked in unabashed wonder as she stepped in. Books lined every inch of the walls, mixed with discarded materials, abandoned projects, and loose papers. A long, cluttered table filled the center of the room, littered with pieces of instruments and other mechanical distractions. Christine's brow knit in fascination as she trailed her fingers over papers covered with notes and designs, then reached towards a large contraption of wood and metal coils.

"Be careful of that. It's a device for generating electrical current, and I can assure you that receiving a shock from it is terribly unpleasant." Christine obediently withdrew her hand and instead examined an area covered in gears and wire, where a half-completed clockwork bird sat in pieces.

"You're quite the tinkerer," she said, almost to herself, as sad as she was impressed. "The music box that you left for me..." Erik understood her melancholy. He had intentionally left the music box out of her room. It had been built to play their most secret melody, the one that had always enticed his student to bare herself and explore her pleasure at the behest of her lying teacher.

"I've made many. Clocks too," Erik said, banishing the memory. It did not seem to cheer her. Christine followed Erik back into the parlor where her eyes returned first to the organ and then to the crowded shelf of scores to the right of the instrument. She reached for the score of *Rigoletto* and touched it forlornly.

"What's wrong?" he asked, fresh anxiety roiling in his gut.

"I know you want me to sing today," she confessed softly. "And I don't know if I even can. I want to, I do, but I haven't sung a note since—"

"Since you learned the truth about your teacher," Erik finished ruefully, self-loathing replacing his fear. At least that was familiar. "And you're afraid you cannot sing without an angel inspiring you. Without faith."

"I do have faith," Christine muttered. "Yesterday, when I was lost, someone reminded me that miracles or angels don't need to actually come from heaven to be the work of fate, or God, or whatever one wishes to call it."

"But?"

"But what if that isn't the same? Or it isn't enough? When I was singing for an angel, the music came from faith and joy and—" She stopped, the word 'love' unspoken. Shame and fear warred within Erik, a discordant symphony whose notes he could almost see writing themselves on the unfinished score open on the organ.

"Then let your music come from something else," he said aloud, earning a look of confusion from his reluctant student. "The beauty of your voice has always come from your heart, Christine. From the feeling you put into the music. But there are more feelings than joy to be expressed. What do you feel right now?"

"Afraid," she answered, soft and honest. "And angry."

"And hopeless and sad," Erik continued, looking towards his reams of music singing songs of despair and longing no one had ever heard. "All of that is in you, especially now, thanks to me. And all of those can be music too."

Christine swallowed, tears now at the corner of her eyes. "I spent three years trying not to feel anything after Papa died," she confessed thickly. "I was so scared of hurting. I'm scared now. What if it's too much? What if I can't find a way out?"

"You will. That is what music does, it takes what we feel, makes it into sound, and helps us understand. Even the painful, terrible things," Erik replied, caressing a score and recalling the thousands of times that music had taken his pain and transmuted it into something more. "That is the magic of art, Christine. We take something ugly and real and transform it into something beautiful and true."

Christine stared at him, something like hope dawning in her eyes. "I don't know where to start," she whispered. It wasn't a protest; it was a plea for someone to teach her.

Erik strode to his shelf of scores, grabbing a well-used one without hesitation and leafing through as he approached Christine. He placed the music in her hands, and Christine stared down at the familiar staves of *The Marriage of Figaro,* open to The Contessa's aria from Act Three.

"I barely know this. I haven't warmed up," Christine protested, scurrying after Erik as he moved to the piano. "I—"

"This is not about technique. It's about what she feels and what you feel, right now." Erik sat at the piano and played the opening arpeggio, looking at Christine in anticipation. "Don't run from it. Feel it. Feel all of it. However much it hurts, feel it, and make it into music."

"*And Susanna does not come,*" Christine sang shakily, her voice so small and rough no one would ever believe all of Paris had applauded her days before. But Erik did not stop her. "*I am anxious to know what the count said to her proposal.*" Her Italian was imperfect, her breath support non-existent; but she sang on, letting the music become more important than the words as she had months ago in a dark theater when a ghost had first heard her sing.

The melody was unsettled, distrusting and despairing, just as Christine was thanks to her false angel's deceptions. The Contessa sang of her fear that the man she loved, who had hurt her in so many ways, would hurt her again. Christine no doubt understood the sentiment.

"*Oh heavens, to what humiliation I am reduced by a cruel consort!*" Christine sang, her voice suddenly ringing with fire through the house on the lake as her hurt and rage finally broke through, her voice far too loud for the delicate notes. Erik winced with the shame he deserved. He had made a fool of her, deceived her, and yet brought her joy and faith; the same as the Count had done to his wife. Christine had every right to hate him for it and that despair filled her song.

"*And now I must seek help from my servant.*" Like the Contessa, she was reduced to seeking hope in the most unlikely of places – with the very man who had caused so much of her pain. Her voice was thick with emotion as she finished the recitative. She closed her eyes, unable to even look at Erik. How could she?

"*Where have the beautiful moments gone, of sweetness and pleasure?*" she sang, beginning the aria proper, the longing melody welling up from her throat like a cry. Like the prayer she had offered in song months ago that only Erik had answered. "*Where have they gone? Those vows of a deceiving tongue?*"

But not everything had been a lie. Not what he had taught her, even today. Erik listened to the beautiful anguish, pain seeping out like putrid blood from a wound. "*Then why, if everything has changed to tears and grief, has the memory of happiness not faded from my breast?*" Her song rose gradually, achingly, but beautiful as the weight of grief was taken from her soul bit by bit with each note.

"*Where have the beautiful moments gone?*" The Contessa returned to the first melody, stuck in her own despair. "*Where have they gone? Those vows of a deceiving tongue?*" The question lingered in the music, the chord and melody hovering unresolved with anticipation, questioning...and hope.

"*Ah, if only my constancy in languishing in love could change his heart.*" As the music changed, bouncing with an unfulfilled promise, Erik watched the light within Christine growing brighter with each note. "*It will bring me hope to change his unfaithful heart.*" The words repeated, but the music changed, rising with each bar to new heights and new hope, until it became something more. The song bloomed from his incredible student's throat, the notes soaring into the darkness of Erik's lonely home. Beautiful and true.

Erik didn't bother with the final bars of the accompaniment as Christine finished. She was beaming with wonder.

"Now, are you ready to begin?" Erik asked as they composed themselves. Christine nodded. "Good. Breathe."

It had taken Shaya under a week to learn the addresses of Messieurs Firmin Richard and Armand Moncharmin after they had taken on the unenviable task of running the National Academy of Music. Their respective stations were evident from the places they called home. Moncharmin had a flat, handsome to be sure, but there were those that would consider its place scandalously near to the ninth arrondissement, home to the more libertine theaters and establishments, a mark against the man. Richard, on the other hand, lived in a house off the *Rue du Faubourg Saint Honoré* amongst the higher echelons who still could not afford a manor in the *Faubourg Saint Germain*. It suited the man who now controlled the finances of the largest opera in France.

Shaya squinted at the dim windows of Richard's stately home, trying to make out movement within. Perhaps he saw a shadow stir, perhaps nothing. This was what hunting Erik was like: staring into the fog and darkness, hoping to catch a glimpse of the monster, and even then, not being sure if it was real or a dream. But in the last few weeks, there had been more glimmers of light, more clues. Christine Daaé was at the center of it, somehow, but she was currently a dead end. So Shaya continued to stare into a different corner of the dark.

The sound of a carriage rattling through the stately street startled Shaya, and he withdrew more into the sheltering shadow of the alley between two manors where he now stood. It was well after supper and no valets or maids would be using it right now. His heart leapt when the brougham stopped in front of Richard's door. A visitor at this late hour meant something. It had to. The figure that emerged might have been hard for a regular Parisian to make out in the flickering gaslight, but not Shaya, who was both observant and a regular attendee of the Opera.

Carlotta Zambelli cut an unmistakable profile in her furs and feathered hat as she swept to Richard's door. She barely waited for the door to open before striding in and slamming it behind her, right in the face of her little secretary, LeDoux. The poor man returned to the carriage, Shaya assumed, to wait. And Shaya waited too.

It took ten minutes for someone to emerge from the house again, but not Carlotta. A butler this time. He had words with someone in the carriage and the coachman gave a nod, the horses a whinny, and they were off into the night – *without* the diva.

Shaya smiled to himself as he watched the light in the bedroom – he assumed – above the street go out with Carlotta nowhere to be seen. The prima donna was making her own moves, and Shaya now knew something that Erik didn't, at least not yet: Christine Daaé was in great danger.

Christine pulled her covers tight around her shoulders and burrowed deeper into the pillow. She hated sleepless nights. Would she ever be able to sleep here, in the unearthly silence that left her mind filled with a strange angel's voice?

By all rights she should be exhausted. After Erik had coaxed her voice back to life like Christ calling to Lazarus, their lesson had been one of the most demanding and exciting in her entire tutelage with him. It was so different to have her teacher there, right before her eyes, his long hands playing expertly, barely a shade different from the ivory piano keys, and his golden eyes ever watchful.

Erik had run her through the entirety of *Rigoletto* backwards, challenging her to summon the right emotion and power without the aid of what came before. It had been hard; even more so given the fact that Erik had only played the other parts on the piano and left her to sing alone, wondering if she would ever hear his angelic voice lifted in song again. Perhaps it was best, given what she knew that voice could do to her. It was amazingly easy, alone in her pretty bed, to remember the ways he had rewarded her after their lessons in the past. How he had sung to her as she'd touched herself and...

Christine sprang from the bed, praying the distance from the soft pillows and mattress would halt the memories of what she and her angel had once been. She simply wanted to sleep without dreams, or at least escape from the confusion of her waking life for a few hours. And she knew just the library to help her.

She found a robe – an incredible garment of red velvet with sleeves down to the floor, lined in silk – and wondered where on earth Erik had found such a dramatic piece of clothing. Perhaps some unfortunate performer in the Opera above was missing it right now. She tightened it over her chemise and opened her door carefully, letting the warmth of the parlor embrace her for a split second before she saw the room was not empty.

"Oh!" Christine exclaimed. Erik sprang up from the chair he occupied by the fire, looking as shocked as she was. She gripped the edge of a shelf by the door with one hand and clasped the collar of her robe closed with the other as Erik stared at her, his eyes wide and his body tense. "I'm sorry! You scared me."

"It's alright. I'm used to it," Erik breathed back, swallowing as he looked at her. Christine cheeks heated. This was certainly not the sort of ensemble a decent woman wore in the presence of a strange man. But then again, she was not sure if she was decent at all, thanks to said man. Erik looked *indecent* as well. His jacket, waistcoat, and cravat were gone, and a few buttons of his black shirt were undone. His dark hair was unruly and several locks hung in his face.

"I couldn't sleep," Christine declared, telling herself to stop staring at the pale, strangely textured skin and his angular collar bone, but unable to look away.

"That's understandable. Neither could I."

Christine carefully took a seat on the couch, forcing herself to loosen her grip on the collar of her robe. It wasn't as if he hadn't already seen every inch of her. Swallowing, she retrieved Erik's book from where he had dropped it on the floor.

"What are you reading?" she asked as she opened the cover.

"*The Iliad*," Erik replied as Christine sighed when she saw the words. "What?"

"This is in Greek," Christine admonished as she handed the book back to him.

"How else would I read a Greek classic?" Erik asked with a slight spark in his eyes.

Christine shook her head. "How many languages do you know?"

Erik, unsurprisingly, had to think about it. "It depends on how you define 'know.' There are a few that I can speak better than I can read. Cantonese was rather frustrating. Twenty or so, if I were to guess." He stopped as he noticed she was chuckling. "What?"

"You speak more tongues and play more instruments than you can count," Christine began, watching him watch her as she spoke. "You're a builder and a tinkerer and a composer and a magician and probably a dozen other things you haven't told me. Erik, you may be the most accomplished ghost I've ever met."

He laughed quietly and looked down at his book. Christine had always treasured the sound of her angel's laughter, for it was so rare. *Erik* laughed easier and joked more than her strict angelic teacher had, and she was beginning to enjoy that as well. Just as she was growing to like the sound of his name in her mouth.

"I find ways to pass the time," Erik said with one of his elegant shrugs. Christine felt strangely compelled to honesty, to see him so relaxed.

"I can't understand what someone so...extraordinary would see in someone like me," she whispered, glancing at the magnificent organ he had rescued that sat watching them from the shadows like a great kraken in the deep. "Was I like her? Another broken instrument for you to rescue and repair?"

When she dared to look at him, his eyes were nearly glowing with emotion. "Christine, no. I may seem extraordinary to you, but despite all my learning and skill, I have also always been alone. This face has cost me a great deal."

"I'm sorry," Christine whispered automatically. "I didn't mean—"

"It was music that saved me. And when I saw you," Erik continued, stopping her pity. "That day fate placed you in my path, I knew you were like me, clinging to music for hope when all else was lost. I wanted to help. Then, that night, I saw you again."

"I knew you were there," Christine breathed, thinking back to her first night in the Opera.

"I came to frighten you," Erik confessed. "But then I saw you sharing your dinner with a rat. And having a lovely conversation."

Christine hid her blush. "You must have thought me quite the fool."

"No," Erik replied instantly. "I saw a girl who, despite everything, was kind, willing to share her meal with a creature others might run from. I saw your pain and I didn't want to cause you more. I saw you. Then, the next day, you demanded that I make you believe. And I could not refuse you."

The words made gooseflesh rise on Christine's skin as she found herself caught in Erik's eyes, remembering the miracle of the first time she had seen them.

"And after that?" she asked in a whisper.

"I didn't follow you or plan to be in the theater that night, I swear," Erik replied, surprisingly contrite.

"Fate put you in my path," Christine echoed his earlier words and recalled what Raoul had said to her: how even a strange angel could be sent by heaven.

"And you sang. You took the music of the composer dearest to my heart and filled it with more passion than I had ever heard on my stage. Just like you did today. Christine, you were not a broken instrument. You were and always will be a miracle. You were a prayer I could not let go unanswered if it was in my power."

Christine shut her eyes, hoping to hide her tears, but she could not hide from the love and wonder in his voice. "So you are a poet too," she whispered.

"Far from it," Erik said, resigned. His eyes were on his book when Christine dared to look at him again. "Homer is far better."

"Will you read to me?"

"In...Greek?"

"I have no doubt you can translate as you go," Christine replied, hiding behind false haughtiness. "And I would not mind hearing any passages you deem of note in the original language."

Erik regarded her for another long moment, then nodded. "As I said, I cannot refuse you." He opened the book and read, his voice as beautiful and comforting as it always had been when he was an angel. "*Sing, goddess, of the anger of Achilles, son of Peleus.* The Poet is invoking a Goddess to start, probably the muse of epic poetry, Calliope. The nine muses, as I'm sure you know, watched over all kinds of art."

"So, they were angels of music, you mean," Christine said and caught Erik's soft smile. "It seems one can find them anywhere."

"So it seems. *'Achilles, son of Peleus, accursed, who brought countless pains upon the Achaeans, hurled to Hades many strong souls of heroes, served them up as carrion for the dogs and all the birds...'*"

She relaxed as Erik read, savoring the music of his words when he switched to the Greek for a few lines. She moved to the couch when she was done, resting her head on the arm nearest to Erik and watching the fire as she imagined the battles of the Achaeans and their foes. It was not long before she closed her eyes entirely, and the story faded away. Like so many times before, sleep took her gently as she listened to her angel's voice.

The fire was low when she opened her eyes again. There was a complicated clock on the mantle above, with rings of symbols and illustrations of the cosmos, as well as a sun that rose and set. It told her that it was four o'clock in the morning. Perhaps the chill had woken her. Or perhaps the man in the chair next to her had made some noise as he slept.

Christine sat up, at last able to look her fill without scaring Erik away. How strange it was, that a man whose life was spent cultivating terror could be so easily unsettled by the eyes of a foolish girl.

Erik's head lolled to the side, making his pale neck look even longer. Even in sleep there was tension in his body, with one hand in a loose fist on the open book in his lap. Christine watched him as he breathed, recalling the first time she had seen him asleep, when she had woken in his bed. It had been his breath that had finally broken her illusions and revealed his humanity to her. And it was his breath that strangely comforted her now.

Erik was not a ghost, or an angel, despite all his masks. He was simply a man, though one unlike anyone else she had ever known. He had lived with an inhuman face, and no doubt endured pain and suffering the likes of which Christine could not even imagine.

Would Erik ever share those tales with her? Did she truly want to hear them?

Christine shivered as the fire guttered to embers. He had to be cold too, and so tired to fall asleep like that. Christine recalled her own first night in the Opera, when she had fallen asleep uncovered on the floor and woken with a makeshift blanket over her.

She moved as quietly as she could to the hook by the door to retrieve his heavy black cape and was careful not to touch him as she placed it over his body. She stared down at him when she was done. *I saw your pain and I didn't want to cause you more*, he had said of sparing her that night. But he had also offered her comfort, in his strange way. A simple, human instinct.

"I see you too, Erik," she whispered to the sleeping man.

3. Ghost Stories

Erik dressed with extra care, listening to the morning silence. He selected a shirt of midnight-blue linen and listened. He fastened the buttons, avoiding the sight of his hideous skin in the dim light of his room, and kept listening. He had heard the sound of water running in Christine's room twenty-seven minutes ago (unless he had been hallucinating it, which was always possible). It had startled him awake, thankfully. He didn't need her seeing him asleep in a chair like a common fool *again*. The first humiliation was worth it, for the gift of her gentle care guarding him from the cold.

Erik shook his head, forcing himself back to reality. He had to focus. He buttoned his vest and tied his cravat, adding an onyx pin at the base of the knot. His clothes were armor and he needed it today. He still had no idea what he was doing at all. For a few hours last night, they had managed something like peace. Now he had no goddamn idea how to get it back.

He combed his hair and listened again. One would expect a house like his to be silent as the grave, in a truly literal sense, but it never seemed that way to him. The candles whispered as they burned, the fire crackled and the logs shifted, the water dripped, and far above, omnibuses and carriages rumbled. If he was quiet enough, sometimes, he could hear the earth herself breathe. And other times, there were more unsettling sounds in the darkness.

Stepping into his parlor now, Erik listened to it all. Within that crowded silence was the almost imperceptible tap of Christine's feet on the carpets of her room. If he closed his eyes, he could even imagine the soft sound of her breath. Then he could remember it against his skin, only nights ago, yet in another life. He shuddered at the thought, panic and passion roiling inside him. After a day in her company, under the pressure of her eyes and close to her warmth, his competing fear and desire were all the worse. What was it like for her? Surely, she didn't feel *only* terror. Not after she had been so kind.

Erik's eyes fell on the piano. Of course. He knew how to soothe his fears and perhaps beckon her from behind that closed door. He seated himself at the keyboard, considering his options. Mozart of course came to mind first, Christine's favorite as well as his, but that was too intimate. Beethoven and Liszt were too passionate. He needed something restrained but comforting; precise and calm.

He set his fingers on the keys and began the first "aria" of Bach's Goldberg variations. It was such a simple melody at the start, building slowly, gentle as snow. He closed his eyes, letting the music wash over him as the piano sang beneath his hands. The aria came to a close and he launched into the first variation, Bach's perfect clockwork of counterpoint and rhythm sweeping him away.

Past the music, he heard the sound of Christine's door. He pushed down his anxiety and kept playing, the music would protect him as it always had. He chanced opening his eyes and barely kept his concentration when he saw Christine watching in fascination. There was no fear in her beautiful face, and, to Erik's relief, he was not afraid either. In fact, he was thrilled.

As the variations grew more complex, he continued to look up at her. She was impressed, he could tell. When he finished the eighth variation with a subtle flourish and paused, like a miracle, Christine smiled.

"You don't even look at the keys," she murmured.

"One gets accustomed to playing in the dark," he said, hoping it was not too sad. Christine glanced away, nonetheless. Erik followed her gaze to the clock above the fire. "Eight o'clock. That's so hard to believe. I'm used to waking up in the dark but down here—"

"It's different. And easy to lose track of time. Hence the clocks."

"You made this, didn't you?" Christine asked, moving towards the complex timepiece. Erik nodded, amazed by the thrill it gave him for her to admire things he had created. Her attention turned to his amended plan of the Opera and she gave a faint smile. "I still can't believe all your haunting is all just trapdoors."

"Not *just* trap doors." Christine jumped at the sound of Erik's voice coming from the other side of the room and spun to look at him. He smirked, lips unmoving, as his voice continued to sound. "To be a first-rate ghost still requires *some* skill, I'd like to think."

"How are you doing that?"

"Ventriloquism is a very useful skill for a magician," Erik replied, throwing his voice to a different corner and earning a grudging smile. "Or a ghost," he finished, his voice in her ear.

"It's no wonder you took up such a career." There was something challenging in Christine's eyes as she spoke.

"I told you: that was an accident. The Opera was already haunted when I came, I merely joined the ranks. This place has room for a thousand ghosts," he sighed, looking up to the painted stars on the ceiling and considering the dark passages and shadows above them. When he looked back at Christine, she was staring at him suspiciously.

"You don't mean to imply that you believe that." Erik gave a dark smile and Christine's green eyes widened. "You think the Opera is haunted? *Actually* haunted?"

Erik shrugged. "Living down here, I've seen and heard things I can't explain. Things I can't simply dismiss as delusions of an over-hearted brain. And, as I told you, all the stories come from a grain of truth."

"I would not have guessed a scholar like you to indulge in such fancies," Christine remarked softly, tilting her head as she watched him.

"I am enough of a scholar to know that what I have learned in all my studies is but a grain of sand compared to the desert of what I do not and never will know. I am not so arrogant to think I know every mystery of the world."

His instinct was to turn away from her as she watched him, but he fought it, instead he tried to gauge the light in her eyes and what her crooked smile might mean. "I've never thought of it that way," she said.

"I have found the world to be a hard and cruel place, but to know or at least believe that there is some magic to it makes it a bit more bearable."

"A false ghost who believes in real ones," Christine murmured in turn.

"A carnival magician who has faith in magic. Like yours."

"Mine?"

"You always knew when I was near, always. That wasn't some trick of mine," Erik explained. "What else do we call that but magic?"

Christine looked down pensively. "You said you were born in France."

"I was. Why do you ask?"

"I was just wondering," she muttered, looking back to him. There was something so breathtaking about the clarity of her eyes. "Are you Roma?"

"Ah," Erik sighed with a smile. She had not used the vulgar and offensive word 'gypsy.' She had said *Roma* in a way that confirmed his theories perfectly. "Again, I must disappoint you. I am not one of your people."

Christine gaped at him, blinking. "How did you know?"

"I suspected when you smiled at the Romani songs I played for you, but I became sure when you told me your father would play you—"

"*The Resurrection of Lazarus*," Christine finished for him. He could still see the way her face had lit up when the Angel of Music had played for her from behind her dressing room mirror.

"Only someone trusted by The People would have had the honor of learning that piece," Erik confirmed. "From what you've told me of your father – a wanderer and musician – I guessed."

"Only on his mother's side," Christine blurted out. Erik cocked his head. That was irregular. Christine scowled. "It is, as you might say, a long, sad story."

"Perhaps you will tell me one day."

"Perhaps," Christine replied, considering him. "If you aren't of The People, how did you learn it?"

"I traveled with them for many years, on and off, moving between different caravans." Erik watched the interest rekindle in her eyes. "As you can guess, my life has never been easy or happy, but my time with the Roma was better than much that had come before. I learned a great deal from them, and they were always more welcoming to me than the rest of society."

"That doesn't surprise me."

"As welcoming as a people without a country could be of another outcast, I still was never more than a visitor. I was—"

"Among them, but not part of them," Christine finished, and Erik nodded. "That's familiar." There was bitterness in her voice and expression as she turned her attention back to the clock.

"They taught me how to work metal, tinker, and more," Erik went on. "I wouldn't have been able to build this without learning from them. I modeled this clock on a much larger one in Prague that I saw soon after I first joined a caravan," he elaborated and she smiled as she raised a hand to touch the fine gold molding.

"Have you eaten?" Christine asked and shook her head before Erik could reply. "Of course you haven't. Get something for yourself too then. And make some of your tea for me as well while you tell me more of the secrets to haunting an opera."

"There is *some* hard work involved," he said as he searched out the makings of tea.

"Ah yes, frightening ballet rats must be exhausting."

"And skeptical novice seamstresses," he corrected. "I do have other duties, you know. I give the managers quite a lot of notes, not that they listen. But I earn my salary."

"Your *salary*?" Erik turned to see the delightful look of consternation on her face. "That story is true too?"

"Like I said, all the stories about me come from somewhere." He liked the way she stared at him now, in amazement and not fear. "I've required a few...financial tributes from the management over the years when they've needed to be taught a lesson. Nothing too extravagant, of course; only what their peace was worth."

"Jammes claims they pay you ten thousand francs a month!" Christine squawked.

"Well of course that isn't true." Erik waited for Christine's sigh of relief. "I got twenty thousand once."

He could not help but laugh at the look of pure shock on her beautiful face. "They pay twenty thousand francs to a *ghost*?!" Christine sputtered. "Fucking hell, that's more money than I've seen in my entire life!"

Erik shrugged. "It was only one time; after a disastrous premiere of *La Juive* that I sabotaged on behalf of anyone who cares for good art."

"What in God's name do you do with money like that?"

"I don't keep it all," Erik protested, raising his hands in mock defense. "I put some of it back and watch them try to fix the books; some I save. And of course, some I spend. Paris is an expensive place to live in comfort."

"I would ask how they can still believe you're a ghost, but I am aware of how convincing you can be," Christine muttered. Erik could swear she looked embarrassed.

"People believe what they need to," Erik tried to console her, but it didn't seem to help. "I don't know about our new managers yet. They haven't paid me a cent and have not listened to my orders."

"I don't know if I respect them or resent them for that." She looked down, picking at her nails and frowning. "I wonder if they have decided what to do with me."

"That's not their decision," Erik reassured her, or tried to. He worried it sounded more like a threat, since it was.

"Is there something else wrong?"

"The chorus is due at rehearsal at noon," Christine replied. "It feels like half a lifetime since I've been to one."

"You know all the music."

Christine gave him a crooked scowl. "I'm more frightened of the people."

"Oh, well, that I can sympathize with."

"So, living underground with ghosts doesn't scare you, but people do?"

"Why do you think I live underground with the ghosts? The living do far more harm than the dead."

Christine's eyes lingered on him long enough to remind Erik of certain such harms, the ones he had been victim to and ones he had caused, and he turned away from her. "Would you like to practice anyway?"

"Perhaps we can enjoy the breakfast you've forgotten about first."

Erik cringed again. It would take a while to get used to sharing his home with someone who ate at regular intervals like a normal person. "Of course," Erik nodded, and Christine smiled.

For a while, they were normal as could be. Erik fetched their food, made their tea, and smiled back at her. It took seven minutes, give or take, before his fear returned and he flinched away from her when she reached for a piece of fruit from their tray. But it had been nice to savor the quiet before the storm.

Christine tried her best to pay better attention on the journey back up to the world of the living, but every dark corridor looked like another to her. Unlike the other times Erik had led her through his labyrinth, he was not holding her hand to guide her.

He had put on his elegant black gloves while Christine had donned the dark hooded cloak he had provided, but he had not offered a hand as he escorted her from his home, nor when she fumbled her way into the boat for their journey across the lake. Now, as the walls transitioned from wood to stone, the free hand Erik maintained while he held his lantern in front of them remained resolutely at his side.

Christine wanted to mention it, but, swathed in the black of his cape and hat, only his mask visible in the dark, Erik was once again the terrifying Phantom rather than the strange, captivating man who had hosted her for the last two days. She far preferred Erik to the ghost who had paused in front of her.

"Here we are," her guide declared. Christine tried to discern what was special about the narrow corridor where they had stopped. The wooden walls were rough and crusted with dust and cobwebs, gas pipes snaking along their seams. But one section of the wall was smooth as glass, like a window from the ceiling to the floor. The dim light of Erik's lantern barely penetrated the chamber on the other side, but Christine was not surprised to see it was her dressing room. The glass was the mirror from which the Angel of Music's voice had come for months.

"I installed this particular door during the war, at the end of the commune's days, to conceal the most direct road down to the lake."

"I wouldn't call that route direct," Christine muttered, hoping to earn a scowl of a smile from the currently inscrutable ghost beside her. Nothing.

"I will show you how to work the mechanism to open it."

Christine watched as Erik reached up high on the right side of the mirror to a sort of latch which he pulled. The glass slid aside without a sound and Erik indicated it was safe for her to step through, back into another world as she crossed the threshold. The last time she had been in this room her life had been so different. She retrieved her matches from the vanity and moved to ignite the gaslights. She had only made it to one before she realized Erik had not moved from the dark passage beyond the mirror.

"You won't come in?"

"I'm not overly fond of mirrors," Erik replied, cool and smooth as ever, but there was something sincere and tense in his tone. "And I should leave you to some privacy to prepare for rehearsal."

"Will you be observing?"

"Eventually. I have to attend to some managerial duties first, I've been far too lax with Moncharmin and Richard lately, given my distraction."

Christine swallowed. So she was a distraction? Or was it an obligation? Did he feel he owed something to the girl whose life he had saved and destroyed? Or did he do this out of the love he claimed for her? Love he had not mentioned since the morning she had unmasked him.

Christine startled as Erik moved without a word and triggered the mirror to close, leaving her gaping at her own bewildered face. "Where will I go after rehearsal? Shall I come back here?" she asked the emptiness.

"You may come here, or head into the cellars," Erik's voice replied, and suddenly he was an angel again with nothing but the entrancing sound of his words to indicate her presence. "Wherever you go, do not worry, I will find you. Good day, Christine."

She closed her eyes and shivered at the way he said her name and the promise that could so easily be a threat. She felt it the instant he was gone from behind the mirror, like the sun going behind a cloud, and reopened her eyes.

Did she look different? Would the friends and colleagues who had not seen her since her debut in *Faust* and what followed notice a change? She did not want to contemplate that. Add that to the ever-lengthening list of things she did not want to think about, including all the debauched things she had done in this room at the encouragement of her angel. She removed her cloak and avoided the blush in her reflection as she retreated from the dressing room where she had exposed herself to Erik's eyes so many times.

Today's rehearsal was set for the main stage, one of several full run-throughs of the new *Rigoletto* before the orchestra joined them for the *Sitzprobe* and final runs next week before the premiere. What part would she be playing in that premiere? Ostensibly she was Adèle's understudy for all her roles, so she knew Adèle's part of Magdalena the whore in the final act. But Erik had been preparing her for Gilda for weeks as if the part were hers, and after her triumph as Marguerite, she couldn't simply be relegated to the chorus. Carlotta had no understudy and had barely been to the rehearsals, wasn't it logical that Christine step in?

"Where have you been!?" Christine jumped at Julianne's voice. Before Christine could even see where the cry had come from her friend seized her in a fierce embrace.

"Julianne, what on earth!" Christine grunted as the other woman pulled back, still holding Christine by the shoulders and examining her. "I'm fine!"

"Three days I've been looking everywhere for you, no idea where you were! Because I *know* you wouldn't be stupid enough to go back to—" Julianne stopped as Christine's blanched. She didn't feel Erik watching, but that didn't mean he wasn't listening. She had forgotten in all the chaos that Julianne was the one person who knew a fraction of the truth. "You did, didn't you? You were with him. The ghost."

"Julianne, please, I can't." How could she explain without betraying the trust Erik had put in her or sounding mad?

"You can't say or he won't let you?" Julianne replied, her dark eyes burning with suspicion now.

"It's not like that. I made a promise," Christine replied. "You of all people understand what it means to me to keep someone's confidences. He trusts me."

"Christine, a man who spirits you away and leaves you weeping and hurt *does not deserve your promises*! Or you!" Julianne hissed.

Part of Christine knew Julianne was right. The same part that heard the Persian's warnings about Erik in her mind each time his demeanor darkened or she thought of what was on the other side of the mask. So many people thought him a monster. But after the last few days, she could not agree.

"Please, trust me, he—" Christine's mouth hung open as she searched for words to placate her friend. "He would never hurt me. If anyone asks where I have been, I will tell them I have been staying with a friend and teacher who treats me with nothing but respect, and it will be true."

Julianne looked like she was deciding whether to scoff or scream. "Respect, is it?"

"Yes. And that is all I can say," Christine replied. She had neither the will nor the ability to explain what the last few days had been like. She worried that when examined in the cold light of day, the pleasant hours spent with Erik full of music and stories would lose their appeal. "Come along, walk with me before I'm late," Christine ordered, and with a sigh Julianne fell in step on the path to the stage.

It was like an explosion. As Christine stepped onto the great stage proper the onslaught of light and noise hit her all at once and she grabbed Julianne's arm in pure shock. It was so bright, loud, and *crowded*. It was as if she had been struck by one of the ocean waves in Brittany, the ones that would sneak up on her as a child and leave her soaked, shocked and breathless, afraid she might drown. It was such a contrast to the shadowy quiet and perfect music of Erik's home.

"Are you alright?" Julianne asked.

"Just overwhelmed," Christine muttered, trying to compose herself and gain her bearings among the crowd. The first thing she noticed was the way her fellow chorus members were looking at her.

Christine had never been popular among the chorus, but she had proved herself a capable musician, kept her head down, and avoided attention. Any odd looks she had received since her unplanned introduction to Paris at the New Year's gala in Carlotta's place hadn't mattered, because she'd had an angel on her side. She noticed the sneers now. She noticed how people raised their eyebrows and whispered when she passed.

In the corner of the stage Christine's only true ally, Adèle Valerius, was in deep conversation with Gerard Gabriel, one of the directors and the master of the chorus. Neither looked particularly happy. Robert Rameau and Carlos Fontana were likewise engaged in conversation, though Rameau at least gave Christine a smile.

"I should go," Julianne muttered, also squirming under the harsh eyes of the company.

Christine opened her mouth to protest, but Julianne was already in retreat. Christine turned, resolved to engage Adèle or Rameau in conversation before the start of rehearsal, but the sight of a different principal stopped her cold. Carlotta Zambelli herself was striding towards Christine with none other than the conductor, Claude Bosarge, in tow.

Carlotta was immaculate in one of the most ornate dresses Christine had ever seen, red accented with gold to match her perfectly coifed hair. Her bustle moved behind her like a queen's train and, despite being taller, Christine felt minuscule and underdressed in her relatively plain blue gown.

"Ah, young Mademoiselle Kristiane, was it?" Carlotta purred as she approached, a cat stalking a frozen mouse.

"Christine," she replied, swallowing down both her fear and indignation.

"Of course. I assumed you had a more Nordic name as a – what are you again?" Christine was suddenly a child again, with playmates demanding to know if she was just poor or a filthy gypsy.

"French and Norwegian by way of Sweden," she replied, jaw tight.

Carlotta smiled smugly and nodded. "Yes, that was it. I wanted to be the first one to share the good news with you." Christine's heart leapt in blind hope as Carlotta paused. "You have the day off."

Christine's guts fell through the floor at the same time as her blood began to pound. "What?"

"Claude and I have been talking, and we agree that the chorus's part is so small that we don't need to keep them here all day and waste everyone's time herding you all about like cattle."

"What?" Christine repeated. Around them people had begun to stare and whisper more pointedly.

"Don't worry, you'll still be paid for the day's work," Carlotta paused to look Christine from head to toe. "I know you need the money."

"What about understudies? I'm the cover for Madame Valerius." Christine craned her head, trying to make eye contact with Adèle across the stage.

"I've had discussions with the directors about that too," Carlotta grinned back. "Haven't we, Claude?"

Bosarge sighed and nodded. "Obviously after hearing you sing a soprano role like Marguerite, it's absurd to keep you as a mezzo understudy, so we'll be finding a different cover for Madame Valerius. For all her roles." Bosarge's usually sparkling eyes were dull as they avoided Christine's.

"Including Siébel," Carlotta finished with a wicked grin.

"But I can sing the roles!" Christine protested, her heart racing in panic. "You've heard me. You don't need to—"

"It's not what suits you. Some time in the correct section of the chorus should do you some good," Bosarge cut her off. "Though I will need to have Monsieur Gabriel take some time with you to make sure you are better able to blend with your fellow choristers."

"The audience pays to hear the principals, not one voice sticking out in all the crowd scenes," Carlotta practically purred. Christine's face went scarlet.

"I didn't know I—"

"Did everyone hear the news?" Carlotta announced to the curious crowd. "You all have the day off and the rest of the week!"

"That's not strictly the case!" Gabriel corrected as he rushed to the diva's side while the chorus erupted in murmurs. "You *will* be needed on Friday for the run-through of *Faust*. We do apologize for the sudden change and the inconvenience, but—"

"Dismissed!" Carlotta trilled. The chorus began to filter off the stage, half of them giving Christine looks of contempt, the other half looks of pity. She wanted to fall through the stage's trapdoors and disappear forever. "Did you not hear me, little one?" Christine looked up to see Carlotta sneering at her. "You need to leave before you get in the way."

"Oh, shove off, you loathsome bitch." It was Adèle who said it, taking Christine by the elbow to lead away. "I can't believe she did that."

"I can," Christine muttered, her embarrassment and fury roiling under her skin. "I humiliated her twice. I'm surprised she didn't fire me."

"She may be biding her time. Or not able to yet, given that you have so many supporters."

"Ha," Christine replied. "I thought Bosarge respected my voice and he—" She stopped, tears suddenly springing to her eyes. "Gabriel too."

"Shush, don't believe what Carlotta's made them say or think. Gabriel believes in you, and so do I, which is why we need you to meet us for supper tonight."

"Supper?" A new panic joined the melee in Christine's stomach. She couldn't go to supper and she couldn't tell Adèle why.

"We're dining with Monsieur Cravalho from the *Opéra Comique*. He heard you at New Year's and may have a place for you there!" Adèle said it with such enthusiasm, but it only made Christine sicker.

"A place at the *Comique*?" Did Adèle really think that Paris's secondary opera house was what Christine wanted?

"They'll be mounting *Carmen* again in the fall! And their Micaëla is willing to share the role! You'd be perfect."

Christine nodded, numb. "It's January. What would I do until then? Would I be stuck in the chorus there too?"

"You would pay your dues the way all singers your age must," Adèle replied with a scowl. "Christine, you may need to accept this place is a dead end as long as Carlotta is here."

"I'll consider your invitation," Christine snapped back. "I may not be there at supper. I'm...meeting a friend."

Adèle scoffed. "The friend you've been with all week? Do you live there now?"

"Don't worry about me," Christine declared and stalked off stage into the buzzing backstage corridors. She wanted to be back in Erik's home, where it was quiet and no one could see her. She was beginning to understand why Erik kept to his shadows. Life was easier when you didn't have to deal with cruel, stupid, vain people.

She wished she knew how to find her way back.

Erik heard his managers before he was even in place under the floorboards, curled carefully in the hidden space beneath the trap door directly behind Richard's desk. The tone of the voices was not promising.

"I am the artistic director; these are my decisions!" Moncharmin was saying.

"The career of one upjumped chorus girl is hardly a decision that affects the artistic integrity of the company," Richard replied with derision in his voice that made Erik's blood boil.

"We were in agreement that Mademoiselle Daaé was a better fit for Gilda!" It was either a stroke of luck or a cruel trick of fate that Erik had arrived to hear exactly what he needed to.

"I recall no such agreement," Richard replied. "Do calm down, Armand. I can assure you that this decision had nothing to do with art."

"Obviously, it had to do with that awful Zambelli woman," Moncharmin shot back. "When exactly did she get to you?" Erik heard a faint huff of indignation from above, but there was no denial. "Aren't you worried about the consequences of this?"

"I've been assured that the patrons favor Carlotta. And the rabble that don't pay for boxes could care less if Gilda is a queen or a chorus girl."

"I meant the other consequences," Moncharmin replied darkly and Erik smiled to himself. He had made an impression on one manager when they had intruded on Box Five during Christine's debut in *Faust*.

"If you bring up that absurd ghost story again, I'll have your head," Richard said.

"It's not a story! You heard what I heard!" Moncharmin countered. "You've seen the notes – the ones which clearly state that it should be Daaé in the lead."

"The dead don't pay to keep this opera open," Richard said with an audible sneer.

"*They can however force this Opera to close if not obeyed*," Erik spoke aloud. He imagined their faces. He had extensive experience with the looks of fear different people could manage. In his mind the men were pale, shocked, especially Moncharmin, with his tidy moustache standing out against his sallow cheeks. Then the blood would return to Richard's face, making him flush from his cleft chin to his bald scalp.

The managers did not make a sound. Had he gone too far? In over half a decade haunting this office, he had never raised his voice there, preferring instead to communicate by letter. But, desperate times, as they say.

"I didn't say that," Moncharmin finally hissed.

"It's unbecoming to hide behind tricks and superstition to make up for the fact your position here is redundant at best. Now, if you need me, I will be observing rehearsals. Carlotta has already notified Bosarge and Gabriel that the chorus won't be needed for today or tomorrow, so *you* will stay here to answer whatever questions those sheep have about not having to work for a day!"

Erik clenched his fists as steps sounded above and a door slammed. He wanted to do more. He wanted to thunder at Moncharmin or rush to the hall and end Richard right there. No quick mercy of the Punjab lasso for him. He would wrap his hands around Richard's neck and see the terror in his eyes, but a dead manager would cause even more problems. And the act would not endear him to Christine.

His heart fell. Richard had said the chorus had been dismissed, which meant Christine was not at rehearsal and no doubt had already heard the news. He had to find her.

It was hard to move quickly when walking behind walls, so Erik was forced to take risky shortcuts. Only once did he hear a gasp as he flitted across a dark hall near the ballet studios. Another sighting to add to his legend among the *petits rats*. Christine's dressing room was empty when he came to it, barely a shadow visible through the glass. She must have gone elsewhere. His heart began to pound.

What if she had left? What if she had taken this opportunity to flee from the monster that had ensnared her and forced her to stay in his home? She could have gone to the police, or the Daroga. Had he been a fool to let her wander alone? No. She wasn't like that. She had been so kind and open in their time in his home, kinder than he could ever deserve. Perhaps she had gone below...

Erik rushed through the shadows of the cellars like a winter wind: cold, precise, and determined. His lantern was in his hand again but unlit. Once one understood the patterns and landmarks of the labyrinth, it wasn't so hard to find one's way. Would Christine have found a light, or would she be looking for him in the shadows?

Erik stopped at the sound of whispers from the corridor in front of him, a spike of apprehension quickly giving way to joy as he recognized the soft, feminine voice guiding him to her with a quiet string of profanity.

"Jesus bloody Christ in heaven, Erik, where are you?" Christine muttered as Erik drew near. "I should have waited in my room."

"That is where I looked for you first," Erik replied from the dark.

"Fucking hell!" Christine yelped, jumping back and spinning to see the ghost she had been berating emerge from the shadows. Erik couldn't help but laugh at her shock and consternation. "Don't laugh! You scared me out of my skin!"

"I'm sorry, old habit," Erik replied warmly as he raised his lantern to light it and Christine glared at him from the edge of the flame's glow. "I didn't mean to scare you."

"Oh, you absolutely did, you rogue," Christine snapped, catching her breath. Erik found himself laughing again. "Well, I'm sorry for my unladylike language. Not that you mind." It was only when she looked away from him that Erik noticed the redness around her eyes and the streaks on her pale cheeks.

"Who has made you cry?" Erik demanded, stepping closer to her out of pure instinct. She looked up at him, her face open and vulnerable, and he wanted nothing more than to touch her soft cheek in comfort. How dare anyone bring tears to the eyes he adored? He didn't though. He held himself back with effort and tension he was sure she could sense.

"Who else? Carlotta," Christine told him. "She took great glee in telling me that I – a lowly member of the chorus – would not be needed for rehearsal. She and Bosarge also informed me that, as a soprano, I'm not suited to understudy Adèle." Christine spat out the words quickly as new moisture appeared in the corners of her eyes.

"That fucking bitch," Erik muttered, and that at least drew a sad smile.

"I came looking for you. I assumed you would know," Christine added. "I was so upset I didn't even think to bring a candle. I'm such a fool." The dejection and regret in her face made the urge to hold her and comfort her all the worse, desire and hurt and love all twisting inside Erik so urgently it hurt.

"You aren't. Carlotta and Bosarge and the managers and anyone that would dare make you think you don't deserve that scheming harpy's position are the fools. And I will make sure they know it."

Christine did not look comforted. "At least you terrified me out of being angry and sad for a few seconds," she offered with a shrug.

"I do try to live up to my reputation."

"At least your head isn't on fire."

"I told you: that's not me," Erik smirked.

Christine's glare hardened again. "Well, don't make me ask. Go ahead and tell your tale."

"It's the ratcatcher that has the head of fire." He tried not to laugh again at the way Christine went pale. "His kind is employed throughout Paris. He shines a bright lantern on himself. All the rats follow the light, and thus, him."

"How many is...'all?'"

"From the experience I had when I ran into him, I would guess it was hundreds, maybe over a thousand. As you can imagine, it's terribly unpleasant to be caught in his path, all those little claws and tails."

Christine made a noise of horrified disgust and Erik laughed, deep in his throat. "Erik, that is not funny."

"Don't worry, he only comes around in the evenings every few weeks, I'm sure he's not here today. Well, I'm almost sure."

"Are you being terrifying on purpose?" Christine demanded.

"As I said: habit. It's hard for a ghost to change his nature," Erik replied with a shrug.

"Or you like to scare people because it means they stay away from you and you never have to worry about them running because you're the one to drive them away."

Erik gaped at her, laughter evaporating.

"I'm sorry!" Christine amended at once, her face falling.

"No, don't be," Erik said slowly. "I am quite unaccustomed to being read so directly. But I certainly deserve it."

"No, you don't." She stepped towards him in the dark and it took every ounce of his self-control not to jump away from her. "I'm sorry. Truly. I shouldn't be so short with you because I'm furious with Carlotta."

"And I am sorry for that. I wish I could have done more to protect you. I assure you this is temporary."

Christine gave a brittle laugh. "Adèle invited me to supper with her, Gabriel, and Cravalho from the *Comique*." Seething fury flared behind Erik's ribs at the confession before Christine raised her hands placatingly. "I'm not going. I'd rather eat one of the fish from your lake than sit through supper hearing about a role I may be suited for in half a year."

Erik sighed in relief. "Well, I guess I shall have to make dinner worth it this evening to compensate." At that, Christine laughed herself, a surprising, warm sound in such a dark place. "Don't be so doubtful. What about a roast chicken and prawns with a nice tokay?"

She grinned and shook her head. "I wouldn't put it past you to be able to make that appear." She paused, regarding him across the pool of light cast by his lantern. "I have to ask: How do you eat?"

"I imagine the same way everyone else does. The mask is not that inconvenient."

Christine scowled at him. "I mean – where do you get food? Or anything?"

"Aha." Erik looked up to the stones above them, where the Opera waited above. "Some things I acquire from the kitchens or elsewhere in the Opera as needed."

"So you steal?"

"I prefer the term 'borrow.'"

Christine scoffed. "But how do you go shopping, as you said, with the ridiculous amounts of money you *borrow* from the management? I can hardly imagine you walking into a fine salon to buy one of your lovely silk vests."

"You don't think the Opera is the only place in Paris that has an underworld, do you? There's a whole second city under the ground and beneath the streets. Tunnels and cellars and sewers. You can move from one end of Paris to the other without ever seeing the sun. I can go anywhere from here; from the sewers where Val Jean was lost, to Esmerelda's court of miracles." Erik paused at the look of unbridled curiosity in Christine's eyes.

"Is it dangerous?"

"It depends. The underground is full of thieves and beggars, and many of the others Paris has abandoned and discarded. There are haunted places too; catacombs lined with bones moved from all the cemeteries that were razed in the name of progress." He paused, waiting a reprimand for his morbid turn, but none came. "They're beautiful, in their way. Mosaics of bone and memory."

"Show me."

Erik cocked his head, dubious. "Are you sure? There are things more frightening than rats in the dark."

"Is there anything there more frightening than you?"

"I guess that depends on your perspective."

"From the perspective of someone or something that might try to hurt me?"

Erik smirked, knowing it made his eyes glitter in the dark, and shook his head. "Nothing."

"Then show me your Paris, *Monsieur le Fantôme*."

Raoul was finally beginning to learn his way around the Opera. Or at least he knew his way from the Patron's entrance on the side to the office and dressing rooms. He believed the regular public wasn't allowed in this part of the building, but he wasn't the regular public. Things were quiet today, which was odd, given that he had been assured by a kindly stagehand that there would be a rehearsal with the entire cast and chorus today, set to end around this time. But the halls were deserted.

"Oh, Lord, what are you doing here?"

Raoul turned at the familiar lilt of Sorelli's voice. She was in her rehearsal clothes, he assumed, since the white toile and blue ribbon were rather plain for a formal costume. She was pale and lithe with a haughty look in her eye that Raoul had become familiar with given her assignation with his brother.

"Do you really have to ask?" Raoul replied.

Sorelli heaved an exasperated sigh that was much like the sighs Philippe had been directing at him since Sunday. "She's gone, I'm sorry to tell you," Sorelli said.

"But I thought Christine and the chorus had rehearsal?"

"Christine is the reason the chorus *doesn't* have rehearsal. Carlotta practically kicked the entire lot of them off stage just to spite your pretty Swede."

"Carlotta? The other soprano?"

"The only soprano," a voice declared from behind Raoul and he turned. It was the very woman in question, Raoul was sure. The way her ostentatious hat sat high above her blonde curls and her narrow body made her look like a gilded stalk of wheat. But what was more confounding was the person that emerged behind her: Raoul's own brother.

"What are you doing here?" Raoul demanded, feeling exactly as he had as a child when Philippe would catch him sneaking out to play with the local children.

"The same thing as you, but with much more success," Philippe replied with a grin as he strode towards Sorelli and took her hand to kiss it. "Signora Carlotta was kind enough to escort me."

"Your brother was telling me that you have quite the outsized interest in the little songbird who contrived to replace me," Carlotta said, her pale eyes boring into Raoul as she made no effort to conceal her contempt. "Such a pity you won't be hearing her for a while."

"I would not be sure of that," Raoul snapped back.

"My dear Comte, thank you for the kind words and insight," the diva said, turning to Philippe. "I shall treasure them. Until next time." Carlotta swept away with a final sneer to Raoul and Sorelli, who was staring at Philippe in pure fury.

"Do not tell me she's got her claws in you too now!" Sorelli said before Raoul could. "We were clear on our rules!"

"Darling, don't be foolish!" Philippe exclaimed. It did not console Sorelli, who snatched her hand away.

"You can come find me when you're done flirting with that Spanish whore or chasing after your blue-balled brother!" With a huff, Sorelli was gone, leaving both Chagny brothers staring slack-jawed down the hall. It took a beat for Philippe to snap to attention and deliver Raoul an annoyed thwack to his shoulder.

"Thank you. Now you have two women furious with me," Philippe admonished.

"The Spaniard didn't seem furious," Raoul grumbled as he rubbed his upper arm.

"I meant Sabine. She's the one who told me you were on your way back here," Philippe replied.

"I wanted to see if anyone had seen—" Raoul cast about again, even though the hope in his heart was faltering.

"My dear brother, if that little minx of yours wanted to see you, she would have sought you out. Her kind aren't shy. I told you when you were a mooning boy not to trust artists like her and that rootless father of hers. You should have listened then and you should listen now."

Raoul frowned, hating how, as always, Philippe was right. "I just wanted to know where she's been and if she's alright. She was upset when I last saw her."

"I'm sure she's fine, little brother," Philippe told him, though he did not sound entirely convinced. "From what the Signora was telling me, Christine is safer away from the Opera for now."

4. The World Below

"**A**re you sure you know where you are going?" Christine asked as they turned down another tunnel. Erik gave her a smile over his shoulder, golden eyes bright as stars in the dark. The light in his eyes was familiar now, as were the shadows.

"Trust me," Erik replied with a wicked tone.

"I won't follow you into a sewer, the skulls were quite enough for me," Christine admonished, though in her heart she knew she was lying. It was terrifying, honestly, but she was already sure she would follow Erik anywhere into the dark below Paris. Somewhere along their strange path, she had found her trust.

"I promise I won't take you to one of those unless you ask. But I don't think you'd enjoy the smell," Erik answered and laughed as Christine scowled.

The night (or afternoon, she truly wasn't sure what time it was anymore) had been unexpectedly delightful and a welcome distraction from the humiliation of rehearsal. Erik had led her through the tunnels to the cellars of what he claimed were some of the more famous and expensive restaurants in the city and they had, as he said, 'sampled' their stores of rich delicacies: soft cheese, delicate pastries, incredible fresh bread, and a bottle of the best wine Christine had ever tasted.

Then: the catacombs. Erik had told her with relish how the network of tunnels below the city had been built up over centuries and how the bones of thousands of deceased Parisians had been used to build walls when the cemeteries had overflowed and then been moved. They had not encountered another living soul, though at one point Erik had held her back as a shadow crossed far ahead of them in the dark. He had shown her caves as well, with natural stone walls marked by centuries of graffiti. People had built entire rooms into the rock. There was even a chapel, somewhere, Erik claimed, with pews hewn from the living earth. But that was not their destination. The tunnel he led her through now was lined with masonry and old, dark wood.

"Ah, here we are," Erik declared as they came to a large wooden door braced with iron at the end of the tunnel. Christine tried to make out the worn crest above the threshold. "This was built in the sixteenth century, I believe," he explained as he pressed the door open. "I was extremely pleased when I found it; I'd been looking for a way in here for months when I did."

"Where is here?" Christine demanded. Erik only chuckled in reply. He raised the lantern higher as they emerged into a chamber, a cellar more accurately, that reminded Christine strongly of the prop room she had slept in at the Opera, though it was much bigger. The flickering light and shadows danced over the shapes of bodies and boxes and – was that a face in the dark? "Erik, *where are we?*"

"Over here," Erik whispered, indicating what looked like a coffin painted with intricate designs and an exotic face. "This is one of my favorites: Napoleon brought it back from Egypt. It didn't belong to a Pharaoh, but perhaps to a rich man. See there, in that little loop. That's the owner's name. It's called a cartouche."

Christine blinked at the sarcophagus in front of her, then looked around again. They were in a storeroom that seemed to go on forever and it was full of statues, paintings, and all manner of other art, stacked carelessly to the ceiling.

"There's more stored down here than they have on view above," Erik commented as he watched Christine survey the cellar. Her eyes passed over a huge tapestry, a collection of small vases topped with animal heads, and dozens of paintings leaning against a wall. "I think that's amazing given that it's the largest gallery – and building – in Europe."

Christine laughed in numb amazement. "The Louvre. We've snuck into *the Louvre*."

"I've never been caught, if you're worried. They don't keep track of things down here." Erik caught her eye and grinned wickedly. "At least I haven't read anything in *Le Monde* about certain pieces going missing."

"Erik, no. Tell me you haven't taken anything—"

"*Borrowed*," Erik countered with a shrug and Christine made an extremely unladylike noise. "Come come, I only moved things from one cellar to another. At least in my home some works of art can be appreciated by one set of human eyes. Or two now, as it were. You did say you liked the pictures in your room."

"I didn't think you had stolen them from the fucking Louvre!" Christine squawked.

"Almost everything here is stolen too," Erik laughed, velvety and entrancing. "Do you think the Egyptians or the Greeks just handed over these treasures? Let me know if you see anything you particularly like. We can carry it back, if it's small enough."

"Dear God in heaven," Christine muttered as Erik strode down a cluttered aisle towards a grand statue of a winged horse with the head of a bearded man.

"We should stay down here for a while; it will be less likely that we'll run into anyone when we go up if we wait."

"*Go up?*" Christine wondered if her eyes could get any wider.

"Don't worry! Like I said: I've never been caught here."

"And if that changes tonight?"

Erik grinned and looked her over. "Then I hope you can run in those skirts."

Christine found herself laughing in awe again. They began to move slowly through the maze of forgotten works of art spanning centuries and, of course, Erik knew all of them.

Her mind reeled as Erik spoke of how the Dutch masters could paint light, how the Chinese had mastered landscapes in ink, and how the Greek statues had been stripped of colors that had made them look alive. When he explained to Christine how the ancient Pharaohs had filled their hidden burial chambers with art and trinkets to carry with them into the afterlife, Christine was sure he was thinking of his own tomb full of treasures, far beneath the ground.

"I've seen them, the Pyramids," Erik told her, wistful. "They're incredible, even at night."

"I would say I can imagine, but I truly can't," Christine replied as they stood before an ancient statue in black stone of a seated woman with the head of a lion, a strange sort of cross in her hand. "I would love to have seen even a fraction of what you have." Erik met her eyes, and she stopped herself from saying that he would have to show her one day. It was too absurd an idea to voice aloud, but for a moment, she wished it could be true.

"Come, it's late enough to go up," Erik said, inclining his head in the direction they were to move. "One could spend months down here or above, and not see it all. I'll show you my favorites."

His favorites turned out to be the Da Vincis. Did Erik feel a kinship with the man, an inventor and artist like himself, so far ahead of his time? (She kept the consideration to herself, not wanting to encourage her guide's ego too much). How many places he had wandered, admiring beauty that he could never touch? How many times had the Mona Lisa smiled back at this ghost through the dark?

"I do wish I could see her in the light," Erik sighed as they stood before Da Vinci's great masterpiece. "Though I feel that way for all of them. You must come some day in the sun and tell me if you notice more."

"I don't think it would be the same without you," Christine said, another thought she should have kept in finally slipping out. It made Erik smile – another treasure she could see in the dim halls.

"You should still go," Erik said softly. "A place like this...it's magic. This temple, full of glorious things that have come down to us through time, little fragments of divine beauty that endure long after their creators have passed to dust. It's so different from music, this sort of art; these solid things that can survive."

Christine had no idea how to reply or explain the way his words made her want to cry.

It was late when Erik led them back into the cellars storing more beauty and rarities than Christine could conceive of. "It is sad, you're right," she mused, touching the cool marble of a Roman bust, "that so much is hidden down here. What you said, about art enduring. It only does that if we remember it, I guess."

"I like to think it still matters," Erik replied as they came to the door and he looked wistfully back at the paintings, statues, and more that Paris would never see. "When we make art, the point is to capture a moment, or a feeling, or a story, and express it. It will have always existed for the artist, even when the world forgets it. Or if they never see it. Or hear it."

Christine wanted to grab his hand and tell him she heard him. That his music – that wondrous music that had sung to her soul for months – *mattered*, even if she was the only audience he would ever have. But he didn't linger long enough for her to say it. She followed him back into his underground world wishing she could summon a sliver of the poetry that came so easily to him to tell him that he would not be forgotten in a cellar too.

It was like a dream, coming back to the lake, and she listened to the drip of water and echo of their breath as Erik poled them over the still, inky water. They came at last to his little dock, where Erik led them to the wall and lifted his lantern.

"I am going to show you exactly how to find my door and unlock it. That will make things far more complicated, should you decide to reveal me," Erik said, breaking the silence that had crystalized between them.

"Why would you do that?" Christine squinted at him as he traced his long fingers over the wall.

"I am handing you a loaded gun to point at my heart, Christine. I hope in giving you my further trust, I can continue to earn yours." He fixed her with his preternatural eyes and her heart stopped. He had shown her who he was behind his mask and now trusted her never to reveal it. And in a way, he had shown himself to be the angel she had known and yet so much more.

"Show me your door, Erik," she said uneasily.

"Here." He lifted his hand to the wall and brought the lantern close, revealing that there were grooves in the surface. Five long lines, in fact. "It's a stave," he explained just as Christine realized it. "The secret of this lock is not a key, but a rhythm." With that explanation, he pushed below the lowest line once, then paused as if measuring a beat in his head. He pressed again, higher on the hidden musical staff by a third interval, twice this time. Again, he waited several beats, then moved up another third for two more taps. And then the wall opened.

Christine smirked. "The Overture to *The Magic Flute*. The 'knock' motif."

"What else?" he replied with a gentleman's nod. Of course Erik had a lock based on an overture full of masonic secrets.

The house on the lake embraced them with its warmth as they entered, the dim golden light of the lamps and candles casting a spell all its own. Christine took off her cloak as Erik stoked the fire and lit more candles, drifting to the piano.

"Would you like me to play for you?" Christine spun at the voice right behind her and Erik stepped back immediately. He had once again transformed without his cloak and hat. He was just a man once again. An extraordinary man who was staring at Christine like she was extraordinary too.

"Will you sing for me?" Christine asked without thinking, and the request seemed to surprise Erik as much as it shocked her to say it. "I haven't heard you sing since..."

"I didn't think you'd want to hear my voice that way anymore." His voice had once had the power to ignite in her the greatest bliss and profoundest longing she had ever known. Of course he would assume she wouldn't want him to use that power or remind her of what her angel had been.

"I do. I miss it," Christine confessed. "And as you taught me tonight, it's not right for a treasure to be kept in a cellar for no one to appreciate."

Erik stared at her, long enough that a blush began to rise in her cheeks. "What shall I sing for you?" he asked softly at last.

"Anything," Christine replied too quickly. "Something of your own composition, if you wish it."

Erik's eyes stayed upon her as he moved past her to the piano and nodded for her to sit. She obeyed instantly, her heart quickening as his long hands alit on the keys. He did not look away as he began to play, a sweeping melody that fell like winter rain from his fingers. He only closed his eyes when he began to sing, and Christine could not help but do the same.

It was more beautiful than anything she had ever heard. Astounding, yet familiar. And now she knew it was not a voice from heaven, but a man. He sang, as he had so many times as her angel, in a language she didn't know. It was lilting and rustic, and even without understanding the words, she knew the song was a lament. A ballad of longing and loss, but also of love. It made her tremble, even as she began to weep.

When her angel had sung to her, his voice had lifted her to heaven while also stoking desires of a far earthlier nature. Now, that same spark was there, but Christine pushed it down. It did not matter that her skin came alive as he sang to her, or how his voice made her blood thicken and dance in her veins. All that mattered was hearing *Erik*, knowing that she was the only person on earth to hear this genius create beauty out of thin air, and it was only for her. It was a miracle.

She could not say how long he played. The world melted away around them until there was just sound and melody and shadow. When the silence fell at last, Christine found herself breathless as she opened her eyes to admire the man who had given her such a gift. The look in his eyes when they met hers was like nothing she had ever seen, a savage mix of fear and something she did not want to name.

"You should rest, it's late," Erik said slowly, rising from the piano without looking away.

She stood, roughly wiping the tears from her cheeks, and nodded. She broke eye contact as she retreated to her room, suddenly shaking and barely able to breathe. When she turned to say goodnight, Erik was there, a meter away. If he came a step closer, he could touch her. Why did she wish he would?

As if reading her mind, Erik took a graceful stride and closed the distance between them. Christine's heart leapt to her throat. Another step and he was inches away, so close she could feel the faint heat of his body. It reminded her once again that he was not an angel or a ghost, but a man.

"I will never forget your music," she blurted out, frozen in his gaze. "Even when I'm a ghost myself, I'll still remember it. And you."

Erik stared down at her, the light of the candles dancing over his white mask and igniting the gold in his eyes. There was shock and gratitude in his gaze. "Thank you, Christine Daaé," he whispered. "To be remembered by you may be the greatest honor of my life."

Erik raised his hand to her cheek, his thumb hovering over where her tears had left their tracks. But he did not touch her. His caress hovered above her skin, like an invisible silk veil was between them. And yet he was so close. Drawing closer. She could feel the cold radiating from his fingers. Christine closed her eyes, a wild, reckless voice inside of her crying out as she reached up to take his hand and force it to cross that final distance.

Erik sprang back faster than the wind as Christine's eyes flew open so that all she saw for a brief second was his mask. And she remembered why he hid his glory here in the dark. She saw his eyes staring at her, glowing gold with unnamable, unbridled emotion, and she remembered as well why she should be afraid of her fallen angel.

"Goodnight, Christine," Erik said, his voice tight and tense. Christine heeded the unspoken command and retreated with a nod, but not another word. As soon as her door was shut behind her, she sank to the floor with the wooden barrier against her back.

What had just happened? What on earth had she just *done*? Or not done, as it were. He had almost touched her. She had almost let him. No, not let him, *made* him. Because she had gone mad and wanted him to. She had longed for the source of that incredible voice, the man of that extraordinary genius, to caress her. And he had run away as if she had struck him.

She did not understand. She did not understand how, after all his crimes against her, she wanted to feel him solid and real and human against her skin. And she did not understand how this man, this strange, terrifying, extraordinary man who had told her a few days ago that all he had done had been for love, was determined to never lay a single finger upon her. And more, never let her touch him.

Did he not want her? He had said all he wanted was her company, but how could that be? Shouldn't she be relieved, if that was the case? Shouldn't she be thanking heaven and hell that he did not wish to seduce her? Why did she feel like she had done something wrong? Why did she want nothing more than for him to touch her when he sang to her again?

Antoine de Martiniac had invited himself to dinner at the Chagny manor, once again. And once again, he had overstayed his welcome into the late hours of the night, drinking their best brandy and smoking Philippe's worst cigars in the drawing room. Raoul, in turn, had exiled himself to the empty balcony overlooking the dormant garden. He didn't mind the cold at all. It reminded him of quiet nights out at sea, when the wind would whip his cheeks raw, but he could see more stars than a man could count in his lifetime.

"Phillipe said you'd be here sulking again." Raoul turned at the sound of his sister's voice, warm as the night was cold. She looked so much like the portrait of their mother that hung above the fireplace, with her handsome, round face and dark, sleek hair. Even when she was frowning at Raoul like now, it made his heart warm to see her.

"I can't snap out of it, if that's what you want me to do," Raoul told her as she came to stand beside him, eyes following his gaze up to the veiled stars.

"I know. I remember how you wept when we sold that old place in Perros. And that was months after she had jilted you the first time," Sabine went on. She had been twenty at the time, and now at twenty-six she was almost a spinster, yet she made Raoul feel ashamed for being the only Chagny who wanted a marriage.

"She didn't jilt me. She—"

"Left. Without ever telling you why and never wrote again. She ignored you then, just like she's ignoring you now. She's not worth it."

"Christine is a complicated woman," Raoul muttered. "I'm sure she had her reasons. And I'm sure she has reasons for avoiding me now. There is all sort of intrigue at the Opera with the new managers and that awful Spaniard."

"Fontana?"

Raoul raised an eyebrow at Sabine. He hadn't known that she paid attention to the principals treading the board at the Palais Garnier. "No, the Soprano. Signora Zambelli."

"What's a Spanish diva doing with an Italian name and title?"

"Italian?" Raoul echoed. "How do you know that?"

"Unlike my handsome but useless brothers, I paid attention to my language tutors. And I did visit Rome last summer while you were away. Miserable place in that season; I nearly melted." Raoul smiled and shook his head.

"I have an Italian friend from my ship. He couldn't stop talking about how Rome was the greatest city in history. He showed me a book of prints, and all I saw were broken buildings and dead empires." Raoul paused, thinking back to the conversations with Vincenzo over bad wine, the thin walls of their quarters barely holding in the crew's laughter.

"Well, ask him about what sort of name Zambelli is," Sabine chided. "I'm sure he's a better influence than that gypsy Daaé. Or those two libertines inside."

"I prefer the term 'connoisseur of Paris's many delights,' Mademoiselle la Vicomtesse." Raoul rolled his eyes at the sound of

Antoine's voice. The man still smelled of cigars as he slunk towards Sabine. "Of which you, of course, are the loveliest."

"A libertine, as I said," Sabine replied with a smile that betrayed her flattery and amusement. Raoul took in the satisfaction on Antoine's pale, angular face. He was an impressively tall man, Raoul always noted, with pale hair and cold blue eyes that reminded one of a glacier. A viper made of ice that somehow continued to charm his sister.

"Of course, my dear Sabine," Antoine replied with a wink as he took Sabine's hand to kiss. Raoul rolled his eyes so vigorously he could nearly see the moon. "I came to bid you a fond goodnight. And invite you to the Opera on Saturday. Again."

"In my own family's box?" Sabine asked, her expression more amused than annoyed. "I will consider."

"We'll need you there to keep this one from leaping over the orchestra to fall at his little Swedish Nightingale's feet," Antoine laughed. "Though I have heard a rumor she won't be long for the National Academy of Music."

"Good riddance then," Sabine said with a meaningful look at her brother. "Everyone will be better off with her gone."

Raoul bristled. "Sabine! There is no such rumor!"

"I wouldn't be so sure, my young friend," Antoine laughed with a sharp look in his eyes. "You have a lot to learn about the Opera. As does your ingenue." The older man turned on his heel with a laugh and left the Chagny siblings standing alone in the deepening chill of the January night.

"What rumors could he have meant?" Raoul muttered.

"I don't know, or care," Sabine sighed. "But I don't think anything I say will dissuade you from trying to find out, will it?"

Erik still hoped that one day it would not be so disconcerting to wake up in the dark, but after years underground, it still left him in confusion and panic to open his eyes to nothing but shadow and no hint of dawn. He groped for a match on the bedside table, cursing himself for not leaving an oil lamp burning low. Another casualty of his constant distraction and tension lately. A flare of flame and the clock told him it was the small hours of the morning. The last he remembered, it had been midnight. At least he had slept for a little while, until the dreams had awoken him again.

Five nights she had been with him now, as she had promised. Five nights, Christine had shared his bread and home and fire in a miracle of trust and kindness. And for five nights, he had dreamed of shattering that trust to pieces and awoken with screams choking his throat.

Each night he dreamed of the searing warmth of her skin, the scent of her hair, the wet evidence of her desire staining his hands between her thighs. It was strange, how in dreams he was so bold. He dreamed of taking her. Whether pressed against the wall or trapped in the ivory sheets of her bed, he would lose himself in her silken heat until she tore off his mask and screamed. She screamed as her nails tore at his skin, screamed as he defiled her. He begged for her to stop, but the screams went on and on.

Erik shook his head and pressed his hands to his ears, muffling the memories and nightmares and forcing himself to come back to reality. It hadn't been real. It would never be real because he would not let it be. He could not.

Then what are you doing? A cruel, cold voice out of somewhere deep in his damned soul demanded of him. *Why trap her here in the tomb with you if not to take her? You know you could.*

"Shut up," Erik said aloud, hands shaking as he confirmed his mask was still safely in place. He tried to rise from the tangle of his sheets, but the other physical evidence of the dream stopped him.

He was soaked with sweat and still breathless from the terror, and yet, he was still hard, his unsatisfied desire throbbing with shameful lust in the dark.

It would be easy, the voice whispered. Erik laid back in his bed, trying to breathe and pretend he was not listening to the darkness for sounds of movement, a room away. If she was asleep, maybe it was safe. Maybe a moment of release would drive away the dreams and he could truly rest. But he couldn't...

Five days he'd spent in her light and warmth. And five nights he'd woken wanting her. He'd refused to succumb to it. He washed in icy water and forced himself to remember a hundred different pains and humiliations. He'd think of the horror and fear in her eyes, not the way she looked at him with the old desire. He was dreaming that. He would dig his nails into his skin and think of his horrible reflection until the blood drained from his traitorous cock. But he was so tired tonight and it was so late and so quiet. *It would be so easy.*

Alone in the dark, locked away from the world, it was safe to remember and to dream. He could remember the way she made him smile and how he could make her laugh. He loved the sound of her laugh. His body began to relax and ache at the same time, as he sank into the memories of her. Too exhausted to fight it any longer, he let his hand descend to his desperate erection.

Erik exhaled slowly, overcome by the sensation and the memory of Christine's smile as he moved his hand over his hot length. He remembered the way she sang for him and gripped harder.

Their lessons were the most sublime part of their days together. He never had felt so transported and ineffably connected to another as when she sang for him with nothing in between them. He dared not sing with her though, it was dangerous enough to sing *to* her. But he could not refuse when she asked for that. He sped up his strokes at the memory, chasing pleasure and escape. She wanted one part of him, the one clean, good part of him that had always been able to cast a magic spell. To ease her tears and stem his pain. The one part of him that was untainted.

You tainted it when you seduced her. No. *When you sang her to sin. When she came on her fingers and you wished they were yours. When you bound her and blinded her and took her innocence.* No... *When you could have done so much more.*

His release came swiftly, dull and pale, staining his sheets with the evidence of his weakness. There was no bliss to it, nor peace, it was nothing but a second to breathe and rest before the shame and fear came crashing down on him again. He had violated her trust again. He had tried to be strong and failed. He had given in and now all he wanted was more.

Coward, the ghosts whispered around him. *Fool. Liar.* Erik shut his eyes and begged for rest again. He couldn't play because every song would sound like her. He couldn't sleep because she would only haunt him again. He couldn't run because he had made her a promise.

Monster. He had to be strong. He had to protect them both. *Monster*, the voices he could not flee repeated again and again.

Christine closed her eyes and lay absolutely still in her bed, forcing herself to catalogue the sensations and textures: the yielding comfort of the down mattress, the warm scratch of her chemise against her skin, the scent of wax, a faint perfume of roses. She focused on the still silence of the shadows, pierced only by the sound of her breath. And his.

She kept her eyes closed, even knowing that doing so would make the prickling sensation of his eyes watching her all the more intense. With her eyes closed, he was only a shadow, a memory. But even as a shadow and an angel he had been able to touch her. Just as he did now. His fingertips were so cold as they drew over her skin.

She released a shaking sigh, a deeper sound of relief and delight hiding behind it. She didn't struggle or move as he pushed away the cloth covering her breast, exposing her tingling skin. Was it silent or was he singing to her again? His music encircled her like fog, his voice sang in that strange tongue. And he touched her. At last, he touched her, firmly and fully, and she moaned, her blood singing back to him.

She felt the weight of him upon her, with her, between the sheets. She heard him whisper her name, then sing it, an entreaty and a command all at once. And it was so easy to obey, spreading her legs as his hand slid down her belly, fingers carding through the hair that veiled her sex and... Yes. Finally. She bit back a moan as he found her, but not with his hands. It was only when he thrust into her that she opened her eyes.

She saw death itself above her, but she could not scream with his hand wrapped around her throat.

Christine sprang from her sheets, her eyes truly open now, as she gasped for breath. She quaked as she scrambled out of the bed, reeling from the intensity of the dream. She was safe and alone in her room and her door was still securely closed. She found herself in the gilded bath chamber and splashed her face and chest with freezing water to wash away the recollection, even as her body continued to ache shamefully for the imagined touch, which made her horror at the memory of his face all the more acute.

She had to be going mad; her days with Erik prizing away what little sense she had. It would be a relief to go home to her own flat tonight, where she could catch her breath and sort out what the hell she was doing with her strange teacher or what he wanted from her. And yet she felt no satisfaction at the end of her promised time with Erik.

Christine looked at her clock as she returned to her room. It was well into the morning, late enough that Erik might be up and about; though she was never sure when, or if, he slept. If she went out to find him, would he read her dreams from her face?

Cowed by even the possibility of him discerning from a blush or a sigh that she had been dreaming about *that*, Christine took her time dressing. She made sure the laces of her corset were tight and every button of her mauve dress up to her chin was secure, as if she could rein in the deceit of her wanton body with enough fabric and determination. Her resolve vanished as soft music drifted to her ears from the parlor. It was the violin again today.

Christine emerged quietly, hoping to steal as much time as possible to take in the art of the virtuoso with whom she had shared a roof for the last few days. She adored listening to him on the organ and piano and harp, but there was something about watching him play the same instrument as her father that transported her to another world.

Today's piece was like listening to a storm, a jagged melody rising and falling like waves. It was somehow familiar and yet like nothing she had ever heard. Christine lost herself in it as she watched Erik's skilled fingers fly over the strings and the fluid, rapid motion of his bow. And if she was blushing when he finally noticed her, it was because of the music and nothing else.

He was not alarmed at her presence today at least, which meant he kept playing. Erik held her gaze, the violin singing under his touch like a wild, ravished thing. It made Christine's mouth go dry, her pulse beginning to race in tempo with the music. In some ways Erik was so elusive, shy even, but when he was in the mood to show off, it was spectacular. The melody rose to a glorious, sweeping crescendo, and Christine nearly leapt to her feet to applaud. But Erik was still staring at her, his breath coming too quickly, and suddenly she couldn't move.

"Was that one of yours?" Christine asked, not trying to conceal her awe.

"Yes, a variation on an old melody that's been in my head," Erik replied, looking away towards where a pile of half-finished music sat on the piano.

"It sounded familiar. Was it something you've played me before?"

"Sung," Erik replied with a tense nod. From deep in his throat came a fragment of the melody and Christine suppressed a shudder at the sound. "*Siúil, siúil, siúil a ruin. Siúil go socar agus siúil go ciúin...*" She remembered now: the first song he had sung to her as an angel to lull her to sleep. "It's an old folk tune."

"From where?" Christine asked, eager and entranced. "That language, it's the one you sing in all the time. What is it?"

Erik's hands were tight on the violin and bow as he avoided Christine's eyes for a long beat. "It's Gaelic. Irish Gaelic. The tune is an Irish song."

"Irish?" Christine echoed in fascination, stepping closer on instinct. Erik tensed at the movement. "Have you traveled there too? I confess, Ireland feels as distant to me as India."

"I have, briefly," Erik replied in the melancholy tone which told Christine there was much more to the story than he wanted to share. But today she was determined to dig more out of him. At the end of their time, wasn't she owed that much?

"Long enough to learn the language? It seems special to you."

"No, I learned it from..." Erik turned to her, his eyes full of clear pain. "It doesn't matter."

"It does to me," Christine countered.

Erik responded by setting down his instrument with surprising force, his hands splayed on the piano's lid, tense and tight as the strings beneath. "It's *not important*."

"Can I tell you something I've only ever told one other person?" Christine blurted out, and Erik turned to her in confusion. "My father was illegitimate. I told you he was only Roma on his mother's side. I'm sure you know how uncommon that is. Her name was Aud, my grandmother. When she was sixteen, she met a boy in a town that the caravan visited. Somewhere near Oslo. I don't know if he was her first love or if he..." Christine swallowed, the shame of it still burning after all these years. "Papa never talked about it much. But all that man left my grandmother with was a babe in her belly and a name. Daaé."

"The Roma aren't welcoming of that sort of thing," Erik remarked, still guarded. "It had to have been hard for her."

"It was unclean, yes," Christine replied. "But her parents let Aud stay, even though she was tainted. She gave her little Stellan his father's name. But it was hard for her, and she died when Papa was still a boy. He wasn't welcomed among The People after that. But he could play the violin, and he played himself into a real music school, then into one fair and orchestra after another, all the way from the north and down into France. He played for the ballet in Nice, where he met a dancer named Michelle and fell in love with her. But her parents wouldn't allow her to marry a poor, half-Roma musician. Her career was bad enough. But nothing could stop them."

Erik had turned to her fully now. Were his brows furrowed behind this mask as he watched a fool babbling in front of him?

"They eloped, moved to the closest thing my father had to native soil, found a house near Upsala, and made a life. A year later I arrived. Mama wanted to name me after her mother, Pauline, but Papa said we should honor my grandfather, Christian, instead, so I was named Christine." She waited for Erik to react or say something, but he only stared, his lips shut tight.

"Papa had learned all sorts of languages among the Roma and in France," Christine went on. "But Mama only knew French, so I grew up speaking all of it. Papa says I'd switch from Swedish to French to Romani in a single sentence sometimes. But I've forgotten most of it now." Christine swallowed, old grief welling up inside her.

"When Mama died, Papa couldn't stay in one place anymore. He had wandering in his blood, he said. We went back to France and to Mama's parents, and they kept me for a few years, on and off. They only ever let me speak French there. But then they died too, and it was only me and Papa. He tried to reteach me, but I was too old. Now it feels like there is this missing piece of me." Christine shook her head. "Which is a long way of saying that *it matters*. If that tongue is special enough for you to sing, it has to matter. I wish you would tell me why."

Erik stared at her, an ocean of sadness in his shining eyes. He opened his mouth, as if the words were finally on the tip of his tongue. But Christine made a mistake: she stepped closer and reached out her hand. Erik flinched away.

"We should go," he declared as collected his hat and cloak.

Christine kept her eyes down as she gathered her own things, her face burning. He hadn't even offered to help her warm up before rehearsal or go over her part. Perhaps he didn't want to remind her that she would be a chorus girl again today, not even an understudy. At least she would be allowed to sing.

Erik led her to the boat and kept quiet as he poled them across the lake. Lake Avernus, he called it, a private joke Christine had not understood until Erik had told her that it was the Roman name of a lake that led the way to the underworld. Now he seemed a strange Chiron, ferrying her soul over Styx. Did this make her Eurydice, as they followed Erik's dark road back up to the land of the living? Her guide was certainly doing as Orpheus had been ordered and refusing to look back at her. Maybe Erik didn't want to damn her to the underworld. Maybe he wanted to return to his solitude without her there to pester and distract him. As if to answer her, Erik looked back as they turned a corner, but she could read no emotion in his glowing eyes.

They came all too quickly to the opposite side of the mirror where Erik deftly opened the portal to let her through. Once again it felt like walking out of the sea to step back into the world she knew and out of Erik's realm of shadows. Christine ignited the gaslight by the door, her hands shaking. It was she who was afraid to turn around now.

"Christine." She froze, her skin coming alive with goosebumps at just the sound of her name in his voice. "It has been five nights."

"It has," she said, turning to him. He looked like a dark god indeed, framed by the black of the hidden corridor as the golden light from her dressing room illuminated his mask. "I guess I shall go home after rehearsal."

He said nothing, but he held his breath, frozen, as Christine approached, daring to get close one more time.

"Though I don't know if Adèle will take me. I may be on her bad side after that business with the *Comique* and Cravalho. And I'm rather sure I forgot to pay rent for the month. And..." *And I wish you would ask me to stay.* The pathetic entreaty continued in her heart as she swallowed and met Erik's hopeful eyes.

"Perhaps, if you wish it..." he began with uncharacteristic hesitance. Christine looked down at where his hand was clasped in front of him in an echo of her position. He had but to reach a few inches and he could touch her. It would be so easy. He had forgotten his gloves and she wondered if that pale skin was as cold as she remembered. His fingers twitched towards hers. "Perhaps—"

"Mademoiselle Daaé! Are you in there?" The voice came accompanied by a pounding on Christine's dressing room door.

In the heartbeat Christine looked away, Erik sprang back and triggered the mirror, so that when she turned again, she saw only her reflection. Left with no choice, Christine rushed to open her door to find none other than Carlotta's obsequious little secretary LeDoux standing outside with his hand raised to knock again.

"Monsieur?" Christine asked, trying to calm her pounding heart.

"Ah, you are here. I've been looking for a while. The managers would like to see you in their office." Christine's heart defied her and began to beat even harder, so much so she felt it in her fingers and toes.

"Why would they send you to find me?" She could still feel Erik watching and, maybe she imagined it, but she sensed his alarm and suspicion too.

"My dear mistress was with them, and I volunteered. She's quite worried by this nasty business," LeDoux explained with a simpering grin.

"Lead on then. I'll follow," she said with a final glance to the mirror. Whatever ordeal she was to face with the managers, she wanted Erik there. Like the fool she was, she wished she could hold his hand.

She had never been to the managers' office before, nor any of the administration areas. It wasn't for people like her – grubby costumers and insignificant choristers. It was the world of the patrons and divas. Such as the one she saw immediately when stepping through Richard and Moncharmin's door.

"Ah, Mademoiselle, we thought we'd never find you," Carlotta purred. Christine could hardly bear to look at her, she was so smug and delighted with whatever was about to happen.

"Messieurs, how may I be of service?" Christine asked, hoping they did not hear the tremor in her voice.

"The Signora has brought a little controversy to our attention," Moncharmin began, placating and pitying. Not a good sign.

"I'm sure you're aware of some of the theories as to your origin that have surfaced in the press," Richard cut in.

Christine nodded. "They say all sorts of foolish things, I'm told. I haven't read them myself." She swallowed. "And of course, none of it is true."

"Really? Because a friend of mine from *Le Gaulois* has quite a story and a reliable source," Carlotta interjected.

The floor was becoming unstable beneath Christine's feet. "What sort of story?"

"That you are a bastard, sired by a gypsy bastard, and roamed all of France before swindling your way into the Conservatoire," Carlotta recited with glee. "From which you were expelled for failing to pay your fees."

"Is that true?" Richard demanded before Christine could protest.

"No, not entirely," Christine stammered. How on earth had someone learned that? "Why does it matter if it is?" Christine turned to Moncharmin, the one sympathetic face in the room. He looked hopelessly at her, then Richard.

"It's just *Le Gaulois*," Moncharmin attempted. "No one reads it."

"First *Le Gaulois*, tomorrow *Le Monde* and *L'Époque!*" Carlotta squawked, fanning herself in a mockery of indignation that made Christine want to scream. But she was too paralyzed to speak.

"This is the National Academy of Music," Richard said with a sigh. "We have appearances to maintain and many patrons to appease. If your origins are truly so scandalous, it would be unclean to keep you in the company."

"In the company?" Christine echoed numbly. She hadn't even touched the stage in nearly a week and somehow that had not been enough for Carlotta to take away from her. "Am I – am I being dismissed?"

"For the moment, yes," Moncharmin stammered, as if it were comforting. "But once this has been cleared up, perhaps—"

"Perhaps nothing. It's done," Richard barked. "You are no longer welcome at the Paris Opera, Mademoiselle Daaé."

5. Blades

Beneath the floorboard of the managers' office, Erik flexed his hands into claws, wishing to every dark power that they could be latched around Carlotta Zambelli's horrible neck right now. How dare she? Was one humiliation not enough? Death was too good for her. She deserved to suffer. She deserved to burn and writhe below the Opera, her terrible reflection her only consolation in a forest of pain.

"Please, don't." Christine's voice cut through the fog of Erik's rage, speaking from above him like an angel still. "You don't have to do this. I can talk to the press and sort this out."

"It's already done, Mademoiselle. You may collect your things from your dressing room, but please do not linger and force us to have you escorted from the premises," Richard said curtly. Erik wished he could wring that bastard's neck too.

"That won't be necessary," Christine replied, her voice tiny and weak. Erik imagined the look of devastation on her face and felt sick. He was responsible for her, and he had let this happen. She said nothing more as her soft footsteps retreated.

"That was unnecessarily cruel, Firmin," Moncharmin admonished.

"It's done now, so let us away," Carlotta trilled, laughter in her voice. "Rehearsal starts soon and I'd adore having you both there."

"Of course, dear Signora," Richard agreed with unusual warmth and Erik knew how the bitch had ensnared him. Was Richard truly such a fool to fall for the whore's tricks, or had she offered him more than her body? Erik didn't care. All that mattered was that the two had conspired to destroy the one person in the world who deserved the Opera's spotlight.

The doors shut above him and Erik didn't wait to emerge from his trapdoor behind Richard's desk chair. The desk itself was strewn with papers and ledgers, not nearly as orderly as Moncharmin's. No matter. With two mighty sweeps of his arm he ravaged both, tossing papers to the floor and spilling ink over leather and wood.

He grabbed a stray sheet of paper and a pen and scrawled his note. The warning was simple: *So, it is to be war? If Christine Daaé does not sing Marguerite tomorrow, you will deliver Faust in an opera with a curse on it.* For good measure, he struck several books and ornaments from the shelves and overturned the chairs before descending again into the hidden passages.

He had to find Christine before she left. She wouldn't just go, would she? He slipped as quickly as he could through the corridors and walls, until he was near the dressing rooms, a few steps away from her.

"What are you doing here?" Christine's voice asked from the hall and Erik stopped. "Have you come to gloat again?" There was only one person she would address with such coldness.

"Oh no, my dear," Carlotta replied. Erik carefully edged along the hall, peering around a corner so he could see Christine facing down the prima donna. "I wanted to see if you needed any help with your things."

"How can you be this cruel?" Christine snapped back. "Are you truly this heartless?"

"I don't know what you mean," Carlotta said with a false smile. "I brought the information about that nasty story to the managers to help you. I didn't want to see it published." Christine's face was stony, though the gaslights reflected in the tears welling from her eyes. Erik had never been one for forethought, but he knew killing

Carlotta right now in front of the woman he loved would not be a beneficial thing. He still wanted to.

"Really?" Christine replied. "I find that hard to believe."

Carlotta stared at Christine, strangely sympathetic. "I remember what it's like, you know. To be young and ambitious and to come from nothing."

"I only want to sing here, that's all," Christine countered pathetically.

"I understand that too. Perhaps this has been an overreaction. If you will meet me after rehearsal, we can discuss it."

Erik's spine stiffened in alarm and suspicion. Why would Carlotta help Christine now, after all of this?

"There's a little café over on the *Boulevard Haussmann, La Grenouille*," Carlotta went on. "Meet me there and I will see if there is anything I can do for you."

"Truly?" Christine asked, sniffling. "Why would you do that?"

"I'm not a monster. We women should help one another, not tear each other down. Until then, Christine." With a sweep of her golden furs, Carlotta strode away, leaving Christine staring down at the floor with her eyes closed.

"You can come out now," Christine whispered and a fraction of the rage in Erik's gut abated.

"I'm so sorry. I didn't know what they were planning," Erik protested as he unfurled himself from the shadows, rendering himself dangerously exposed. "We shouldn't talk here. Someone could see us."

"And confirm the rumors that Christine Daaé can summon and control the great and terrifying Opera Ghost?" Christine said, finally looking at Erik with accusing, teary eyes. "What of it? It's not as if that matters now."

"Christine..."

"You said you'd protect me," Christine snarled. "I guess that was another lie."

Erik staggered back, guilt mingling with his ire. "I swear, they'll pay for this. The managers and Carlotta. I've warned them and—"

"They don't listen to you!" Christine exclaimed. "They don't care about you or me! God in heaven, my only chance now is making peace with that awful woman."

"You cannot meet her. It's a trick!"

"What more could she possibly do to me?" Christine scoffed. "Maybe if I can appeal to her better nature, *I* can salvage this." She glared at him, the unspoken accusation – that she would have to grovel to save herself because Erik had failed – cutting him to the bone.

"Christine, your willingness to see the best in people is one of the parts of you I love the most, but there is no good to be found in that woman." Erik was not prepared for the aghast laugh that Christine gave in reply.

"Love? You speak of love *now*?" Christine asked as Erik cocked his head in bewilderment. "You claim you love me, but you don't show it."

"What?" The fury in Erik's heart was gone, replaced by utter confusion and fresh agony. "How can you—"

"You won't talk to me. You won't answer any question that's too intimate. You won't tell me anything about you, not really," Christine accused, eyes bright now. "All your talk of trust and you still spend every day and night hiding from me. For God's sake, you won't even touch me!"

"Why would you want me to?" Erik demanded back, confounded. "You don't want me to touch you. You can't. I have only tried to treat you as a gentleman would."

"But you're not a gentleman! And I'm not a fine lady and – and I have no idea what I am to you! Or what you even want from me!"

Christine snapped her mouth closed at the volume of her voice as Erik stood staring in shock. "Are you my suitor, Erik? Or am I just some other curiosity for you to lock away?"

"I have hoped to be your friend and—"

"And protector? Well, you've botched that job. And I don't need a teacher anymore, thanks to your *friendship*." He was used to cruelty, but it stung more, coming from her.

"Please, give me a chance to fix things," he begged.

"How will you fix things? You won't even go out above ground! So, I'll fix it myself, thank you very much." With that she turned and stalked away, leaving Erik, once again, alone in the dark.

The fur at the collar of Raoul's coat would not stop itching him in the winter wind. It was one of those bitterly cold days where the sun was incongruously bright but the air was frigid, turning the whole barren world into a shard of ice. Even though he was wearing gloves, Raoul had to rub his hands together to keep the feeling in them. He was seriously beginning to regret his decision to wait for Christine by the stage door. Being caught in the Opera again was better than freezing to death for the barest chance he might see...

Raoul blinked, then grinned, as a familiar shape emerged at last from the artist's entrance to the *Palais Garnier*. It was her. Finally, after days of waiting and wondering, it was Christine. And she looked utterly miserable. Her cheeks and eyes were red as if she had been crying and her head hung dejectedly low.

"Christine!" Raoul called, rushing to his old friend. She looked up at him in shock as he bounded towards her. "Christine, are you alright?"

"Raoul? What are you doing here?"

"Waiting for you, of course! I've been looking for you for days," he answered, catching his breath as he met her. Even with tears staining her cheeks and her hair in the plainest of styles, she was as beautiful as ever. "I was so put out when I heard you weren't at rehearsals, but they said I could wait here."

"For me?" Christine echoed, staring at him like he was speaking another language.

"And I'm glad I did. You seem distressed. What's happened?" Raoul wished it was appropriate to embrace the way they had as children, clutched together in dark attics and stables telling ghost stories.

"I-I've been—" she swallowed, new tears forming in her eyes. "I've been dismissed. The managers found out about Papa and—" She heaved a sob, her composure breaking.

"That's absurd! You're the greatest singer they've ever had! They can't dismiss you!"

Christine looked at him with the most desperate and lonely of expressions and – propriety be damned – Raoul would not let it stand. He pulled Christine into his arms, hugging her close. She nearly collapsed into him, her own arms wrapped so fiercely around him he almost couldn't breathe. He didn't care that people on the other side of the *Rue Gluck* were staring. He was holding his beloved at last! It was wonderful.

Too soon Christine pulled away, her face flushed as she dabbed at her cheeks. "I'm sorry. I'm always falling apart when we meet." Christine looked over her shoulder at the Opera. "Would you walk with me?"

"Of course." Raoul fell into step with Christine down the *Rue Auber* toward the *Rue Scribe*. He could not help but grin at her as they walked.

"I must confess I am glad fate keeps putting you in my path, old friend," she smiled back.

"Old friend?" Raoul echoed with a chuckle. "I hope to be more than that, my darling Christine. Have I not made my intentions clear?"

"You have," Christine just about sighed. "You wish to be my suitor. Or are, I guess. I wish I knew better what that meant."

Raoul laughed again. She had always possessed such a strange way of saying things or looking at the world. "What do you mean? Surely you must have many suitors already." It was half a joke and half an attempt to suss out his competition. "Though I do promise to outmatch all of them."

"Do you?" Christine asked back. "Tell me then: what would you do to win me? What feats would you attempt to court me and win my heart?"

It was Raoul who found himself blushing now. "Well, I would call on you in your parlor, of course, if it was proper," he stammered, and Christine looked interested. "We could dine together. And I would take you on outings if you'd allow it."

"What kind of outings?"

"Perhaps to a museum. Or a walk in the park, or a garden. Maybe even a boat ride in..." Raoul was not prepared for Christine to laugh at that, in a strange, sad way that made him feel excluded from some private joke. "Don't make fun. I am new at this too."

"I'm sorry. I didn't mean to offend you. I found it funny that perhaps I have had a suitor without knowing."

"Like I said, I'll do better than him, in every way," Raoul declared. Christine raised her eyebrows high. "I'll prove it, right now. Let's find some hot food and we'll plan how to get you back on the stage where you belong. I can help. Or Philippe can. If it's that awful Zambesi woman—"

"I can handle her myself," Christine sighed. "I have an appointment on the *Boulevard Haussmann* to hopefully do just that, but until then, I would be happy to share a meal with you. You can finally tell me what these last few years have been like for you. I want to know everything."

Raoul grinned at her, his heart leaping again. "And I want to tell you. Nothing would make me happier."

There seemed a cloud over the Opera, Shaya noted, despite the bright sun outside. Everyone was in a mood, glowering at their feet or each other and barely noticing him as he wandered the halls. He knew the place well (as well as any of the 1,500 employees at least) but he still had to think about where he was going and how to get there. For Erik, he assumed, it was second nature, as it had been in the palaces the monster had haunted when they first met. Erik had brought darkness on the brightest days to those places too.

Shaya tended to walk slowly as he made his rounds. It was the best way to happen on a conversation or assignation that could provide him with a new clue. His goal today was to verify the health and wellbeing of Christine Daaé, who had been missing since he had last seen her. But he was more than happy to pick up more along the way.

"What a farce," a male voice with a slight accent declared from around the corner. Shaya paused. Perfect. "That bitch thinks she can just run rehearsal now!"

"Someone has to, with Gabriel and Mercier misplacing their spines," another man replied in a much lower tone. "Carlotta gets to do anything she wants with Richard and Bosarge under her thumb."

"Including making us sing the whole opera out of order so she can leave early to do who-knows-what?! I have a bigger role than her and you don't see me complaining!"

It was Carlos Fontana, the tenor who sang Faust, Shaya realized. That meant his companion had to be Robert Rameau, the bass who took such relish in the part of Méphistophélès.

"That's because you're as afraid of her as they are," Rameau said.

"And you aren't?" Fontana huffed.

"No, I'm not," Rameau replied. "I'll be having words with Armand about this." Did he mean Moncharmin?

"Be careful being too familiar with our illustrious artistic director, my friend," Fontana said darkly. Shaya's ear perked up all the more. "Speaking of—"

A commotion in the hall interrupted the conversation.

"Why have the police not been called!" an unmistakable woman's voice cried. "That little trollop's cabal are threatening me! I want them found!" Strangely, Carlotta had lost her accent in the heat of the moment.

"Whom are we arresting?" Rameau asked with a bored drawl as Shaya dared to peek around the corner. Carlotta was flanked by both managers, her simpering secretary trailing behind.

"Whoever ransacked our office while the door was locked," Moncharmin replied, speaking to Rameau like he was the only one in the room.

"Good luck sending the police after a Phantom," Fontana chuckled.

"Or Daaé, since you've fired her," Rameau added, and Shaya was certainly interested in that. No wonder Erik was throwing fits. His pet had been sacked.

"I have endured this abuse for years now and I will not allow it any longer!" Carlotta screeched and raised a finger into Rameau's face. "I was considering letting that gypsy whore simply linger and fade, but not anymore. And if I hear you mention that damn *ghost* again, I'll have you out on the street too!"

"We have the guards sweeping the building," Richard said with a sigh. "Surely that's enough."

"Not even close," Carlotta snapped and spun to the managers. "As usual, I'll have to deal with this myself."

Shaya needed to hear no more. His mind raced as he made for the exit. Would this be the day Erik made a fatal mistake? Would the dismissal of Daaé finally draw him out of the shadows and into a cell or a grave where he belonged?

After days of dining on cold food stolen from the Opera stores with a man who barely ate, Christine took immense pleasure in a hot supper in a crowded café with a boisterous, hungry companion. The noise was still overwhelming to her, as was the heat and the brightness of the winter sun until it sank past sight. But it was also welcoming and warm to be part of the crush of humanity again and to share it with a friend.

Raoul had been at sea on and off for two years, earning his officer's status and making several naval voyages that his siblings hardly approved of. Raoul's tales were so different from Erik's. They were bright and boisterous, full of feeling but lacking detail. Not like Erik's poetic stories of a world explored in secret and at night. Raoul talked of one subject that Erik never did: the people he had met and befriended, something that came so easily to him, of course. Currently he was regaling Christine with a tale of badly translated Portuguese that had seen Raoul's friend run out of a tavern for accidentally propositioning the innkeeper's wife.

"He's Italian, you know, from Naples," Raoul was saying as Christine sipped on the dregs of her coffee with milk. (Drinking it had been a small rebellion, given that Erik claimed both coffee and milk were bad for the voice. Well, that didn't matter now.) "I saw him for supper yesterday! He had quite a few things to say about your horrible Spaniard."

"Why would he know Carlotta?" Christine asked, the shame and anger of earlier rekindling. Raoul gave her the shining grin he had always sported as a teenage boy. It was only more dashing now.

"I asked him, about that name of hers – Zambelli – and the fact that everyone calls her Signora like she's Italian, not Spanish!" Christine blinked. How had she never thought of that? It was as odd as Carlotta's terrible mélange of an accent.

"I always wondered if she was less than truly Spanish. Do you think she's Italian?" Why had Erik never investigated her? Not that he could do much from his sepulcher beneath the stage.

"Well, that's the thing! He doesn't think she's either. He heard from a friend about a scandal some years ago in Naples where some tenor or impresario named Zambelli gave away a lead role at a prestigious theater to some woman who sounded like a broken penny whistle!"

"That sounds like how Carlotta would find her start," Christine muttered. "Was this woman Spanish?"

Raoul's smile broadened. "No, much worse. *American*."

Christine yelped in laughter. Who knew if it was true, but oh, if *Le Gaulois* could hear that news. "If she doesn't make peace tonight, that's an interesting thing to know."

"If it's true," Raoul admonished and Christine sighed.

"I don't know if truth matters. What they said about me was only half true." She squinted at her dinner companion. "Raoul, you're the only person I ever told about Papa. Did you ever share that? I can't think how else Carlotta or her cohorts could have known, but I know you'd never do that to me."

Raoul looked down at his empty plate and Christine's stomach turned. "I...did tell Philippe and Sabine, but that was years ago. I didn't mean to, though! I was trying to make the case for why

I should have been allowed to—" Raoul stopped, a blush better befitting a schoolgirl than a grown man coloring his cheeks.

"To what?"

"Marry you, of course," Raoul replied, and it was Christine's turn to blush. "Don't you remember our plans? We had such dreams that summer and then you left. And then Father died and—"

"What do you mean left? Your family objected to me. My father agreed with them, but I didn't *leave* you." Christine still remembered the conversation in front of the fire in Perros. Papa had just started showing his illness and had made it exceedingly clear that they were no longer welcome at the Chagny manor.

"Philippe told me you changed your mind and...and that you left."

"He lied, Raoul." Christine's mind spun at the revelation. Was this why Raoul had never written to her or sought her out until now? Did he think she had chosen not to be with him all those years ago?

"I never knew," Raoul whispered. "Christine, I'm sorry." She might have been moved by the contrition in his handsome face had a new, darker idea not occurred to her.

"Philippe and Sabine never liked me. And you said you told them the truth about Papa and now some reporter knows it. Do you think that they told someone?" Raoul looked absolutely stricken by the idea, which was not promising. "Raoul, what is it?"

"I saw Philippe with that woman. I don't know what they were up to. But I'll ask him and I'll go to the managers too and make it right, I swear."

It was so easy to talk to Raoul. He withheld nothing, neither the truth nor his heart.

"It's alright. You needn't worry for me." Christine glanced out the café window towards the sunset. *La Grenouille* was nicer than she was used to, but it was still a typical café with an awning over the sidewalk and windows that would be open in the summer.

"It's getting late. Do you think she's actually coming?" Raoul asked. "I'm happy to wait with you. Or escort you home. I wouldn't want you wandering around in the dark."

Christine suppressed a laugh. If only he knew how Christine might find herself lost in the darkest reaches of Paris tonight. Though the idea of groveling back to Erik after berating him earlier was as unappealing as going back to the flat she barely thought of as home. She didn't want to face Adèle right now either. Maybe Julianne would take her in for the evening.

"Christine?"

Raoul was still waiting for her to answer, she realized. "I'll be fine. I can take care of myself."

"You can, of course, but you don't need to when I'm here." Raoul said it with a tender smile, taking her hand across the table as he did. Christine felt so many things it was dizzying: annoyance and flattery, longing and guilt, all at once.

"Your family will be wondering where you are," Christine muttered, withdrawing her hand. The best way to deal with these feelings was simply not to go anywhere near them. That seemed to be Erik's strategy.

Raoul scowled playfully but nodded as he retrieved his coat and hat. Christine nearly sighed in relief before he turned to her again, his brown eyes gleaming with hope as bright as his smile. "When will I see you again?"

"What?"

"A good suitor never leaves his lady without the promise of another meeting, that's what Philippe says, though he put it differently. And I *am* your suitor now, you can't deny it." He took her hand again, such an easy gesture. His hand was soft, or at least softer than Erik's, though there were callouses from his days at sea.

And it was so warm. Just like his arms had been when he'd held her today. She could still feel that solid embrace, still smell the starch of his shirt mixed with soap and skin.

"I don't know," Christine stammered.

"I have to go to the performance tomorrow, unfortunately. I'll boo Carlotta if you like," Raoul went on. "But I'll call on you the day after perhaps? Or maybe I'll see you there."

"Raoul, I'm not sure if I—"

"And I want you to tell him, whoever this other man is, your teacher or suitor or whatever, that he has a rival who will not be easily dissuaded."

"I doubt that will be helpful," Christine muttered. God help her if her suitors met. And of course it was Raoul who had convinced her (once again, without meaning to) that Erik was more of a suitor than she had assumed.

"I hope next time I see you it is under better circumstances, no more of this finding you on the street in distress," Raoul said, squeezing her hand. "I won't stand for it."

"I make no promises."

Raoul grinned again before, to Christine's shock, pressing a chaste kiss to her hand that made her heart leap. "Goodbye, my dear Christine," Raoul said and did not wait for her to reply before exiting the café with a spring in his step. And leaving Christine cursedly alone with her thoughts.

She was an idiot in every way, she berated herself as she let her head fall into her hands, the right still warmer than the left from Raoul's grasp. Somehow, she had become entangled with not one, but two men who could not be more different. Raoul was the light of summer, of days on rocky beaches or rolling green hills. He was safe and good and stable. Open and honest.

Erik was fire on a dark winter's night. He was moonlight and magic songs that entranced and entrapped. He was a fascinating genius and a maddening mystery. She should run now, while she had the chance. But she knew she wouldn't. If Erik asked her to – if he called to her again in his angel's voice – she would return. Part of her hated that truth, the same part that wanted to stay safe in the sunny embrace of Raoul de Chagny. And part of her wanted nothing more than for Erik to use that power to its fullest extent and end her indecision.

Christine looked up after what felt like forever. The sky was entirely dark, and the maître d' was giving her dark looks. The shame and hurt of earlier returned in full force, accompanied by a healthy dose of anger. It had been a trick. Rehearsal was long over, and Carlotta had sent her to sit in suspense for hours only to be abandoned again. A final slap in the face.

Christine rose from the table and exited into the street, pulling the dark cloak close around her shoulders. Maybe this was the only way Erik would ever embrace her. *Why would you want that?* The voice in her head that asked sounded suspiciously like the man in question.

In protest, Christine turned resolutely towards her flat and not the Opera. A night at home in her own bed would do her good. She stumbled when a body blocked her.

"Ah, Mademoiselle Daaé." Once again it was LeDoux who interrupted Christine and stood in her way. "We are so glad to have caught you."

"We? Where's your mistress?" Christine demanded, following a nod from LeDoux. There was a carriage parked further down, blocking an alley next to the café.

"The Signora does not wish to make a scene or be mobbed by her admirers. Please come this way," LeDoux said. Every hair on the back of Christine's neck stood at attention, anxiety trembling in her bones. She could simply walk away... No. She had to do this. "Here we are."

Christine found herself led into the alley, a dark place between *La Grenouille* and a shop of some kind. She took in the setting nervously, shivering in the chill. The stink of old food and new lingered in the air, and the paving stones were cold even through Christine's shoes. At the end of the alley were two burly figures wreathed in cigarette smoke.

"If you wanted privacy, I don't think this is the place," Christine muttered and turned. To her shock, it was Carlotta who stood blocking her way out and grinning, with LeDoux nowhere in sight.

"But this setting suits you, my dear," Carlotta said with a glee that froze Christine's blood. ". Among the muck of the gutter where you belong."

"You aren't here to negotiate a truce, are you?" Inside Christine was screaming at herself for being foolish enough to hope. At least Erik was not here to say he had told her so.

"Of course not. I was going to just leave you here before your little cabal made more threats." Carlotta stepped towards her, slowly and intentionally, and Christine braced herself. She could smell the men in the alley behind her and did not want to get any closer, so she stayed stuck to the spot.

"What are you talking about?"

"That little note from the supposed ghost calling down a curse on my Opera." Carlotta sneered. "I should have expected as much from a gypsy wench. I wonder if the papers will even care what you are, now that your career is over."

"Do you think they'll care what you are?" Christine snapped back and Carlotta looked interested. "What is your real name? I have to ask."

"What do you mean?" Carlotta's eyes narrowed dangerously.

"I know Zambelli is a fiction, certainly. But Carlotta; not a very American name. Is it Charlotte?"

Christine was not prepared for the way Carlotta's face turned to stone at the sound of that name. She had made her second grave error after coming into this alley.

"Did you know I had a sister?" Carlotta said, poison in her eyes. "Parents aren't supposed to love one child more but, well, she was the baby, and they doted on her. She could do no wrong in their eyes. So she got away with making life hell for me."

Christine swallowed, keeping her eyes on Carlotta even as she had the terrifying sense of being watched from behind. Carlotta continued to advance, her eyes boring into Christine.

"She would play the most awful tricks on me. Leaving tacks on my chair and glue in my brush. Then one day, do you know what I found? That little monster had put a toad in my bed. Terrible, huge, slimy thing. I can't even begin to think where she found it. I pulled back my sheets and there it was. I knew she was waiting outside in the hall for me to scream. But she made a mistake. All her little tortures hadn't made me delicate like her, they'd made me strong. So, I didn't scream. Do you know what I did?"

"I don't think I want to," Christine replied, teeth gritted tight. If she chose the right instant, she could push past Carlotta and run. She was stronger and younger; she could do it.

"I put it in her bed. In pieces. I used my sewing scissors to do it. You should have seen the blood. Oh, the scream she let out. It was one of the most wonderful things I've ever heard."

"So is that what I am to you?" Christine demanded even as she heard a huff and the scuff of a boot behind her. "Another sister for you to torment?"

"No, my dear. You aren't the one pulling the strings, I know that." Carlotta gave a nod as Christine moved to run. Rough hands seized her arms and another clamped over her mouth as she tried to scream. Carlotta only laughed. "You, sweet girl, are the toad."

Christine screamed in earnest now, but the sound was swallowed by the hand on her mouth, its fingers digging into her cheeks. She struggled against the unseen captors even as Carlotta laughed.

"I'm going to make sure whoever left you in my path gets a message. These dear gentlemen have already been paid and they know what to do." Carlotta smiled sweetly to the men who held Christine. "Though I do encourage them to be creative with how they teach you your lessons." With a toss of her head, Carlotta turned away, her singsong laugh echoing against the alley walls as the men dragged Christine back into the shadows.

Christine struggled with all her strength, fear as she had never known it rushing through her. She was damned and doomed and she should have listened and she should have stayed in the light and she should never have come here or to Paris and she was going to bleed and break and die.

The man with his hand on her mouth pulled her with him towards a wall as the other man came around to the front. He looked familiar, like one of the stagehands who all of the women of the Opera were warned to avoid. Against her captor's hand, Christine screamed again, the sound no louder than the noise of Carlotta's carriage rumbling away.

"Stop making so much noise, dearie, I don't want to be interrupted," the man rumbled as he produced a tarnished knife from his coat. "Maybe if you're good, I'll leave your pretty face the way it is."

"Didn't Carlotta say to break her jaw? Can't have her singing again," the man behind Christine growled. She knew that voice for sure, but the words were far more terrifying. She tried again, in vain, to break free, and in turn the hidden one squeezed her arm so hard tears sprang to her eyes. She wanted to beg and weep and scream, but he wouldn't let go.

"Right you are. Pity. I liked listening to her," the man with the knife said and drew back his hand in preparation to strike. Christine screwed her eyes shut and braced herself for the pain but instead heard a crash and a man's scream. Her eyes flew open and she gasped behind her captor's hand at the sight of a shadow throwing the other man into the wall with incredible force. The shadow turned and Christine's terror was replaced by awe.

Erik stood in the alley, white mask glowing in the gloom, like an avenging angel wreathed in a cloak of night.

"No! Not you!" the man holding her cried and threw Christine to the ground. Pain shot through her knees and hands as she crashed to the cobblestones, and it took her a second to regain her bearings. When she looked up, she saw that Erik had stopped her assailant's flight, his hand around the man's neck before he threw him against the wall. Christine recognized the brute at last: Joseph Buquet, chief of the flies.

As Buquet stumbled to the ground, his compatriot rose, knife catching the light as he steadied himself. Erik flexed his hands and Christine was filled with a new sort of fear. The fight began before she could think and it was nothing like her limited experience and imagination had envisioned. The man lunged at Erik, his knife slicing through the air and missing by a mile as the Phantom dodged away. It went like that three times and Erik had the upper hand in skill and speed until, out of the dark, Buquet joined the fray with a cry. And then it was chaos.

Erik was fast and nimble, but in the dark with two assailants, one armed, it was a brutal fight. Christine cried out as one man grabbed Erik and another struck him roughly across the face, thankfully not dislodging the mask. In a split second, Erik was free and delivered a kick to Buquet's shin that made the man scream in pain and anger as he fell to the ground in the right place to take a kick to the chest.

The other lunged at Erik with the knife, but Erik caught his arm as it aimed at his abdomen and Christine winced at the sound of something snapping. The man howled in pain, dropping the knife, and pulling back his arm. It now hung at an unnatural angle, but Erik wasn't done. He seized the man again and dashed him against the stone wall of the alley, face first, and he collapsed to the ground.

"No. No!" Buquet screamed as Erik advanced on him. He grabbed a handful of muck from behind him and threw it blindly, stalling Erik long enough for him to scramble to his feet and flee into the street, Erik glowering after him. Christine finally let out a quavering breath in relief and Erik turned to her.

"Are you alright?" Erik asked, rushing to her and kneeling. To Christine's shock and incredible relief, he took her hands without hesitation.

"I'm fine," Christine stammered, trying to breathe as Erik gently touched her face.

"You see, I do come above ground sometimes," Erik muttered and held her gaze before the man on the ground moaned. "We have to go."

"Where?" Christine demanded as Erik pulled her up by the wrist and rushed with her from the alley. "How?" Her question was answered in the most improbable manner when she saw, waiting for them like it was the most normal thing in the world, César, the white gelding (and true star) from the Opera's stables. "You *stole a horse*?"

"Borrowed. I had to get here quickly."

Erik lifted her with a hiss at the effort, and Christine told herself it was not the time to think about his hands on her waist or how close he was when he took his place behind her and urged César into a canter.

They had to be a strange sight, two figures in dark cloaks sharing a white horse, but it was past dusk, and the people of Paris had little interest in anything beyond their own journeys home through the cold. In no time they were at the stable gates, the exact place Christine had entered the Opera all those months ago.

"Here," Erik said as he dismounted and helped Christine down, massaging his side as he did, as if the effort hurt. "Thank you, César," he added, patting a hand against the horse's white flank. And leaving a handprint that was unmistakably red, even in the dim lantern light. "Well, that's ominous," Erik muttered before stumbling back to lean on the stable wall, hand clutched to his side.

"Erik!" Christine cried, rushing to him.

"It's just a cut," Erik protested through gritted teeth.

"Let me see," Christine ordered as Erik sank to the ground. He made a sound of protest as Christine pushed back his hand to reveal the wound. There was a great deal of blood, but she could see that the knife that had undoubtedly done this had cut through Erik's layers of clothes and deep into the flesh beneath. "Jesus Christ, this is not just a cut!"

"I'm—"

"Take off your jacket, we'll use it to slow the bleeding for now," Christine commanded. Erik obeyed with clear difficulty, then a fresh hiss of pain as Christine tied the garment tightly around the wound. "Keep pressure on it. We need to get you home to tend to it. Come on."

Erik did as he was told, staring at Christine with a combination of annoyance and wonder as she helped him up and draped his arm over her shoulder. She lit the lantern and held it as she opened Erik's hidden door into the cellars, letting Erik guide them slowly downwards on the path to his home. They turned too quickly after one staircase, and Erik grunted at the effort.

Christine glared at him in the flickering light. "You are not allowed to bleed to death and leave me alone down here."

"I shall try," Erik muttered in return.

At last, they reached Erik's door. He leaned on the wall, holding his side as Christine triggered the musical locking mechanism as he had taught her. Finally, they entered Erik's parlor, where he immediately stumbled towards one of the chairs by the fire and collapsed a foot short of it.

"I should be clearer," Christine chided, throwing off her cape and rushing to him to prop him against one of the chairs. "You are not allowed to bleed to death on my watch *at all*."

Erik gave her a look that was warm and dubious at the same time. "I do not intend to die today. It would make a terrible ending."

"Where are your medical supplies?" Christine demanded, tearing her eyes from his besotted gaze. It was ridiculous to blush when there were far more important tasks at hand. Erik looked confused.

"In my room, in the bath. There's a box under the wash basin. I can get them," Erik protested, trying to rise.

"*Stay*," Christine said with force in her voice that pushed Erik back to the floor. She spun away before he could protest and stalked away.

She had only been in this room once before, and she would be damned if she wasted time thinking about waking up in Erik's bed or anything else that had happened there while she had the man's blood all over her hands. His bath chamber was far more ornate than hers, but it was easy to find the wooden box full of vials and bandages. With a quick search, Christine found a surgeon's needle and thread in the store. She quickly washed her hands – which were unsurprising, but unfortunately – shaking terribly, before seizing the kit and several towels before heading back into the bedroom.

Where of course Erik was leaning on the frame of his bed.

"I told you to stay put!" Christine cried, flying to Erik's side and depositing the box on the bed just in time to catch him as he faltered to the mattress.

"I thought I'd meet you halfway. And the brandy is in here." Christine realized Erik had also somehow procured a dusty bottle of liquor from who-knows-where. She helped him onto the bed, and he wasted no time in taking a long draught of it. "I'll attend to the wound. You don't need to watch."

"Like hell you will," Christine growled, to Erik's clear shock.

"I'm...fine," Erik replied with clear effort, his breath shallow.

"You've been stabbed, you fool!"

"I've had worse!"

"That does not make it better!" Christine yelped, horrified. "Now give me that." She grabbed the bottle from Erik and set it on the nightstand. "Keep the pressure while I get these off," she ordered, untying their makeshift tourniquet from his abdomen, then resolutely setting to unbuttoning his ruined shirt and vest.

Erik moved to stop her, panic evident in his eyes and slack mouth, but Christine stopped him with a fresh glare. He was tense and stiff as she pushed away his hand to inspect the wound as quickly as she could. The deep cut was on his right, below his ribs (which were terribly visible), and the length of her little finger. She used a towel to clear away the blood and, without warning, grabbed the brandy and splashed it over his side, provoking an indignant yelp from her patient.

"That's twenty years old!" Erik cried.

"It's not like you paid for it," Christine snapped back as she took her own swig and she did have to admit it was good. She pushed a towel into Erik's hand. "Use this to keep the pressure on. I need to get ready."

"It's still good brandy," Erik argued as Christine returned the liquor to him so she could rummage through his impressive store of ointments and herbs.

"Do you have anything cheaper?"

"No."

"It is not my fault you're a snob then."

"I am not *a snob*," Erik protested.

"Everything in here is labeled *in Latin*," Christine shot back, drawing out the needle and thread and trying to let her irritation steady her hands.

"It's scientific," Erik huffed.

"It's *pretentious*!" Christine cried, and Erik gaped at her. She bit her lip, sure she had gone too far, and settled herself next to Erik on the bed. Their thighs touched in this position, and she could feel how incredibly tense Erik was as she prepared her needle. "I'm going to sew this up. It will hurt."

Erik took another deep drink of brandy and braced himself as Christine nodded for him to take away the towel staunching the blood. She glanced at him, maybe for reassurance, maybe to comfort him. The intensity of his eyes only served to remind her how intimate and unusual this was. Of course it would take mortal peril for him to finally let her feel his skin. Christine swallowed as she prepared for the first stitch.

"I do, you know, want you to touch me," she muttered as the needle pierced skin.

"*What?*" Erik gasped in confusion and pain. Christine did not look up and kept stitching, pulling his pale skin back together.

"You think I don't want you to touch me. You asked *why* I would want it," Christine went on, every ounce of her strength focused on keeping her voice and hands steady as she continued her task. "Well, I do want it. Though I can't really say why."

She could feel Erik staring at her as he tried to steady his breath. "Are you saying this to distract me?" he asked through gritted teeth as she secured another stitch.

"Yes," Christine replied. "But also because it's true, and I don't know when I'll have a better chance to make you listen to me, you stubborn fool."

"Why are you mad at me?" Erik gave a quiet grunt as the needle did its work.

"Because I'm mad at myself. This is my fault," Christine replied in a whisper. She could feel Erik's gaze boring into the top of her head, as if he was trying to read her thoughts like a book.

"I let him lunge at me," Erik told her slowly as she finished the final stitch. "It was the easiest way to disarm him."

"You *let* him stab you?" Christine pulled out one of Erik's vials, grateful that calendula was a Latin name.

"I told you, I've had worse," Erik said as she dabbed the wound with the ointment.

"You keep saying that as if it makes this better!" Christine snapped, grabbing bandages while she avoided Erik's eyes. "You wouldn't have had to get yourself skewered if I had listened to you. If I hadn't been stupid enough to talk to that bitch."

"You weren't stupid, you were optimistic," Erik protested, and Christine looked up into his ardent eyes. "I told you, it's one of the things I love most about you. Your willingness to see the best in the worst people."

Christine looked down again, blushing. "Get these off so I can bandage you up," she muttered, tugging at his shirt and vest. It was absurd, asking him to disrobe to make the moment less awkward.

"No, we can work around them," Erik protested, the tension in his body returning. She wanted to protest, but there were other battles to fight tonight. Awkwardly, she wrapped the bandages around his abdomen, trying not to look and invade his privacy. She failed, and more than once she noted how his pale skin was marked just as his face was, crossed with strange textures and raised lines, like—

"Ah," Erik winced as she tightened the last bandage and Christine was forced to look up at him again. Was that why he was hiding? Was that why he did not want to be touched? Was his body as bad as the face behind the mask? Christine found herself staring at the mask again, and the lines and odd texture that peeked out at the edges. Some of which were stained with vivid red.

"Erik, you're bleeding."

"Not as much as before, thanks to you."

"No, not that." She raised a hand towards his mask. "Your face..."

Erik winced away immediately. "*No*," he growled, fear and panic in his eyes.

"Just let me check and clean it! It could get infected or—"

"Oh yes, we wouldn't want a scar!" Erik's breath was coming fast now, but Christine refused to let him escape this time. She caught his jaw with her hand, as gentle as she could possibly be while holding his gaze. It reminded her of calming a wild animal caught in a trap.

"Erik, please, trust me. I'll be quick and then you can put it back on," she said softly. "I've already seen."

"I don't want to see you look at me," he protested again, barely a whisper.

"Then close your damn eyes," Christine commanded.

Erik stared at her as seconds ticked by. She hoped he could see in her eyes that she had no intention of hurting him or letting him say no. Erik grabbed the bottle of brandy again and took a long swig, then nodded. Slowly, he closed his eyes.

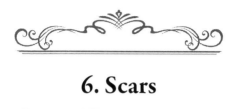

6. Scars

It was madness, Erik knew, to be more afraid of Christine's relentless gaze than an armed man ready to kill him in the street. Even so, he found himself awash in terror. His heart pounded and cold tingling engulfed his body as Christine's fingers carefully fixed around the edge of his mask.

"You can trust me, I promise," Christine said, gentle and calm. The pain of his wound could not distract him from the panic that overtook him the instant the familiar pressure of the mask was gone, replaced by cold air on his bare face.

At least she did not scream, he told himself, refusing to imagine the gruesome sight she saw. He winced at the first touch of a rag against the gash on his cheekbone, but he didn't move away. If he stayed still and did not fight, it would be over quickly...

"Do you shave?"

Erik's eyes flew open in utter bewilderment to meet Christine's curious gaze. "What?" he asked breathlessly.

"You're a man. Men have beards. Do you have to shave?" Christine repeated, as if it was the most normal thing. Erik could only blink at her. "I imagine it would be awkward, without a mirror or with a mask on."

"Only rarely," Erik found himself replying, staring up at Christine and trying to find the horror and repulsion in her face. But her expression was completely neutral. "Hair doesn't like to grow on scars," he muttered as she dabbed his face with the cloth that came away red.

"Hm," was Christine's only reply.

Erik could not understand. Perhaps unwisely, he took another swig of brandy to steady his nerves. The drink burned down his throat and dulled his senses enough that he could breathe. He could not close his eyes again now; he was too fascinated and terrified by the woman brave enough to touch him and look on his face without fear. Or at least without showing it.

"Do you have witch hazel?" Christine asked.

"*Hamamelis mollis*. In the middle."

Christine rolled her eyes. "Pretentious." She moistened her rag with the ointment and carefully dabbed it on Erik's cheek. "I'm sorry, by the way," Christine said, voice as gentle as her touch. "Even if this wasn't my fault – and it was – I'm sorry you were hurt on my account. I don't want to cause you pain."

Erik stared at her as she withdrew her hand, uncomprehending. How was she possible? How could she do this? How could a face as perfect and beautiful as hers hold such concern as she looked upon the monstrousness of his?

"I keep telling you, I'm used to it," he said, the words fleeing his mouth before he could stop them. Perhaps brandy was a bad combination with blood loss.

"You said you were born like this, but if these are scars..." Christine began haltingly, tracing one long line at the edge of his face with the lightest touch. It still made Erik shudder and retreat on instinct, and Christine's brow furrowed. "Erik—"

"You asked about the song," Erik said, looking down and away so that his hair fell in his face, shielding him from her eyes. "I learned it from my mother. She was born in Ireland."

He heard Christine's sharp intake of breath. He wanted more brandy but didn't want to move again.

"She had been broken by the cruelty of the world already when I was born, this grotesque thing she had never asked for," Erik went on, voice unsteady. "She would go in and out of madness. One day she would be wild and violent, the next week she would not leave her bed. She called me a changeling, sometimes, when her mind was afire. She would say the fairies had taken her real son and replaced him with the withered corpse of one of their own. She'd scream at me and shake me, demanding I reveal my true nature. She hated my face and she—" Erik stopped, the pain and horror of the memory choking his lungs and stealing his voice.

To his amazement, Christine grasped his hand. "What did she do?" she asked gently. And like magic, her voice gave him comfort and the touch of her hand did not sting. Erik took an unsteady breath.

"She'd claw at me and strike me. And once...she tried to cut it off. My face." He dared to look up into Christine's eyes and was still amazed at the depth of pity he saw there.

"Oh, Erik."

"It's strange, really. I was the one that drove her mad, and yet I was the only one who could calm her when she was at her worst. Or get her to move when she wouldn't come out of her room. She loved music, you see. She'd sing to herself. She had a beautiful voice, even when she was weeping. It's one of the first things I remember." In his mind, Erik could hear it still. "*There were three ravens sitting on a tree, with a down, a down, hey down, hey down,*" he sang barely above a whisper.

"When I realized I could sing too, I'd sing to her. It was like magic. She'd come back alive or calm down. I've always wondered if she was right. Perhaps I am some otherworldly thing..." Erik shook his head as Christine squeezed his hand. There was moisture on his face that was not blood.

"Sometimes I didn't want to sing to her," Erik went on. "I didn't think she deserved to be brought back, after what she'd done. But the maid who cared for us would make me. She left marks too. And at night I'd sing to myself too. I'd sing myself to sleep in the dark, old songs of my mother's home that I'd never seen. I loved them, because for all her madness and cruelty, I loved her."

Christine's thumb glided over the back of Erik's hand in an unfamiliar, soothing gesture that made him shudder. He tried to push away the memories, but they crowded around him like ghosts.

"When I was small, I'd sneak out of our house. I wasn't allowed past our gate or into the village, but I wanted to be free, even then," he said wistfully, surrendering to the impulse to simply tell Christine everything. "I'd go to the church and hide outside. I knew it was where people went to find God. And I heard the music of the organ and the choir and I remembered of how my voice could soothe my mother and save me, and I was sure that the music *was* God. It was so beautiful, and even a monster such as I could share in it."

"That's beautiful," Christine said. Still holding his fingers with one hand, her other hand found his wrist, and he shook again, from the touch and from another shadow of the past.

"Years later, in the worst place in the world, chained and tortured, music saved me again." The feel of shackles in his memory was overcome by the tender pressure of Christine's fingertips on the marks from long ago.

"These are scars. Your skin..." Christine gasped and looked up, not at his face, but at his half-bared chest. She pushed back his ruined shirt to reveal the old burns that radiated from his shoulder and mingled with narrow scars far longer than the one he'd have from today's adventure. Her fingertips grazed the ruined skin, and the heat was searing. Erik startled back again as Christine's eyes widened in understanding.

"I'm sorry," he muttered, not sure what he was apologizing for.

"Is this why you're afraid of me touching you?" Christine asked instead, horror and pity in her voice. "You have only ever been hurt? No one has ever touched you with kindness?"

"No one who has lived to tell of it," Erik replied. He did not know if it was the brandy or the pain or the warmth or her closeness had loosened his tongue so disastrously. She did not seem terrified though, only sad.

"Erik, if I ever made you think I'd hurt you; or if I did hurt you, I'm sorry."

Erik's mind flashed to the awful sight of her raised hands and the feel of her fists on his shoulder the last time she had seen him unmasked in this room. "I deserved it."

"No, you—" Christine bit her lip, her hand still hovering above his chest, so warm he could still feel it. "I'm still sorry."

"I've learned to expect pain from...other people," Erik said, keeping his eyes on Christine's extraordinary face.

"If it is something you have learned, can it not be unlearned?" Christine asked carefully.

Erik cocked his head, unintentionally revealing more of his face to the light and her observance. "What?"

"Could you not learn to be...touched with tenderness?" Erik stared at her, unable to understand. "With the right teacher." With those words, she cautiously laid her hand upon his scarred flesh.

"Christine," he choked out, the sensation of her hand on his skin sending waves of feeling through him that were not unlike an electric shock. "Christine, I—"

"Breathe," she commanded, and what could he do but obey? He breathed deep as her hand remained still and steady against his chest, the sensation so alien and overwhelming he could barely comprehend it. Could she feel his heart pounding in panic behind his ribs? "Tell me how that feels."

"Warm. Burning," he gasped out. She turned her hand, letting her cool knuckles graze his collarbone.

"Better?"

How could he possibly answer? Simply being touched by her was everything. It was torture and exquisite pleasure all at once, and his addled mind could not make sense of it. He nodded instead and it looked like she smiled. But that was a dream because no one smiled as they looked at him. No one was so gentle as they touched him.

His breaths shuddered along with his body as her palm and fingertips found his skin once again, and this time it did not burn. Her delicate hand slid slowly towards his shoulder, pushing his shirt back as she did. He had never felt more exposed in his miserable life than he did in this moment, as she drew his garments away from his body along with all his defenses.

He kept breathing, kept watching her as she attended to the other arm, her gentle hands so incredibly soft and warm against his skin. And suddenly he was totally exposed. Her eyes and fingertips explored the map of pain and captivity etched over his chest, arms, and face.

"And this? How does this feel?" she asked as she touched the burns over his left shoulder, following to where they extended to his back. He wanted to tell her. He wanted to share the story behind every mark and tell her that this was hell and heaven all at once. But he was too overwhelmed to speak as she continued to touch him as no one ever had. All he could do was nod and close his eyes on the tears that had blossomed there.

He had to be dreaming, he told himself, as her hands swept slowly over him and up his neck. He had lost too much blood and had too much brandy. Or maybe he'd simply died and this was a cruel trick making him think he'd found heaven before he was cast into the inferno he deserved. But it was so real. Her hands were brands against his skin, but they were not there to hurt him. They were kind. She was so much kinder than him.

"I promise, I'll never hurt you," Christine whispered. He opened his eyes at the impossible words to find her incredibly close. "I promise."

"I do not deserve such a promise nor such a lesson," he breathed back. The world swirled around them, her eyes the only steady point in the tempest. Her eyes. They were so beautiful.

"I will be the one to decide that," Christine replied, and with infinite delicacy, she touched his face as she leaned closer. She traced the scar his own mother had given him, traced his sunken cheek to the edge of the stub of his skeleton's nose. She pushed back his hair from his forehead, and Erik could see the tears in her eyes as she drew closer still, rising like the angel she was.

And without more warning than that, Christine kissed his forehead.

It was too much. The feel of her tears on his bare skin, on his brow, like a new sacrament. The velvet pressure of her lips. The heat of her breath. It was everything and too much. Erik heard himself make a sound, as if from far away, a piteous sort of sob sure to repel her with its lack of dignity. But she did not recoil. She did not retreat. She did not die.

Christine Daaé twined her fingers in his hair and kissed him again, and Erik was sure this was heaven, even as the world twisted and thundered around him. She kissed him. Then there was nothing but black and silence.

Nothing...but her.

Shaya had learned that a man such as himself was one of two things in a city like Paris: obvious or invisible. There was no shortage of foreigners in the great metropolis, and people with skins of every color walked the streets. But where you were in the city mattered in terms of if a Parisian saw someone like him as a nuisance, a threat, or nothing at all. Tonight he was close to the posh flats of the *Rue du Faubourg Saint Honoré* where the fine residents looked askance at him. It would be much the same near his flat on the *Rue Rivoli*, he thought to himself, as he came to the crossroads with the *Rue Royale* where a simple right turn would set him on the course towards home.

He was happy to leave if he was being honest, even if his spying had yielded nothing. He had been so sure some agent of La Carlotta would report back to her after the events of the day, but hours across from her door had produced nothing but boredom and sore feet. He was glad to be done, and yet still unsatisfied. Shaya turned left, back towards the Opera. Perhaps there would be something to be gleaned there.

The route came automatically to him after so many years and allowed him time to think and stew. What might Carlotta have done to Christine Daaé? What revenge lay in store for her if Erik truly valued his Swedish songbird more than his own discretion? Soon enough Shaya found himself turning off the *Boulevard des Italiens* and into the grand *Place de L'Opéra*. In all truth, he found the massive building – with its excessive colonnades, grand copper dome, and endless filigree – ostentatious and overbearing. The Prophet had been right to prohibit depictions of living things in art, for it would have spared him this palace to excess, adorned in nudes and pagan gods.

There was no one coming in or out of the Opera since there was no performance tonight. The whole plaza would be full of life tomorrow, but now it was quiet. Shaya rarely went in through the front, anyway. He always had better luck at the back entrance. Or through the stables on the *Rue Scribe* when Lachenal, the head groom, was dozing at his post as he tended to. However, the raised voices coming from beyond the stable door indicated tonight Lachenal was *very* awake.

"It's a curse, I tell you!" Lachenal was yelling.

"It's probably just paint, you fool," an impatient woman's voice replied. Shaya peered warily around the corner. Lachenal was red-faced and sweating, standing next to the white horse from *Le Prophète*, speaking to a woman with tightly curled black hair whose face Shaya could not see.

"It's blood!" Lachenal cried, pointing at the horse. "I tell you, César disappeared again and I knew the fiend had taken him – without a note or a 'by-your-leave, Jean-Paul!' And I'd had enough, so I went to alert the new managers to complain and demand *locks* for the paddocks. And everyone in the office was up in arms about how the Ghost has placed a curse on us all!"

"I think you're exaggerating," the woman sighed.

"Course the clods had no time for me. So I came back and César was here: marked in blood!" It finally occurred to Shaya that the César of which Lachenal was speaking with such concern was the white horse. The horse himself was uninterested in anything but the sack of oats he was enjoying.

"Maybe you missed him?" the woman attempted, and Lachenal threw up his hands. "Why would the ghost mark your horse? That makes no sense. Ghosts don't bleed."

"I never said it was his blood!" Lachenal exclaimed. The woman gave another powerful sigh, turning away from the groom enough that she caught sight of Shaya and her eyes went wide. Shaya's interest leapt as well – he knew the girl. He had seen her several times in the company of Christine Daaé.

"You!" the woman gasped. Shaya knew that tone and what it meant. He turned immediately to retreat onto the *Rue Scribe*. "Wait!" the woman called after him, grabbing his elbow. "Were you looking for Christine too?"

"What?" Shaya asked, turning back.

"Or were you looking for your friend the ghost?"

"He is not my friend," he growled. There were many rumors about him that were tiresome, but the one Erik had sewn and nourished that he was an ally of the Phantom was the one Shaya hated the most. "Who are you? Why do you think I'm concerned with Christine?"

The woman looked him over, clearly deciding if he could be trusted. Her dark skin marked her as one like him; condemned to be invisible and marked. That did not make them natural allies, however.

"My name is Julianne and I'm her friend. And she's—" Julianne bit her lip before saying more.

"Vanished again?" Shaya finished for her. Julianne blanched. "I suspected as much. And she has not seen fit to tell you where she goes, I would guess."

"She says she's safe with a friend..."

"Do you believe that?"

"I don't know what I believe right now." Julianne looked him over again, from the toes of his boots to the steepled top of his Astrakhan hat. "Is Christine in danger?"

"I truly cannot say," Shaya replied. What did this woman know? "But she is certainly not safe. What has she told you about her so-called friend?"

"Nothing I would tell a stranger who lurks about halls and spies on people," Julianne snapped. "I'll protect her myself."

"Do you really think you can?" Shaya laughed.

"I'll take my chances," Julianne replied, chin held high as she turned and disappeared down the street. Shaya turned the other way, finally ready to go home. There was nothing more to be done tonight if Erik had indeed spirited Christine away again to do who-knows-what. Shaya shuddered at the idea and pushed it from his mind. The idea that Erik had corrupted another innocent soul was too loathsome to consider. Shaya would not let it happen again.

Christine woke slowly, keeping her eyes closed. She was not sure what had awoken her; the cold, her body's own clock, or the soft breath of the man beside her. She remembered all too vividly the last time she had awoken to the sound of that breath and the anguish that had followed. It made her gut squirm with shame now to think of how she had berated her fallen angel, of her blows and screams and the way she had torn off his mask. It must have reminded him of the mad mother whose name she did not know. No wonder he had been left hiding from her like a child, singing to himself.

Bracing herself, Christine opened her eyes to gaze on Erik, unmasked, once again. His was not an easy face to look at, even knowing him as she did now. Perhaps it was like his past, she thought, as she took in the collapsed ruin that served for a nose, the deep eyes, and terrible scars. If she looked long enough at the horror of it with compassion and not fear, she could endure it. She wanted to.

It was extraordinary to see him peaceful like this, exposed and vulnerable. It felt like prying to take as much time as she needed to stare. It had seemed that way last night, so she had closed her eyes. Strange, how that had been her solution, rather than simply leaving him. The idea of abandoning him to sleep alone and in pain had never crossed her mind until now and she was glad of it.

She stared her fill, feeling the way she had wading into the sea as a girl. It had always taken a few agonizing minutes before her skin had stopped feeling like ice and her lungs had adjusted to the cold. Now, after a long stretch of feasting her eyes, she could see past the scars and the death to something of the man beneath. But too long in the cold water could still kill. So she rose and turned away, composing herself.

It was seven in the morning, according to the clock Erik kept for himself in his curious room. It was similar to the one in the parlor, with a rising sun on a dial to show it was morning. But beneath the clockface was a rotating menagerie of animal figures making their way in and out of a clockwork forest. She could not imagine how long it had taken him to build it, like so many other things in his home.

Erik was still deep asleep, so she heeded her body and returned to her own room to tend to her ablutions, wash, and change out of the dress that was still smeared with his blood. It made her sick with worry and guilt all over again to look at the stains, so she gathered her dress and their cloaks and washed them as well as she could in her copper bath.

By the time she returned to Erik's room, hands cold and withered from laundering and belly full, it was past eight and her patient was still asleep. It was good for his healing, she knew that, but it was so lonely in the quiet house without his music or furtive presence. She settled herself in a worn chair set near an oil lamp where a book had been abandoned carelessly on the armrest. It was a worn copy of *Candide*, Christine observed as she examined it. At least it was in French, she mused as she scanned the first page.

She was twenty pages in when a groan came from the bed, more annoyed than pained. She looked up to see Erik stir, wincing as he pushed himself upright.

"I was worried you'd sleep the whole morning," Christine said calmly. Even so, it startled her patient. He blinked at her, golden eyes somehow even more extraordinary without the mask to frame them.

"You're still here," Erik breathed.

"Where else would I be?" Christine tried to keep her face implacable and her voice steady as Erik looked at her as if she was some holy apparition. "I wanted to make sure you didn't expire during the night."

"I appreciate the concern," Erik said dubiously, watching Christine as she rose and approached. The blanket she had placed on him fell back from his body, once again exposing his awful scars and the bandaged wound on his side. Gingerly, she sat on the side of the bed, slow and careful in her movements so as not to alarm her patient. Just as carefully she touched his shoulder, the left one that was mottled with scars, and Erik's breath hitched.

"I had the strangest dream," Erik said deliberately, not even blinking as he watched her, as if to confirm she was real.

Christine's heart began to speed as she remembered her boldness the night before and the feel of Erik's skin beneath her lips. "What was it?"

"You kissed me," Erik whispered, reverent and awed.

"And you fainted."

Erik's mouth fell open, and Christine wondered idly if he could blush. It was hard to tell in the dim light and with the gash on his cheek was still a vivid stain against the deathly pallor of his face. "In my defense, I had lost a lot of blood," Erik said at last.

"I was afraid that you'd died," Christine replied shyly. Had it been too far, kissing him, even so chastely? She stroked a hand down his chest to the knife wound he had endured for her.

"I thought I might," Erik said, and there was utter devotion in his face as he did. "I could have died from happiness and wonder right there." Christine caught her breath, scolding herself for the idiocy of thinking this man did not love her.

"That would have been very inconvenient," Christine muttered, touching his bandages to examine them. "How do you feel?" Christine asked, noting that the dressing would need to be changed soon and wondering if Erik would fight her on that.

"Like a hungover fool who took a knife to the gut," Erik grumbled, raising his hand to massage his brow then starting in alarm when he found his mask still gone. "Where is it?!" he demanded, eyes wide and horrified.

"Over there. It's alright!" Christine reassured him as he scrambled to where she had discarded his mask beside the bed the night before. "I'm not scared. You don't need to—"

"I do," Erik said as he replaced the mask, securing it with the wires that went behind his ears she had never noticed before. It was remarkable how it changed him from a vulnerable creature into a powerful man. A man who made her stomach flutter when he looked at her.

"You should be alright to clean yourself up a bit before I change those," she muttered as she stood. Suddenly it felt unseemly to be so close to a man in such a state, who looked at her in such a way. She turned to go, hoping to hide her rising blush. To her utter shock, Erik gently caught her wrist.

"Christine." He said her name in that magical, unquestionable way, and she had no choice but to turn back to him, feeling herself shrinking as he rose from the bed to tower over her, her wrist still trapped in the circle of his fingers. "Do not mistake me. I know that, by some miracle, you won't run from this." He gestured to his face. "But to be seen as I am...is another lesson it will take time to learn."

She was going to be the one to faint now. He was close enough to touch again and part of her wanted to do just that, to continue to teach him not to fear her caress, to feel the textures of his skin and scars again and prove to him he could touch her in turn, as he had before when he was but a shadow.

"Good. That's...good," she said before her memory took her too far into the details of what his touch had felt like against the most intimate parts of her person. "I'll leave you to dress."

Christine had never moved so fast in Erik's home as she retreated into the parlor. So much had happened since the last time she'd woken in Erik's house, thinking about it made it feel like her head was about to split open.

In the span of a day, she had lost a job, gained (or regained) a suitor in the person of her first love, been assaulted and nearly faced worse, seen her *other* suitor who pretended to be a ghost take a knife to save her, stitched him up, finally learned a fraction of his story and kissed him. Then slept next to him! In his bed!

It was a wonder she was still standing. In fact, she wasn't. Somewhere in her crisis, she'd collapsed onto her favorite chair by the fire with her head in her hands. At least Erik was distracted; it gave her time to truly appreciate her panic.

What would Raoul think of you if he knew where you spend your nights? A voice in her head asked. *Would he be so eager to overshadow your other suitor if he knew the vile things you've done? How would he look at you if he knew of the way your angel commanded you to spread your wanton legs and how you still wish—*

Christine shook her head and shivered. The fire had faded to embers in the night, and she busied herself with restoking it, wishing her doubt and shame and desires were more kindling she could shove into the flames. Why was she in such a state all of a sudden? She'd been so calm while Erik was asleep. Why was she so brave before and such a bumbling, blushing fool now? Why was it so different when he had the mask on?

"Am I allowed to get myself some tea?" Christine jumped at the music of Erik's voice cutting through the tumult in her mind. She stood and turned to see where he leaned on the door frame, thankfully wearing an unbuttoned dark shirt.

"I'll do it, you sit," Christine ordered and busied herself gathering food and rummaging through Erik's copious stores of tea. All too soon she was handing him a cup and once again caught in his adoring stare.

"Thank you," he said with disarming sincerity.

"It's your own tea," she muttered back, screaming at herself inside her head to just act normally. Not that anything with Erik was ever normal.

"No, thank you for helping me and...for taking care of me. I'm not used to it. I should be more grateful for such kindness." Had his voice become more beautiful in the night? Had his eyes grown brighter?

"You need fresh bandages," she muttered and rushed away to his room for supplies. It only occurred to her when she took a seat next to him on the couch that this would mean touching him again.

"I can—"

"Let me," she commanded softly and unquestionably. Erik relaxed and caught her eye.

"Thank you again," he whispered, and she could feel it on every inch of her skin.

"You're welcome," Christine murmured back as she slowly began to unravel the bandages, allowing herself to savor the ridiculous thrill of letting her knuckles graze his skin. "I still can't believe you *let* yourself get stabbed to get the upper hand."

"It seemed like a good idea at the time," Erik replied with a familiar shrug.

"Hand me the calendula," Christine ordered. Erik complied with a wry smile that made her want to touch him until he fainted again.

"I didn't have the presence of mind last night to ask where you learned how to do stitches and dress wounds," Erik said as he handed her a vial of golden oil. "Or which herbs prevent infection."

"When my father became truly ill, when I was about seventeen, he needed medicine and care we couldn't afford," Christine explained as she unwrapped the last old bandage and discarded it into the fire. "A doctor in Perros took pity on us and let us stay as servants, in exchange for caring for Papa. He was a very kind man. He loved music and enjoyed hearing us play or sing. After a while, I started earning our board and Papa's care by helping him in his practice as a sort of nurse or assistant. Mostly cleaning scrapes and dressing wounds." Christine dabbed at Erik's wound. It thankfully did not look infected at all. Carefully, she began wrapping fresh strips of linen around Erik's midsection. "And most of the injuries I saw were idiot boys who thought something was *a good idea at the time.*"

"They were probably all throwing themselves off cliffs so the town doctor's pretty nurse would patch them up," Erik commented. Christine's gaze shot up to him, cheeks ablaze. "Should I not say such things?"

"No, it's fine. I'm just not used to compliments. Like that. From you. But it's not unwelcome." She needed to stop talking or she was going to say something stupid.

"I don't really know how to do this," Erik confessed, holding her gaze. "Be a—"

"A suitor?"

He shook his head with a soft laugh. "A *person*," he countered. "It's been a very long time since I've tried."

"You're doing well enough," Christine muttered. She was done now and there was no need to be so close to him. Yet she didn't move.

"I have a good teacher," Erik replied with warmth she so rarely heard from him, and it stoked the fire in her core. "She's quite remarkable."

"So is her teacher," Christine whispered back, suddenly so aware of how close her face was to his mask and the way was looking at her mouth. *Fuck.*

"Christine." There was just enough darkness and danger in his voice to jostle her back to reality and she sat back, then stood up for good measure.

"I – I wish you had coffee. It would be nice after a night like that," she declared, steadfastly ignoring whatever kind of annoyed or confused look Erik was giving her. "And I don't need a lecture on it being bad for my voice. It's not like I'm singing tonight."

"Why would you say that?"

"You may have forgotten with all the uproar," Christine said as she turned, annoyed at his flippant tone. "But I am no longer employed in your opera, *Monsieur le Fantôme.*"

"As it is my opera, I shall be the one to decide that. I promised the management that if Carlotta performs tonight, it will be a disaster."

Christine gave a bitter laugh as she sat back down, this time on a chair a safe distance from Erik. Her blood heated for another reason now as she remembered the humiliations of the day before. "If only. I'd love to see that miserable bitch get a fraction of what she deserves."

"Such venom. I like it. And I promise you, she will. I don't make idle threats." The way he said those words should have frightened her. But right now, it thrilled her and that alone was terrifying.

"I've never hated someone like this before," Christine confessed.

"You haven't known many lead sopranos then." She shot Erik a look and he shrugged. "Don't be afraid to hate her. Think of what she wanted those men to do to you." Christine shuddered. "Like you said, she deserves what's coming."

"And what is that? Do you plan on telling me?"

"As soon as I come up with it, yes." Erik took a sip of tea. "I think something public is in order, don't you?"

"Show everyone in Paris what a loathsome toad she is," Christine spat.

Erik cocked his head. "A toad?"

"It was something she said to me." Erik's eyes were hazy now, lost in some dangerous thought. "Why?"

"You've given me an idea... I don't have to tell you the details if you'd like to remain innocent." Erik held her gaze, the soft light of the parlor deepening the golden glow of his eyes. There was a fire there, as always, but today Christine felt it in her heart as well, as it tempered the raw metal of her rage and her hate into ruthless steel.

"Tell me."

"Is he back yet?" Raoul asked the valet as he came into the breakfast room. The man shook his head grimly.

"Why are you so eager to talk to Philippe?" Sabine asked from her place at the table, as she peered over the morning's copy of *Le Monde*. She sighed as she took Raoul in, as if she could see how his love had grown in the past day. "Her. Of course. You better not mean to ask him permission to marry that trollop."

"I don't want to ask permission to–" Raoul found himself blushing as only his sister could make him. "I have certain hopes and intentions, of course, but we've only just started to court and—"

"You're courting now? I thought she wasn't even seeing you."

"No, we had supper yesterday, and it was sublime!" Raoul was only allowed a breath to recall what joy it had been to simply be with Christine again – as old friends, and now something more – before Sabine scoffed again.

"I'm sure she made you feel that way, the little minx," Sabine muttered as the salon doors burst open and Philippe tumbled in, still in the clothes Raoul had seen him in the night before. Of course Antoine was with him, looking even worse for wear.

"Which little minx made you feel what way?" Philippe bellowed, stumbling towards Raoul. "Has some little whore finally plucked you? Let us celebrate! It's been long enough!"

"Philippe!" Sabine gasped as her older brother grabbed Raoul's face. His breath stank of spirits almost as badly as his clothes smelled of smoke. He pressed Raoul's cheeks hard as he examined him with bleary but discerning eyes, then sighed.

"No, I don't think you have been, you still blush like a girl," Philippe slurred, dissolving into laughter. "Too bad. We could have shown you some real fun last night."

"Of for heaven's sake!" Sabine yelled. Finally her older brother noticed her, and her glare sent him stumbling into a chair while Antoine laughed at the threshold.

"You have no sense of fun," Philippe pouted. "Either of you."

"Food! We need food!" Antoine cried, startling the valet with a playful blow. "And coffee!" he called after the man as he fled.

"Did you tell some second-rate journalist about Christine's family?" Raoul demanded of his obviously still-drunk brother.

"Why would I care about her family?" Philippe asked back with a hiccup.

"Because her father was a gypsy mongrel." Raoul spun to stare at Sabine. His sister's face was hard and implacable. "She'd be unsuitable even if she wasn't an actress, which I should not need to remind you is only one rung above a whore."

"She is not like that!" Raoul fumed. "She is a good Christian woman!" This drew a snicker from Antoine and an eyeroll from Sabine. "Did you tell someone about her?"

"I did."

Raoul rounded on Antoine at his words. "Why? How did you know?" Antoine pointed blearily towards Philippe and snickered again. "Why?"

"Because such a woman does not befit our station," Antoine said with a shrug. "And I hoped revealing the taint on her blood to all of Paris would protect this family. You know what those people took from us. I wouldn't want to have that woman's reputation ruin your sister's." Raoul looked between Antoine and Sabine, who, to Raoul's horror, actually seemed impressed.

"As if whatever you two were up to last night or get up to with your *friends* at the Opera doesn't ruin your names," Raoul snapped.

"It doesn't, because our women know their place and we know the rules," Philippe snarled and Raoul shrank down. "Sabine, dear, would you mind leaving this discussion to the gentlemen?"

Sabine sighed powerfully but rose to leave, giving Antoine one more infuriating smile as she did. "I'll see you when it's time to leave for the theater," she commented, reminding Raoul that he had to share a box tonight with all of the people he very much wanted to strangle.

"When will you get it through your head that no one cares if you take a tumble with a ballet rat or a soprano – it's what they're there for. But you can't go about thinking they can ever be anything more," Philippe declared as soon as the door was shut. "I don't care if you make Daaé your mistress, but you cannot make her your wife."

"You know that telling me I can't do something is the surest way to encourage me?" Raoul shot back. "You said I didn't have the stomach for the sea or the wits to survive without you clucking after my every move and see what I've done."

"Ah yes, taking our noble family name across the seven seas!" Philippe crowed.

"I don't care about our name, or Father's legacy, or Christine's lineage, you boar, I only care about her." Raoul did not like the way Philippe and Antoine looked at him, with a combination of pity and disgust. "And I don't appreciate your continued insistence that her morals are so loose. She would never!"

"Admit it, boy," Antoine sneered. "She's a whore like all the rest of them. The sooner you learn that, the sooner you'll be free to enjoy her for what she is."

"Just because you have no soul doesn't mean the rest of us have sold ours," Raoul seethed and charged out of the room.

He wanted to get out. He wanted to go to church and wash off the stain of Antoine's presence and his brother's moral rot. He wanted to go to Christine and hold her again and let her reassure him that she was good, as he knew in his heart she had to be. She was not what they said. She was not corrupted. She was an angel.

The pain did not bother Erik as they walked. The sting of his wound had barely been a worry all day because he had been with her. Admittedly, the journey up from his home to Christine's dressing room had been more tiring than usual, but that simply meant they had to go slower, which gave him a few more precious minutes with the woman who continued to astonish him at every turn. They had planned and practiced all day, spending the hours in quiet intimacy he could barely fathom, and he was not ready to part.

"You're sure they won't have given the room away already?" Christine asked as they ascended the final flight of stairs on his secret road. "I wouldn't put it past them."

"The managers and Carlotta may be fools, but everyone in the company knows this room is haunted," Erik replied as they arrived behind the mirror. "We can go another way if you like."

"No, it's fine," Christine whispered, turning to him. It was a small space behind the mirror and naturally forced them to be close. Yesterday Erik would have recoiled at the way her movement brought her near, and the instinct was still there, but her assurances and the magic of the kiss she had bestowed on him gave him the strength to remain still. In the cool dark of the passage, even through their cloaks, he could feel her warmth. She looked up at him, face illuminated by the golden light of the lantern as he held it aloft. He'd never seen someone more beautiful.

"You remember where to go?"

"Yes, you were extremely clear in your instructions," Christine replied with an annoyed smile. "Will you be alright? No tearing those stitches I worked so hard on."

It was a strange thing, to be fussed over and cared for. "I am, you needn't worry. They're much better than your costuming work."

"I told Louise I knew the general theory of sewing when she hired me, I just neglected to mention what it was I had experience mending."

"I'm eternally grateful for your skill," Erik replied, smiling back at her.

And then, as had happened many times that day, he found himself staring at his remarkable student and wishing he was brave enough to properly kiss her. He did not try to hide the desire. He glanced at her lips and noted the way her breath caught and the flush of her cheeks. He wanted to cross that distance, claim her as truly his... But he couldn't. One kiss to his forehead had nearly ended him; he feared a real kiss would stop his heart entirely.

"You should go," Erik whispered, looking down to avoid seeing her disappointment or relief. To his shock, she raised her hand to touch his side, tender against his wound.

"Be careful, please," she whispered.

Erik wanted to tell her he would endure a thousand such injuries for another moment like this, blessed by her concern and gentleness. Bold in the darkness, he took her hand, raising it up close to the mask she had so bravely removed the night before. He couldn't kiss her lips, not yet. Instead, he kissed her wrist, his lips pressing against her pulse point so he could feel her heartbeat, tasting the heat of her pristine skin.

Then he let her go, drawing back as she stared at him, thunderstruck. He triggered the mirror and nodded for her to move.

"Go. You'll be magnificent," he promised as she staggered back. Another movement and she was once again separated from him by glass before he retreated back into the dark, leaning against the wall for support as he struggled to catch his breath.

In all his life he had never dared to take such a treasure. He closed his eyes to remember it: the heat of her skin as it faded from his lips. Perhaps there would be more time for their lips later. But now, there was work to be done.

7. Sweet and Bitter

To Raoul, the Opera seemed especially crowded tonight. He was not the best judge, perhaps, being a newer patron, but it was as if every subscriber who was anyone had made it a point to attend the latest performance of *Faust*. Given that he was steadfastly ignoring Sabine, Philippe, and Antoine, Raoul had a good vantage point to listen to the gossip. Some people were there to see the new soprano who had been such a sensation at New Year's and the last performance, and others were there because they had heard Carlotta would be making tonight a special triumph. Raoul wondered who the false Spaniard had paid off to spread such a lie.

"Raoul, did you hear me?" His sister's voice cut through his thoughts, and Raoul turned to her with a sigh. She looked quite handsome in her blue-black silk gown dripping with black crystal beads, though it was conservative compared to some of the other women in their capes and glittering gowns trying to outdo the gilded ceiling of the *Salon du Glacier*.

"No, I wasn't listening," Raoul confessed. "Did you need something?"

"Only your decision on if you will be visiting the *Salon du Danse* after curtain," Antoine answered, as smug as ever. "Perhaps you'll find something else on the market there to replace your errant Swede."

"She's spent most of her life here in France," Raoul grumbled. "But I should like to speak to the managers if they will be there."

"You don't need to wait." Philippe raised his glass of champagne to indicate where Moncharmin and Richard had entered. Richard looked placid, an improvement over the glower Raoul had seen him sport before, but Moncharmin looked as harried as usual.

"Excuse me then," Raoul said, ignoring Sabine's sigh of protest. In a few steps he had blocked the two men's way and they looked as happy to see him as his family was that he was speaking to them now, which was to say annoyed and exhausted. "Messieurs, I wish to speak with you on the matter of Mademoiselle Daaé—"

Richard raised a hand, sighing. "We have no reason to discuss a woman no longer employed by us. But do feel free to bring your petition to the *Comique*."

"Now, Richard, we have discussed the possibility of—" Moncharmin began and fell victim to a glare from his partner. He sighed and looked at Raoul. "My apologies, Monsieur Le Vicomte."

"Monsieur Moncharmin." All three men turned to see a concierge, an older woman with dark eyes who held herself with a bearing that was both noble and defiant.

"Didn't I fire you too?" Richard muttered.

"I do not work for *you*," she responded raising her chin proudly. "I have a letter for Monsieur Moncharmin, from my true employer." The woman handed Moncharmin an envelope with black lining. Was it a death announcement or a mourning note? Richard and Raoul both stared at Moncharmin as he opened and read the missive and the color drained from his face.

"Well, what is it?" Richard demanded.

"I must attend to some business backstage," Moncharmin muttered then turned on his heel and left them all staring after him. The concierge looked pleased as she shot Richard a smug look.

"My door shall be locked tonight. Do not bother intruding again," the woman said and turned without ceremony to exit the salon, a spring in her step.

"I say, Richard, you seem to lack authority over your people," Raoul remarked. "Perhaps it would be in your best interest to change course. With Mademoiselle Daaé as a start."

"Let the man rest, Raoul, he has more important things to attend to," came Antoine's voice as he tugged at Raoul's elbow. "It's time to take our seats."

"Do enjoy the performance, Messieurs," Richard muttered with a begrudging nod. "I'm sure our reigning diva will impress us."

"I doubt it," Raoul snapped back.

Antoine rolled his eyes. "Come, let's take our seats. It shall be quite the performance."

Shaya took no pride in being a subscriber to the Opera, and he certainly hoped Erik did not know about the money his adversary had wasted on the privilege of claiming a box with a middling view on the top tier of Garnier's jewel box of a theater. Nevertheless, he was glad of it tonight. There was a foreboding in the air that did not only come from Gounod's brooding music. Another thing Shaya would never admit to Erik was that, of all the operas he had endured, *Faust* was his favorite by far, though he was dubious of the effectiveness of the morality tale as it made Faust and Marguerite's descents into sin so compelling.

Another matter Shaya was sure Erik would agree with him on was the terrible etiquette of the audience. As the massive chandelier blazed above like a second sun, the audience barely stopped chittering even as the action continued on stage, so much so that there was barely any difference between the climax of Act I and the brief interval. Things escalated when Carlotta finally made her appearance of course, with a vocal claque in one section applauding her single, overly-ornamented phrase of music.

Again Shaya was struck with the uncomfortable shame of agreeing with Erik in his opinion of the diva. He had learned to appreciate the music of Europe many years ago, in part thanks to Erik's affection for it, and he knew enough now from years attending the Opera that Carlotta's instrument was indeed commonplace. It cut through the audience's chatter like a jagged knife, shrill and lacking any of the warmth and color of Christine's sound.

Shaya glanced, as he had all night, towards box five on the grand tier, the only empty space in the house. Or it looked so to those who did not know it played host to a specter. He wondered if Erik was there now, in the shadows. Or was he somewhere else, plotting his promised disaster?

Act III began with Siébel's sweet love song. It was a rare moment for Adèle Valerius to shine. The audience barely gave her attention though. After Faust and Méphistophélès left their devilish gifts for Marguerite next to Siébel's pathetic flowers, the tension in the audience rose.

Finally, the supposed "maiden" herself stepped onto the stage. Carlotta's mere appearance provoked applause from her claque, and the prima donna broke character to smile and nod in appreciation. Shaya rolled his eyes. The music was pensive and ominous as the diva made a circuit of the stage before taking her place at the spinning wheel. She began the recitative and Shaya held his breath with the rest of the audience. *"I would truly like to know, who the young man was. Was he a grand lord and what was his name?"*

Shaya breathed a sigh of relief as Carlotta sang and the whispers of the audience ebbed as the rhythmic march of the violins gained speed with Marguerite's spinning wheel. What had he been expecting anyway? As the music grew more agitated, Carlotta began the Ballad of the King of Thule in earnest.

"*There was a King of Thule,*" she began, then suddenly that crystalline voice became something...else. "COU-AC!"

Shaya's heart stopped in his chest. The entire audience went still. Carlotta's face went pale beneath her rouge. The terrible noise she had produced had been more than a crack, more than an errant note. It was as if a toad or some other horrid creature had been set in place of her voice. The orchestra played on as Carlotta looked about her, then nodded in resolve. Shaya held his breath. Perhaps it had been a mistake.

"*Kept in memory of his beautiful* – COU-AC!" The audience gasped at the horrible sound, so foul that no one could ignore it. Carlotta clutched her throat, as if to expel the loathsome toad that had somehow lodged itself there. "*A cup* – COU-AC! – *etched in* – COOUUUAAACCCC!!"

The diva kept trying, standing up now and toppling her spinning wheel, giving all her effort to overcome the curse she was somehow under. But each attempt was more terrible than the last. Even the notes she could manage to sing rather than croak were strained and choked. Carlotta's face reddened in horror and rage as the orchestra played on, though a few instruments trailed off as she flailed about on stage, croaking and coughing.

Shaya knew it was not a curse that had been set on Carlotta. He recognized Erik's tricks; his expert ventriloquism that had driven men mad as the monster had played with them. That was what he was doing now, playing with Carlotta like a cat with a mouse it was about to devour.

And then, the final blow. From one of the premiere boxes came a snicker. Even from afar Shaya recognized the young man who was the source of the sound. The young Vicomte de Chagny was bursting with glee in his box near the stage. And his laugh was like a match to dry kindling. In mere seconds, the entire audience was howling as Carlotta continued to screech and croak on the stage.

"Stop! You must- COU-AC!" Carlotta rasped, and the orchestra screeched into silence. Shaya was the only one not laughing as he looked between Carlotta and the shadows in box five. "What is – COU-AC! Who – COU-AC!" Carlotta's face was red, the tendons in her neck starkly visible as she attempted to yell only to be drowned out by laughter.

"She is singing to bring down the chandelier!" came the cry in a voice that cut through the din that. A voice Shaya would know anywhere.

Shaya's eyes flew to the great mass of crystal and brass above the audience. No, dear Allah, no. Erik could not mean that threat! On stage, Carlotta gave a silent scream and rushed into the wings as the curtains fell.

And Shaya prayed. He prayed this revenge was enough for Erik. He prayed for the lives of the laughing patrons in the seats below. And he prayed that Christine Daaé was far away, or at least cowed and afraid of the disaster that had been unleashed on her behalf. If not, she was already damned.

Erik had relayed to Christine a quote from an English playwright recently, opining that all theaters were madhouses, but an opera house was the ward for the incurables. That certainly rang true tonight. Backstage it was utter chaos as the curtain closed. Carlotta had rushed off stage left, exactly as Christine had anticipated. She herself was tucked away stage right, between a few flats. It was much like the first time she had listened to Carlotta butcher *Faust*, but this time Christine had truly enjoyed the diva's performance. She laughed to herself again, remembering the look on Carlotta's face as Erik showed the whole of Paris what she really was.

"We need a doctor here!" someone called from the tumult around the ailing diva, and Christine smiled again. There was another commotion behind her as she finally dared to emerge from her hiding place. Adèle, Rameau, and Fontana were gathered in a clump around Armand Moncharmin, all yelling at him at once.

"I won't go on! Not with her! Who knows what will happen!" Fontana cried.

"I told you this would happen," Rameau was adding, while Adèle looked particularly furious.

"If you hadn't sacked Christine, we could—"

"Mademoiselle Daaé is here!" Moncharmin yelled above all of them, his eyes finally falling on Christine and relief spreading over his face. He pushed past the crowd and grabbed Christine by the hand.

"What on earth—" Adèle whispered in shock.

"Monsieur Moncharmin invited me," Christine said before anyone else could speak. "He was worried about how delicate Carlotta's health has been and regretted his earlier decisions regarding my place as her understudy," she added, holding the manager's gaze meaningfully.

"Yes, exactly." Moncharmin nodded and looked around as if expecting someone else to cut into the conversation. Christine controlled her smile and the urge to tell him that the ghost he feared was currently far away. Alas. "And – yes! It was a good thing I did. Get yourself dressed! You'll be on as soon as you're in costume!"

Without ceremony, Moncharmin rushed onto the stage. Christine heard the murmurs of the audience ebb as the manager signaled for their attention.

"*Mesdames et Messieurs*! I regret to inform you that La Carlotta has fallen ill and cannot complete—"

"Let's get you to your dressing room, my dear." Christine spun to find Adèle at her elbow, ushering her across the stage towards the singer's dressing rooms.

Their route took them directly past Carlotta's door. Christine could not help but glimpse inside to see the once-powerful diva sprawled on her chaise, her face red and her makeup smeared with tears. Through the door, the woman caught sight of Christine and opened her mouth to scream. No sound but a terrible rasp came out. Carlotta began to point, like she had seen a ghost. Christine only smiled and nodded before striding away, Adèle close behind.

Julianne was waiting for her at her dressing room door, looking thunderous.

"You could have told me you were here," Julianne grumbled as she rushed Christine into the room.

"I'm sorry, I didn't want to cause a stir," Christine began.

Julianne scoffed. "I was looking for you in. Figured it would take an act of God to keep you away. And somehow, you're walking through walls again."

"I came in the same way as everyone else," Christine lied.

"At least Moncharmin had some sense and prepared," Adèle agreed, and Julianne shot Christine a dubious look. "Come on, get her ready before there's a riot!"

Julianne sprang to action, and with Adèle's help, Christine was dressed in no time. "Don't you need to warm up?" Julianne asked suspiciously.

"Already done," Christine smiled, and that earned her another look.

"You really were ready to go on at a moment's notice," Julianne remarked.

"And a good thing too! Could you believe the sounds that woman was making?" Adèle laughed. "Her voice finally matched her soul."

"I couldn't have said it better myself." Christine smirked and gave her mirror one more glance. She couldn't feel Erik there. He was waiting with the rest of the audience for her to go on, not behind the mirror shrouded in the shadows where he had dared to kiss her.

Her stomach leapt at the memory, as it had again and again in the hour since he had crossed the divide between them. She grasped her wrist on instinct, running a thumb over her pulse and feeling it race as she recalled the softness of his lips on her skin. It made her legs feel unsteady and kindled an ache in the deepest part of her. An ache she had not allowed herself to feel, except in dreams, since her angel had fallen from heaven...

"Come on, girl!" Christine jumped at Adèle's voice. "All of Paris is waiting for you."

Christine nodded and rushed from the dressing room, her friends by her side. All of Paris waited for her to do the one thing she had spent her whole life dreaming of, to take the prize she had fought for. She was thrust onto the stage at Marguerite's spindle as the curtain rose, revealing the glittering crowd of people watching her, waiting for her to fail or triumph.

She knew Raoul was there. She knew that somewhere backstage Carlotta was in a fit knowing Christine had not only survived but was the one who had replaced her. The managers were watching. Every dancer and singer and stagehand and musician who had sneered at her or secretly supported her was waiting for her to open her mouth.

And none of them mattered. The only gaze that mattered was Erik's. She could feel it upon her as the music began, dark and pensive. She thought again of his kiss, of the touch of his hand, and the sound of his angel's voice. And she sang for that. "*I would truly like to know, who the young man was. Was he a grand lord and what was his name?*"

She sensed it when the audience let out their breath in relief. She did not care that she was about to prove them wrong, instead she reached into her soul, the way she had been taught by a genius who lived far beneath this stage, and sang out everything she felt.

"*There once was a king of Thule who, faithful unto the grave, Kept in memory of his ladylove a vessel of chiseled gold,*"

Marguerite paused, entranced by the memory of the man who had dared to kiss her hand. In two days, two men had done the same to Christine in such different places and ways. Yet it was only one who ignited the music in her soul. She looked at box five and sang out her soul to him.

Erik had never seen such a triumph in his theater. Between Carlotta's downfall and the utter brilliance of Christine's performance, there was no question now as to who the brightest star in the Opera firmament was.

Before the curtain even closed the audience was on their feet, and Erik with them. The other bows were rushed and cursory, the other principals giving way to Christine as she curtsied with tears streaming down her perfect face. Erik too. For pride. For joy. And for love.

There was nothing he wanted more than to leap from his box – the jump was not too far – onto the stage and snatch her into his arms. He wanted to kiss her properly and never stop, let her have every inch of his skin and scar. He wanted nothing but her, and every second of applause that delayed her return to him was torture, but seeing her joy and the adulation of Paris laid at her feet was also ecstasy.

At last he retreated into the hollow column that gave him access to his box and moved as quickly as he could through the walls and corridors towards dressing room thirteen. Soon he was behind the mirror, but he was not the only one waiting. Christine's dresser, Julianne Bonet, was stationed inside and staring warily at the mirror.

"I'll ask again: am I alone?" she spoke to the glass, much to Erik's shock.

"Do you expect me to say yes?" Erik replied coolly and watched Julianne jump. "Did you have a question?"

"I have a declaration," Julianne snapped back, straightening her spine. "I know you're more human than all of this—" she gestured to the mirror "—let's on. I know you bleed and you hurt Christine before and somehow, she's still part of whatever game you're playing."

"It's not a game, my dear Mademoiselle—"

"I was not done, Monsieur!" Erik would have been annoyed if he was not so impressed. "If any harm should come to her, I don't care how frightening or powerful you are, I will hunt you down and get her justice. I'll keep my mouth shut as long as she seems happy, but if that changes, I will be your enemy."

"Be at peace," Erik replied when it was clear he could speak. "There is no one in the world more precious to me than her. I only wish to protect her and...cherish her."

Julianne nodded and looked satisfied. She turned from the mirror and gathered up a gown from the wardrobe, the same violet confection Christine had worn at the New Year's gala. Erik remembered the way she had blushed in it when she had taken it off before this very mirror, baring herself and her soul to her angel in penance for smiling at another man. The same boy who had intruded on her after *Faust* before. Surely, he would not be there tonight. She had rejected him, hadn't she?

Erik's heart seized as he heard a commotion outside the doo. Christine entered with her arms full of flowers, a crowd of well-wishers on the other side of the door, and Armand Moncharmin right beside her. Erik sighed, relieved and annoyed.

"Ah, good, you'll be ready," Moncharmin said as he spotted Julianne with the dress.

"Monsieur, I'm very tired," Christine protested.

"You won't have to stay for long, I assure you, but your presence is required. As an employee and a principal in the company," Moncharmin said meaningfully. "Many of the patrons were great admirers of Carlotta and may have been understandably upset by her sudden *illness*. Happily, they are quite taken with you now but as you can tell, their support can be fickle." There was an unmistakable edge to the man's voice.

Christine's face began to harden in understanding. "I suppose it will be an excellent time to announce that I will be singing Gilda at the *Rigoletto* premiere on Friday?" Erik grinned in pride at Christine's shrewdness.

"Of course," Moncharmin smiled. "It would delight me. I'll leave you to change. Your escort should be here soon. I've discussed it with him. I have to find Richard."

"My what?" Christine asked, but Moncharmin had already left.

"Looks like everything is going according to plan," Julianne muttered as she pulled Christine behind her dressing screen. Erik was grateful for the modesty. He was already distracted enough. He caught the curious look Christine gave her friend. "I hope it's all worth it. And that you know what you're doing."

"Julianne—" Before Christine could protest, the door sprang open again, and Christine yelped in modesty at the intruder. It was Robert Rameau, of all people, already dressed for the reception.

"Monsieur!" Julianne shouted. "There is a lady dressing!"

"Oh come come, it's a theater and I don't care," Rameau brushed them off as Christine rushed to get into her gown. "I've come to escort you and make a proposal."

"A proposal?" Christine stammered. Erik was intrigued. He knew exactly where Rameau's inclinations and affections lay, and it was not with Christine, nor any other woman.

"I'm sure you're aware of the many rumors about you, my dear, especially concerning the mysterious lover you claim not to have," Rameau drawled as he took a seat at Christine's vanity, stroking his goatee. Christine for her part looked dubious as Julianne finished her laces. "No one knows who it is that's stolen you away from that Vicomte who keeps asking after you up and down."

Now that made Erik's fury rise and – was Christine blushing? Perhaps he needed to send a message to that entitled little fop.

"What is your point, Robert?" Christine asked, finally emerging from the screen, a vision in purple, like a crocus in the final days of winter.

"Can I speak with you alone?" he asked, glancing at Julianne, who turned to Christine with a challenging look.

"It's fine, Julianne," Christine said, her eyes on the mirror and nothing else. "I'm perfectly safe."

"You better stay that way," Julianne muttered as she left the room.

"Alone at last," Rameau smiled, standing and taking Christine's hand. It was so easy for normal people to simply touch her, wasn't it? "My dear, I am sympathetic to you. If there is someone you wish to, shall we say, conceal. It can be hard being the paramour of an opera star, especially if they are a powerful person."

"What are you implying?"

"Not implying, proposing," Rameau said, his rakish façade finally falling. "I know there is a war brewing in the Opera, and you've won a great victory. I want to be on your side and help you. And to be honest, I need you to help me too. I also have an assignation that requires some...concealment."

"You mean Monsieur Moncharmin?" Christine asked without judgment. Rameau gave a sober nod.

"Let us help each other. I am a great performer, as are you. Cast me as your lover and you as mine for all who would enquire or ask, and we will keep everyone safe." Erik tilted his head in interest. It was not the worst of plans. Christine turned to the mirror. To Rameau it would look like her examining her reflection, but Erik understood it. She was asking permission.

"It's fine," he whispered as soft as possible, his voice in her ear, and she nodded.

"We will be seen together tonight then. And leave together. Your carriage can simply drop me off behind the Opera. I'll find my way home."

"Well, we don't need to work out that many details yet."

"We do," Christine replied. She turned to Rameau to offer her arm. "It seems I have made a deal with the devil."

Rameau laughed, a sonorous, rumbling sound. "I doubt it is your first, my dear Christine."

Erik listened to the sound of their voices as they retreated down the hall. He knew it would hurt, to watch her in the *Salon du Danse*, in the arms of another man – even if it was one that would never be a threat – but he could not stop himself from following. Something terrible was in his heart, woven with the memory of the boy. The one who still haunted Christine's steps and life. The fear of seeing him touch her again stabbed Erik with more pain than the healing wound at his side. It was nothing compared to the pain he'd endure for her. Or cause. Did the young fool not know that Christine belonged to one alone?

Raoul had experienced so many emotions in the span of one night he felt as unraveled as in his first days at sea. He had gone from annoyance to resentment of the crowd's applause for Carlotta, to utter delight at the woman's strange fit of hysteria on stage that had revealed what a monster she was. Then to joy at hearing Christine again. She had been utterly wonderful, even better than before.

There had been such passion in the way she sang, such romance. Her duet with Faust had left Raoul fuming with jealousy that Carlos Fontana had been the object of even her false ardor, for it had been so enticing. And her final scene calling to the angels had been truly like hearing heaven. He wished he could tell her that she did not need to look to the beyond to find an angel of music, she was one.

But Raoul had to find her first. It had been nearly impossible to get backstage, and he was sure Sabine and Philippe had taken as much time as possible leaving the box and discussing their arrangements to get home, Antoine in tow. Finally, here he was, shoved in the packed *Salon du Danse* behind the stage while the ballet rats and ladies of the chorus brazenly flirted with any man in a respectable jacket. Raoul ignored them all until he saw one dancer he had seen with Christine's colored maid who claimed to be such a close friend.

"Excuse me, Mademoiselle?" he asked the girl with dark blonde curls.

"Jammes. Cécile Jammes," she said with a smile. There was a smaller girl next to her who seemed overwhelmed by the entire event. "And this is Meg Giry. You're Raoul de Chagny. Meg, don't bother with this one. All he cares about is Christine. She's all anyone cares about these days." The venom in the dancer's voice was truly terrifying.

"Jammes, be nice," Meg muttered beside her. "He may want to talk to us."

"Have you seen Christine?" he asked instead. Jammes sighed and dragged herself and her companion away. Raoul only had an instant to lament his lot before turned to the entrance of the gilded salon and at last saw the one person in all the world he wanted to see. Christine was there, radiant and smiling. And with another man.

Raoul should have been accustomed to jealousy by now, but to see her with the fiend was something else. Was that the bass who played *the devil*? Raoul strode through the crowd, blazing with indignation. Did she have to be so brazen? Christine had known he was in the audience tonight! There had been moments when he was sure the undeniable passion in her voice was for him.

"Is this him?" Raoul found himself demanding, stepping in front of Christine.

"If you mean the talented devil who failed to corrupt this shining soul – on stage at least – I am," the basso replied.

Raoul frowned. "I was speaking to Mademoiselle Daaé."

"Monsieur de Chagny, I do not believe you have met Robert Rameau, my...dear friend." Christine's cheeks were bright, and Raoul knew she was not the sort of hussy who would rouge them, which meant she was blushing in shame at her discovery.

"I asked you a question," Raoul said, and Rameau gave a derisive sort of laugh that made Raoul disappointed that duels were illegal. "Is this *him*?"

Christine swallowed, looking between the two men who sought her, and nodded tightly. "We needn't make a scene."

"You're not good enough for her, do you know that?" Raoul demanded of the cad.

"I do. I am but a humble peasant in the presence of a queen of the stage," Rameau replied, easy and dashing. People were staring at them, Raoul realized. Rameau raised his crystal glass high and shouted: "To Christine! The savior of the Opera and the brightest light in the Opera's firmament!"

A cheer went up and Christine gave a shy smile. Raoul could only stare at Christine as pain split his poor heart. "Can we speak alone?" he asked, pathetically. He didn't want all these gawkers to observe more of his misery.

"I don't think that's wise," Christine replied nervously. "Robert and I—"

"Let me refill your glass, my dear. I'm sure whatever you and this dashing youth have to say won't take long," Rameau said with a smile, taking the completely full glass of champagne from Christine's gloved hand.

Raoul knew it was bold, but these opera folks and lascivious patrons had seen worse. He grasped her arms, trying to reclaim the closeness they had shared only the night before. "Christine, I was sincere last night. I'm willing to fight for you."

"Please, Raoul, I don't want to be fought over," Christine protested, drawing away. "I can't talk right now."

"Because he is here? Does he know about us?"

"There is no us!" Christine said with a firmness that shocked Raoul and struck his heart.

"I always loved that you were kind," Raoul muttered and watched how his words of adoration made her look over her shoulder like an errant child. "I never would have guessed you would be so cruel. That you would play with hearts like this."

"Raoul!" she protested, but he had no ear for it. He turned on his heel and marched from the salon. People looked at him; the little dancer, Meg, called after him. He kept walking, determined to forget this damned brothel of a place forever.

"A re you sure you'll be alright here?" Christine's latest suitor asked with concern that was touching and patronizing. "I can take you to your flat, wherever that is," Robert offered.

"I'll be fine, my lodgings are not far off," she muttered. Her head was still buzzing with everything that had happened tonight. And the day before. And the week before as well. It was honestly a miracle she was not crying on the floor somewhere. Part of her wanted to be.

"Even so," Robert said, taking her hand kindly. "Be careful, Christine."

"I will be," she said and left the carriage. As she walked beneath the gaslight on the *Rue Scribe*, the black cloak belonging to a ghost draped over her shoulders, seeking out the entrance to the underworld, she wondered if she had lied.

Was she being careful? Or was she playing with hearts, as Raoul had accused her? An hour ago she had stood basking in applause, Carlotta's reign ended, and felt invincible. Now she felt like a lamb throwing herself in front of a lion whose hunger she had been foolish enough to pray for.

As if reading her thoughts, a shadow along the edge of the building moved as Erik materialized from the dark. And again Christine questioned her sanity as the Phantom held out his hand to her, his eyes glittering in the gaslight. There was something irresistible in the gesture, and it terrified her.

"You found me," she said, taking his hand without hesitation.

"I always will," he replied, and she knew that the feeling of him watching her during the party had not been a dream.

He did not speak as he led her below, the shadows retreating from the light of his lantern like frightened animals. It was colder down here tonight, or perhaps it was the danger and disappointment radiating off him that made Christine shiver.

"Do you know if Carlotta is gone for good?" Christine asked when they were deep in the cellars.

"I wasn't paying much attention to her after you took the stage," Erik replied, voice as cold and dark as the stone around them.

They came to the lake and skirted the edge towards Erik's home quickly. In a blink, they were in the parlor again. The fire was only embers and the candles had burned low, all the warmth of the place gone. Still, Christine removed her cloak and gloves as Erik did the same before turning to the fire.

"Erik, please talk to me." Christine took a cautious step forward. "I know you're upset. About Raoul—"

"*Don't* say his name," Erik growled, rounding on Christine and rising to his full height. "Why does he still pursue you? I thought you drove him away." There was something in Erik's words, the ownership and entitlement of them, that kindled an even hotter fire in Christine than the one crackling in the grate. And it burnt away her fear.

"He is my friend, my oldest friend in the world," Christine said slowly. "And you're jealous of him."

"Of course I am!" Christine jumped at the venom in Erik's voice but did not back down. "He is perfect. Handsome and rich and *normal*, and he wants to steal you from me!"

"I cannot be stolen, Erik, I am a person, not a pair of candlesticks!" Christine snapped as Erik shrank at the matching ire in her tone. "I am here, right now, with you. Not him. Doesn't that mean anything?"

Erik stared as if seeing her for the first time, the menace that had radiated from him a moment before melting away. "It means everything," Erik whispered.

"Then why don't you trust me?" Christine asked, inching closer.

"I don't trust *him*," Erik replied, much to Christine's shock. "You shouldn't either. You've refused him and still he pursues you. Men like him won't stop until they have what they want."

"Men like him?" Christine balked. "I know him; he'd never do anything like that."

"He was born with a title, raised among gold and glory," Erik went on, a new sort of darkness in his voice. "His kind take everything they want and leave nothing in their wake but ashes."

"You hate them, don't you? The nobility and the rich?" Christine asked in return, thinking back to things from warnings from her angel to Erik's time as a communard. "Why? Why would you, of all people, insist on hating and judging someone because of how they were born?"

"Because I know them, Christine," Erik said with surety that was chilling. "They made me."

"What?" Christine braced herself as Erik stepped closer, his body coiled and tense as he held her with his glare.

"Once upon a time, in a little town near Sligo, in Ireland, a farmer lived with his family. He tilled the earth all week and took his family to sing in the church on Sunday. He had a daughter, and she had a voice that delighted the whole village. They did not own the land they worked, it belonged to the English lord of the manor, who they never saw until it was time to pay their rent. The English didn't let them speak their tongue or sing their songs, but they did it anyway. And no one was better than that girl. Her name...was Sarah."

"Your mother," Christine whispered. Erik turned away from her, eyes closed as he leaned against the mantle above the fire.

"She wanted more from life than a backward village at the edge of the world, and she hoped her voice and her spirit could take her there. That was even before the famine drove her whole family to the new world, the ones that lived. She didn't go west.

She went east, to Dublin, then to London. The only work for a sixteen-year-old Irish girl there was as a maid. But she was smart and hardworking and impressed her employers.

"She impressed herself all the way into a fine house where she waited on the noble women, including a guest. A Baroness. She was so fascinated by young Sarah that she hired her away on the spot and took her home across the channel to the family's fine chateau, near Rouen. Sarah hoped she could save enough working there to go to Paris. No one in Paris would care if she was Irish, like they had in London. There would be a chance."

Erik turned to Christine, regret now in his eyes and voice. "She didn't make it, did she?" Christine guessed aloud.

"She was happy there, for a few weeks. She loved the gardens and all the flowers she had never seen before. She even caught the eye of a stonemason who was building a new chapel on the grounds. Everything was hopeful and good, until the spring came, and with it the son of the old Baron and Baroness. And he took a liking to the pretty new Irish maid."

Christine gulped, her stomach dropping as she understood.

"I do not share the luxury your father enjoyed: the possibility that my conception could have been something born of love, or even mutual desire," Erik went on. "I know what my father did to my mother. He pursued her, and when she refused him, he raped her. He took what he wanted because she was just a foreign maid, not a person. And he enjoyed taking what he wanted. He liked the fight."

"Erik..." Christine imagined that if a scar had a sound, it would be akin to the timbre of his voice as he told the tale. She wanted to touch him, to console him somehow, but she did not want to stop him.

"And she never stopped fighting him. For months he abused her. And she couldn't get away. She couldn't tell anyone. It was only when the Baroness realized her new maid had somehow gotten with child that she was forced to confess. She beat the truth out of my mother and then exiled her son to Paris, but now she had a grandchild to deal with and the woman carrying it.

"My mother was a good Catholic girl; she'd agreed to come to France because of that. So she thought her soul was already damned, why not damn it further? She went to a woman in the village for help to get rid of the child that monster had put in her. It didn't work. I think it did something else. She wanted to try again or kill herself; she told me that many times. But the Baroness stopped her, even over the protests of her husband.

"I don't know what kind of threats or deals were made, but by the end of the summer my mother was married off to the stonemason – a useless lout named Carl who saw the arrangement as an easy way to stay on the payroll. He didn't mind that my mother was pregnant as long as the Baroness gave him his money. They were hidden away in a little village, across the Seine, and my father was told that Sarah had been sent away. Perhaps the story could have been different if it hadn't been for this."

Erik gestured to his face and Christine blinked back tears.

"I was born in the dark of winter, and that was what finally broke her; to see that the child her tormentor had left her with was a different kind of monster. She went mad when she saw me. She had to be forced to nurse me, or so I learned later. She would tell me how she gave me my first mask, so she could look at me and let me live."

Erik's eyes were closed as he relieved the memories and so he did not see when Christine took his hand. He looked up at her in disbelief as she held it to her heart, wondering if he could feel it breaking for him behind her ribs.

"To her credit, my grandmother was the only relation who wanted me alive, in her way. She collected foreigners, the Baroness, and so she sent a half-blind maid from Finland to keep us alive. Aneka. She gave me a name when my mother wouldn't. She'd tend to me, along with the other animals, and, somehow, I lived. My earliest memory is sneaking into her room and listening to my mother sing, and Aneka shooing me away like I was a dog when she found me."

"They both hurt you?" Christine asked in horror.

"Everyone hurt me. My mother, Aneka, Carl – the man I thought was my father until he confessed in a drunken rage that I was a baronet's bastard. He and my mother hated each other by the end. The only affection they shared was for the same wine. He'd come and go, take the money from the Baroness, then wander off for months to gamble it away.

"My mother took pleasure in antagonizing him. It was to spite him that she spent all of our stipend on a little piano one season, before he could take it. He beat us both for it, but the piano stayed, and I taught myself to play. It wasn't my first instrument; I'd already learned to make melodies on my mother's tin flute. Carl hated it when we played, so we played louder to spite him more. And it was to spite the world that she taught me to read and write. She taught me the language she had learned in secret as a child, so I could know what she was saying when she'd fall into one of her fits and scream at the walls. It was strange, once she was gone, I hated the quiet."

"What happened to her?" Christine asked, so afraid of the answer but desperate to know. Erik looked at her, a bitter smile playing at the edge of the mask.

"My father," he replied, confirming Christine's worst fears. "The old baron died when I was eight, and when he did, the money stopped. Carl didn't like that, and so he decided it was a good idea to barge up to the chateau and demand the new Baron support his bastard. He didn't come back by nightfall, but one of the Baron's valets did. He demanded we present ourselves, my mother and I.

"It was my first time meeting my real father. I'd always wanted to see the monster my mother blamed for me. I wanted to know if one could perceive the evil in him, like people could in me. But he was handsome. I remember the disgust on that handsome face when my mother ripped off my mask to show him mine."

Erik's hand was tight around Christine's fingers now, his breath shallow. "You don't have to go on," she offered, her other hand stroking his arm as gently as she could manage. "It's alright."

"You need to know what he did. What *they* are capable of," Erik said through gritted teeth. "He had sent Carl to the cellar, beaten and drunk. But he had us up in his private rooms. When Mother demanded that he pay what she was owed, he grabbed me and threw me in a wardrobe of all things. I guess anything with a lock would have sufficed. I can still remember the dark. The smell of his fresh linens and shoe polish. And I remember the way my mother screamed. Even as a child, I knew what he was going to do."

"Oh dear God," Christine whispered.

"She had sworn, my mother, she had *sworn* to never let a man do that to her again. Especially him. So she fought. I screamed too and beat against that door until it broke, and he looked up. It gave her time to get away. She didn't run to the hall or the door. She knew he would catch her. She ran to the window instead."

"Erik," Christine gasped and threw her arms around him. It was instinct, truly, to want to hold a broken soul closer to her and pray that it could erase the pain of the past. He was so tall her head was right against his heart as she held him tight, and she could hear that heart pounding.

"I ran down to her. Maybe she had survived it. She looked like she was asleep," Erik went on, his arms finally wrapping around Christine. "I had always been able to wake her up. To bring her back. So I sang to her. She had been my jailer and my tormentor, but she had also been my hope and my life. She was my world, and she taught me from birth that the world was cruel and unjust. I loved her and I didn't know what I would do without her. But she didn't wake up..."

"Erik, I'm so sorry," Christine whispered, looking up at him and touching the mask.

"*He* did that. He killed her, as sure as shooting her. And so did I." Erik's eyes glistened with tears as he spoke. "I am cursed, Christine. She always said it, and she was right. It's in my blood and it shows on my face. I will always be tainted by the man that forced her to birth a monster."

"You are not a monster," Christine said, adamant. "Monsters are not born. They're made."

"And I always will be the monster they made me," Erik murmured, but Christine shook her head.

"I don't believe that. I won't." He did not stop her, or tense, when she lifted the mask from his face, letting it fall to the floor beside them as she touched the scars a lifetime of pain and his own mother had left. It made her heart shatter to think of it.

"You don't know it all," Erik protested, tears flowing down his desiccated cheeks. There were no words in the world that could change his mind, Christine knew it. "You don't know what I—"

Christine kissed him. Finally, she closed her eyes and kissed his withered lips because it was all she could do and all she had wanted for days. He didn't respond at first, except to go rigid in shock, but she didn't stop. He tried to struggle and cower, but she twined her fingers into his hair to keep him from escaping. She would not let him leave her tonight.

"I know you, Erik," she whispered against his cheek and kissed him again. This time, he melted into it, his arms locking around her as secure as stone. It was like his music, kissing him; dizzying and dreamy. His mouth was inexpert, as was hers, she was sure, but it didn't matter. She tasted his breath and their tears as she parted her lips and let him devour her. His arms held her, strong as the sea, and she was ready to drown.

8. Memory

Certainly, Erik had died this time. No one would kiss him, let alone kiss him like this. And yet it was real. Christine's lips were against his, sublime and perfect, and if he was indeed not dead, he was a trespasser into heaven. He wanted this forever, and yet he was greedy. He wanted more. He touched her, pulling her close and letting his hands slide over the satin of her dress as her lips explored the ruin of his face. He found the skin of her back, her shoulder. He ran his fingers through her silken hair. She sighed and parted her lips further, her tongue darting to lick his lips and he grew even bolder, kissing her perfect cheek and her jaw, his mouth trailing towards her neck.

She arched towards him with a soft cry, something between a gasp and a coo. He knew that sound, he had heard her make it in the secret depths of the night so many times. It was a song that ignited his blood, and gods above, the taste of her skin was sublime. He wanted to hold her tighter, to make her whimper and sigh forever. She pulled him close in turn, so incredibly close, and for one blissful second, desire rushed to his groin before pain screamed from his side.

"Ah, fuck!" he cried as he stumbled back, grasping at his wound and returning blessedly back to his senses.

"I'm sorry!" Christine yelped. "Please don't faint!"

"I'm not going to faint!" Erik snapped, barely able to conjure the concentration to glare at Christine. Her face was full of concern, but all Erik could see was how debauched she looked;

175

reddened lips, flushed cheeks, and mussed hair. A vision of temptation. "I'm fine," Erik lied, still smarting.

"I'm sorry. I don't know what I'm doing," Christine muttered, looking bashful and affronted.

"Neither do I." Erik balled his hands into fists at his side. He knew what he *wanted* to do, more than anything, and that was to keep touching her, keep kissing her until he faded to dust. But he couldn't. He couldn't trust himself with that pleasure, especially not with the memory of the sin that had created him so fresh in his mind. "Let me attend to the bandages. You should rest."

He saw her disappointment out of the corner of his eye as he retreated, his idiocy stinging as much as the wound on his side. The pain was useful though, it kept his treacherous cock in check. It wasn't half as pleasant to change his own bandages as to have Christine tend to him, but that was the point. And if he pulled them too tight around him, that was good too.

He waited in his lonely room, whispers of the past both near and far echoing in his head. He remembered his mother, how the worst stretches of her madness had not been the violence or the cruelty, but the tenderness. Those times when her demons had made her blind, and she had thought Erik was someone else, the child she was supposed to have from the life she never got to live. For a few precious moments, his mother would smile and reach out to him, but the touch of his hand or the reminder of his mask would always ruin the illusion. And she'd hate him all the more when she realized. Would Christine run too, when she knew the whole truth of him? Was he lying to her now as surely as when he had pretended to be an angel, taking the mercy and trust he did not deserve from her like a thief?

"Are you just going to stand there staring at nothing?"

Erik spun to see the object of his brooding waiting in his door. She was a vision, as always; an angel on earth, clad in her creamy dressing gown and nothing else.

"I thought maybe you had gone to sleep," Erik said. "You must be tired after so many long days."

"I am. But I have trouble sleeping in the quiet," she replied, and to Erik's shock, stepped into his room. "Luckily I know someone who can help."

"What are you—" Panic seized him as she walked past him and climbed into his bed, where the sheets were still mussed from the last few days. "Christine, please, I—"

"Just let me hold you tonight, nothing else," she whispered, looking up at him shyly from where she had curled herself into the covers. "Please?"

"How can I say no?" As carefully as he could manage, he joined her in the bed. It was gradual, the way she arranged herself against him, gentle and cautious so as not to hurt or frighten. It still did hurt, of course. His skin still screamed at the new sensation of tenderness. But the panic and ache subsided quickly, replaced by awe and joy at the feeling of her in his arms, her head on his chest, against his heart.

"I was there too. When Papa passed. I watched him...leave. So I know how it feels. For the whole world to fall out from under you in a second. I knew it was coming. I'd known for years, but it still hurt more than anything before or since. He told me not to be afraid, that he was going home to Mama. The last thing he said was that the Angel of Music would protect me. I ran to the beach, after. And I looked for his soul and my angel in the waves he had loved to watch."

Erik closed his eyes on fresh tears; for Christine and her pain and the lies he had told her about her angel. And for himself, for the broken child still bent over his mother's body, knowing he was the reason she was gone.

"I'm sorry," Erik said, and it seemed so useless.

"But I kept breathing," Christine went on. "Do you remember when you told me that I was strong because I simply kept breathing and survived? I never thought until today how strong you must have had to be to keep breathing."

"You have to breathe to sing," Erik murmured and pulled her closer. He could feel her tears through his shirt.

"Will you sing me that song – the one from before?" she asked softly. "It makes me think of home."

He didn't know which home she meant, Sweden or Perros, or somewhere else. The only home that mattered to him was this, right now. "Me too," he replied and began to sing.

"*Siúil, siúil, siúil a rúin. Siúil go socar agus siúil go ciúin, Siúil go doras agus éalaigh liom. Is go dté tu, mo mhuirnín slán,*" he began, and she relaxed against him. "*Oh I wish I was on yonder hill, it's there I'd sit and cry my fill, until every tear would turn a mill,*" he crooned to her, for the first time placing the refrain in the tongue she'd know.

"*Come, oh come, come, my love with me; Come quick, and soft, through the door we shall flee. And safe forever may my darling be...*"

Many people came and went from Carlotta's flat on the *Rue du Faubourg Saint Honoré*, throughout the morning, but none were the sort that Shaya wanted to talk to. There had been many well-dressed men, perhaps patrons, who had come to the door only to be sent away, and a few other old men with leather bags who had been admitted only to leave frowning half an hour later. Doctors from all over Paris, Shaya assumed.

Most interestingly, Shaya had seen Richard storm in at around nine in the morning and storm back out ten minutes later, face like thunder. Shaya dearly wanted to know what had been said and the condition of the diva in the flat. That sort of information took time to acquire, but he'd always been particularly good at getting the truth.

Nearly a decade ago, a fur trader had come to court with a wild story of a magician of the like no one had ever seen, both in skill and in ugliness. And Shaya had been the one assigned to investigate the claim, for surely such a treasure belonged in the glorious collection of the Shah himself. He did so enjoy surrounding himself with the unique. From poets and scientists to tigers in golden cages. Alas, the creature the fur trader had spoken of proved to be more like a deadly tiger than a poet.

Looking back, Shaya wished he had not been so good at his job. If he could, he would tell his younger self to forget the fur trader and the Shah's foolish whims. It was not the first time he had wished that. The first time, he had been looking down at the body of the one person in the world he was truly meant to protect, dead because of Erik the magician.

Shaya shook himself from his reverie as he saw movement across the street again. This time it was not the front door that had opened, but the servant's entrance at the side of the building. A miserable-looking maid rushed out, struggling to get on her bonnet and gloves. Shaya jumped at his chance, crossing the empty street and following the young woman.

"Excuse me, Mademoiselle, do you work for Signora Zambelli?" Shaya called. The woman turned to him, suspicious and wary. She looked exhausted, as if she'd been awake all night.

"Currently," the maid replied. "Why do you want to know?"

"I wish to know how she's doing after last night," Shaya replied. Honesty worked best with savvy people, and this girl seemed like that type.

"You with the papers?" The girl asked, squinting. "You don't look like a reporter."

"I am interested for my own reasons," Shaya replied. "But I will make it profitable for you, should you tell me all you can." He opened his hand to show the woman a few francs, likely more money than she made in a week, and her eyes widened.

"Give that here!" She snatched at the coins.

"Information first, if you please," Shaya said, clasping his hand, and the woman scoffed.

"Fine. But I better not see this in the papers, or the mistress will have me whipped before I'm turned out on the street." Shaya raised an eyebrow. From all he had heard of Carlotta, it was hard to have sympathy for the ordeal she'd experienced the night before. "But she'd have to write that and she ain't that patient."

"Write it down?"

"She's got no voice!" the maid crowed, as if it was the most delightful thing. "There has to have been half a dozen doctors in and out of here, and none of them can say where it's gone or why. The hag claims she was poisoned. She keeps writing that over and over anytime she wakes up from the stuff they're giving her. *Poison*. Doctors think it's hysteria. That's what I heard one say before she threw a lamp at him."

"Does she say anything else?" Shaya asked, the weight of having all his suspicions confirmed settling on his shoulders. "Or write, I guess."

"Only two things: she writes 'ghost' and a name, 'Christine.'"

"She thinks Christine Daaé is behind this?"

"Who knows what the bitch thinks! It doesn't matter now. She's done for." Shaya blanched in alarm and the maid laughed.

"Oh she ain't dying. But one of them doctors said she may never get her voice back, and that's as good as dying for a lady who lives on her voice, ain't it?"

"I would not disagree," Shaya muttered as he handed the girl the coins. "Thank you."

"Good luck with whatever it is you're doing," she said and walked away. Shaya turned in the opposite direction, following his well-trod path home. He needed some rest, in all truth, and it was long past time for morning prayers.

Some days he wondered if it mattered when he missed one or more of his five daily turns towards Mecca. Allah knew his prayers; they had been the same for seven years. He prayed for strength in his cause. For righteousness and steadfastness. And for justice. Always for justice. And some days justice had a very different name and he prayed for revenge.

It was Christine who woke alone this time. She knew it before she opened her eyes. Despite the blankets atop her, there was a warmth missing from the bed, and she missed it. At least Erik's music was there in his stead, the lilt of the piano wafting from the parlor in a familiar melody. She mused on it as she stretched, considering how Erik's skin was often so cold but at his core, he was as warm-blooded as any man. He must have left a while ago because she could feel no trace of that heat on the sheets beside her.

She wished she could. It was an idle desire, born of a relaxed mind at the edge of slumber. Maybe she had dreamed something of the kind too, nestled against him and feeling so safe and cherished. In the still of the morning in his bed, with an angel's music in her ears, and his kiss in her memory, Christine wished and dreamed many things. She wondered how it would feel to kiss him until his skin was warm under her touch, and how deeply he would kiss her and touch her in return. The place she wished he would touch flared with an ache between her thighs.

It had been so long since she had let herself remember the way her angel had touched her in the darkness. The thoughts had come many times, yes, but she had pushed them away. But now she let her mind explore, along with her hand, and the piano sang with the melody that she recognized now. The one her angel had sung to her in their most intimate and sinful moments.

She listened to her angel play their secret song, floating on waves of perfect melody, and groped at the throbbing spot through her nightdress. She wouldn't do more. She couldn't. Not in *his* bed. She couldn't bring herself to go past that barrier of linen and feel how wet his music and the memories made her. But it felt so good to touch herself. And yet it paled in comparison to what the angel had given her. To what Erik could give her still.

Christine's breath was quick and shallow now, as she rubbed hard, desperate for more, her legs a vice around her hand. She listened as Erik's melody grew in intensity, and she called on the memory she had resisted the most, of her first night in this bed and his mouth on her sex, his deft fingers within her, bringing her higher as that melody entranced her. She had kissed that mouth. She didn't fear it, nor the man it belonged to now. If she was brave, perhaps...

She bit her lip, the idea of letting Erik taste her again pushing her closer to climax as the music rose to a crescendo...then stopped. Christine gasped, denied release, trying to hold on to the momentum, but it was gone. She withdrew her hand, panting and about ready to crawl out of her skin with need. She could hear the faintest sound of Erik's quill on parchment. Of course he had to stop to write things down. She groaned in frustration. Then blanched as the unmistakable sound of the piano bench being pushed back thundered through the house.

Shit. *Shit.* He was going to come back in and find her in this state and Christine wanted to dig herself right into the catacombs to escape. He knew what that music meant and was going to walk in and know what she had been doing the instant he saw her with cheeks flushed and, Christ in heaven, she could feel her damn nipples hard against the fabric of her night dress and he could so easily see them. She was going to die of shame!

Acting on pure instinct, she sprang from the bed and rushed to the bath, shutting the door behind her just as Erik called her.

"Christine?" She turned on the water by way of reply. "Oh. I'll, uh, leave you to that." She shoved her face into the frigid stream and screamed at herself inside her head. She was a fool and trollop and an idiot and probably damned. She stood up, face dripping, and expected to see her reflection in the mirror. But there was none. Remembering where she was and why there was nothing reflective at all in this otherwise well-appointed bath that sobered her fully.

She closed her eyes and breathed deep. Erik wasn't the kind to judge her, but he was the kind to see her run away into *his* bath rather than look at him and think it was because of some offense of his. Christine sighed and finished seeing to her needs in the bath as quickly as she could and hoped she was composed enough to pass for normal when she came out. She did not find Erik in his room, but instead back at the piano, scrawling away at his latest composition. He looked comfortable and ruffled, his dark shirt unbuttoned at the collar and his vest open. Once again, he was wearing the mask.

He looked up at her when she cleared her throat.

"I'm sorry, I wanted to get myself decent," she half-lied when she saw the worry in his eyes.

"I understand. I'm sorry if I woke you. I was inspired," he said, and Christine smiled shyly.

"It's beautiful." Christine ventured closer, peering at the music and trying to discern Erik's tangled notations. "Unlike your handwriting."

"I think it's passable for someone with no formal instruction in the art," Erik grumbled. "And it's not like I've ever had to worry about anyone but me ever reading it."

"Do you ever sign your work?" Christine asked, growing so bold as to leaf through the sheaves of music piled on the piano.

"I'd need a longer name for that, and I've only ever gone by Erik, so, no." Christine leaned on the piano lid, trying to discern his thoughts. It was much harder to do with his mask on, and she found herself missing the expressiveness of his bare face, despite its horrors.

"You said your name came to you by accident, what did you mean?"

Erik immediately looked down at the keys in a manner she might have thought sheepish if he was anyone else. "It's not important."

"Well, now I must know."

"Must you?" Erik shot her a gentle glare and Christine gave him what she hoped was her most supplicant look. He heaved a powerful sigh and looked to the ceiling. "Fine. But you mustn't laugh."

"Why would I laugh?" Erik's second attempt at a glare was more successful and Christine schooled her face into seriousness. "I won't laugh. Or I'll try."

Erik looked dubious as he began. "It was Aneka, the servant who I told you about. We lived on the edge of the town in an old farmhouse, so we had a few animals she took care of. Chickens and goats, and a few cats to keep the mice at bay. I liked the cats best, especially a big ginger one. Aneka named them all. Names from her homeland after Vikings and Scandinavian saints. My mother didn't want to give me a name, but Aneka noticed that I'd look up when she called..."

Christine fought to keep from smiling as realization dawned. "When she called the..."

"The cat. I somehow decided I had the same name as...the cat." Erik looked back at her, challenging. Christine fought to keep her mouth a straight line as the infamous Phantom held her gaze. She kept her composure for only a heartbeat before exploding in laughter. "I shouldn't have told you," Erik said, but there was no venom behind it, in fact, she could see him smiling. She liked that.

"Why don't you play me something else and I'll try to forget?" To her surprise, Erik rose from the piano and moved towards his hoard of instruments and chose one Christine had never seen him play before, but she was curious to hear. It was a simple flute, a pennywhistle really.

"This was the first thing I learned to play," Erik mused. "Would you like to hear it?"

"Yes, please."

Raoul had missed the water. A decrepit pub near the banks of the Seine was not the same as the deck of a ship, but it reminded him enough of the freedom of the last few years that he didn't mind. It was the company more than anything that made him ache for that liberated time, as the sailors he had not seen for months caroused around him.

"So, my friend, are you tired of your silver spoon and gilded cage yet?" Vincenzo asked. He had been the one to tell Raoul the tale of Zambelli, not that it did much good. Now his tanned features were brightened by a wicked smile in the dim light.

"That's a bad mixed metaphor," Raoul grumbled.

Vincenzo laughed and took a swig of the cheap wine that always flowed when he was around. "So the answer is yes? Sounds like I win our bet."

"What bet?" Raoul grabbed the bottle and took his own swig. It tasted like jam mixed with vinegar.

"Don't you remember? Before you got off in Le Havre, I bet you that you'd be begging for a new commission within six months!" Vincenzo grinned as Raoul rolled his eyes. "Don't tell me you were too drunk to remember."

"You're the one who gets that drunk," Raoul said, knowing it was a lie. It didn't feel like it though. The person he was allowed to be at sea was a different man who did different things and had different worries and rules to follow. He missed being that man.

"You're only saying that so you don't have to pay me twenty francs."

"Now I know you're lying because you don't have twenty francs to bet."

"Not when I know I'm betting on a sure thing." Vincenzo snatched the bottle back. "And you coming back to us is a sure thing. Now that your heart's been broken, you can come to your senses and join us on the new expedition."

"Has it been announced?" Raoul asked, perking up. Vincenzo's teeth were bright white as he grinned.

"Didn't you hear? We're going to be the new heroes of the North Pole." Raoul had not heard that. "Don't you want to escape this silly city and see what the edge of the world looks like?"

"I'd like that. I'm tired of Paris," Raoul muttered.

"Paris doesn't deserve you," Vincenzo purred, and Raoul's cheeks heated. "So, was it the singer? I still can't believe you found her after you wouldn't shut up about her for the first month at sea."

"At this point, I wish I hadn't. She has another suitor and I don't know if I can trust her."

"Who's snagged her? I bet I know him," Vincenzo said. Indeed, the Italian cared more for opera than Raoul ever had. It must have been in his blood.

"The bass who sings the devil in *Faust*. Rameau." Raoul was not prepared for Vincenzo to burst out laughing.

"He's not her lover," Vincenzo replied when he caught his breath.

"How do you know?"

"Because, my dear boy, I've seen him at, shall we say, certain *places* where women are not welcome. Or needed. And he was having quite a good time." Vincenzo winked and Raoul hid his face, not just because of the scandalous implications, but because he was utterly confused.

"So his tastes don't run towards women? Have you and he—"

"Oh he's far too full of himself for me. You know I like them shy and seasick," Vincenzo grinned, and Raoul rose from the table so quickly he ran into it. Vincenzo laughed heartily again. "You're easily offended on land. More reason for you to get back to the sea."

"I need to go. I have things to think about," Raoul mumbled and rushed out of the pub.

Why would Christine lie about the other man? Raoul should have known it wasn't Rameau who was entangled with her. He had heard *that* man's voice in her dressing room and it had been unlike any voice he'd ever heard if he was to be honest. What on earth was this scoundrel hiding and what game had he forced on his friend?

They had spent the entire day in music. It was magic to Erik, the way it could make time run differently. How it could transport them to the green hills of Éire to Venice's canals and dark forests of the north. They had sung through *Rigoletto*, and for the first time since he had revealed himself as human, he had dared to sing with her. Perhaps her kiss had made him braver than ever before, but he was glad of the risk. It was magic as well to sing with another, to blend their breath in song nearly as intimately as in an embrace. It was the incredible desire to repeat that embrace that had made him end their lesson before he overstepped and did to her what the Duke had done to Gilda.

He wanted that too, of course, to embrace her again. Kissing her had felt so viscerally real and perfect. So had waking up next to her. But even that had been a torment when he had found himself hard and flustered by the pressure of her body against his. He'd retreated from his own bed and tried to wash away his desire with icy water. It had quelled the physical frustration, but not the lust. And so he'd played, the very song he had seduced her with as an angel, letting the music take his awful desire and make it into something beautiful. But he had stopped short when even that became too tempting.

A civilized day as teacher and student had proved an antidote. They had studied and laughed, and Christine had been insistent that he rest and heal. It had been wondrous, but now, huddled by the fire, gazing at her beauty in the golden light, he wanted nothing more than to kiss her again. He was on the couch alone, and she in her favorite chair by the fire, looking at the clock above the mantle, thoughtful and curious.

"How did you get from a little village here in France to Prague?" she asked, alerting Erik from his reverie. "And don't tell me it's a long story. Or a sad one."

"Are you sure?" Erik's stomach twisted at the darkness of the memories, the walls of the room seeming to grow closer around him. Sensing his apprehension, Christine rose from the chair and joined him on the couch. She was not so close as to trigger his instincts to run or recoil, just near enough to take his hand.

"I'm sure. I've been wanting to ask all day what happened...after." She squeezed his hand, pushing back the memory of his mother dead on the cold ground before it could overtake him. "I want to know."

"I don't remember much about the next few days after my mother died. The B aroness t ook o ver, e xiling h er h orrid son somewhere else. They b uried m y m other o n the g rounds, b y the chapel Carl helped build. And then my grandmother gave him a thousand francs to disappear forever with me. He dragged me to Le Havre. I do remember seeing the ocean for the first time. It was so big and wild and it made me feel so small."

"And it made the world a little less frightening, when you realized you were such a little thing compared to the sea and the earth and the sky," Christine murmured, eyes cloudy with memory.

"Exactly," Erik breathed. "We crossed the channel to Brighton, then traveled to London. Carl's English was terrible, so he made me translate half the time, and the people we met were more than suspicious of a Frenchman with a young boy in a mask. When we got to London, we took rooms. I wouldn't see him for days. He drank and gambled away the money in a few weeks, barely fed me. He intended us to go to Dublin and find someone from my mother's family to leave me with. But then..."

Erik swallowed. It had been a long time since that first brief stint in London. He had been young and foolish enough then to hope it was a new beginning.

"What happened?"

"H e was spending time among the seedier theaters and saw advertisements for a peculiar sort of show. One night, he came back to the room and fed me something that tasted wrong. I fell asleep and woke up in a cage in a rail car without my mask."

"A cage?" Christine echoed in horror. Erik nodded tensely, hanging onto her soft hand and letting it anchor him before the past washed him away.

"I was scared. I screamed. But I wasn't alone. There was a woman there with the blackest skin I'd ever seen. She told me not to be afraid, and that if I was good, no one would hurt me. I don't think she meant to lie. Her name was Rose, and she informed me that she, like myself now, was the property of Klaus Steiner, an impresario." Erik spat out the words. The decades had done nothing to dull his hate. "He had been on tour with Rose and a few others in London but we were on our way to his home now, to Vienna, where he kept his museum of living *oddities*. His human zoo of freaks."

"Vienna?"

"Steiner owned an establishment there. It was grand from the outside, but everything behind the curtains was rotten and terrible. There was a dozen of us in various forms of bondage to him. There was a man, Gus, with a third arm; this withered thing on his side that he could barely move. Phineas was covered in tattoos from head to toe. Ezra was covered in hair like a dog's or some other creature. He escaped after a year. I envied him.

"Rose he exhibited as a *Hottentot* Aphrodite, or a Congo queen. She was neither. She'd been born in America and bought as a child. She didn't know that owning people was illegal in Austria. None of us did and it didn't matter. Steiner kept us in check with more than laws. Chains and cages and the whips of his assistants." Erik's free hand strayed to his wrist and the scars from the manacles that had bound him. Christine's fingertips followed, and he looked away from the tears in her eyes.

"And there was Sebastian, another deformed boy, but he was different from me. He looked like a figure of clay the gods had twisted in the womb, human but distorted. He couldn't speak or understand orders, but he was kind and gentle. He'd only listen to his sister, Constance. She took care of him and did her own act throwing knives and axes. But Sebastian was difficult to make cooperate, so I was to be Steiner's new star. *Der Lebendige Tod.* The Living Death."

"How old were you?" Christine asked in horror.

"Eight, when I came to Vienna. Nearly nine. I know because it was winter, and it was freezing in the place he kept me. He thought he could break me quickly, with steel and pain and cold. But I'd seen worse. I refused to even speak. But that meant I couldn't sing to console myself. But then, he put me in..."

Christine grasped his hand and he held on tight.

"It was built as a carnival maze, but it didn't make any money, so Steiner repurposed all those mirrors into a new sort of prison for freaks like Sebastian and me. The worst thing he could make us do was look at our own terrible faces. He shut me in that little room with a lamp and walls of mirrors in his cellar. It was a torture chamber."

He stopped, shutting his eyes against the memory of his face multiplied a hundred times, screaming in those awful mirrors.

"Erik," Christine's voice cut through the dark, and he looked up. He was still there, still home and safe with her.

"Rose was the one to let me out, after I broke and said I'd do whatever Steiner wanted. I wasn't allowed out of the cellar though. I stayed there, wishing I could just die and be done with it. And then I heard it: a sound like something straight from heaven. It was slow and steady. Only violins, and another sound, melancholy and small but so beautiful. A clarinet. In a melody that rose above everything, like the voice of God once again coming from the dark. I had found myself below the concert hall next to our theater, and do you know who they were playing?"

Christine smiled through the tears on her face. "Mozart."

"The Clarinet Concerto in A, the adagio. It was perfect. Like no music I had ever heard before. And I knew then I could live. And I had to stay so I could be close to these sounds and discover how to be part of them, to make them even. I learned later that I was in Mozart's city. And so to learn and survive, I stayed there."

"It made you a composer."

"Vienna made me many things. I learned everything I could from anyone I could. Languages, music, magic, and ventriloquism from the Roma who would come in and out of the theater to fill in the show. I hated simply being exhibited for the patrons to scream at, so I became more. I'd do illusions and sing. Until they screamed at the end when they saw my face, I was just like the musicians next door.

"I'd sneak out to hear them and others all over the city once I was older. I'd be thrown in the torture chamber when I was caught, or beaten and whipped, but it didn't stop me. By the time I was thirteen, I was stealing paper to write my own music. Mozart had composed operas and symphonies by that age, I was already behind. I left some with the conductor next door. He sent it back to Steiner. That was the final straw. Steiner decided he'd had enough of my defiance and since the usual ways weren't working, he decided to try a new tactic: hurting someone I had come to care about."

"He knew he couldn't hurt Rose. She'd married a strongman Steiner had entrapped through a debt, Gregory his name was, and Steiner was afraid of him. So Steiner hurt Sebastian instead, over Constance's objections. I told him to stop, we all did. But he wouldn't. I can still hear his weeping, his begging without words. Then Constance attacked, with the knives he had bought her. After that it was a blur of screaming and fighting. Sebastian threw a lantern and a fire broke out. We all made it out alive. Except for the man who had held us captive."

He could still feel the heat of it, and the rush of freedom he'd felt when he watched that place crumble.

"Is that where these came from?" Christine touched his left shoulder, where beneath his shirt the skin was mottled with burns.

Erik shook his head. "Those were...more recent."

There was fresh concern in her face. Erik did not want to tell her she should feel fear instead. "But you were done. You could all leave."

"We were free of Steiner, yes, but not free of what we were. There aren't many normal jobs for people like us, so most everyone set off looking for another freak show that would pay better and abuse less. I didn't though. I went looking for my friends among the Roma and begged them to take me with them. And amazingly, they did. I traveled with a caravan from Vienna to Prague and many places after that."

"It feels useless to tell you that I'm sorry for all that's happened to you," Christine murmured. "But I am."

"It means more than you can know that you even say it," Erik replied. He looked up at the clock modeled on the one he had marveled at as a foolish teenager who thought he could find a place in the world. "It's past ten o'clock and you have rehearsal early tomorrow. You should get some rest," he said, forcing himself to rise, remaining as formal and gentlemanly as he could manage.

"Oh. Yes," Christine said, standing as well and retreating towards her door, shy and slow. "Thank you for today. For telling me and trusting me."

"It is I who should thank you, for what you have given me," Erik replied and dared to look at her. There was unmistakable anticipation in her eyes. And perhaps, if he was going mad, desire. It drew him like a magnet, his feet taking him to her before he could stop. His hands moved of their own volition too, alighting on Christine's waist as her breath hitched.

All day he had kept himself from this. All day he had tried not to remember kissing her, so as not to lose himself in the need to do it again. But it was impossible now not to want it, not to see her parted lips and remember their softness and heat. He wanted to claim that mouth and every bit of her that went with it.

"Erik," she breathed. The sound of his name – *his* name – spoken with such want behind it shattered the last of his resolve, and he kissed her at last.

It was better than before, and he wanted to catalogue and preserve each detail. He wanted to revel in how her hands snaked around his waist as she pulled him close; how her touch did not hurt or burn but made him feel like a missing part of him had found its way home. He wanted to transcribe the notes of her soft whimper as he pushed her against the wall and his palms swept up over her breasts. He wanted her forever and he wanted all of her.

She tilted her head back, allowing – nay, *encouraging* – him to kiss the delicate skin of her neck and taste her racing heartbeat.

"No king or emperor has ever received so fine a gift," Erik murmured against Christine's skin, drunk on her searing warmth.

She sighed again as his lips made their way down her neck and, almost unbidden, the song that had been in his mind and blood all day began to hum in his throat. It was *their* song, the one that had seduced her so many times before, when he had been an angel. He was not an angel now, as she responded to the secret melody, her body arching into his. His mouth came to the edge of her dress, and he wanted to sing to her while he tore the fabric off. But he was not that mad. Not yet.

He had been too long separated from her lips, and he pressed closer to her as he kissed her again. She opened her mouth to his, and he dared to dart his tongue past her lips, deepening the kiss. But of all inconveniences, his mask caught awkwardly against her cheek and pressed against her face. How he hated the damn thing.

"You can take it off," Christine whispered, drawing back and staring up at him through her lashes, her eyes dreamy and dark. "You should."

"I..." It was she who kissed him now, her fingers twined in his hair. Her heat awakened a desperate need, the same need that had driven him from the bed this morning. Blood rushed to his groin and he felt himself begin to harden, the organ pressing against Christine's body even as her fingers found the edge of his mask.

"No," he cried, springing away and turning his back to her so she would not see his obvious *distress*.

"What's wrong?" Christine panted. He looked at her over his shoulder and winced at how utterly sinful she looked: hair tangled, cheeks and lips flushed. He had done that and been eager and ready to do so much more.

"You should get some rest," he muttered, looking away and gritting his teeth as the hardness in his trousers begged to disagree.

"Erik..."

"Goodnight, Christine." He walked as quickly as he could to his own room, wincing at the sound of her door slamming shut. And still his lust remained, aching and hot and shameful as he leaned against the wall. It would be easy, he knew, to deal with it; to make himself come with his pathetic hand to the memory of her kiss. But that would be a violation; a desecration of her almost as terrible as what he had so narrowly avoided.

There was one place he could go to cure himself: the one room in his home he had never shown her and never would. But it was too great a risk. It was just as effective at quelling his lust to remember his reflection repeated around him a thousand times. The misery of Steiner's cellar and the tortures of the commune and the horrors of the Rosy Hours of Mazenderan were still with him. He had built them for himself because he deserved them. The memory alone served to douse the fire in his groin.

How could he keep doing this? How could he be so mad to think he could simply kiss a woman without becoming a monster who wanted nothing more than to snatch her maidenhood like a thief? Why did he think this time was different?

He had spent so long thinking his life could be more than what Steiner had told him it could be. And yet decades later, it was all the same. He lived in the cellar of a theater, a torture chamber of his own making keeping him in check. He acted as a caricature of death and longed for the touch of a kind hand to ease his suffering. But even that he did not deserve. Not anymore.

Shaya did not, as a habit, frequent taverns. He was banned by faith from spirits and he detested the smell. When he made an exception, it was for nights like this, when he knew the denizens of the Opera would be spending their coins close to work. There was always gossip and tonight was no different.

Every tongue was wagging with the story of Carlotta and how she had finally pushed the Phantom too far by slighting Christine Daaé. Daaé of course was a witch or a gypsy, or a gypsy witch, who had ensnared the ghost as her dark servant. Either that, or she was having an affair with any number of men in and out of the Opera. So far tonight Shaya had heard that she was the mistress of everyone from Gerard Gabriel or Claude Bosarge to Charles Gounod or the minister of fine arts. But the most likely candidates were the men she'd been seen with regularly – Raoul de Chagny and Robert Rameau.

"She left with Rameau last night," a woman was saying at the table behind Shaya. "The little slut."

"As if you wouldn't spread your legs for that devil," a man hooted back. The crowd erupted in laughter, but the mirth was cut short by a commotion near the door.

"Let me in and give me my wine!" A man was yelling at the entrance, while two more men held him back.

"You need to be at home, Joseph," a huge stagehand (Alonzo was his name, Shaya believed) rumbled. "You're not well."

"Fuck off, you fat clod!" the man – Joseph – spat. "I'm not sick! That thing tried to kill me *again* and I want a drink!"

This interested Shaya. Unobtrusively, he made his way towards the door where the proprietor of the establishment was making it clear that Joseph was not welcome. Shaya recognized the man now. Buquet was his surname, an odious man who oversaw the flies. The one Erik had thrown down to the stage months ago. And now his face was purple with bruises.

"It's alright, my friend. Let me buy you something at a kinder establishment," Shaya said, stepping through the crowd and leading Buquet away.

"Who the fuck are you?" Buquet slurred.

"A curious friend who'd like to know how you were injured," Shaya replied, leading Buquet down the street. "Was it the ghost?"

"What hurt me was no ghost. It was a *demon*," Buquet said. "Broke Franc's jaw and his arm. Nearly killed me too. He was a monster."

"Was this in the Opera?" Shaya asked in horror.

"No, Carlotta didn't want it there," Buquet answered with a cough as he leaned on a wall. Shaya's interest sharpened. "Wanted Christine away from him. Lot of good it did us."

"So the ghost came to help Daaé?"

"She's his mistress, that whore." Buquet spat on the ground then finally looked at Shaya. Really looked at him. "And you – you're his apprentice! Or minder!"

"No, I'm—" The blow connected before Shaya could protest.

"Trying to trap me again, are you?" Buquet howled as he punched again, connecting with Shaya's stomach and knocking the wind from him. "Heathen Turk! Go back to the devil with your master the ghost!"

Buquet swung again, but this time Shaya was ready. He spun away and drew his revolver, pointing it squarely at Buquet's forehead, and the man froze. "I am not his friend. I'm his enemy just like you, you fool. And if you had any sense, you'd know that you've happened on the best way to trap him. Threaten Daaé and he'll come running."

Shaya delivered the man a kick to the chest and retreated. He rubbed his jaw, fury and suspicion rising. Erik *was* willing to reveal himself to protect Daaé as much as he was willing to protect her. Whether Christine was a whore or a captive, it didn't matter—

He didn't finish the thought. The blow to the back of his head overtook him first. Then fear and pain. Then panic. *Where was his gun?*

9. Captive

Christine could not say, in all honesty, that she had not slept well. This was because she was not even entirely sure that she had slept. She'd tried, of course, once her confusion and anger had faded. She'd lain in her lovely bed and tried to listen to anything besides her conscience telling her what a foolish slattern she was. After hours of shame and questioning how Erik could kiss her *like that* then push her away, she'd finally dozed.

But in those half-conscious dreams, she'd found no rest. Instead, she'd been braver than her waking self and strode right back to Erik and demanded his voice and his arms. In her dreams, Christine had torn off the mask and kissed him again, trapping him in his bed so he couldn't run. And then the dream had changed, and she'd woken hot and gasping, and once again, fiercely unsatisfied.

In the cold watches of the night, she'd given in, touching her wet, aching sex, trying to recall her angel's songs and the heat of his tongue and the feel of his long fingers inside her and she'd been so close... But she couldn't come. No matter how she tried. She'd screamed into her pillow in defeat and prayed for dawn.

Now she found herself stumbling to her damn rehearsal, again furious at her teacher for refusing her the mercy of coffee, grateful to him for being gentleman enough to hold her hand on the dark path, and annoyed at how much touching him made her think of the heat of his kiss and the frustration that had followed.

"We're here." Christine looked up at Erik. It was hard to tell that one part of the dark passage was glass, with no light coming from her dressing room.

"I wonder if I should have gone out some other way and come in. People may notice if I keep appearing out of nowhere," Christine muttered. She hated and treasured how small the passage was and how close it made them stand. She has only to breathe too deeply and they'd be chest to chest. Would that make him run away again?

"Surely no one's paying that much attention," Erik said lightly.

"So you don't think I should spend a night at home?" Erik tilted his head. "I mean at Adèle's."

"Oh." He looked so crestfallen, and Christine wanted to kick herself *and* throttle him. "Do you want to?"

"No," she answered immediately. She didn't want to spend another night in torment either but she couldn't tell him *that*. "I was just wondering. I don't want to draw too much suspicion."

"Perhaps after rehearsal you can leave with Rameau again. Let him take you to supper. Be seen. And after you can return...to me."

"Do *you* want that?" Christine asked, the pit in her stomach ready to swallow her whole. Behind the mask, Erik's eyes narrowed.

"I want nothing more," Erik whispered.

Christine swallowed, ready to protest that he didn't *act* like that was the case, but the reproach faded as he looked, unmistakably, at her mouth. It made her want to scream, the unresolved need in her gut coiling even tighter. She was going to strangle him or combust on the spot if he kept looking at her and didn't do anything and she was going to die if he did and—

The kiss stopped every thought in Christine's head. The world whittled down to his lips on hers, banishing everything that wasn't *Erik*. She flinched as the damn mask dug into the flesh around her lips, but the discomfort was minor compared to the pleasure of his mouth claiming hers. She made a soft sound as he encircled her in his arms, enveloping her in shadow and making Christine feel as if she could dissolve entirely into him, like a counterpoint joining with a melody. All too soon he withdrew, taking the breath from her lungs as he parted his lips from hers. His eyes glowed as he looked down at her, his hand upon her cheek.

"Come back to me," he whispered, the command in his voice unmistakable.

Christine nodded automatically, her whole body singing with desire. It was a tune he knew, one he could whisper to her right now and she'd spread her legs for him in the cold and the dark. The obscene image overtook her mind as she turned, blushing, and staggered into her dressing room. When had he opened the mirror? Before she could ask, it was closed again, leaving her breathless and alone.

She didn't want to see her red cheeks and mad eyes, so there was no reason to stay near her mirror. She didn't even take off her cloak before she set off into the halls. Because she wanted to keep the garment that had belonged to him and held her when he couldn't. Or wouldn't. He had run from her *again*, and she didn't know if she was furious or grateful.

She was the first to rehearsal and she kept her eyes on her score as she waited for the other principals to arrive.

"So the new Marguerite becomes the new Gilda at last." It was Adèle of course. "Are you alright? You look as sour as a wet cat."

"It's been a confusing few days," Christine muttered. "And I'm sorry for not coming the other night and not talking to you enough about—"

"Don't worry, my dear, I respect a woman who knows what she wants and sticks to it," Adèle replied, and Christine wanted to burst out laughing. As if she truly knew what she wanted. "Or lets it stick it to her, as it were."

"For heaven's sake, Adèle." Christine buried her face in her hands. "I'm not being *stuck*."

"Of course not," Adèle laughed. "Just like Gilda isn't getting it from the duke before the story even starts. At least you know your noble's real name."

Christine stared at her friend for a beat before realizing who she meant and shook her head. "No. Oh no! Raoul isn't – I mean—"

"Pity. Nobles have the best equipment I've found. Good breeding in every sense of the word. If the boy's anything like Antoine, I'm sure he'd be quite the stallion between your thighs," Adèle sighed, looking wistfully to the heavens. "That pretty cock of his is the only reason I keep that charlatan around."

"Adèle!" Christine squawked.

"You wouldn't think it was impressive when he's at rest, but when he's hard—"

Christine blanched. "When he's..." Christine stopped herself as Adèle burst out laughing.

"My sweet girl, you really aren't getting stuck, are you?" Adèle patted Christine's shoulder. "I'll tell you more about it over supper. Which you *are* having with me, no excuses." The older woman turned away with a throaty chuckle.

Christine wanted to protest, but she had been ordered to go out to dinner, hadn't she? She also wanted to scream, but she wasn't sure about what. She wanted to roll herself into a ball and she wanted to sleep. And she wanted more than anything, though she tried to push away the desire, for Erik to kiss her again.

Erik came through the auditorium, hidden in the orchestra pit, to see where the chandelier had been descended for maintenance. It wasn't often that the workers lowered the great, gilded thing down from the ceiling to clean and inspect. It was quite a feat to relocate the 700-kilo mass, requiring the coordination of several stagehands attending the five counterweights that kept the chandelier hanging safely above the theater. Erik surveyed the empty seats and boxes, only to see that they were not entirely unoccupied.

To Erik's surprise, the man he was most interested in seeing was already in Erik's own box. Perhaps Armand Moncharmin wanted a meeting as well. Erik disappeared into the trap door in the orchestra and made his way to the ladder concealed in the hollow column leading to box five.

He remained hidden when he arrived at the box, observing the way that Moncharmin kept standing, sitting, and tidying the seats as he did. He bent to brush some dust off the edge of a railing.

"Madame Giry will keep the box in order, I assure you," Erik said and took immense pleasure in watching Moncharmin leap in terror. "I do not recall making an appointment, Monsieur."

"I wanted to reach out!" Moncharmin stammered. He spun slowly, looking around the box as if he could find the phantom that spoke. Erik did his best not to laugh. "I have a letter." He held up the paper in his hand.

"Are you going to read it to me or leave me in suspense?"

"It's ten thousand francs. I couldn't find more, just yet, but Monsieur Poligny has assured me you will take it as a gesture of good will."

"Leave it on the shelf," Erik ordered and Moncharmin complied all too quickly.

"Of course Mademoiselle Daaé will sing Gilda and Marguerite from now on. I wanted to see if there was anything else you suggested. To improve the Opera." Well, Erik liked that. Finally a manager had been taught his lesson.

"You should consider replacing the gas with electric lights, it's much safer. And wouldn't you like our Opera to be the talk of the continent?" Erik bit back a chuckle as Moncharmin fumbled in his jacket for a paper and pencil and began taking notes. "Though you will need to turn the chandelier off if you intend to mount Wagner within the year."

"*Wagner?*" Moncharmin scoffed. "We'd have a riot!"

"Not if you start off easy. *Lohengrin* perhaps. Paris has an appetite for something new, and their greatest theater should give it to them."

The man was sweating and pale now, so overcome it was almost pathetic. "And you think your Christine could sing Elsa?"

"By the end of the year, perhaps. She could share the role." Erik mused. It would be a challenge, but to bring new music to the people... Christine could do it. "It is simply a suggestion. Perhaps at the next gala she could try something new. Test the claque."

"I'll consider it," Moncharmin muttered. "We won't announce another gala until the masquerade. And only if *Rigoletto* goes over well."

"I look forward to the next triumph, Monsieur," Erik intoned. He watched Moncharmin nod and rush from the box. He waited a safe time to take his salary – or ill-gotten gains as the Daroga would call them – and stow the envelope in his inner pocket.

His instinct was to go directly to the rehearsal studio, but it had been a while since he had properly inspected the state of his kingdom. He looked in on the dancers, with their mothers hovering in the corners while the Opera's resident painter, Monsieur Degas, sketched them in charcoal. Erik wondered if the man would ever draw Christine and how easy it would be to steal the work. He was holding a small fortune in his pocket; perhaps he could buy it.

He checked in on the other painters of the Opera: the scenery artists, finishing their work on the *trompe-l'oeil* that would serve as the distant hills of Mantua in a few nights' time. Next, costumers shining coats of armor, then the stagehands arguing in the flies. It was apparently a disaster up there since their chief had gone missing again. How tragic.

At last Erik came to the rehearsal studios, just in time to hear the duke and Gilda in a duet. Fontana was in good form today, Erik noted from the hall as he waited for the incandescent beauty of his pupil's voice to find his ears. And Christine's entrance came...late. An error she had never made. Erik stood straighter in his hiding place. Her support was off as well, and though her pitch was good, there was hesitance in her voice.

The piano stopped as Gabriel rapped on his music stand. "Mademoiselle, let us try again, from your entrance. On four." Again, Erik waited, and again, Christine entered a half-beat off, no conviction in her voice.

Erik leaned back against the wall, flummoxed. She had seemed tired this morning, distracted perhaps. He had no doubt exhausted her in the last few days, between caring for him and burdening her with the horrors of his youth. He listened as his brilliant student's voice continued to rise and fall with inconsistent strength and intonation, occasionally empty and trepidatious like he had not heard from her in months. It was all the more shocking given how brilliantly she had sung yesterday. But that had been before he'd kissed her. Before he'd crossed the line he never should have dared go near. It was the most brazen thing he had ever done, but there had been such anticipation and want in her eyes. Had he misinterpreted again? Had he ruined everything?

"You could try to smile. Someone will think you're here against your will." Raoul looked up at his brother and made a face. He didn't care that they were in a fine café.

"I *am* here against my will," Raoul replied. "You know I'd rather be anywhere than near that place." He glared down the avenue at the hulking outline of the Palais Garnier. For a while he'd found it beautiful because it was the place where Christine was, but now he had decided to despise it. It was an ugly, gaudy building anyway.

"At least try the duck," Antoine teased, kicking Raoul under their table. "Or would you like some pigeon? I know you have a preference for songbirds, little brother."

"You are not my brother," Raoul snapped. "Not yet."

"He's as good as," Philippe scoffed. "Whether Sabine marries him or not, when two men die together, that makes their sons brothers."

"Our fathers died in a fire, not a war," Raoul snapped. He failed to see how Philippe saw their fathers' fate as something to bind them to Antoine and not a reason to hate the man. Indeed it had been at the Martiniac estate where the disaster had occurred. If not for Alfred de Martiniac's negligence, Georges de Chagny might still be alive. "And I'm not hungry."

"Well, I want dessert. And here it is, right on time," Antoine said with a wicked grin, nodding over Raoul's shoulder. He turned and his heart jumped as he met the stunned eyes of Christine Daaé, entering their café on the arm of Adèle Valerius. Raoul turned to Antoine in confusion. "A peace offering."

"Raoul, I'm sorry, I didn't expect—" Christine stammered as Raoul stumbled past several tables to get to her.

"I did," Adèle replied, pushing Christine towards Raoul. "Antoine let me know he'd be dining here with these handsome brothers, and I figured you might be interested."

"Adèle, I..." Christine looked torn, even more so when Raoul took her hand.

"I am so glad to see you outside of that place," Raoul said, overcome by Christine's beauty and modest blush. He pressed a bold kiss to her hand as he bowed deep, all his confusion and resentment dissolving.

"I have to go," Christine declared and fled from the café. Raoul did not think twice about following.

"Christine, wait!" Raoul called, chasing her into the busy street. He easily caught up to her, catching her by the shoulder, and forced her to turn to him. "Please stay! Have supper with me again! I shouldn't have been such an ass the other night."

Christine kept looking around as if she expected to be watched, but the street was empty. "No, Raoul, I should be the one to apologize. Robert and I—"

"Aren't involved, I know," Raoul finished for her with a grin. "It's quite compassionate of you to lend cover to a man like that, though I don't think you should spend too much time with him."

"A man like that?"

"It is not worth discussing in polite company," Raoul said with a smile and a sigh, noting Christine's worried eyes. "It makes me worry for you all the more, that you are being forced into this deception by whoever else it is who pursues you."

Christine bit her lip and looked away. "No one is making me do anything."

"I will say it again, whoever it is who seeks to supplant me in your heart, I will face him and defeat him in any contest you put before us. Just let me know who my rival is." Raoul took her hand in reassurance. "My darling, I want nothing more than to protect you. You called this man an angel, but no angel would make you engage in so many deceptions."

"And you have only ever been honest with me," Christine muttered with a sad smile. She looked so forlorn, all Raoul wanted to do was take her in his arms and comfort her. And so he did. Christine immediately returned the embrace, sighing as she rested her head on his shoulder.

"I hate him, you know," Raoul confessed into her dark hair, breathing in her scent. "Not only for trying to take you from me, but for how he has hurt you and upset you. I would never do that."

"I know you wouldn't," Christine replied and it sounded like she was close to tears.

"Christine." Raoul caught her chin with his finger to make her look at him. "I don't know what sort of spell this charlatan has you under, but I'm determined to break it." Raoul's heart began to race as he recalled the fairy stories he and his playmate had shared as children. "In fact, I know how to break it."

"I'm not under a—" Christine protested before he kissed her. It was so different, to kiss her as a man who knew all his desires, compared to the foolish boy he had been when she had given him her lips before. It was familiar and thrilling, yet wonderful, the way she stiffened then relaxed in his arms. He should have done this ages ago.

With a gasp, Christine pulled back, batting Raoul's arms away. "I can't! I'm sorry!" Christine cried, sprinting away into the night.

"Christine—" He rushed after her, but she was too fast, disappearing into the dark, her black cloak like a shadow. Raoul wanted to throw himself into the Seine in shame and scream in confusion.

"I'm sorry, sweet boy," Raoul turned to see Adèle Valerius looking after her friend with equal disappointment, standing in the café door. "We all tried. I do think you suit her better than whoever it is she's gotten herself mixed up with."

"Do you know who it is?" Raoul demanded desolately. He could still feel the echo of that stolen kiss, and it made his guts twist to think of any other man touching her in the same way. "Has she mentioned anything to you?"

"I've never asked about this good genius of hers," Adèle replied with a sigh. "There's never been any point. We might as well be asking after a ghost."

Raoul did not like the sound of that.

The horses whinnied as Christine rushed through the stables towards Erik's secret door. Her hands shook as she triggered the lock, the feel of Raoul's kiss still burning on her lips, like the sting of a blow. The door finally worked, and she thanked heaven that there was a lantern waiting on the rusted hook rather than a ghost in the shadows.

Raoul had kissed her. He'd held her and been honest and open and good and kind he had kissed her. And for a brief, hysterical moment Christine had wanted it. Then her mind had turned to Erik and how different his lips were from Raoul's and her guilt had driven her from the arms of the boy she had wanted to marry, so long ago. Her guilt was not solely for the kiss, but for the thought that Raoul would never seduce her or confuse her. He was so simple.

Christine paused in the dark corridor. She'd never found her way into the cellars alone, but honestly, she was ready to stay here for the foreseeable future. It was all easier that way. She wasn't ready to see Erik. Not after Raoul's kiss. Or Erik's kiss and command in the morning. Or the night before.

"Just keep going down, it can't be that hard," she told herself, forcing her feet to move. Almost immediately she came to a junction she did not recognize. Which way did Erik usually go?

Left? Yes, she was almost sure it was left. Her surety evaporated as she continued, her footsteps echoing ominously in the dark. Everything and nothing looked familiar since each cold wall and piece of stone looked exactly alike in the meager light of the lantern.

"Where are you?" she asked the shadows, telling herself she was shivering from the cold and not trembling in fear. Erik hadn't even told her where to go, he'd simply *commanded* her to return, and she'd done it like an idiot! And goddamnit it was *his fault*, even if she was running away from Raoul as much as running to Erik and she was so fed up with these men spinning her head about she wanted to scream!

Christine stopped still in her tracks, listening to the darkness. Was that an echo? No, it came again: footsteps from ahead of her in the black. Erik never made any noise.

She turned and ran, trying to hide the light of her lantern from whoever had dared to enter Erik's realm. The very fact that someone was there – alone, at night – was enough to tell her they were dangerous. What if it was the rat catcher? If she encountered him, that was yet another reason to wring Erik's neck when she found him.

"*Where are you, damnit?*" Christine hissed as she reached the bottom of another flight of stairs, but the only answer was the echo of her labored breath. She waited, every muscle tense as she listened for another sound. The silence stretched out around her. Maybe she was safe. She lifted the lantern slowly.

"No."

Christine tried to scream as a gloved hand covered her mouth. An arm locked around her, pulling her back and forcing her to drop the lantern, which sputtered into darkness. She struggled against her captor, completely blind and terrified.

"Hush! They're still coming."

Christine froze, recognizing the urgent whisper and the strong arms around her. Slowly, Erik moved his hand from her mouth as the sound of steps came again from the distance. Christine could make out a distant flicker of light coming down the stairs. Before she could panic, Erik pulled her gradually away from the light, holding onto her so tightly he was nearly lifting her from the ground. She realized quickly why he was doing it – it made her steps almost as quiet as his.

A jolt, then they stopped. They must have come to a wall. Erik held her tight, and she remembered him pressed against her last night, something stirring between them, and the sound of a secret song in his throat. It made her legs unsteady, but the sound of another step in the dark filled her with new fear.

"Don't let go of me," Erik ordered in her ear. Christine nodded. "Now."

They were off like a shot, careening through the pitch darkness, following the path Erik knew by heart. Her guide caught Christine roughly as they came to an abrupt stop, pulling her back as she splashed into freezing water. At least they had found the lake. Christine had no time to swear or complain, as Erik rushed her along the edge. He opened the hidden door with lightning speed and did not let her go until they were safely locked behind it. Christine staggered into the parlor and held on to the piano, panting.

"Who was that?" she asked as she caught her breath.

"I couldn't make him out," Erik answered, lingering by the door and listening. "But he was certainly looking for something."

"It wasn't your Persian friend?"

"He's not stupid enough to wander about alone down here," Erik said and turned to catch the glare Christine leveled at him. "Without an invitation," he amended sheepishly, hiding his eyes.

It did not make Christine any less furious. "I'm sorry, I didn't mean—"

"I need to change. I'm all wet," Christine snapped and stalked to her room, anger rising along with her shame at the memory of Raoul's impertinent kiss. Anger was easier. She kept it up as she stripped off her sodden dress. She was angry at both men for confusing her with their kisses, but only one was there and he had been willing to hold her close to keep her from harm but not to satisfy needs in her he had fostered.

Christine violently tied the red velvet robe around her waist, waiting for the sound of music to come from the parlor. Certainly, that's what Erik would use to entice her out or calm her down. It was his favorite spell, just like Raoul said. It always had been. Erik had used their secret song last night so briefly and, in an blink, she had been willing to let him do *anything*. Now, in the silence, she realized how terrible that was.

She strode from her room before he could start playing and found him staring into the fire instead. He had discarded his jacket, something no gentleman would ever do in the company of a proper lady. And yet he still wore the mask, the one thing Christine wished he would discard. It was so much easier to resist him and pity him when she could see that awful face.

"I'm sorry I wasn't there to escort you," Erik said warily when he looked up. "Why did you come back early?"

"I wasn't hungry," she lied. There was no reason to tell Erik she had seen his rival again or what Raoul had done. None at all. Erik looked over her. What she could see of his expression was serious and concerned.

"We need to talk," he intoned like she was an errant child who had wandered too far from home. "I listened to a good deal of rehearsal."

Her stomach fell. She had forgotten *that* humiliation in all the chaos. "Oh."

"What was wrong? I've never heard you sing so inconsistently. You were distracted and unsure. Why?"

Christine had to laugh. "You have the gall to ask that?" Erik stared in reply. Did he honestly not know? "You kiss me like you did this morning and want to know why I was *distracted*?"

"So it was me," Erik sighed, infuriatingly obtuse and pathetic.

"Of course it was you! I've barely been able to think straight since last night." Christine's cheeks heated with the remembrance and it only stoked her anger, as did the way Erik slouched in guilt.

"I should not have been so forward, I—"

"I'm not mad at you for kissing me!" Christine exploded and she didn't care that Erik winced at the volume of her tone. "I'm mad at you for – for using this power you have over me then casting me away a second later!"

"What?" Erik looked so confused Christine wanted to shake him.

"You undo me, Erik. Don't you know that?" she demanded. "One moment I know my own mind and what I want, the next I can't even think. And it makes me furious because nothing has changed! I'm still that foolish girl who begged for an angel to touch her. When you sing, when you kiss me or you command me, I am *powerless*. And I hate it." She was breathing like she had run a mile.

"Christine," Erik began, a storm in his eyes. "I would never force you, I swear."

"But you could! You have but to sing the right melody and..." The memory filled her with such desperate rage and need at the same time she wanted to crawl out of her skin with it. "You had me bound and bare under your hands. Twice. I begged for it. You could so easily have me like that again, and you mean to say you won't?"

"Why do you think I stopped last night?" he asked urgently, coming closer to her, as close as possible without touching. "I stopped so I wouldn't force you. I still can't imagine how you could want—" he gestured at his body and then his face. "This. Now that you've seen."

"Didn't you hear me?" Christine snarled, and Erik leveled her with a look that was equal parts challenge and supplication. "I want to decide what I want."

"Then tell me what you wish and it's yours," he said softly, beseeching and contrite. "You hold the power, Christine."

"Truly?" she demanded in turn, forcing her voice not to shake. "Prove it."

Erik did not look away from her. Rather, he held her gaze as, slowly, he knelt before her Christine gasped but he did not stop at kneeling. He bent his head low and took up the hem of her robe. His eyes still locked with hers, he kissed the fabric.

"I am your slave, a dog at your feet," he murmured and bestowed another humble kiss on her hem. "You can do what you will with me. If you will have me, let me show you how I am yours," he whispered, echoing the prayer she had made to a false angel in the dark.

Christine took a shuddering breath, sure she was a second from fainting. It was only the lingering vestiges of her rage that kept her standing, even as lust tightened around her lungs.

"Stand up," she ordered, voice shaking. Erik immediately complied, gold eyes still locked with hers.

Christine had never felt more powerful, yet less in control of herself. She wanted to fall right there and give herself entirely to the man who had been her angel, as she had before, when she had bared every inch of her body to her mirror and let a shadow touch her, tie her hands and make her come. She wanted to strangle him and scream that his pretended obedience meant nothing when she still *wanted* that again. Instead she kissed him with all the force she could summon.

Every time they had kissed before had been gentle, full of longing and wonder. This was different. That had been candlelight, this was a bonfire. She yanked Erik to her by his vest, savoring the tentative way his arms encircled her in contrast to the vigor of his mouth on hers. It made the need between her legs scream to life with such ferocity she nearly collapsed.

Christine pushed him towards the couch. She was untamed, hungry, wild. Erik's calves met the edge and he stumbled backward so the couch caught him. Christine followed him and straddled his lap, trapping him between her legs even as she continued to kiss him, and he moaned against her lips. The sound went straight to her core, and suddenly kissing him wasn't enough. Her fingers were clumsy as she fumbled at his buttons, but soon enough she'd divested him of his waistcoat and shirt. To her delight his scarred skin was warm under her hands.

Erik's hands were far more skilled undoing her sash, pushing away her robe, and trailing up to her breasts. He grazed her tight nipples through the fabric of her nightdress and again her desire flared. She still wanted more. She needed friction. So Christine sought it, pressing her hips against the prone body of the man beneath her so that pleasure flew through her. But Erik's hands swept to her waist, holding her back.

"No," she ordered, grabbing his wrists and freeing herself from his restraining touch.

"Christine, please," he gasped as she moved against him again. And then she felt it. The night before she had thought it was in her head when something had moved against her when they pressed close. But there was no mistaking it now. It was his cock she could feel growing hard in his trousers.

"Is this why you ran away?" she asked breathlessly, kissing Erik's neck and grinding herself against his rising desire. "Were you like this?"

"Yes," he hissed as she released his wrists and peered into his wide, awestruck eyes.

"Were you hard when you had me before?" She was suddenly drunk on the revelation of what *she* could do to *him*.

"Yes," he gritted out as she continued to move against him, balling his hands into the fabric of her chemise.

"And what did you do? What do you do when you're like this?" Erik gripped her hips again, slowing her once more, as he bit his lip. "*Tell me*," she growled, grabbing his hands and thrusting hard against his groin.

"I touch. I—"

"Make yourself come," she finished for him, a thousand revelations sparking in her mind. "Have you done that – touched yourself – while I've been here?"

He hid his head against her shoulder in shame, the mask cold against her skin. Christine gave another hard roll of her hips and he gasped then nodded frantically. "Just once. I-I was weak."

"I have too," Christine sighed, licking at the shell of his ear as she did. "But I couldn't. I couldn't finish. Thanks to how you've *ruined* me." She did not wait for him to protest as she slipped her hand between them, exploring over his bandaged abdomen and then lower to the straining front of his trousers. Carefully, she began to unfasten his belt.

"Christine, you can't," he protested as she fumbled with his buckle, reaching to stop her. She batted his hand away with a glare.

"Was this what you used? The first night you brought me here?" Christine asked as the belt finally snaked free. Again Erik nodded. "How did it feel? Touching me while I was helpless?"

"Intoxicating," he groaned as his hands slid up her arms again, trying to pull her into another hungry kiss, but she stopped him.

A wild, reckless idea took hold of her, and she looked deep into his eyes, where the golden light was dimmed by his wide pupils. She held Erik's gaze and he did not resist as she pushed his arms until they were behind him. But he did gasp when she began to wrap the belt around his angular wrists.

"Trust me," she whispered and drew back, triumphant and delirious. He was fully restrained, her powerful teacher. Christine's hands swept up his arms. He was lithe and strong, nothing but taught muscle, and she knew he could easily escape these bonds if he wished. But he didn't. Right now he was hers.

She looked down at him as he blinked at her from behind his mask. How she had come to hate the thing. His eyes grew wide and worried as she gripped the edge. "Trust me," she commanded him again as she carefully prized off Erik's last defense.

"Christine..." he breathed, closing his eyes as she kissed the scar along his cheek.

"Bound and bare beneath me," she sighed. It was intoxicating indeed.

She let it overtake her, the moment and the desire and the power of it all. Without resistance now, her hands moved over his chest and downward as her lips met his. And then she found it, the hard length of Erik's lust that she ineptly freed from his trousers at last. He gasped when she touched him and then it dissolved into a moan.

Christine wondered if Erik could feel the heat of her blush when she pressed her cheek against his, or if he only felt her fingers as they cautiously explored his cock. It was so different from the rest of him – velvet soft, yet hard and hot. She caressed the organ, gentle and curious, wondering what it would do to him. He whimpered, his head falling back.

"How do you do it?" she asked, finding that she was breathing hard and her head was spinning. "How do I touch you?"

"Around," he managed to reply, with great effort. "Put your hand...around."

She followed his instruction, wrapping her hand around him as well as she could at this angle. She knew what she liked when she brought herself pleasure, the friction and pressure. Was it the same for a man? Slowly she moved her hand up the length of his cock, slowing at the ridges of the crown and the tip where a bead of moisture had escaped. That provoked another gasp of pleasure from her prisoner. Then down again, as he shuddered beneath her. She moved her hand over him again and again, slow and tight.

"Fucking hell," Erik whispered, his hips bucking under her, and Christine smiled at his frustration. "Are you trying to kill me?"

"Not yet," she replied, amazed at how brazen she had become with him captive between her thighs. She pitied his frustration though. Her own arousal throbbed, spurred by each moan and movement of the man beneath her at her mercy.

"Faster...please..." Erik begged and she kissed him as she complied. Her hands spread the wetness from the head as she pumped his cock between them. "Fuck. Oh God," Erik muttered, his breath rapid and his entire body tense.

Christine added her hips to her ministrations, and Erik strained against his bindings. He was ready. She could feel it. "Now," she commanded.

"Christine!" he cried and convulsed as she caught his mouth in a desperate kiss. He shook under her, cock twitching in her hand as something hot spilled from him and onto the rumpled folds of her chemise.

She pulled back, observing how his eyes were unfocused as he looked before sagging against her, breathless and spent. She'd made him come. It had been her will and her choice and she savored it. He nuzzled against her, kissing blindly at her décolletage.

"You can touch me now," Christine sighed, his mouth igniting her skin. Without even a second of hesitation, Erik snapped his bonds. His hands were everywhere immediately: in her hair, on her arms, then pushing her chemise up and over her head so that at last her breasts were bare to his attentions. It was Christine's turn to cry out as his mouth found her nipple and he licked and sucked at the sensitive nub.

She was right back under his power again, she knew it, pliant and desperate in his arms as his hands kneaded her ass and gripped at her thighs. Now it was Erik who reached his hand between them to find her wet, eager sex.

The sound she made at the first touch of his skilled fingers was something like a scream, but deeper and needier. She moved against his hand as he explored, frantic want overcoming her. He was careful, methodical, teasing her with gentleness until at last he breached her and she keened again, grasping his face between her hands.

"Stop!" Christine cried, and instantly, Erik was still, his every muscle tight as a bowstring. He caught his breath, pulling away to stare up at her.

"Did I hurt you?" he gasped, his hand retreating carefully from her cunt. Christine saw that same supplication in his eyes as when he had knelt before her. And now she truly believed it.

"I wanted to know...if you really would stop," Christine whispered back, chest heaving as she used the last ounce of her strength and control to speak the words.

"Are you satisfied then?" Erik asked, jaw rigid and voice choked.

Christine shook her head, ready to break apart at the slightest touch. "That first night here, you made me come with your mouth," she sighed into his ear, voice and body trembling, and he tensed against her. "Do it again."

Erik seized her with a speed that left her reeling, lifting her bodily from the couch as she locked her legs around him. He kissed her like a man possessed as he bolted with her to her bedroom and deposited her on the mattress. She spread her legs, eager and aching as he kissed his way over her breasts and belly and then finally, *finally* his glorious mouth found home.

The moans Christine let out as Erik licked and sucked at her came from some deep cavern of animal desire, as did the way she found herself moving her hips. He held her loosely as she thrust towards his mouth, chasing the waves of pure pleasure his attentions elicited. She was his instrument and he was drawing music from her like never before.

"Yes, dear God, yes, there," she heard herself babbling between cries. "More. Please. More." He obeyed and she gripped the sheet in complete bliss as his long, perfect fingers filled her, matching the rhythm of his tongue and lips.

She felt the climax approaching, building deep within her from the place he touched. She felt it shaking her, overcoming her, subsuming her in pleasure and ecstasy like thunder. For days she had been a clenched fist, a coiled spring, a cocked gun. And at last, as Erik hummed and lapped between her thighs, she let go. She let the orgasm take her and came with a long, guttural scream like she had never let out before. For a glorious moment, she was entirely free.

She floated, her mind clear and calm at last, simply a wave on a sea of contentment. Erik collapse beside her, his ragged breath slowing. It was so simple to roll herself to him, curl against his chest, and pull a blanket around them,

"I—" Erik began, but she raised a hand to silence him.

"Stay with me, just stay with me," she ordered. He relaxed again as she settled herself under his arm and listened to the slowing beat of his heart. "Sing to me. Sing me to sleep."

"As my lady commands," he murmured, and in the quiet dark beneath the Opera, her angel's voice rose and surrounded her.

Shaya felt the pain before he even opened his eyes, screaming from the back of his head and possibly other places as well. He was in a bed. At least, it felt like a bed, and he was dry and warm. The last time he had awoken he'd been cold. Where had he been?

"Don't even try to move," Darius's voice cut through the pain and Shaya winced at the sound. He dared to open his eyes, despite the warning, and the light was blinding.

"How did I..." Shaya mumbled, his mind still swimming. He remembered a street. A gun. And a man.

"The doctor said you'd be confused for a while, maybe even a few days," Darius replied as Shaya finally focused on the other man's concerned face above him. "So I won't fault you for asking that for the third time."

"What?" Shaya would have been alarmed to know he couldn't remember asking this all before, but his head hurt too much.

"Concussion, he said it was, and a bad one. Cost us ten francs for that information, and I could have told you that," Darius grumbled as he went in and out of focus. "What he couldn't tell me, nor could the police, was what you were doing knocked out in the street, nearly frozen to death."

"Who found me?" Shaya asked back.

"Alonzo. He's a stagehand. You were near the Opera." Darius sighed as Shaya struggled to sit up and came to his aid. "Was it him? The monster?"

"No, it was one of his enemies," Shaya replied, the encounter with Buquet finally coming back to him. "He thought I was Erik's agent or friend."

"And he nearly killed you for it," Darius snapped, ever the mother hen.

Shaya rubbed his forehead, as if it would make the throbbing fog in his brain dissipate. "At least that gives me some hope."

"What do you mean?"

"He wants revenge on Erik and I told him exactly how to get it. Maybe he'll be successful." Shaya laughed to himself at the idea. "Though I doubt it."

"Well you won't be seeing him or the fiend anytime soon; you're on bedrest for the week."

Shaya rose in consternation. "I don't need to be on—" A wave of dizziness took the words from his mouth. "Damnit," he hissed as he fell back in the bed.

"Rest, sir. Get some rest and know that others have taken up the cause."

"Ha." Shaya shut his eyes on the headache. "The fool doesn't even know the worst the monster is capable of."

He heard Darius's low sigh and dared to look at his old servant and friend. He was not prepared for the sorrow in Darius's brown eyes. "Sometimes I wonder if you were wrong to let him live. I know you believed it was the honorable thing to do but—"

"He saved my life," Shaya muttered, the memory more painful than his injury.

"And he cost your brother his," Darius shot back, and Shaya turned away from him as well he could.

"I've told you not to speak of him," Shaya whispered.

"You could have avenged him years ago. And yet here we are," Darius shot back.

"Erik's life is my vengeance, for him to live alone knowing what he has done. The grave is too great a mercy." Shaya said it like a prayer and shut his eyes tight. He did not want to remember all the mistakes and blood that had brought him here. He did not want to brood on how he was an exile now, thanks to the man he hunted.

"Then why does it matter if he's caught or not?" Darius demanded. They'd had this argument before, but like many things right now, Shaya could not recall how it ended.

"Because he deserves to rot in a prison cell, not rule an opera and corrupt sopranos," Shaya growled. "He deserves suffering."

The piano keys sang softly beneath Erik's hands, and he let himself savor the vibration of the ivory, the smooth action of the pedal, the reassuring thump of felt hammers against coiled wire. It was almost as perfect as the feel of Christine beneath his hands. He allowed the memory to mold the music, closing his eyes and letting the melody rise and sing of loneliness and consolation. It grew from the dark like the first bud of spring, waiting for the sun. But he couldn't find it.

He stopped playing and frowned at the notes scrawled before him on the staves before he crossed out a few with a grunt. It was still not quite right.

"You were getting closer." He looked up at the sound of Christine's voice from her door. She was wrapped in a blanket, her pale shoulder exposed her hair loose. She was, as always, the most beautiful sight Erik had ever seen, and he caught his breath as she walked towards him. "It's three o'clock in the morning you know," she chided as she sat next to him on the bench.

"I'm sorry. I woke up and I was hungry. Then I was inspired," he explained, buoyed by her tolerant smile.

"I guess we did go to bed early," Christine muttered and took up some of the cheese Erik had left on the piano lid. She nodded her chin towards the unfinished composition. "Play it again, without the arpeggios."

Erik obeyed, returning to the beginning of the piece – an etude or a rhapsody, he was not sure yet. Playing with her next to him was new, but not unwelcome, and the warmth of her beside him added something new, inspiring different chords beneath the melody. But as he came to where he had stopped, he was still unsure of how to go on. "It's missing something," he sighed.

"Because it's a duet," Christine said simply, her eyes not straying from the notes. "You need another instrument as a counterpoint. Here." She pointed at a measure. "And then let it have the melody while you repeat the first chord progression."

Erik turned to her, amazed and annoyed, and she met his eyes innocently as she took another bite. "That's brilliant."

"You would have come to it on your own I'm sure," Christine smiled, just a bit smug.

"In my defense I don't usually compose for multiple instruments," Erik said, and Christine tilted her head curiously. "I don't like that I'll never hear it played properly. I'd love to write trios, quartets, symphonies, oratorios. But I ask myself what use is there in that when I'll only ever hear it in my mind."

"Beethoven couldn't hear his music at the end."

"But he at least knew it would be played. I, on the other hand..." he sighed, then started as Christine leaned her head on his shoulder.

"I'm not the finest player, but I could play with you if you wrote us something for piano and violin. I used to accompany Papa. Or you could write me a song." Erik stared down at her perfect profile, overcome. Each day he thought it was impossible to love her more, and each night she disproved him. "I'd be honored to play the work of a true genius."

"You flatter me," Erik whispered.

"You of all people know what a sublime gift you have," Christine replied. "Here. Try it again." She nudged him and he began again, but this time, she joined him, her fingers tentative against the keys as she added her own variation and counterpoint, humming softly along with the notes. And it was perfection. It was the brilliant light of the sun, glowing upon the cold earth. And beneath that light, beauty, love, and life began to grow. It swept Erik away; not only the sound, but the joy and wonder of playing it with her. It was magic.

He stared at her when the cadence concluded, just as breathless and awed as he had been the night before as a prisoner in her arms. "You are a wonder, Christine Daaé. A miracle."

"Now who is the flatterer?" she muttered, but he saw the shy blush on her face. He wanted to make it deepen. "Aren't you going to write that down?"

"Later," he breathed as he raised a hand to feel the warmth in her cheek. She echoed the gesture, and only then did he realize he had forgotten to replace the mask. Christine had not even flinched when she looked at him. "I swear, it is you who are the true angel."

"If you're not planning on working, you should come back to bed," Christine said, eyes and voice languid.

"I'm not very tired," Erik replied and was surprised by the impishness in her smile.

"I did not say anything about sleep."

He did not need any more command than that to sweep Christine into his arms. The blanket fell to the floor as he seized her, lifting her as he stood. She kissed him as he carried her back to her bed and fell upon her. He took his time, savoring every centimeter of her alabaster skin under his rough hands. She did not seem to mind the texture. Indeed, there were places he touched her where the coarsest parts of his hands provoked the most pleasure. He wanted to give her more.

"What would you like me to do, my angel?" he whispered in her ear, leaning above her.

"Your fingers," she panted. "I want your fingers while you kiss me."

Again, he had no choice but to obey.

It was a wonder, the way she opened to him. She was slick and quivering, eager and tight as he massaged into her, kissing every part of her he could find.

"Erik, oh God," she moaned, and to his shock, her own hand found its way between them again to where his hard cock waited in his trousers. She was clumsy with it, but it didn't matter. She was touching him, her hand encircling him and sending him reeling with pleasure and want. It spurred him on, and he fucked into her with his fingers in a matching rhythm. "Erik! Fuck!" she cried, her body tight and tense.

He drew back and watched her climax, adoring the twitch and tightening of her cunt. And that was enough for him too. He came in hot spurts over her bare stomach, his vision blurring with ecstasy.

How could he dare be so blessed? He did not deserve her smile or her touch, let alone the privilege of her pleasure. And that she would return that precious gift... It was unthinkable. Yet here they were, spent and panting. Here she was, exposed beneath him with his seed staining her skin.

He kissed her again, drunk on the sight. He kissed her neck and her breasts and her belly as she sighed and groaned. He kissed her thighs and listened to her cry of shock melting into delight when he licked at the sensitive folds of her sex. He kissed and licked and suckled and fucked her with his tongue, provoking spasms and cries as her climax rose again and again. He kissed her in worship and wonder, determined to bring her to the brink and beyond. Anything and everything to keep her here, with him. His angel in the dark. Forever.

10. Cursed

Christine wondered if she would ever get accustomed to being a spectacle. That was always what she felt like at rehearsals nowadays; like everyone in the entire Opera was watching her and judging her. She had picked a strange career for someone who didn't particularly like being observed and stared at. She'd rather be back with Erik, bare and exposed to only him, rather than up here among the thundering crowd as they shuffled off stage, nervous for the premiere of *Rigoletto* tomorrow. She'd dreamed of being a real diva for so long, but now that she had achieved that impossible goal, all she could bring herself to want was to return to Erik in his windowless house, where he served her like a supplicant between her thighs.

"What are you daydreaming about?"

Christine blinked and Julianne gave her a suspicious glare. She remembered coming to her dressing room and Julianne reminding her not to walk off in Opera property, but if they had been talking, she didn't remember what about.

"Getting home and going to bed," Christine replied. It wasn't entirely a lie.

The last few days had been a dream and whirlwind all at once. She had floated through the technical rehearsal on a cloud, barely speaking to anyone in the long stretches of inactivity while the sets were put in place. It had been a long, grueling day, but she had not been so tired returning to the house on the lake that she couldn't accept her teacher's praise and generous rewards. She'd let him please her until she could barely murmur for him to stop, and then he had taken his own pleasure pressed against her in the dark, grinding against her until he spilled over her back.

The next day and the following had been the same, the harrowing noise and chaos of rehearsals giving way to the glorious music and magic below, where the Opera's darkest legend lived to serve her. He kept her mind occupied as much as her lust, it had to be noted. Erik would read to her or play. The only times that were more sublime than when his hands and mouth were upon her were when they sang or played together.

"Christine, did you hear me?" Julianne said. Christine turned back to her friend and shook her head. "I said, I didn't think you'd been at home lately," Julianne (apparently) repeated, her customary worry in her face.

"It doesn't matter," Christine muttered. If there was anyone she could tell about what had been happening within the walls of the strange house she'd begun to think of as home, it was Julianne. But to speak of it would make it all too real, and Christine was not ready for that. Christine straightened the jacket of her dress, wishing that she could feel Erik watching through the mirror and that she could just disappear through it rather than keeping up the charade of leaving the Opera like a normal performer.

"Are you alright? Truly?" Julianne asked, her face still concerned beside Christine in the reflection.

"I think so," Christine replied. She was grateful for the knock that sounded at her door, and even more relieved when Julianne let Robert in.

"You look as lovely as always, my dear," Robert said with a grin. "Are you ready for supper?"

"Yes, though I can't stay out too late. I'm quite tired," Christine replied, taking Robert's hand as he led her into the hall. Julianne shook her head dubiously as she left them.

"As am I. The final days before a new production opens are always a nightmare," Robert sighed. "It always feels like nothing will come together and then suddenly, like magic, it's an opera."

"It is magic, isn't it?" Christine remarked as she caught sight of the stage. It was still a hive of activity, with dozens of stagehands yelling as backdrops were lifted up into the flies. She could swear some of them were looking at her, like everyone else. They continued on, and Christine resolved to ignore it.

"It does tend to help when the newest diva is in excellent form," Robert remarked warmly as they continued through the gaslit halls. "I'm glad you overcame whatever it was bringing you down earlier this week."

Christine squirmed at the reminder. "No one said anything to me about it."

"Of course they didn't, they're too scared of you," Robert laughed.

Christine turned to him in alarm. "What?"

"After what happened to Carlotta, no one would even dare look at you the wrong way, for fear of being cursed too," Robert explained lightly, his stride not even faltering as they came to the stage door.

"I didn't have anything to do with that," Christine muttered, wondering if Robert knew it was a lie. The way he raised an eyebrow in response wasn't promising.

"Of course not. But even if that's the truth, this is a theater, the truth doesn't matter. Only what people think they know," Robert said as he held open the stage door for her. "You have power, whether you're a witch who's ensnared a ghost or a normal whore like the rest of us."

"I'm not—" Christine balked again then snapped her mouth closed. It would be another lie to deny both those things.

"I'm not judging, my darling," Robert countered, and Christine believed him. "We all take whatever advantage we can to get where we want to be."

"I like to think I earned my career," Christine grumbled as they circled to the front of the Opera. They were bound for the most popular café among the singers, *Entr'acte*, located within *Le Grand Hôtel*, across *Le Place de L'Opéra*. Christine liked how the dark wood of the rooms reminded her of Erik's home.

"We all like to think that," Robert went on. "But no one in the theater is here solely because we deserve it. The two of us are lucky, to have found lovers to uplift us who we also enjoy."

Christine swallowed. It was strange to think of Erik as a lover. It was such a small and inadequate word for what he was to her, and at the same time, the idea made her blush.

"I don't recall saying anything about...him," Christine began as Robert led her into the café and they took a place in a secluded booth in the back. There were other singers and musicians there already and they all pretended not to stare at the couple. Robert chuckled at her shyness, a wonderful low rumble as only a true basso could produce.

"Indeed you haven't," Robert sighed. "Though I must admit, I am terribly curious about whoever the Gualtier Malde is to your Gilda. Or if your Faust has deflowered his Marguerite."

Christine looked down at the dark wood of the table to hide her blush. Gilda was very much like Marguerite: a woman tricked into the bed of a man who wished to corrupt her. She didn't think Erik was like the duke, rather he was much more like Robert's own role, Rigoletto himself. A deformed man who hated the nobles he had to serve, who wanted to keep a woman locked safely away. But he failed.

"No one has deflowered me, Robert," Christine whispered, scratching at a notch in the table.

"Really? I wouldn't have guessed that by the way you sing." Christine looked up at Robert and he shrugged. "You sing with the passion of a woman who shall we say, knows the ways of the world. Or at least how nice it is to be fucked."

"I – we—" Christine's tongue was too big for her mouth all of a sudden, even more so when Robert chortled again. "He and I, we've done *things*. But we haven't—" God, where was one of Erik's trap doors to disappear into when you needed one? "Never mind."

"Well, if you've found yourself a man who'll please you and not demand more, that's a remarkable treasure indeed," Robert said. "Though I do hope you are returning some of the favors he gives you in kind."

Christine blanched as Robert smirked, just in time for a waiter to finally arrive to serve them. She was glad of the distraction. She had to admit in all of her time with Erik in the last few days, she had pondered more than once when he would take her fully. Perhaps he was waiting for permission of some kind, or for both of them to be ready. They were both virgins after all and neither of them knew what to expect from any of this.

"I hope you don't mind that I ordered for you," Robert was saying when Christine looked up. "You were lost in thought."

"Well, I have the devil whispering in my ear, you can't blame me," Christine shot back and Robert grinned.

"Always happy to be of service. Now, in case your other devil asks something for you, I do have some experience there," Robert went before he took a long sip of the wine that had appeared in front of them at some point. He pushed the other glass towards Christine. "It's not so different from singing, in all truth, it's all about relaxing your throat."

Christine took a gulp of the wine, horrified and amazed as she listened.

E rik was not entirely sure how they had made it to this place. Not solely in terms of how it was even possible that a woman like Christine would ever let him touch her, let alone kiss her and caress her. But physically he was not sure how they had come to be on the floor of the parlor, halfway under the piano, clothes strewn around them. It was certainly a better location than *on* the piano, where things had started.

He didn't mind being down here with her. It was more than pleasant to fall back on the rug, sated and breathless, and look to find Christine in the same state. She smiled at him and immediately he remembered the lack of his mask. He knew there was no reason to hide from her, after she had seen him so many times, but even so, he ducked from her gaze and hid his face against her bare breast. It was as natural as anything to kiss her, right above her heart.

"Was that not enough?" Christine asked, gentle humor in her voice as she twined her fingers into his hair.

"Are you tired?"

"I know I should be, but no." She hummed in encouragement as his mouth trailed along her chest and his tongue found her breast. She sighed, pulling him closer as he licked and sucked at her, savoring how her nipple grew taut and hard between his lips. Thankfully, what they had just done kept his cock from doing the same, for now.

"Good," Erik whispered as he drank her in.

"Do you ever miss them?" Erik looked up to find Christine's gaze was upon the parlor ceiling. "The real stars? Don't you wish you could see them?"

"I can see them any clear night," Erik replied, and to his surprise, Christine rose on her elbows to look at him.

"What? How?"

He had to laugh, which only made her deepen her glare. "The Opera has a roof. It's the best view in Paris in my humble opinion." He was not prepared for the smile that spread over her face.

"Show me."

"Now?" Erik glanced at the mess around them and their state of mild undress. "Right now?"

"Do you have a previous appointment?" Christine stood without waiting. "It was clear today. I want to see your stars, Erik."

"Unfortunately, you will need to wear slightly more," Erik admonished, taking an indulgent beat to observe Christine unadorned from behind.

Christine scowled at him over her shoulder. "It's not too cold. You won't need the mask," she countered as she grabbed her skirt from where it had been discarded.

As with so many things, Erik was helpless to deny her.

The ascent from the cellars was quick and quiet. The Opera was almost entirely empty this time of night, save for a brave (or stupid) fireman. Erik still tingled with nervousness to be above ground unmasked, recalling how it had only taken being seen by one idiot for accurate rumors of his appearance to spread. Luckily, he did not think he had to worry about Joseph Buquet tonight, or, if he was lucky, ever again.

Buquet's realm of the flies themselves was dark and quiet, barely lit by the ghost light on the stage far below. Erik kept Christine close, holding her hand as they ascended past the ropes and rafters, up narrow, shaking stairs, and finally, to the limit of the building. The door to the roof was inconspicuous, but when they stepped through, Christine gasped. Erik smiled as he followed her out into the chill February night.

Christine's eyes were on the sky as she moved along the edge sloping roof towards where the silhouette of Apollo thrust his golden lyre into the sky. They were on the highest level, behind and above the great dome of the auditorium. Erik stayed close, keeping Christine's hand in his as her eyes took in the blanket of stars above them.

"Mother of God," Christine whispered. "It's beautiful."

"It is," Erik agreed softly, not looking away from her perfect profile. "They used to be brighter, before they started adding more electric lights to the streets."

Christine's gaze lowered to the expanse of the city below them, blazing even brighter than the stars above with a million lamps and fires. "It goes on forever."

"I come up here, once in a while, to feel free. Like I can step into the sky." Erik sighed. "I worry though that someday soon I won't be able to see these stars, when the light of the city grows even brighter."

"That's awful," Christine muttered, looking wistfully at the sky.

"That is what they call progress." Erik listened to the sounds of the city below: the rumble of carriage wheels on cobblestones, the distant noise of voices fighting or rejoicing, and the quiet song of the wind.

"Can I tell you a secret?" Christine asked, and Erik nodded for her to go on. "I can see how lovely it is, up here, but it's blurry compared to your ceiling below. Papa always said I was nearsighted, and up here it's evident he was right."

"Have you ever had spectacles? You'd look quite charming in them."

"No. I've never bothered."

"Well, I don't necessarily need your vision to be better," Erik sighed and Christine laughed, the warm sound carrying through the night above the rumble of the city.

"How far can you see during the day?" Christine asked, turning to him, her face innocent and curious. Erik focused his eyes on the stars, unable to bear seeing her expression when he replied.

"I wouldn't know. I've never been up here then."

"Erik." He heard the pity and concern in her voice. "How long has it been since you saw the sun?"

"I see the sun all the time," he muttered.

"I don't mean through a window or clouds or from the shadows." He startled at the feel of her hands on his bare face, forcing him to look at her. "When was the last time you felt the sun on your face?"

Erik closed his eyes, taking in the cold of the wind and the warmth of her hands on the skin that was so often hidden by the mask. And he remembered the heat of a summer's day. And the searing fire of a summer night.

"Six and a half years," he whispered.

"When you came to the Opera?"

Erik nodded. "I came here at night, but that day...was the last time I saw sunlight." The scars of that disaster prickled on his skin. "Please don't ask about that day. Not now."

"Do you miss the sun?" Christine asked instead.

"I don't know," Erik replied, thinking back to brightness and open air. "I never belonged in the light, and I try not to think about it."

"Does that work? Not thinking about the living world."

Erik turned to her, noting how the gaslighting and stars illuminated her face, so like the first night he had spied upon her. "I told myself it did. Until I met you."

Christine smiled shyly and looked away. It was strange to see her be coy, after all they had shared. But perhaps words of love were different. He didn't ever dare to speak his heart, knowing his feelings could never be returned. They did not deserve to be.

"Can we stay here a while, before we go home?" It did make his heart surge, to hear her call his house home.

"Whatever you wish," he whispered. She tightened her grip on his hand and leaned her head against his shoulder, looking towards the heavens again.

"Papa used to sing to the stars, when he thought I was asleep," she murmured. "Old Swedish songs that he saved for himself, the ones he pretended not to know during the day. I think he was singing to my mother, somewhere up there. I hope she heard."

"In the old days, in churches, you couldn't speak prayers. They had to be sung for God to listen," Erik mused in return. "Perhaps it is the same with ghosts in the stars."

"And angels."

Vincenzo's tobacco was cheap and damp, Raoul noted as he stared out the window and took a long inhale from the cigarette his friend had rolled for him. Vincenzo himself remained in the rumpled bed, carefully crafting his own.

"Are you just going to stand there brooding?" Vincenzo asked before he licked the delicate paper. Raoul scowled and took another drag. He had given up the habit of smoking for the most part on his return to Paris, save for cigars with brandy in the evening at Philippe's insistence. Apparently tonight was for giving into all sorts of vices he had left at sea.

"I should get home. Philippe will think I've gone off to the Opera again," Raoul sighed.

"Oh yes, you wouldn't want him to think you were up to something so below your station," Vincenzo laughed. "I do keep meaning to ask if you've given up your songbird for good."

"I don't know," Raoul answered, honest for once. "She turns me about. One moment she's the good, kind girl I remember, and the next she's an elusive vixen whose words I cannot trust."

"Sounds like every woman."

Raoul glared at Vincenzo over his shoulder, still sprawled like the picture of indulgence in the bed. "What would you know," he grumbled. "I do think it would be better for my soul and my heart to be rid of her. But I just can't stop loving her. Not after how she kissed me."

"So only you get to corrupt her then?" Vincenzo laughed. "You have so many plans for a woman you hardly know."

Raoul bristled. Everyone liked to remind him of that, but none of them understood how long he had nursed his love for Christine Daaé and how much he was prepared to defend it. Especially after their last encounter.

"I want to save her from all of it," Raoul sighed. "The Opera and its backstabbing and scandals. Whoever this man is who has forced her into such lies and deceit."

"You want to save her soul *and* fuck her?" Vincenzo chuckled. "You'll have better luck finding the North Pole with us. Have you made your decision on that yet?"

Raoul shook his head, grinding the butt of the cigarette into the windowsill. "I still have hope that she'll be mine. And if she does want me, we could marry and start a new life."

"She has a career. So do you."

It was Raoul's turn to scoff at that. "I told you; she has morals. She surely wouldn't want to stay in the theater."

"Then propose to her, hear her rejection, and be done with it," Vincenzo said before taking a long inhale and blowing the smoke back into the musty room. "And move on. Don't you have seats for *Rigoletto* tomorrow?"

"How do you know about that?" Raoul demanded, advancing on his friend and snatching the remaining cigarette from him to finish.

"You know I love opera. Though it's a travesty to have Verdi – proper *Italian* opera, mind you – sung in French and filled with little dancers. But you Frenchmen insist on your ballets."

"Don't be a snob; you're too poor to afford a ticket," Raoul admonished and Vincenzo merely laughed again.

"So that's a yes, you are going." Raoul glared at the other man, which was hard to do when the object of his ire had not yet put his shirt back on. Neither had Raoul, but that wasn't the point.

"I have to see her. I'm worried for her," Raoul explained as he slumped onto the bed and snuffed out Vincenzo's cigarette on the nightstand. "I know in my soul that she's in some sort of danger. I can feel it."

"Then go and come tell me of your grand success after. And if the tenor is any good. I do like that part." Vincenzo smiled as he began to sing, and not badly at all. "*La donna è mobile, qual piuma al vento.*"

"What does that mean?"

"Women are as fickle as a feather on the wind," Vincenzo answered with a wicked grin. "You'll learn, my friend. You'll learn."

Christine's mind was a fog as Erik held her close in the dark behind the mirror, pressed against the cold wall as he kissed her.

"Christine?" Both of them jumped at Julianne's voice and accompanying knock from outside the dressing room. "Are you in there? I have to get you ready."

"I don't want to make you late," Erik whispered, leaning in so close his mask touched Christine's forehead. She hated that he had worn the thing, but he insisted on it since the premiere of *Rigoletto* was a 'formal occasion.'"

"I don't care," Christine confessed. "I'd rather be here."

"The managers would be quite disappointed not to have their newest star for their opening," Erik replied. "As would be the audience."

"I don't belong to them," she breathed back. His body was flush against hers, and yet not close enough, a devilish part of her said.

"You belong to no one." He said it warmly and then kissed her as if to prove it was a lie. Christine's mind returned to her supper with Robert and his reminders of all the things her strange love affair was lacking.

"Perhaps...tonight," she found herself murmuring against Erik's jaw, the mask cold against her flushed skin. "After the performance. I could be yours. Entirely. If you wish it."

She was not prepared for Erik to draw away in what she could only guess was shock. It was almost impossible to see his expression in the darkened passage, but his glowing eyes were wary and nervous as he looked down at her.

"Do you not...wish for that?" Christine stammered, her cheeks heating for an entirely new reason now.

"I did not think you would want such a thing so – so soon," Erik muttered back and she could tell he was evading. Perhaps if she could see his cheeks there would be a blush there too. "What we have done – or do – it's just as pleasurable. Even more so, in my experience."

It was Christine's turn to look through the shadow in confusion and surprise. "In your experience? What *experience* is that?" Erik's mouth hung open and Christine's consternation rose with every second of silence. "Are you not a virgin as well?"

"I—" he began, then stepped away from her, hiding from Christine's scowl. "I have lived a life."

"Yes, a life you won't tell me about past your youth," she shot back. It was unfair and she knew it, for she had herself been too frightened to ask.

"Christine, I—"

"How many?" The words left her lips before she could stop herself. Erik only stared in reply. "How many women have you had?"

"People. I've been with three people like that," Erik answered tersely.

"And?"

"And *what*?"

"And what happened to them? How did it end?"

"*Horribly*," Erik shot back with venom that set Christine back on her heels. "You need to get ready. I will find you later." Erik turned without a word, not even bothering to take the lantern or trigger the mirror before he disappeared into the pitch dark of the secret corridor.

It was up to Christine to let herself into her dressing room, and though the room was warmer than the passage behind the mirror, Christine felt cold. For the first time in days in days she was truly and fully awake, conscious enough to see the mess her lust and need to believe in this man had put her in. She had kissed and touched Erik, thinking it was some holy gift she could give him, something to offset the horrors of his life and he had been with others before her! Was that the real reason he had been so slow to touch her?

"What's happened?" Julianne's voice cut through Christine's worry as she strode into the room, costumes in hand. "Aren't you excited for a premiere?"

"Just get me dressed," Christine muttered.

She avoided her reflection in the great mirror while Julianne laced her into her intricate gown of silver and purple, laces all up the arms and flared bits at the shoulder. For her it was a beautiful frock, for Gilda it was no better than chains. She did not speak to Julianne much as she helped her with her make-up and the braids in her hair, and she warmed up automatically once her friend was gone, barely thinking about the exercises. Erik had already sung with her today. They had sung Mozart and she had almost swooned to hear his Don Giovanni ask for her Zerlina's hand.

"Five minutes!" a stagehand's voice called from beyond the door and Christine steadied herself. How was she to sing tonight with this tempest in her mind? She closed her eyes, hoping to keep back her tears, and a telltale prickle danced down her spine.

"You will be wonderful." The voice of her angel, as always, seemed to come from all around her, even though she knew he was simply a man behind a mirror. She let out a sigh of relief at the sound.

"I am sorry, if I have hurt or deceived you, I will try to make it right when I can. But now, tonight, do not think of my wrongs. Think of our music and live in that."

"I will," she replied like a prayer.

She floated in the memory of his voice to her place backstage. Much as with her role as Marguerite, Gilda was not needed for much of Act I. It was later, after the duke's hunchback jester was cursed and encountered the assassin Sparafucile, that it was revealed Rigoletto kept a daughter locked away from the terrible attentions of men.

Christine thought of Gilda as she waited backstage, hidden in a dark corner among the flats and curtains; of how trapped she had to feel. Christine pitied the poor girl as she became her. And then, finally, she was free as she began to sing.

She sang of the name of her beloved, *caro nome,* conscious of the terrible irony that the soaring notes of joy were inspired by a lie. It was not Guailtier Malde that had courted Gilda, it was the duke who would steal her and defile her. And yet, Gilda was ready to give her life to save the man who took her virtue. She was ready to die, but was it even her choice? Her father, Rigoletto the jester, was the one who had been cursed. Not her. She was just a victim of a man's folly and hate.

Still she sang on, letting her heart soar with the notes, not even hearing the applause when she was done. The patrons cheering and the thousands of people watching did not matter. She didn't sing for them. She sang for Erik as no one ever had. Her heart surged, because she knew that whoever he had touched before, they had not given him this. Only she would give him her soul in song.

E rik stayed for the entire ovation, watching from the shadows of box five on the grand tier. The crowd was rapturous for all the leads, Fontana's rakish count, and Rameau's cursed hunchback. But the volume of the applause doubled when Christine bowed. She had been more fantastic than he could ever have hoped, and the crowd stayed on their feet clapping for a full five minutes before the great red and gold curtain fell for good.

There was no chance tonight that he would be able to spirit Christine away before she had to parade herself through the *Salon du Danse* among the patrons and well-wishers. At least from there Erik could watch her, pretend he was the one on her arm, smiling in pride as the bourgeois and boring kowtowed before her.

It was to his hiding place behind one of the salon mirrors that Erik stole, not to Christine's dressing room. He did not need the temptation of her bare skin at the moment. He did not want to think about what sort of conversation awaited them when they were alone either. There was still so much she didn't know, so much he didn't want to tell her. He wanted to exist just a little while longer in the light of her compassion before she learned how little he deserved it.

One by one people filtered into the grand chamber, many of the ballet dancers still in their white skirts of toile, calves scandalously exposed to the leers of the patrons at their sides. Men and women from the chorus mingled as well: dour basses, vacant-eyed tenors, scheming sopranos, and altos who were too smart for all of this but usually passed beyond anyone's notice.

The directors came next, with Gerard Gabriel looking relieved, and Henri Mercier looking exhausted. As usual, Charles La Roche of the ballet thought himself too important to be there. Perhaps he did not like the reminders that his dancers of barely fifteen years of age were being handed off to interested patrons by chaperones acting as little more than pimps.

Claude Bosarge received a smattering of applause when he stepped in. It would have been more had the musicians of the orchestra been invited to soirées such as this, but lowly *instrumentalists* would be a stain on the glittering assemblage. Finally came the managers. Moncharmin was bubbly with excitement and Richard frowned like the marble bust of a dead Roman. The only life he conjured was to nod at the richest patrons.

Erik didn't look too closely at the patrons; or tried not to. But he could not help his interest when a particular pair of men entered. It was that boy, the so-called *Vicomte* who continued to dog Christine's steps along with his blustering brother. The brother went immediately to Sorelli, shooing away the *petits rats* that had congregated around the prima ballerina. But the boy looked around the room expectantly, eyes keen and curious. Did he hope to annoy Christine once again?

The boy and the rest of the crowd turned to the door when a murmur went up and Christine entered, on Robert Rameau's arm. It was like sunrise, as well as Erik could remember it. She was radiant in a gown of red taffeta, edged with lace and beads. Her white gloves reached up to her elbows, but the gown's small sleeves exposed her pale shoulders and Erik could only dream of what a pleasure it would be to kiss that vulnerable skin. To think, barely a week ago he had been afraid to even touch her...

The fantasy faded the instant he saw the boy race towards Christine, an expression of adoration on his face. What was he doing? Erik watched as Christine's expression fell when she saw him and he adopted his haughtiest attitude with Rameau. Was he asking her to talk alone?

Christine demurred, but the boy was insistent. Erik tried to read their lips, a skill he had never truly mastered, but he could tell when the boy said something callous and insulting to Rameau. Even so, Christine nodded for the bass to leave. And then she did not resist as the boy led her away from the crowd and, serendipitously, towards the corner where Erik was concealed.

"This isn't private," Christine protested, looking nervously around them at the crowd and then at the mirrored wall. Did she know her angel was there? Was that why she was so nervous?

"I don't care." The boy grasped Christine's gloved hands, pulling her closer as he implored her. "I've made it clear before, I don't care who knows my feelings for you or my intentions." Erik frowned in the dark. What on earth did that little scoundrel intend?

"Please, not here," Christine whined.

"Christine, I'm sorry for overstepping the other night," the boy went on, ignoring her and taking her hand.

"Raoul, please." Erik did not like the way Christine said the name, plaintive and overcome.

"You drive me to wildness; you must know that." There was real ardor in the words, and Erik considered if he might be able to break through the mirror that separated him from this rival and choke the life from the boy right there. "You let me court you, take you to dinner, and play the suitor..."

The world went out of focus. What was that boy talking about? Taking her to supper? How many times had Christine seen the little lout?

"I know I should not have kissed you. I'm sorry for being so forward."

"Raoul, dear God, not here!" Christine pled, but Erik could not make out her face through the sudden fog in his vision. "I do not wish to speak with you!"

"I don't believe that," the boy said, even as Erik blinked and moisture slipped under his mask. He was crying. "Just tell me who it is that has so bound you to him that you are afraid to even speak his name. Such a man cannot be trusted."

"You know nothing about him," Christine admonished in a pitched whisper, trying to draw her hands away but unable to escape.

"I know you do not act of your own will, or else we would be together," the sniveling fool continued. "I would see you unbound, my love. I would be the one to release you. I know what you felt for me once, what I know you could feel again—"

"I *am* free," Christine insisted and it did not slake Erik's rage. She wasn't free. She was his, wasn't she? "I am mistress of my own actions, Raoul; I am not subject to anyone, including you," Christine declared, finally wresting her hands from the boy's.

"Christine, I love you. Do you not care?" Again the boy took her hands, pulling her to him with an ardent look in his eyes. Dear God, he looked about ready to kiss her.

"No..." Erik breathed, and Christine sprang away from her insolent suitor and rushed away, leaving the boy staring at the walls in confusion. It would be wrong, to kill him right now. It would not endear him to Christine and would cause a scene, but oh how Erik's hands itched to be around that perfect, pretty neck right now. How easy it would be...

You are more than an executioner.

Erik gasped, the memory so clear it was like hearing a ghost, but not the wretched shades of the cellars. A familiar one who had believed him more than a killer, more than a monster. Just as Christine did.

But she did not know what he had done. She would run like the rest or die like the speaker of those words if he dared tell her or touch her too long. Still, he would be damned if he let any other man come near her.

Erik stalked away from his hiding place, mind afire and heart aching. He had to find where she had gone. He had to find out why she had lied and deceived. He had to know that she was still his.

C hristine could not go down to run away from Raoul and all the eyes of Paris watching her. She could not go to her dressing room, for Erik would find her there too easily. She couldn't go to the flat, because Adèle was there tonight and would demand to know why Christine was sleeping in her own bed for the first time in weeks. So she went up, following the path to the roof that Erik had shown her the night before. It was easy to just keep climbing, racing away from the disappointment in Raoul's eyes and Erik's horrified whisper with every step.

The flies were cold and dark, heavy with the scent of hemp and oil and dust. A hundred thousand yards of rope stretched around Christine as she ascended the narrow metal steps, ever higher. Her breath was ragged from her pace, but if she stopped, she would have nothing but her thoughts and her crimes against the men who loved her. The fools.

She tripped on the hem of her ridiculous gown and grabbed the flimsy railing for support, making the mistake of looking down to the empty stage so many stories below. She swore, her heart racing in terror, and finally halted.

What did she think she was doing? There was no running from the mess she had made and the hearts she was sure to break. She could feel the air stirring, the sense of eyes upon her that she had felt when Raoul had tried to speak to her. She waited, holding back her tears and trying to think of what to say.

She looked up at a sound from in the flies, alarmed that whatever distress she had caused had made Erik reckless enough to be heard. But she didn't see him approaching. She shivered again, anxiety and fear seeping further into her mind.

"Are you running away from me up here?" Christine spun to see Erik behind her on the narrow catwalk.

"I needed to think," she half-lied. She could see the pain in his eyes.

"You lied to me." His voice was weak as he said it. "You've been seeing that boy."

"I didn't lie, I just—"

"Forgot to tell me the truth. I have been reliably informed that's the same as lying, if not worse." Erik took a cautious step towards her, eyes alight. "How many times have you seen him? When?"

"A week ago, the night you were hurt. And once after that but – but that was Adèle, she ambushed me with him." Christine swallowed. "I've tried to tell him to give up."

"Not very effectively, he was about to propose!" Erik snapped back. "Do you think he would feel the same if he knew about you and me? Really knew?"

Christine's face and heart hardened. "And would you be the one to tell him? That would require a certain amount of forthrightness from you that is not your forte."

"This again? I have told you—"

"You've told me some things, but not everything. You won't tell me about how you came back to the Opera. You won't tell me about Persia."

"Because if you knew what happened, you would run to that terrible boy and never come back!" Erik replied desperately and Christine threw up her hands.

"Is that what happened to your other lovers? Did they go running when they found out some terrible secret from your past?"

"They died!" Erik cried, and the words echoed into the emptiness of the flies. "All of them. They died *because of me*. Do you not understand that I am cursed? That everyone I have loved or dared to touch has met a damnable end? Your pity cannot erase what I am."

Christine's breath slowed as she stared at the man she had been so willing to let into her bed, who had already confessed such horrors to her in the dark of his hidden world. Was he protecting her? Did she have a chance now to run before she was ruined? Before she fell too far? Maybe Raoul would take her back.

"Erik, I—"

A low laugh cut Christine off and her blood froze.

"So, the monster has a name." They both turned in horror at the words, looking down from their unsteady perch to see none other than Joseph Buquet leering from a catwalk below.

"Dear God," Christine whispered, her body seizing with terror.

"Don't you take the Lord's name in vain, you little whore," Buquet spat, pure hate in his eyes. "To think, you spread your legs for that *thing*. You know I thought he was a demon, face like that, but no, I was wrong. You're just a man!"

"Are you so sure of that?" Erik growled, bracing himself like a snake about to strike.

"Oh yes." Buquet grinned. "Who do you think will pay me more for your name? Carlotta, or the managers? Or the police?

What'll they do to your little whore when they find out about you, *Erik?*'

"You don't learn, do you?" Erik intoned, Before Christine could blink, he sprang from their catwalk into the open air, catching a rope as he flew towards Buquet. The master of the flies' face went slack in fear as the shadow of the Phantom alit beside him.

"Fucking hell," Buquet yelped and ran headlong down the quivering catwalk, but Erik was close behind, rope still in hand.

"Erik!" Christine cried, racing to the flimsy metal stairs to get down. She watched the chase from the corner of her eyes, her heart pounding in panic. She arrived at Erik and Buquet's level and rushed across the catwalk in time to see Erik seize his prey and loop the rope around Buquet's neck. "Oh God!"

Erik spun with the man in front of him and Christine stopped dead at the sight of the master of the flies staring at her in abject horror, as Erik choked him from behind. She froze as the realization overcame her; the utter certainty that Erik was ready, and worse, capable of killing Buquet right there. And it was not the first time he had taken a life.

"Erik, no. Please, just let him go," Christine whispered, trembling as she stepped closer, trying to calm the killer that she had let into her bed. For an endless moment, Erik held her gaze, his golden eyes glowing with deadly rage. And then, in a blink, it was gone. Replaced with horror that matched Christine's.

"You will tell no one," Erik commanded in Buquet's ear with unquestionable authority as he drew his makeshift noose tighter. "You will leave my opera and never return. If I ever find you near this place again, my face will be the last thing you ever see. Do you understand, Joseph?"

Buquet gave gurgling noises of assent, his purple face making some semblance of a nod. Erik looked to Christine once more, awaiting her command.

"I believe him," Christine said. With a final squeeze of the noose, Erik let Buquet go, throwing him to the catwalk where he collapsed, gasping for air with his arms braced around his chest.

"Get out of here, now," Erik ordered.

Buquet continued to pant, rising slowly from his knees and meeting Christine's eyes just as his hand slipped into his vest. He grinned and Christine gasped when she saw the pistol. The world slowed as Buquet spun, the rope still looped about his neck, drawing his weapon to aim it at Erik. Christine cried out in warning and lunged towards Buquet.

She could not grab him, he moved too fast, but she managed to push instead. For a second she felt the coarse texture of his shirt and smelled his sweat, as the catwalk bounced and shook beneath their feet. A second of contact and pressure and he fell, tumbling away into empty air as the gun flew from his hand, his wide, terrified eyes filling with terror. The rope still around his throat pulled taught and the wet snap of his neck breaking echoed through the flies.

Joseph Buquet's body swung before Christine's horrified eyes, lifeless.

11. Until I Am Sleeping

Erik leapt to Christine, grabbing her tight and clamping a hand over her mouth before she could scream.

"Don't look. Don't look!" he whispered, pulling Christine away from the grisly sight of Buquet's corpse, dangling like a sandbag among the ropes. He chanced a look at her to confirm her eyes were screwed shut, tears escaping from the corners. "There are still people about, do not make a sound."

She nodded, and he released his hand from her mouth. He spun her towards him, touching her face with all the gentleness he could summon, and she gasped in a breath. She opened her weeping eyes and Erik's heart broke for the second time that night.

"We have to move. Right now," he commanded and did not wait for her assent before leading her away, making sure she did not look back. Erik did though. He glanced over his shoulder to the sack of meat that had been Joseph Buquet until moments ago. Far above, in the highest part of the flies, there were giant bells. They would never sound in mourning for their former master.

Erik led her down the twisting path to the stage, holding her close when they came to the main floor where he ushered Christine quickly as possible to her dressing room. It was cold and empty when they entered. When he grabbed Christine's cloak from its hook and placed it around her shoulders as she stared into the shadows, her eyes unfocused and her body limp. He caressed her face, and she blinked back to life as he held her gaze.

252

"We can't just leave him," she said, voice small and terrified, eyes drifting upwards. Erik forced her to look back at him.

"Christine, listen to me. You have to leave, right now, before it's found. You must be seen exiting the building by as many people as possible and get home."

Christine shook her head wildly. "No, please, I can't. You-you have to come with me." Her voice broke into a sob and she grabbed his arms, holding onto him with desperate pressure. "Please don't leave me alone. *Please.*"

Erik stared at her, at a loss. He had done this. Buquet was dead because of him, and now Christine bore that sin on her heart. And he could not abandon her to the dark, not now.

"Alright," he replied, concern for the woman he loved overcoming his panic and fear. "Come, we have to go now."

He pulled the hood over her head then stole a wine-colored scarf and wrapped it around his face before pulling the brim of his hat low. If he was to do this, he would take no risks to himself, and more importantly, to Christine. Wrapping a protective arm around Christine, he guided her back into the hall.

He kept them moving at a steady pace, not so fast as to arouse suspicion, but not so slow as to increase their own panic. He leaned in towards Christine when a fireman passed them, his heart racing all the while. He noted Christine and said nothing to Erik. A stagehand, an alto, the attendant at the stage door. All of them saw Christine and the shadow at her side. Not soon enough, they stepped into the frigid air on the *Rue Auber*. Christine shuddered beside him and he tried to keep himself from doing the same. His mind flashed to the sight of Buquet turning, pistol in hand, and Christine's cry. She had been trying to save him.

He pulled her closer to his side as they made their way to the bright *Place de L'Opéra*. Erik braced himself against the rumble of carriages and the sparse people still about at this time of night.

He was used to venturing out at a much later hour, but no one paid them much mind as they traveled quickly down the *Avenue de L'Opéra*. Christine caught his gaze in confusion as Erik turned them at the *Rue des Petits Champs*.

"You know where I live?" she asked meekly.

"Of course," Erik replied.

Their steps grew slower and more unsteady as they continued on their way, and Erik could feel Christine beginning to tremble at his side. The shock was wearing off. Finally, they turned left, almost at the *Rue Notre Dame des Victoires*, and Christine stopped, gasping for air and staring down the street. She was looking at the dark façade of the Basilica of *Notre Dame des Victoires*.

"Oh God," Christine whimpered, collapsing against Erik in the sight of a house of the holy. "He's dead and I – Oh God!"

"Christine, no!" Erik grasped her by the arms, holding her up with all his strength and shaking her so that she looked at him. "Stay with me!"

Christine made a choked noise in response. She was pale and wheezing, like she was drowning on dry land, eyes wide and unfocused, her whole body shaking in Erik's grasp.

"Christine, *breathe*," Erik commanded with all the authority of the angel she had known, and she froze. Erik took a deep inhale, and she mirrored him automatically. He breathed out and she did the same. "Good. Keep breathing." Again they breathed together, then again, Christine growing calmer with each inhalation and release. "That's my girl, keep breathing for me."

He was not expecting her to throw her arms around him, embracing him with such force it squeezed the breath from his lungs. But he did not stop her. He embraced her in return, wishing above all that he could hold her like this long enough to drive away every horror that she had seen because of him.

"Let's get inside," he whispered in her ear, and she nodded against his chest. She laced her arm with his and held him tight as they passed the church and came to the door of her building.

"I don't have my key," Christine said, staring at the lock. She did not flinch when Erik pulled a pin from her hair, nor show any sign of surprise when he picked the lock within seconds. He kept her close on the way up the stairs and they thankfully found the door to the Valerius flat unlocked.

"Adèle is home," Christine muttered.

"We should—" Erik began to reply, when light spilled into the parlor from an opened door, revealing Adèle Valerius' silhouette.

"Christine, is that—"

Before Erik could panic, Christine pulled him into her arms and kissed him, drawing him tight against her so that his back was to Valerius and Christine was against the wall. Erik's mind could hardly process his fear and desire and worry all at the same time, but Christine kissed him with more heat and desperation than she ever had before, and as she did, the world faded around them. It was wrong, he knew it, to love the feel of her fervent mouth in the shadow of what they had just done and seen, but nevertheless, he adored it.

"Well, I'll leave you to that," Valerius said from a thousand miles away.

Erik was faintly aware of the click of the door shutting again, and the loss of the light, but all that truly mattered was Christine's desperate embrace that refused to release him. "Where is your room?" he managed to ask as he drew back for breath. Christine grabbed him quickly and pulled him by the wrist through the dark parlor to her door.

Her room was dark, with no illumination but the faint orange glow of the gaslights on the street outside through her thin curtains. Erik had no time to examine what little he could see because as soon as the door shut behind them, Christine was in his arms again, tearing away his mask.

It was so much better to kiss her without it, so good that he barely noticed her pulling off his hat, scarf, and cloak. Hers had been discarded too, it seemed, for he felt the bare skin of her back and shoulders as he embraced her. She tore away her white gloves clumsily between them and then set to Erik's tie and top buttons with shaking hands. In shock and horror, Erik jumped back, catching Christine by the wrists and holding her at bay.

"What are you – what are we doing?" he asked, breathless. He could barely make out her face in the amber-tinged dark, but he could see the anguish in her eyes.

"You have to keep going. You have to keep touching me," Christine pled. "I'll die if you stop."

"Christine, I—" He was shaking too, he realized.

"It makes it all stop, when you touch me," she went on, batting Erik's hands away and resuming her task before silencing his protests with a fresh, starving kiss.

In seconds his tie was cast aside, and she had undone his top buttons, her mouth following close behind her fingers, kissing his exposed skin and making him gasp. It was madness, he knew it, to give in to his lust now, but she was right. Nothing else mattered when they touched.

He helped her tear off his jacket, his vest, and his shirt, leaving him with nothing but the bandage she had given him to conceal his scars. He devoured her neck as he undid the buttons and laces down her back. He had done this before – undressed her – but never in such darkness and never with such need and urgency between them. Bodice, skirt, corset, chemise; he divested her of them all, kissing and groping each exposed swath of skin as he did.

Finally she was bare for him, and he lifted her to his arms, caring for nothing else in the world but the way she wrapped around him. He was hard and he knew she could feel it as he laid her down beneath him so he could gain one second of relief rutting against her. He reached between her legs, savoring how she cried and arched against him as his fingers dipped into her molten heat.

"Erik, please, I need..." she whimpered. "You have to..."

"Tell me," he panted, pushing deeper as she writhed. "Tell me what you need."

"Fuck me."

Erik froze above her, braced on the bed, trying to find her eyes in the dark. "Christine, you can't want that."

"I do. I need you. I need you more than anything right now," she murmured, her voice thick as if she was weeping again. Before Erik could protest, she pushed him, flipping their position so that it was he who was prone on the bed as she began to unfasten his trousers, kissing gently at his bandaged wound. "I don't care about a curse. I'm already damned,"

"Don't say that," Erik groaned as his cock sprang free and Christine discarded the last of Erik's clothes to the floor. "You're good. You're—" Christine stopped him with another kiss, firm and deep. He could taste her tears though; he could feel them against his bare cheek when she pressed her face against his. Or perhaps they were his.

"I don't know what I am, not anymore," she confessed. "But tonight, please let me be yours."

"Mine," Erik sighed as his resolve crumbled at the feel of her hand stroking his cock, sending torrents of pleasure and desire through him. In the dark she was his. "You're mine. That's all that matters."

She straddled him, fully in control and command, her thighs soft and hot against his hips. Her hand was steady now, spreading wetness from the crown of his cock, sending lighting through his blood before she rose and guided him to her slick entrance. He held his breath in amazement, half-sure this was a dream. But it was too real as she took him inside her.

It was slow, so agonizingly slow and perfect and good as she lowered herself, taking in his girth one careful centimeter at a time. She moaned as she sank down and Erik forgot how to breathe as her heat enveloped him. This was nothing like any time before. It had never felt so right and so heavenly. It had never made him feel so like his heart was ready to explode with love and regret and desire. At last she stopped, and he was fully within her, ready to die from the warmth. But he didn't. Not yet. Rather, he gasped and groaned as she began to move. If there was something beyond heaven, now he was there.

"Is – Is this right?" Christine panted, her hips slowly finding their rhythm.

"God yes," he managed to respond. Above him she was barely a shadow, and he reached up to touch her, cupping her breasts as he watched her outline move against the hazy dark. That made her cry and he loved it. He loved the feel of her, the wet slide and tightening of her cunt as she rode him. He loved her strangled exclamations as his hands moved to the place where they were joined, finding the sensitive, hidden nub that made her quiver and keen.

"Yes, there, please, oh God, Erik, please," she chanted, her hips increasing in speed as Erik thrust up into her while trapped beneath her. She doubled over with another cry that was lost as she kissed him, hungry and feral, her hands in his hair.

He wanted to speak. He wanted to say how he loved her. He wanted to beg her mercy for what he had done to her, for how he had defiled her and clouded her light. But there were no words, there was nothing but his body screaming in pleasure and her body tight and tense around his. There was only this. But he wanted more.

Erik flipped them this time, animal instinct taking over, and Christine's legs wrapped around his waist. Finally free, he did what she had commanded and fucked. He drove into her, hard and fast and deep so that she whimpered and gasped with each thrust, her flimsy old bed trembling with the force. She looked up at him, and he was so glad of the dark that concealed his face. He could see her eyes, like onyx, reflecting back the meager light. Could she see his glowing back at her? Could she see the fear and the awe?

He wanted to speak, but there were no words for this. There was barely music that could express the depth of how it felt to be lost in her arms, to give her this, to hold her like an anchor as the storms of grief and pleasure tossed her on their rough waves. His pleasure was spinning to a peak, he could feel it, but with all his might he kept himself in check, even as Christine's body stiffened, and her cunt tightened around him in the most sublime way.

"Let go," he whispered, eyes on her in the dark. "Let go, my love."

And at his words, Christine came. She gave a raw, unbridled scream as her climax took her, convulsing in pleasure beneath him. With his last shred of sanity, Erik grabbed tight at the base of his cock as she spasmed in ecstasy around him, threatening to make him explode. He fucked her through her pleasure, as long as he could, and she cried out as he withdrew.

He slid his cock against the juncture of her hip and thigh, blindly rutting against her. In a breath, the orgasm claimed him with more force and pleasure than any before. He managed to open his eyes and look down at her as he spilled over her belly in a hot flood.

The fog of pleasure held him for an incandescent moment, receding slowly as they caught their breath. He was still poised above her, unable to see her beauty with his eyes but it was just as magnificent to trace her moist cheeks with the pad of this thumb.

"Don't let go of me," Christine whispered.

"Never," Erik replied, and pulled her tight to him, laying back so that she was in her preferred position with her head against his heart.

"Don't let me fall, Erik. Hold me until I am sleeping," she breathed against his skin. "Don't let me drown."

"I will hold you until the end of the world," he swore in return and tightened his embrace. Careful so that no other ears would hear their secret song, he sang softly into her ear. *"Close your eyes and forget all the world, in the dark you are mine, my love. From darkness you call me, and to darkness I lead you. But you are light, ever mine as I am yours."*

She was his now, entirely. And he would obey her: he would never let go.

Raoul had wandered every salon and hall of the Opera in the past hours. All these rooms looked the same to him, with their gilded mirrors and murals of heathen gods. He didn't care that there were five hundred different colors of tile or marble, or how the nymph in the fountain by the rotunda smiled as he passed. It was all noise and waste and moved nothing in his heart as he wandered the salons emptying of celebrants and workers. None of them were Christine.

The *Salon du Danse* was nearly empty, save for a few ushers or maids (or whatever servants were called who cleaned up Opera houses) gathering empty glasses and one discarded glove. This was hopeless. Christine was long gone, and he had driven her away. He left the salon through a side door that took him close to the backstage areas and found to his surprise the way to the dressing rooms was open and empty. One last try would not hurt.

"Where are you taking me?" a whisper came from the stage, alarming Raoul. It was a woman's voice. His curiosity piqued, he followed the sound and the laughter that followed.

"Somewhere private, trust me." Raoul recognized that voice and when he turned the corner it was confirmed. Christine's maid, the negress, was pulling the ballerina Jammes toward a small spiral staircase leading above the stage. Jammes her name was.

"You!" Raoul yelled, bounding towards the women, who jumped at his voice. They would know if Christine had gone or if she was at least safe.

"Oh God, not you," the maid said with a frown. Beside her the dancer sighed as well, looking put-upon as she rolled her eyes. "I haven't seen her since I dressed her for the party, but I heard she left—" The dancer's scream cut off the maid's words.

Raoul followed the ballerina's eyes and covered his mouth in horror. Above them hung the body of a man, face purple and arms limp. He was dead.

"Oh Jesus Christ," the maid gasped. Raoul sprang into action, running to the horrified dancer and taking her by the arm. "Go find a policeman or a fireman, now!" he yelled at the maid. She looked as if she was about to be sick, but she nodded and rushed away. "You, do you know who that is?" Jammes looked at the body again and Raoul was worried she would start screaming anew.

"Buquet. It's Joseph Buquet," the dancer replied. "Chief of the flies."

Raoul glanced up again at the dangling body above. "Why would he kill himself?" He hadn't meant to say it out loud, but the ballerina scoffed at the words.

"He didn't kill himself," Jammes replied.

"Who would want to kill him then?"

"The Ghost." Jammes said it like it was something that made perfect sense.

"Excuse me?"

"He saw him! Months ago! He told everyone what the ghost looked like without his mask," Jammes explained, her distress rising.

"Ghosts do not exist, Mademoiselle," Raoul said as firmly as he could manage. Surely the girl was mad. "And they certainly don't murder people."

"You know nothing!" Jammes snapped back, shaking her head so that her dark blonde curls shook. "You, the managers, you 'll make up a story to feel better and keep the peace, but when news spreads that Buquet is dead, everyone will know who did it: the damned Phantom of the Opera!"

The girl shoved Raoul and ran, leaving him alone on the stage. Well, alone unless he counted the poor lost soul strung up above him. Raoul wished he had a cross to grasp, or somewhere other than an empty stage to kneel, but it would have to do. His knees smarted at the hardness of the floor as he bowed his head.

"*Ave, María, grátia plena, Dóminus tecum. Benedicta tu in muliéribus, et benedíctus fructus ventris tui, Jesus,*" he whispered, hands clasped. "*Holy Mary, mother of God, pray for us sinners, now and in the moment of our death,*" he finished as pounding footsteps approached.

"Dear God," a man's voice exclaimed behind Raoul. "Someone get a message to Richard and Moncharmin."

C hristine dreamed of the flies. She dreamed of herself tangled in their ropes, unable to move as Buquet fell again and again. They strangled her screams as he drew his gun and the shot echoed through the Opera. Then it was Erik who fell, bleeding and unmasked, but there was no ground below them, only an abyss of dark water. And then she was falling too.

"No!" She awoke with a cry in the near-complete darkness of her little room in Adèle's flat. She shot upright, shaking and unable to breathe. "Erik!?"

He was beside her in a heartbeat, pulling her close. "It's alright. I'm here. It was just a dream."

"It wasn't," she whispered against his bare shoulder, the old burns there a strange texture as always against her cheek. "He's dead. Buquet is dead." It made her sick to say, but she could not run from the truth, not here in the dark without her lust to drive away the memory of one sin with another. "Because of me."

"No, because of me." Erik took her face in his hands, and all she could see in the dark was the light of his loving eyes. "You did nothing wrong. It was an accident."

"I pushed—"

"To save me," Erik intoned, and Christine choked back a sob, seeing Erik fall in her dream. "I'm the reason he was there. I'm the reason he did not run."

"A man is still dead because of *us*," Christine protested.

"A man who would have destroyed us both," Erik countered, and Christine's heart fell once again at the certainty in his voice. And the lack of any guilt. She remembered his eyes as he choked Buquet, the utter coldness and resolve. How could those same eyes look at her with such regret and devotion now?

"I know what you're feeling," Erik went on softly as Christine shivered. "You were numb at first, as if it wasn't real. There had been some mistake, or maybe there was something you could say or do to erase what happened. And now you are realizing you can't. You feel sick, like you want to crawl out of your own skin, because the person you suddenly are, you don't even recognize."

Christine recalled being in his arms, how it had made her feel perfect and free to only be his. Even now she wanted it again: to kiss him until there was nothing else, to listen to his voice so that every other thought was quiet.

"Does it get better?" she asked softly. Erik inclined his head so that their foreheads touched as he nodded.

"Tomorrow, or the next day you'll begin to realize that it couldn't have been any other way. This was the fate he chose long ago. You won't believe it the first time you tell yourself he deserved it, but you will think it. And soon, you'll know it's true."

Christine closed her eyes on fresh tears, the undeniable truth behind Erik's words settling in her soul. "You've killed before."

"Yes," Erik whispered. "Many times."

"In Persia."

He nodded again. "And before."

"How many?" Somehow, she had always known. It had been the way the Persian had called him a monster. And the way Erik regarded himself. She had known in her heart he was a killer for weeks, and still she had taken him to her bed.

"Christine, are you sure you want to know?" Erik asked. Christine pulled him back towards the mattress with her, so that their heads rested together on one pillow, their bodies pressed close.

"Tell me," she ordered, knowing that he would not refuse. "Tell me everything at last."

Erik took a deep breath, the light of his eyes disappearing as he closed them in preparation. "I blamed myself for my mother's death, and when Steiner died in the fire, I took joy in not running in to save him," Erik began carefully. "But the first death I caused, truly, was my first lover's. If she can even be called that.

"After Vienna, I traveled for years, joining different Romani bands across the continent, learning all I could and entertaining at fairs as a magician and musician as well as a living corpse. I was welcomed enough to survive, but not to belong. Back then I was naïve enough to think that one day that could change. That if I looked long enough, I would find a place where I belonged. And I was a young man, I had desires, but I could never act on them. Or so I thought until I came to Venice.

"It was Carnival, I was seventeen, and the whole city was masked. I could move about freely, as I never could before. I sang at the finest parties, picked the pockets of the richest dukes, and drank and laughed with people who were alive and beautiful under their dominos and masks. I met her at a party on that final Tuesday before Lent, about this time of year, I guess. I never learned her name."

Erik paused, and the light of his eyes disappeared again as he closed them, remembering. Christine took his hand, clasping it gently to her breast.

"She was much older than me, I know that. But she enjoyed my voice and said I looked young and strong. I was drunk and stupid, so I went to her bed when she invited me. I wanted to know what it was like, to make love. It was...pleasurable, but brief. Afterwards I was in a daze, so I did not notice when she reached for my mask. I can still hear the way she screamed when she saw me. I tried to run, but before I could, her husband rushed in."

Christine shivered, already guessing the terrible end of the tale.

"He was drunk too," Erik continued. "I cannot say what sort of man he was, but it was not me he went after first, but her. It was not a fair fight between the two of them. He grabbed her, he struck her again and again while I screamed at him to stop and tried to intervene. And then threw her so she hit her head against the marble top of her vanity. He threw her so hard. She was dead before she hit the floor. I can still see that too, the way her skull caved in..."

"You didn't kill her," Christine protested, and the light of Erik's eyes returned, searching hers in the dark.

"No. I killed him, the husband, when he turned on me. To this day I cannot say how I won that fight. Perhaps it was because I hated him so much in that moment for what he had done. I saw my father in his face. But we fought, and I ended it with my hands on his neck. The next thing I knew, he was dead. Then I ran."

"You were defending yourself," Christine said automatically then recoiled at her words. How could she so easily dismiss such a crime?

"I told myself that while I was vomiting into a canal. I believed it by the time I fled the city. Once I reached Rome, I knew he deserved it." Erik paused for a deep breath. "Just like Buquet did."

"What happened after?" Christine asked, feeling sick herself.

"I wandered the world, cursed and marked like Cain himself. I traveled all through the Mediterranean and into Arabia, and then India. Each place I went, I explored and learned, but I never could stay too long. I always drew suspicion and revulsion. At least in parts of the East, if I covered my face and myself in the right clothes, I could pass for a strange, tall woman. But women in those places were barely treated with more dignity than I was as a freak, so I rarely did it. I was always an outcast, often met with violence. But I didn't kill again. Not until Punjab."

"I made mistakes there. I stole from and insulted too many British oligarchs. I found myself in a secret enclave of Ambarsar, fighting like a gladiator of old for the colonizers' amusement. It was blood sport, but rarely did anyone die. They'd surrender first. It was there I met a man, Nehal. He was a seasoned fighter who defended himself with nothing but a length of rope. He used it like a lasso, strangling his larger and faster opponents until they beat the ground in submission. He beat me with it, and afterwards, I asked him to show me how it worked."

"Why?" Christine asked, her mind filled with the image of Erik fighting like an animal in a pit for the amusement of the rich.

"I was curious to learn how something that so simple could be so lethal. I have a certain affection for that which more than what it seems," Erik replied. "And soon enough I had a chance. There was a British officer who came often, and he had a large hand in keeping us all there, like slaves. He didn't like the old man with the lasso winning over and over, so he went into the ring with him and shot him in cold blood. So I took up the lasso and I used it on Nehal's murderer. It started a riot, that man's death. In the chaos, we all escaped. I was free. And I took the lasso with me."

"You still have it, don't you?"

"It has defended me for many years, but it did not take another life for a long while after I left India. I traveled through China, all the way to Hong Kong, where once again I found the British seizing a land that was not theirs. So I stowed away on one of their ships and drank their ale on the sea journey back to London, around the horn of Africa. By the end of the voyage, the sailors were convinced the ship was haunted and I quite enjoyed being a ghost.

"I had spent so long wandering that I wanted nothing more than a place to belong, a place to call home. I hoped I might find it in my mother's homeland, or perhaps meet someone of my own blood I did not hate. So from London I traveled England, and then went to Ireland for a year. But everyone with my mother's name had left their village long ago for America. And so I returned at last to the land of my birth for the first time, wondering if it was possible to go home."

"And you came to Paris, and found a home among the communards," Christine continued for him. "I understand better now, why you joined them fighting for a new order."

"My life had been filled with pain, thanks to the greed and cruelty of men in power. I wanted to destroy them, and I thought I had found compatriots of the same spirit and that we were making a better world. Until they began to do more to their prisoners than hold them captive. And I helped."

For the first time, it was Erik who shuddered at the memory. What could be so dark that even he was repulsed by it?

"I knew pain and torture so well by then, from what Steiner taught me. It was easy to let my imagination do its worst. Especially when I told myself it was righteous." Erik shook his head. "The communards grew as cruel as they were incompetent, and I tried to get away from what we had begun. They had other bases of operation besides the Opera, less fortified. And like any soldiers' camp, there were women willing to sell themselves nearby, hoping for enough coin to survive the siege. And I indulged with one woman who was there."

"Do you remember her name?" Christine was surprised at how much she resented a whore from a decade before.

"Mireille. Such a pretty name," Erik replied wistfully. "It was at the end of things when I fucked her. It was empty. But a week later, the siege was broken, and the commune fell. I went back to our base, and I found so many dead. She was among them. They'd hung her."

Immediately Christine burned with guilt for her jealousy. "That wasn't your fault either."

"I never felt anything for them, the women before you," Erik murmured, touching Christine's face in the dark. "You should know that."

"You said there were three," Christine asked, bracing herself. "Three lovers. What of the third?"

Erik sighed, his eyes downcast in the shadow and Christine could sense his pain and regret in the air. "The third I met in Persia. And yes, I did love him, for a little while."

"Him?" Christine echoed, more curious than shocked. In a way, it made sense. Why would Erik care at all for who he touched or loved if given the chance? "It wasn't your Daroga, was it?"

"No," Erik replied with a shadow of amusement in his voice. "It was his brother. Shaya was the one that the Shah sent to obtain me. I had found my way to the great fair in Nizhny Novgorod, and my reputation had spread along caravan routes all the way to the court of Naser al-Din Shah Qajar of Persia. The Shah was eager for the most rare and unique amusements. I said no at first. I didn't want to serve at the whim of a bored royal, no matter their country or creed.

"But Shaya was convincing, speaking with such love of his land and how the Shah wanted to bring it into the modern, continental world and show Britain and France and the Ottomans that Persia was still as great as it had been in the time of Darius or Xerxes. And he said the Shah was building a new palace, a place of dreams that I could consult on. So I went, thinking I could find my place and be more than a carnival freak or a failed rebel. I could be a builder there, a man of influence even. I should have listened to my instincts."

Christine shivered at the words and the threat in Erik's tone.

"I amused the Shah with my skills and he even laughed at the horrors of my face. He liked horrors. The women of his harem – the ones he kept locked in their own secluded world, barely able to see the sky – liked to hear me sing outside their windows. Shaya was assigned to spy on me in his role as one of the Shah's secret police. I didn't mind; I liked to dine with him and his brother, who was one of the Shah's chief builders. His name was Ramin."

Christine closed her eyes at the sound of regret in Erik's voice.

"I had been there a few months when the Shah began to become bored with me, and I with him, honestly. It was only Ramin that kept me there. I had found a friend whose curiosity and intellect were close to my own. To him I confessed many of my misadventures of the years before, of Punjab and the Commune. He in turn took to consulting me about his designs for the new pleasure palace on the sea, at the Shah's resort of Mazenderan. We were there, at the old palace, when the Shah decided on a new game for his pet monster. Shaya had told him, you see, the stories I had relayed to Ramin. And the Shah wanted to see how a man could be killed with just one length of catgut. I said no at first. I did not want to be that monster. Ramin tried to stop it."

"But," Christine provided for him, looking up. She could see Erik better now, as if her eyes were adjusting to the dark.

"But he put me in a courtyard. I can still see it, with its perfect arches inlaid with the names of Allah. The Shah was on a balcony above with courtiers at his side, including Shaya, who was some sort of distant noble cousin. But facing me on the ground was one of the men Shaya had helped arrest while doing the main function of his work – finding dissidents against the Shah. The man was a traitor condemned to die, but he was armed. Whichever of us made it out of that courtyard would be allowed to live."

"And you killed him," Christine whispered.

"Since my mother tried to expel me from her womb, I have always been stubborn against death. I don't know why, really, but I have always fought to live, no matter what. And so I would not let death take me there. When I strangled that man with my Punjab Lasso, the court applauded as if it was a new magic trick. I was glad Ramin wasn't there to see."

"But it didn't stop there, did it?"

"I became the monster I had always been told I was. My will was law, and everyone feared me. Everyone except the Shah, Shaya, and Ramin. The Shah was a cruel, paranoid man. He had been a reformer in his youth, inviting Europe to dine at his table while they colonized the rest of Africa and the East, but they had no respect for him and exploited his country. So, he grew petty and small-minded.

"By the time I came to his court, Naser al-Din had become the weakest kind of ruler – who only cared about maintaining his power and authority, no matter how his people suffered. I came to Persia in the midst of a terrible famine. Thousands starved throughout the country, but the Shah did not care. He continued to fill his court with gaudy spectacle and build his palace, while unrest grew and dissidents plotted against him. Shaya tracked them down. I gave them death.

"The Shah always gave the victims the same offer and the same warning: survive and walk away a free man, but beware if you see the demon's face, for that means you are already dead. I killed fourteen men for him, and each time it got easier. Each time I became more of a monster because I enjoyed the power it gave me to hold their lives in my hands. The world had hurt me so much for so long. I could finally take my revenge in those rosy hours in Mazenderan."

Christine shivered at the echoes of the past in Erik's voice. The relish she could hear.

"Shaya grew afraid of me, but Ramin...he feared for me. For my soul, or so he said. He told me so many times it was a crime, a waste, to put an artist like me in the place of a common executioner. But I was more than that. I was an angel of death, a terrible, magnificent, powerful thing. I told him I was what I was always destined to be. He disagreed. He said I was meant to be so much more.

"I worked with him on the new palace. At the Shah's insistence, I was to do on purpose what I had done piecemeal and in secret at the Opera: design a mystery box, a giant magic trick where he could move about unseen to do his own spying upon all that would defy him. He also wished for a place to put those that displeased him, male and female. A place to confuse and punish. To torture.

And so I thought back to my time in Steiner's cellar and the commune and I built him a maze of mirrors to drive men mad."

Christine shuddered, and in Erik's distorted face she could see his disgust, or so she hoped. The outline of his body was visible now, set apart from the shadow by gray light.

"I never saw it at work," Erik continued despondently. "The Shah's paranoia turned on me. He ordered that the light of my eyes be put out forever, so no one would know the secrets of his new realm. He ordered Shaya to do it, but Shaya made the mistake of telling his brother. And it was Ramin who saved me before Shaya and his men could strike.

"We ran, the two of us. And Ramin's name was added to the list of those who were to be killed for their knowledge, along with all the builders who had worked on the palace. Shaya refused to kill his own brother and innocent workers, so he was branded a traitor too.

"We went to the sea, the shore of the Black Sea, Ramin and I. I had always admired him, enjoyed our time, and he had always been there to tell me I was meant to create beauty, not death. He even said my face was not so bad, if one got used to it. I laughed at him, in that little house by the sea. And he said it would not be impossible for someone to...to care for me. To want me.

"Shaya knew before either of us, what Ramin felt. I still don't understand how someone that good could see anything worth saving in me in that terrible place, knowing what I was and what I had done. But he did. I mocked him at first, called him a fool who would turn on his god and his people for infatuation with a monster. And he told me that love was never a sin."

"You said that to me, about Jammes and Julianne." Christine watched Erik nod in the light that had begun to creep through the curtains. Soon it would be dawn. "You and he were lovers then?"

"For two nights. And on the second one, I was foolish enough to hope that we could escape. But the curse found us. Shaya found us. He berated Ramin for destroying their family's name and lives for the sake of a monster, he cursed me for corrupting a good man with my evil. They fought, Ramin telling Shaya it was he who had lost his soul serving an evil man. And then the rest of the secret police found us.

"There were two of them. Both armed. They did not have Shaya's tact or conscience. They shot Ramin first and turned their guns on us. Shaya and I were too fast, he shot the one who had killed his brother, and I killed the other with the Punjab lasso before he could take Shaya's life.

"Shaya could have killed me there. I had just destroyed his family and condemned him to exile or torture. But I had saved Shaya's life. And he wanted to do what Ramin would have done and be a man of honor. So he let me go.

"He told me I would have to live with his brother's blood on my hands, along with all my other crimes. When Shaya returned to court, whatever lie he told failed, and he was imprisoned then exiled. Only his royal blood saved him from death. He followed the tales of me until he found his way to Paris, three years ago, but by then I had already been driven farther into the dark than he would have ever guessed."

"You came back to Paris six and a half years ago." It was time for the final confession.

"It took me a while. I had to hide, travel slowly. I couldn't perform, for word might reach the Shah that the living corpse with the voice of a siren was doing magic in the East. I went through Turkey, tried my hand at a mechanical career there, but that gained attention and I knew I could not stay anywhere long. I was too tainted.

"I kept running, joined with a Roma band heading west, and found myself in France once again. Here I thought I was safe enough to sing in the fairs once again, and eventually, in the summer of 1874, our caravan was invited to be the entertainment for a garden soirée near Rouen, hosted by a man with a name I recognized."

"Your father." Christine's heart began to pound in fresh horror. In the dawning light, she could see the burns on Erik's shoulder and arm.

"I still wonder if he knew who I was when he hired us. But I recognized my father that day in the sun. I stood there at last before a crowd of nobles, sharing their blood, with the man who had cursed me before birth sitting among them in the manor gardens so close to where my mother had been buried. And I took off my mask and felt the summer sun on my face. And he knew.

"He called me a monster, a thief, and a criminal. He had me seized and locked in a cellar. The lasso was of no use, and there were so many of them. His people had guns and no regard for my life or the Romani who had come with me. So I did not fight. They beat me anyway. But I escaped my bonds easily at night. I needed a distraction for the men set to guard me. So, I set a fire. I don't know how the fire spread so fast, but before I knew it, the whole manor was in flames. I could hear people screaming, guests for the party trapped in their rooms..."

Erik's voice faded even as the light in the room grew brighter, his words and eyes echoing with the sounds of death and destruction he had caused.

"I heard someone calling for help close by, and I tried to go back. I wanted to help. Prove I wasn't like them. But a beam fell and my way was blocked. I was trapped. Then I heard it: my father's voice, calling for his son. I found him, in the grandest bedroom of the house, where he very well could have raped my mother all those years ago, pinned under a bookshelf. He saw me through the flames and begged for help, begged for his life. He offered me money, his name, and his lands. He offered me everything. And I turned away and left him to die."

Christine bit back the words of comfort she wanted to offer. It was wrong, to say such a man deserved that fate, to die alone in flame. But didn't he? After all the evil he had done? It made Christine's own heart burn with guilt just to think it. And did that mean Erik deserved the same fate, for all his crimes?

"I was hurt badly trying to escape. Burned and beaten, I still refused to die. I stole a horse and rode as far as it would take me. I moved at night, hiding and growing weaker, but I finally made it to Paris where I found my way to the Opera. From there you know and guess the rest."

Christine looked into her lover's face, the picture of death, scarred and broken by so much tragedy. It was strange to finally know the truth about the man who loved her, who had saved her life and trapped her soul. Now at last she saw beyond all his masks, to the ugliness she had always known was there and tried to ignore it in the dark. But now it was dawn.

"What will Shaya do when he hears about Buquet?" she asked. Somehow the fear was distant, while Erik held her in the twilight.

"He's been waiting for me to prove I am still a monster. When he hears Buquet was hanged, he'll want words with me I expect. He'll know I killed him."

"But *you* didn't," Christine protested. "It was—"

"It was me, Christine. He is dead because of me. Please, do not let that sin weigh on your soul. Let me have it, another body added to my list does not trouble me anymore." Of all the things Erik had told her in the last hour, that chilled Christine the most. "I do not regret that man's death. He hurt you. He would have kept us apart and the world is better without him in it."

It made her sick to finally hear the last truth: that Erik was willing and ready to kill for her. To keep her. Out in the street a carriage rolled by, the horses' hooves clopping steadily as the vehicle rumbled behind them. Paris was beginning to wake. Erik looked towards the light growing beyond the curtains.

"You have to go, don't you?" Christine whispered, her heart filling with fear again. She knew today she could not go with him. And perhaps, she should not.

"There is much I'll have to attend to today," Erik said sadly. "Meet me at sunset, at the stables. Then I'll take you..." he paused, rolling his lips.

"Home. You'll take me home."

He nodded. Without another word he rose, shying away from even the dim light of day as it touched his eyes. Christine rose as she watched him dress, marking the long scars across his back from lashings long ago, the way they faded into his burns, like rays of sun into a cloud. They were nothing compared to the damage upon his soul. His back straightened as he put on his mask, and the room grew colder. He looked back at Christine, still nude beneath the sheet covering her.

"Keep breathing today, please," Erik entreated. The light in his eyes was no longer visible, now that the night had passed, but the adoration and worry were still there. The love.

"I promise I will," Christine whispered. He seemed unconvinced as he drifted to her and pulled her into one final, aching kiss. It was an entreaty, that kiss, a desperate call to her heart to survive the day and return to him.

"I love you," he breathed as their lips parted. "I love you more than I have ever loved anyone before. I want you to know that."

"I would never doubt it," she replied. She knew, somehow, that he did not expect her to say it back, but even so, it scared her to think of the words crossing her lips.

"Until I see you again, my angel," he said with a final kiss on her brow. She closed her eyes as he left and kept them closed until the click of the door closing made her jump like a gunshot. She wrapped herself in her sheet, running to the window to watch him go. She saw him for only a second, a shadow on the street below that disappeared into the cold alley behind the church in an instant. She fell to her knees, gasping.

He was gone and she had to face the day alone with a man's death on her conscience. She would have to stand and dress with the ache in her groin and thighs from how a killer had fucked her. She would have to walk through Paris, to his opera, knowing what he had done and the things she would so willingly let him do to her again. Her fear choked her, but she forced herself to breathe, as he had commanded her.

Christine did not know what terrified her more: being without the one capable of driving back the dark that threatened to consume her, or the man himself, who had brought that darkness upon her.

12. Persephone

Erik came home via the sewers and tunnels into the fifth cellar. He didn't bother with a lantern; he knew his way in the dark. He knew he was close to the lake when he heard them. He hadn't listened for the ghosts in a while. Their whispers and cold breezes were simply part of the underworld which he inhabited, like the sound of water dripping in the damp blackness, or the scent of earth and stone. Maybe they knew he had confessed and spent the night thinking on his crimes. Or maybe they had a new companion to welcome with open arms. Erik did not fear Joseph Buquet's spirit; only the consequences to Christine of separating said spirit from its body.

He stopped in his tracks, just as he reached the glow of the furnace fires that never slept, thinking of her. This was the only place in the cellars, save his home, which was warm. And yet he was sure he could lean right against these steel beasts and not feel the same heat he had when Christine's body was made one with his. He would do anything now, for her. He'd kill a hundred, a thousand, at her command. He had given up on regret many years ago, but it shocked him now, to think how he would discard any shred of conscience he had if it was at her command.

He came up through the sets and storage below the stage, listening for activity. There *shouldn't* be anyone there so early in the morning after a performance, and on a Saturday no less. But there were voices and footsteps above. Serious, low voices and purposeful steps. Buquet had been found.

Erik hid under a trapdoor – one that was there intentionally, for theatrical magic and not one of his. He peeked up through a crack at the edge to make sure the path was clear then stole out of the opening like a shadow, hidden behind a flat at the back of the stage. He had to find the gun Buquet had dropped—

"Will you be needing anything else of me, Monsieur Mifroid?" Erik froze at the sound of the boy's voice. *What was he doing here?*

"No, Monsieur le Vicomte, you have been most helpful," a man replied, Erik assumed it was the Mifroid who had been addressed. He sounded tired and surprisingly bored.

"Too helpful, one might even say." It was Richard's voice that cut in, and he rose slightly in Erik's estimation for the mockery of the so-called Vicomte in his tone.

"I felt a sense of responsibility, Monsieur. As both a patron and the one to discover the body," the boy replied. Now that was interesting.

"So you've mentioned," Richard sighed.

"Any idea if the man had family?" Mifroid asked. "The body will need to be claimed within a day, or it's into a pauper's grave for the poor soul."

"At least you won't need to call a priest for the burial," Richard noted. "Suicides do save on that expense."

"Monsieur Richard!" the boy gasped. Erik rolled his eyes in the shadows.

"I will investigate, *Monsieur Inspecteur*, and send word." For the first time it was Moncharmin who spoke. He sounded utterly exhausted.

"Good day, Messieurs," Mifroid said with a click of his heels and Erik heard his steps depart. "I'll be waiting by the wagon for it. You can cut him down now."

Erik looked up reflexively to see Buquet still swinging above, paler and more bloated than he had been hours before.

"You heard the man! Get this thing down and out to the cart!" Richard yelled, and there was a scuttle of movement. Erik retreated further backstage, as steps approached him as well, all the while looking for the gun anywhere it might have fallen. It would not do to have a weapon lying about or leave a clue that Buquet had gone to the flies with more on his mind than ending his life.

"The exit is this way, Monsieur de Chagny," Moncharmin's voice came, firm but insistent near where Erik hid on stage left. "You can use the stage door. The same one I will assure you *again* your dear friend Mademoiselle Daaé was seen leaving last night."

"Will she be returning here today?" the boy asked, trying to sound casual but failing.

"No, not for a few days," Moncharmin replied.

"You're honestly going to keep the Opera open when a man has died in your theater?" The churl sounded so offended. How did he survive in the world?

"Some of us cannot afford to mourn for long," Moncharmin replied. "Good day, sir."

Too slowly, the boy's footsteps faded. Erik turned back towards the stage, wishing there was more light so he could search, and that everyone else would just leave.

"*Monsieur le Fantôme*, are you near?"

Erik startled at the sound of Moncharmin's question. What on earth?

"I should like to speak with you, if I may."

"Then speak," Erik replied, stepping from behind the curtain to face Moncharmin. To the manager's credit, he did not jump at the sight of the ghost.

"I have much to do today, Monsieur, as I am sure you do as well," Moncharmin said with a sigh. "I have to track down Cécile Jammes, who was there with the Vicomte when the body was found. Make sure nothing is in the press. You understand."

"Of course," Erik replied, squinting at the man as he fumbled in the pockets of his coat.

"I only wish to know if this incident was...a beginning or an end."

"It was a suicide," Erik corrected. Moncharmin nodded politely.

"Of course, the police agree, but my question still stands, out of an abundance of caution." Erik stared at the man. There was very little fear in his tired eyes, just a sort of resigned sadness.

"It was the end, Monsieur. I assure you," Erik said slowly.

"That is a relief," the manager sighed as he pulled something from his pocket and placed it on the ground. It was the pistol Buquet had used. And now that Erik could see it better, it was familiar. "I hope this does not fall into the wrong hands again."

"I will see it disposed of. You have my word."

Moncharmin turned with a stiff nod and retreated, leaving Erik alone in the wings of their theater. The gun was lighter in his hand than he would have expected. In truth, he handled firearms rarely. They were cruel, inelegant weapons that gave the power of death to so many who did not deserve it. He examined the handle, worn from many years of use and confinement in a coat pocket. The inscription on the wood confirmed what he suspected, a character that meant 'justice' in Farsi. But how had Shaya Motlagh's gun come into Joseph Buquet's hands?

Erik stole into the shadows, his mind full of scenarios and suspicion. But the sound of voices above brought him back. He looked up from his hiding place to watch as a crew of stagehands lowered their former compatriot's body towards the stage. It took a while, and the men grew silent as they cut the rope and the limp corpse flopped to the stage, its head lolling to the side unnaturally. Alonzo, the largest of the stagehands yet somehow the gentlest, was the one to pick up the thing and wrap it in a sheet, a makeshift shroud, then lift it onto the ladder that had been brought to carry Joseph Buquet on his final journey from the Opera.

Erik watched as they carried him on the temporary ramp set up above the orchestra pit, into the audience of empty seats of red velvet, beneath golden lyres and laughing muses. So strange that the man would leave the Opera by a route he had likely taken only a few times in his miserable life, if at all.

Erik watched the mockery of a funeral procession through the auditorium: pallbearers carrying a man they had likely hated, so he could be thrown into the cold ground with no one there to mourn. Just as he deserved.

Christine's stomach drove her from her room. She didn't think she could keep much down but she hadn't had a morsel since well before last night's performance. She had no idea if Adèle even had food in their meager kitchen, but even just tea (or better, coffee) would help.

"There's my young lover awake at last," Adèle purred from her chair by the fire the moment Christine opened her door and Christine cursed internally. At least the older woman had a pot of something steaming in front of her. "I can see how you'd be tired after all that exertion."

Christine looked down to hide her blush as she rushed across the room for a cup. "I didn't realize we were that loud."

"You should know by now how thin these walls are," Adèle chuckled. "At least I don't have to ask you if it was good."

"You're going to anyway, aren't you?" Christine shot back as she took a seat. Maybe it was better to gossip with Adèle than hide in her room and wait for the hours to pass, thinking on her sins. Well, her other sins.

"Of course I am," Adèle said, pouring for her. Thank God, it was coffee. "So, how big is he?"

"Oh Jesus Christ in heaven, Adèle!" Christine yelped. "I – he—" Blushing again, she held up her hands coyly and Adèle's eyes went wide. Christine made a ring of her finger and thumb (since if she was to share this, she should at least be thorough) and Adèle squawked in glee.

"I might hate you!" Adèle chuckled. "How bad did it hurt taking all of that your first time, whenever that was?"

"Last night was the first time," Christine confessed softly, and Adèle stopped laughing. Christine took a deep sip of coffee, her pulse quickening as she remembered it. She'd heard it was supposed to hurt, but she had forgotten that fear last night as she had taken Erik into her and he'd made her feel so perfectly and wonderfully full. "It didn't hurt, except a bit at first, but it was nothing like I've been warned."

"He must have had you properly dripping then," Adèle remarked, looking at Christine over the rim of her cup. "Lucky girl. Did you take precautions?"

Christine nodded, recalling the shock of Erik withdrawing before his climax and the feel of his hot spend over her skin.

"Good girl. Keep it up. I won't have you ruined right when your career is getting started. And I hope you aren't too in love with this good genius of yours either. That would be the worst."

"No, I'm—" Christine protested but stopped. She didn't know. She didn't want to be. "I'm not."

"Good girl. Nothing more dangerous than that. Now tell me more about his nice big—" A frantic knock cut Adèle off. "Who could that be at this hour?"

Christine's stomach fell as Adèle went to the door. She had to compose herself for whatever news their visitor brought. She had to look casual and curious and not scared, so she called on everything she had learned on the stage to be an actress.

"Is Christine here?" Julianne's voice asked before the door was even open all the way.

"She is but—" Adèle barely spoke before Julianne forced her way into the room and ran to Christine.

"Are you alright?" Julianne demanded, grabbing Christine's hand. For her part, Christine tried to look worried and confused.

"I'm fine," Christine lied. "What's going on?"

"I should have come sooner," Julianne said, and Christine could see her eyes were bloodshot and her complexion ashen. "I was up all night calming Cécile down. We found him. She saw him first!"

"Saw *who*?" Adèle said, thankfully, so Christine did not have to speak. She was afraid if she opened her mouth, she'd be sick.

"Joseph Buquet!" Julianne exclaimed to Adèle then turned back to Christine. "He's dead."

"What?" Christine managed.

"He was hanged above the stage. In the flies," Julianne replied. "We found him. Jammes and I. Along with your pretty Vicomte! He was looking for you."

"Raoul was there?" Christine's head spun. What would Raoul think? What would he do, knowing a man had died in the Opera? What more peril would his imagination place her in now? And how could his assumption ever come close to the truth?

"He stayed to talk to the police," Julianne explained, swallowing.

"The police?" Christine was about to faint; she was sure of it.

"They have to be called, even for a suicide, I think." It was Adèle who said it and her voice was surprisingly calm.

"Or if it wasn't," Julianne corrected.

"What else could it be?" Christine listened to herself say. "You said he was hanged."

"Why would Buquet kill himself?" Julianne snapped back. "Christine, don't you understand? Everyone knows who Buquet crossed." Julianne looked frantically between Christine and Adèle, as if afraid to speak.

"If the Ghost killed Buquet, then I'll be the first to tell him thank you!" Adèle spat, and both Julianne and Christine looked at her in shock. "Do you know how many rats he forced himself on? There's a reason they stuck him in the flies, far away from the girls. But that didn't stop him. Don't you remember Rochelle? Emilie? Lucile?"

"He was a drunk and a brute," Christine agreed aloud. "He nearly did the same to me. And you."

"Christine!" Julianne gasped.

"Good riddance. The world is better without that monster in it," Adèle crowed.

You won't believe it the first time you tell yourself he deserved it. Erik's voice rang clear in her mind as Christine fought a shiver and made herself nod. "Good riddance indeed."

"Christine, if it was the Ghost, that means the Opera is more dangerous than we thought," Julianne said slowly, filling each word with meaning as her eyes bored into Christine. Her friend was scared for her, and for good reason. Christine was scared too, but somehow, she managed to shake her head.

"I doubt it was him," Christine replied slowly, hating that it was not a lie.

"And where were you last night?" Julianne asked in a pointed tone. "While your suitor was finding dead bodies."

"Why does that matter?" Adèle answered. "She was here. Having a lovely time with another suitor far less concerned with the police."

Christine threw her face into her hands, hiding from the shock in Julianne's eyes. "Adèle, for God's sake, not everyone needs to know my personal affairs."

"Then you and he should have kept it down. The whole street knows your affairs now," Adèle laughed. When Christine looked up, Julianne was staring at her with the deepest of concern and uncertainty.

"So, he is your lover," Julianne said quietly. "Your Angel of Music. After he left you sobbing in my house not two weeks ago!"

"I don't think you're one to judge others on who they fuck, Mademoiselle Bonet," Adèle reprimanded as Julianne ignored her in favor of keeping her eyes on Christine. They were full of disappointment.

"I am my own person. I can take care of myself and make my own decisions," Christine declared. Now that was a lie too. She wasn't her own, not after last night. Perhaps she never had been.

"Are you really?" Julianne asked back. "Because you don't behave like a woman acting in her best interest. From where I stand, I see a fool who cares more about her stupid career and spreading her legs for whoever is puppeteering her than the people getting hurt!"

"How dare—" Christine's hand flew back of its own accord, red-hot anger and shame blotting out her vision.

"That's enough!" Adèle bellowed, and Christine froze before the slap could launch. Suddenly she could see again, and there was nothing but horror in Julianne's eyes as tears filled Christine's.

"Like I said," Julianne growled through gritted teeth. "I don't know you anymore." Christine opened her mouth to protest again, but Julianne spun and stalked away before she could, slamming the door behind her.

"What on earth is she on about?" Adèle asked as Christine collapsed into her seat, hiding her face. "The girl needs to learn her place."

"I'm going out," Christine said suddenly, rushing to her room and grabbing her cloak. Or was it still Erik's? It didn't matter anymore.

"Are you sure?" Adèle asked, following Christine to the door. "You haven't even eaten."

"I'll get something somewhere else. I just need air." Christine stopped with her hand on the handle of the door, catching her breath.

"Will you be back here tonight or otherwise occupied?" Adèle asked, eyebrow high.

"I don't know. But don't wait for me." Christine said no more as she rushed onto the street. It would not be too hard to find Julianne, she could not have gone far. But what would be the point? There was nothing she could say to dissuade her about the danger Christine was in or the way she had changed. Because it was all true. Erik would never hurt her, she knew that, but what if he was right? What if he was cursed and she was already marked by it? What about those he would hurt for her?

She turned right, heading away from the Opera. She walked in the cold, as fast as she could, turning at random until she found herself at last on the banks of the Seine, near the gardens of the Tuileries. She took a place on a bench, among the barren trees that would not bloom for a month at least. It was freezing, the wind biting at her cheeks and the slate gray sky threatening snow above. She pulled Erik's dark cloak around her tighter, wondering if she would ever see spring again. Or if she deserved to. Still, she breathed deep, the winter air like ice in her lungs.

Raoul's mind was full of ghost stories as he wandered the streets. He didn't want to go home. What would he do there other than brood on phantoms and death? The Opera was haunted apparently, by a ghost who took a box and cursed prima donnas and spoke through the walls. He had listened to various workers relay the stories to the bored Inspector Mifroid, and while he had assured the man that he himself was a good Catholic who did not hold with superstition, Raoul could not deny that something was going on in the Opera. Christine had disappeared more than once. He had heard a voice in her room and found no one there. But how did that connect with her teacher, this *angel* who wished to seduce her, who proved as elusive as a ghost himself?

And now a man was dead. A man who, according to several of the mechanicals interviewed by Mifroid, had been a special enemy of the so-called Phantom. Had he been killed or was it, as Mifroid and the managers seemed bent on assuming, a suicide? Ghosts did not kill people because ghosts were not real. But there was something wrong at the Opera. Christine was in danger. Raoul knew it in his soul.

Christine, who he loved with his whole poor heart. Christine...who was walking towards him down the *Rue De Rivoli*. His heart leapt.

"Christine!" he cried, rushing to her. She looked at him as if she was seeing a ghost and barely moved when he embraced her. "Oh thank God, you're alright!"

"Why should I not be?" Christine stammered.

"You must not have heard. A man *died* in the Opera last night. I was the one to find the poor soul," Raoul exclaimed, watching Christine's face grow even paler, if that were possible.

"No, I heard. But I don't see what a suicide has to do with me," she muttered. Raoul took her hands. She had forgotten her gloves and through the leather of his own he could feel the cold in her skin.

"Christine, that place is dangerous!" Raoul exclaimed. "I knew it was corrupt and lascivious there, but I've heard such stories lately. The place you wish to make your career in cost a man his life, either through driving him mad or something else. You can't be there. You *shouldn't* be there."

"Where else would I go?" Christine asked with a hollow laugh. "I have worked my whole life for this career. I cannot just leave."

"You could marry me." Raoul said it before he could even consider the question, but the instant the words were past his lips, he knew nothing had ever felt so right. "You wouldn't need to work! I can provide for us, either through my family or the sea! We'll find a way and be together."

"Are you...*proposing*?" Christine asked, face slack. He hoped it was joy that moved her.

"I was ready to marry you six summers ago, and I still am," Raoul replied with a grin.

"You're mad!" Christine exclaimed, tearing her hands away. To his horror, she laughed, shaking her head. "Everyone has gone mad."

Raoul had never in his life moved so quickly from joy to utter despair and shame. "This is because of him, isn't it? Your mysterious angel."

"No, it's because we've barely spent a day together since we've met again!" Christine shrieked, another little knife in Raoul's heart. "You don't know me!"

"I know you better than anyone," Raoul said and did not let her laugh again. "I know your heart. I've seen it. I hear it when you sing. I know you are good and kind and pure and honest. Despite what that place tries to make you, that is who you are. That is the girl I love."

"You don't know me," she repeated in a whisper, her face a map of tragedy.

"I will ask of you one favor then," he said, holding back the tears stinging the corners of his eyes. "Tell me there is no hope for us, none at all, and that you would never marry me, so I can depart Paris with a clear conscience and broken heart."

"You're leaving?" Christine asked, now alarmed.

"I have been offered a commission on a voyage to the North Pole. It will take at least half a year."

"You could die," Christine said, and her worry gave Raoul some hope. "You want to take a voyage *that could kill you* because of *me*?"

"Tell me not to, Christine. Tell me to stay, *for you*." He was begging, but he kept his spine stiff. He would not bend and scrape for her love if it came down to it. He did still have some dignity left.

"You cannot ask this of me *now*," Christine said, cradling her head as she shook it. "Dear God, Raoul!"

"I'll give you time then," Raoul replied. "I'll wait for you. At the Madeleine! Tonight! I'll be there at five o'clock. If you don't come, then I'll have my answer."

Christine stared at him, her expression unreadable. Raoul could not bear it and he wanted nothing more than to kiss her, even if it was for the last time. But before he could she turned and ran, disappearing from his grasp once again. He hoped it was not forever.

Erik had meant to visit Shaya. He had known of his old friend and current adversary's flat on the *Rue de Rivoli* for many years now. It had been his full intention to see if the man was alive and remind him to keep better track of his dangerous property. But then he had seen the boy rushing towards something. And then he had seen them together.

To Christine's great credit, she had done nothing Erik would not expect of her. She had been polite and kind, though she had seemed overwhelmed and appalled in turn at whatever ridiculousness the little noble had been spewing. Erik had not been able to hear them, hidden in a gallery, behind a column across the wide road. Whatever the dandy said before leaving had left Christine shaking her head and aghast. Erik wanted to go to her, to hold her again. But it was bright day, even with no sun, and he was himself. He could never accost Christine in the street the way that boy had.

So he followed the boy instead. Luckily, the young man moved on foot, though he was spry and hasty. Erik was fast too, even moving in the shadows. He still had Christine's scarf from the night before to cover his face, and no one looked twice at him in the February cold. They were headed towards the *Faubourg Saint Germain,* Erik realized, where the "nobles" that had survived three revolutions and a century of disdain from the rest of France still lived in fading luxury. Of course the Chagny house was one of the grandest manors. There was a woman waiting on the steps, who had the same chestnut hair and strong features as the boy, and she was elegantly dressed. A sister perhaps? She ran to embrace the boy as Erik snuck closer to listen.

"—we've been worried sick!" she was saying.

"I'm fine, Sabine, I was—"

"At the Opera! Always the Opera!" The woman called Sabine cried. "Philippe's escapades are bad enough, but you're supposed to be the one who comes home! Were you off with that hussy you're obsessed with?"

"Don't talk that way about her!" the boy exclaimed, and when Erik peeked out from his hiding place behind a manicured bush, the poor young thing looked terribly offended at a slight on

Christine's virtue. The thought of how the boy might faint if he knew what Christine had done the night before made Erik smile.

"I'll talk about her any way I like!" the sister snapped. "She's not a good girl—"

"She might be your sister-in-law tomorrow!"

It was like a gunshot had gone off. The whole street was quiet as the boy's declaration sent a tremor of fear and rage through Erik. No. He did not mean that...

"What on earth are you talking about?!" Sabine demanded, to Erik's gratitude and relief.

"I asked her to marry me. Just now. I told her I'd meet her tonight at the Madeleine and if she doesn't come, I'm joining the expedition to the Pole."

"Are you out of your mind!" Sabine yelled. "That's not how you propose! And that – that's stupid and rash! I'm telling Philippe. He'll disinherit you if you marry that whore like this!"

"He can't stop me."

Erik flexed his hands. No, the boy's dolt brother could not stop him. But Erik could. He did not have the Punjab Lasso right now, but he did not need it. He had a loaded gun in his pocket. Wait. It was already in his hand. It would be so simple to do...to end it all right here. Erik pulled back the hammer, readying the weapon.

"She's not going to come! Your precious Christine will see this ploy for the foolish, selfish nonsense it is!"

Erik froze, the name of his beloved bringing him back to reason. He could not kill the boy, not if he hoped to keep her and protect her from more horrors. It was too rash and it was unneeded. He didn't have to worry about the boy, he just had to trust Christine. He did still trust her, after everything. Didn't he?

"Get inside, you idiot," Sabine was saying as Erik blinked back into reality.

"You'll see—" the boy began before the door shut. Erik stalked away, thanking whatever god or angel had put him in the right place at the right time to learn this. The same one perhaps that had put Christine in his path months ago and changed his life forever. He did not know, even now, if fate had been bestowing a blessing or a curse when he had first been given the chance to save her. Perhaps it was a matter of perspective. But he would not squander that blessing. Nor this one.

S haya was not sure if it was the smoke and noise of the tavern that made his head spin, or the lingering injury that he was quite tired of healing from. The favorite watering hole of the Opera denizens was particularly loud and crowded today, and that was not just Shaya's head playing tricks. Nor was the way that people looked at him and began to whisper when he entered and headed for the back to listen and linger.

"Bad business, if you ask me," someone muttered.

"He had it coming, however it happened," another person said, and Shaya's ear perked as he took a seat. He did not expect to be served and that was fine.

"He believed in hell, don't know why he would have gone that way," came another snippet of conversation. "He cared whether he was damned or not."

"You think a man who did what he did to Rochelle cared about his fucking immortal soul?" a woman asked. Were they discussing a suicide?

"He was killed, mark my words," a different voice said. Shaya abandoned all pretense of not listening and turned. "And we all know who did it. The Ghost tried to get him before. He was just finishing the job."

"Do you mean Joseph Buquet?" Shaya asked aloud as his heart began to pound. "Is Joseph Buquet the one who's dead?"

"That's what they say," the woman replied, sneering at Shaya. "Some dancer and her patron found him in the wee hours while they were sneaking off for a tryst."

"How?" Shaya's pockets suddenly felt terribly empty. Buquet had his gun. If he'd used it... "How did he die?"

"Hanged himself. Right up in the flies," a man answered.

"I told you, he didn't do it, the Ghost did!" the other said.

"Are you sure?" Shaya demanded, cornering the first man who had spoken. He was huge, Shaya realized too late. "Are you sure he was hanged?"

"I helped move the body. I'm fucking sure," the man growled, and Shaya stepped back. "Why you so interested, Turk?"

"Ain't you a friend of the Ghost's?" the woman asked as eyes all around Shaya narrowed. "That's what I hear."

"No. I'm—" Shaya stammered.

"You're not welcome here, friend of that demon's or no. This place is for good Christian folk." Shaya was not sure who said it. It didn't matter. He had heard everything he needed.

He ran from the tavern, his mind reeling even as he felt as if his head were about ready to split in two. Erik had killed again. He knew it in his soul. The day Shaya had feared and awaited for years had finally come.

Christine walked until her feet ached and her hands were numb from the cold. She wanted to lose herself or be lost. She had to keep moving or she knew she would fall and never move again. So she kept walking for hours. And yet she was not surprised to find herself on the *Boulevard Haussmann* looking at the back of the Palais Garnier when the sun began to sink lower into the sky.

Erik would be waiting for her soon. So would Raoul. Whose heart would she break? Whose life might she end? Would it feel easier the second time? Erik would know.

How could she consider going back to him now? After all he'd done, after the tragedy he'd laid at her feet. How could she consider leaving him behind, knowing the havoc that would follow if she did?

Her feet took her to the *Rue Scribe* automatically, her body drawn like a lodestone to where Erik would await her within the next hours. She could just go now, descend into the dark and find him. It would be easy. Everything with him was so easy when he was there, so simple in its own way. It had been the simplest thing in the world to give him her maidenhood, as if she had known from the beginning it would be him. It was the easiest decision, to call out Erik's name and push away the man that meant to kill him. She would do it again, she knew that too. She would save Erik and take him back to her bed, with no question.

I know you are good and kind and pure and honest. Raoul's words still echoed in her ears. What a fool he was. A beautiful fool who had offered her the perfect escape. With him, she could forget everything, start a new life and be that girl he loved. She would be safe, even if she would not truly be free.

Christine leaned against the cold stone of the Opera and watched the people coming and going along the street. Good Parisians on their way home or to a café or meeting those they loved. A young man strode confidently, in a rush. He had to be off to meet a paramour, for he carried a little bundle of flowers in his hand: white snowdrops and yellow daffodils. They had to be the first ones of the season, early even. The excitement on his face as he rushed towards his future reminded her so much of Raoul. The sun finally broke through the clouds to cast weak rays on her face. The sun Erik would never share, the light that Raoul offered her. There would be no grief with him.

What would Papa want for her? He had never approved of Raoul. But he had never wanted any man to take her away from him. He had kept her sheltered and secluded and told her again and again that love was poison as much as it was a joy. He had warned her to never love what she could lose. Maybe he had been right.

She closed her eyes and listened to the noise of the city. Horses. Trolleys. Vendors. Carriages. A million footsteps and voices. It was so loud up here, compared to Erik's world beneath her feet. A world full of soft silence and perfect song. She could almost hear it if she tried to listen. Erik's angelic voice, singing her the song of seduction he had crafted for her ears alone. She shivered and then blushed at how even that memory could awaken her desire.

She opened her eyes, looking at the people on the street. Normal, good people like Raoul who would call in a doctor or a priest if they knew the things she was thinking. The things she'd done. And even with her eyes open, the music was there, making her skin prickle and her stomach knot with anticipation. Once again, her feet moved of their own accord, towards the stable door and the darkness within that beckoned her with a song.

It was not in her memory. The shadows were singing for her in the waking world. Erik was calling her to him.

Was Raoul waiting already? Was he kneeling in the church, pleading Christine would come or praying for her soul? How could he know that a dark angel had that soul already, bound to him in a contract she had signed long ago? She walked with steady purpose through the stables, following the song, the sun at her back, until she came to the edge of the shadows. The limit of the living world. Erik opened his eyes so that they shone like twin torches in the dark before he took her hand and pulled her from the light.

His voice acted on her like a drug as she followed him, dulling every sense and thought but the ones he wished her to have. He led her down, deep into the earth where his kingdom went on forever, his voice drowning out the whispers of the ghosts that shared it. His hand was as cold as hers where he held it, but together, they grew warm as he guided her home. To the house beyond his Lake Avernus, a palace or a tomb for a dark king.

He pulled her close, her back to his chest, as soon as the door was shut behind them, and he touched her. She nearly collapsed at the pleasure just that gave her. He pawed at her breasts as he snaked his hand around her waist to keep her close and upright as he sang his lust and love into her ear. She helped him to undress her, impatient to give him access to her skin. Soon enough, her clothes were in a puddle at her ankles as his hand found her wet sex between her thighs.

Ecstasy sang through her blood as he touched her in all the places his voice ignited, bringing her nearly to the peak right there. His voice was unquestionable. It was the whole world, full of love and beauty, and his long fingers were on her and inside her, and she was his instrument to command. And so she came, gasping, with her lover holding her tight as his song crescendoed in her soul.

But it was not enough. She knew there was more and she could feel his desire hard and hot against her back. She was hungry for it.

She kissed him when she turned her to him, but not his lips. She wanted him to keep singing the same way she wanted him to be deep inside her again, driving away the world above and its pain. Her naked body was trembling from the climax as she kissed his throat and she tore at his cravat. She kissed the scars on his chest as she pushed off his jacket and shirt.

"No mask," she commanded, and with shaking hands, he complied, his voice quieting as the mask clattered to the floor.

"Keep going. Keep singing." Again he obeyed, song filling her soul and making her brave. Or mad. Maybe there was no difference.

The first feel of his cock in her hand was perfect, and Erik's voice faltered for the first time she had ever heard as she gripped his rigid length. She stroked him again and was delighted as his music became a cry of need. But her cunt was empty and she ached to be filled.

"Take me to your bed," she ordered and before she could blink, he lifted her into his arms and carried her into his chamber, where a few candles burned low. She kissed his bare cheek, not afraid of the revealed wreck of his dead face. But he flinched away, hiding himself as he sang against her breast. He sang to her as they fell into the sheets, sang to her as he turned her onto her belly then lifted her by her hips so she was bent over before him. And he sang, low and gentle, as he pushed himself inside her and she keened in slavish pleasure.

Did the song continue as he fucked her? She didn't know. It was there, in her head and her spirit as she gasped and cried with each thrust as Erik drove his cock into her, penetrating her more deeply than she had ever imagined possible. He held her tight, his fingers digging into her hips as he claimed her. Her nipples grazed the bed, her hands tangled in the sheets, and she had no thoughts or needs beyond now, beyond him, beyond the way she had become his music, his rhythm, his alone.

She came again, lights exploding behind her eyes as her body bucked and writhed, before she collapsed, sated and limp. She whimpered as he withdrew from her and ground himself against her back before he trembled above her and she felt the hot stain of his climax over her skin.

As much as she adored the music, so did she adore the quiet after, as Erik pulled her to his chest and settled them among his sheets below the bower of ebony branches. She sighed as he kissed her lips at last, so glad to be free for a while. He kissed her long and deep and slow, as gentle as night.

At last, she opened her eyes to look on his deathly face, half hidden by his dark hair, a breath from hers on the pillow.

"You should let me cut this for you," she whispered, catching a long lock between her fingers and pushing it away. "Soon you won't be able to see your piano keys."

"Can I trust you with scissors?" he asked back, with something like a smile.

"I don't know." Christine touched his cheek. If felt so strange against her palm, and yet it was already so familiar. Just a face, really. Nothing more. "You came for me early."

"I was worried." She could see the sincerity in his eyes, and the anxiety. Did he trust her at all? Should he?

"Raoul asked me to marry him," she said before she could think better of it. Erik winced and nodded.

"I know." Of course, he knew. The Angel was always watching. And yet she still needed to confess.

"I've seen him twice outside of the Opera. We had supper the night I went to see Carlotta at *La Grenouille*. Then after Monday's rehearsal, Adèle tricked me and I saw him again, briefly. But he kissed me. I should have told you."

"It doesn't matter now," Erik replied, placing his hand against her cheek, echoing her position. "I knew you would come back. I knew you'd come home."

"I have to, don't I?" Christine breathed, closing her eyes and noting that now, his hand was so warm and alive against her skin. Such a strange thing, here in the underworld. "I'm bound here. To this. To you. Like Persephone. For I have tasted the food of the dead."

The church was cold. Just another reason to hate this place, Raoul thought, as the chill seeped into his bones as he waited in the stiff pew. The cold did not dull his shame or his heartbreak. He glared at the altar, his disgrace turning to anger as he looked at the statue of Mary Magdalene. He'd always hated this place for how pagan it looked, and because he did not think it was right to so venerate a whore. Though it was a fitting place for a woman like Christine to worship, if she even prayed.

"Let's go, little brother."

It did not surprise him to hear Philippe's voice. He looked up at his brother with a frown and followed him down the empty aisle, casting one last scowl to the altar over his shoulder.

"Let's get you a drink," Philippe sighed as he led Raoul to their carriage. There was pity in his brother's voice and face as they rattled through the streets, and Raoul hated it. What a fool Philippe must think him. What an idiot he was, to sit in the pew in the sight of God for hours, waiting for a woman he should have known would never come. He'd done it all right too. He'd made his confession beforehand and said his Hail Marys and Our Fathers so that he could enter his new life with an unburdened soul. And then he'd waited and waited, his parents' wedding bands in his breast pocket, like a lead weight.

"Well, say it," Raoul grumbled as the carriage turned. "Tell me how you warned me."

"It wouldn't be sportsmanlike," Philippe replied but he couldn't hold back his smirk. "Even though I did."

"Maybe he kept her away," Raoul lamented. "It's possible."

"And it's possible she was offended by a rushed proposal and elopement," Philippe said. Raoul could tell he was actually trying to be kind. "But you must consider the possibility that she was never yours to win or save."

"No," Raoul lamented as he glowered out the dark window. "Her soul belongs to an angel." Raoul laughed softly to himself, bitter and cold.

"What's so funny?"

"That an angel has damned her," Raoul replied.

13. Entwined

Erik didn't want to leave her. There was so much music in his mind, ideas itching on the tips of his fingers ready to burst forth from his piano or scrawled on the page, but Christine Daaé's head was on his arm and she was warm and real against him. He could not leave her. He never wanted to be parted from this, from this moment in the quiet of the morning (at least, he thought it was morning, it was always hard to tell down here and he could not move to see his clock without disturbing her). Even when she stirred against him and opened her eyes, there was a pang of regret in his heart for the end of the peace and safety of having her asleep against him.

"I didn't expect you to be here," Christine said groggily, rubbing her eyes as she looked up at him. There was not a trace of fear or disgust as she took in the awful sight of his face.

"Why not?" he asked, pushing the loose hair from her face.

"You're usually gone when I wake up, off to compose or create."

"I considered it, but I'd rather be here," Erik confessed. "I didn't want you to be alone."

"Are you worried for me?" Now that she was awake, the sadness had returned to her eyes, settling over her like a fog that Erik wanted nothing more than to dispel.

"Yes. Very much so." He ran his thumb along her cheek, and the faintest of smiles warmed her face. "I'm going to take care of you today. No lessons. No worries about anything from up there."

"Who would believe it? The fearsome Opera Ghost clucking over me like a mother hen."

"You know I came close to being named for a chicken instead of a cat," Erik said softly, and her smile spread. "I befriended Erik the cat because he was more willing to be caught than the chickens. And he pecked less. But I liked them too." A soft laugh bubbled in Christine's throat. "Can you imagine? The fearsome Opera Ghost as you say, with a foul-tempered roster named Olaf as a namesake."

At that, Christine laughed, truly, the sound as perfect as an aria, as joy brightened her face and Erik's heart. She was the most beautiful thing he'd ever seen.

"There you are," Erik said, twining his fingers into her hair. It was bliss when she kissed him, dizzying and perfect as always. He lost himself in it, his mind clouding with love and desire as he let his lips trail down to her jaw, her neck, her ears, and her collarbone.

"Erik," she sighed as he kissed down her chest, nipping and licking at the tender rise of her breast and taking her nipple into his mouth. "Don't stop."

"Never," he whispered in return, turning his attention to her other breast and making her cry out as he grazed the taught nipple with his teeth. It amazed him, how good it felt to touch and be touched by her. He loved the way she responded to him; how her body arched as her legs spread and he took his place between them. He was growing hard, but that could wait. They had time, all the time in the world, and he was going to take advantage. She was wet and open when his fingers found their way between her folds while his mouth moved past her ribs. He loved her this way, when even the barest touch to her cunt would make her gasp. He loved that the first swipe of his tongue made her buck, her hips chasing him as he teased her. He loved the taste of her, of honey and spice.

"May I make you come, before I fuck you?" he whispered against her thigh, holding her legs open and massaging the soft base of her ass. She made a noise of shock that dissolved into a moan as he lapped at her then pulled back. "Perhaps more than once? And then you'll finish on my cock, if you like."

"Yes, oh God," Christine replied, her voice strangled as Erik set to his task.

He knew what she liked, but his knowledge was hardly comprehensive, and he was, as always, an eager and thorough student. He knew that if he wanted her to come fast, it was a matter of focusing right above her entrance, on the stiff protrusion of nerves that was like a lightning rod for her pleasure. He sucked there and listened to how she keened, noted how when he touched her just right, inside, her hips shuddered and her body would begin to shake as she chased her pleasure. Her breath sped up as she trembled on the edge as he filled her with his fingers and tongue, and imagined how sweet that tightness would feel on his aching cock.

"Erik, please!" she cried. What was she begging for? She had to know by now he'd give her anything. He sped up the ministrations of his tongue in response and there, right there, he'd found it. She arched and shook, riding the waves of the orgasm he drew from her like a perfect crescendo.

"Good," Erik purred against her belly. "Again."

"I don't know if I can," Christine stammered, but he did not relent. It was easy, bringing her back to that peak, when she was so sensitive that just his tongue inside her made her scream and tremble again. He loved it. He loved the wet stain on his mouth from her arousal, he loved how pliant and boneless she was when he pulled her down the bed and lifted her hips so she could sheath his cock while he knelt on the bed.

"And now, one more," he commanded as he proceeded to piston into her, rapid and fierce.

"I – I can't," she whimpered, but already he could see her signs. Her breasts were flushed, her thighs were a vise around his waist. Her hands were tangled in the sheets and her eyes were shut tight. He was glad of that. He didn't want her to see him and have the horror of his face taint this moment. All she had to do was feel.

"You can. For me."

She was so tight around him that he was ready to spill and join her in ecstasy, but the memory of his own face that stayed his pleasure. It was enough to feel her quivering around him as her cries rose in rhythm with his thrusts and he worked his thumb above where he was lost inside her. And then suddenly she was still, her back rising, her breath caught on an inhale.

"*Erik*," she gasped as her body undulated in a wild sort of dance, arching and curling back in on herself as her cunt grasped tight on his cock. It was the hardest thing in the world to pull himself from her, to not live in that perfect pleasure, but he managed it just in time. He watched his seed spill over her thighs as ecstasy blurred his vision before he collapsed beside her, the world nothing but pleasure and light and sound.

"Jesus, my ears are ringing from that."

Erik blinked, pushing up from the mattress. He could hear ringing too. "That's not your ears." The rhythmic peal of a bell was unmistakable, now that he was paying some goddamn attention. "Fuck."

"Erik, what's that sound?"

"Someone is on the lake. Or in it," Erik answered as he sprang from the bed. Where the hell were his trousers?

"What do you mean? Who could—"

"It's the Daroga," Erik answered and looked to see Christine had gone pale as he tugged on his clothes.

"How do you know?"

"No one else would be stupid enough to come down here or angry enough at me to risk my traps."

"Your *traps?*" Christine echoed in horror.

"I'm going to get him out, don't worry," Erik replied as he rushed to the door. "Stay here."

"Absolutely not!" Christine cried, following after, wrapped in a sheet. "He could—"

"He won't hurt me. Especially after I save his goddamn life again." Erik didn't bother with too many buttons for his shirt. It wouldn't make a difference in the water. "I'll be fine. I promise."

Erik didn't dare look back at her as he rushed from his home or think of what might happen if he broke that promise. He could hear the splashing and swearing the second he exited his house.

"Erik!" Shaya screamed as he breached the surface, right in the little patch of light from the grate up to the street. Beside him, the boat had capsized, overturned by the traps Erik had set for anyone who dared to use the craft and not follow the correct route. Those same traps now ensnared Shaya to pull him down to the depths.

The water was as cold and dank as Erik remembered when he dove in, thick with silt and grime and who knew what else. He swam to the boat as fast as he could, his muscles screaming. With a deep, angry breath he dove below the surface. It was almost impossible to see in the water, but the muffled, bubbling sound of screams and struggle guided him. He freed Shaya's wriggling foot from the trap and hauled him to the surface. Hanging onto the overturned boat as a support, he began to swim to the shore as Shaya gurgled and spat out fetid water beside him.

"I told you to never try to cross my lake, you ninny," Erik hissed as he pulled himself to the narrow shore, dragging the Daroga after him. Shaya coughed up another lung full of water and glowered as Erik righted his boat. "You couldn't just lurk and sulk about my opera like usual? You had to risk your life to pay me a visit?"

"Joseph Buquet!" Shaya finally yelled. Erik turned with a defiant challenge in his eyes. He knew they were glowing, and he saw the horror in Shaya's face when he realized Erik was unmasked. "Why did you kill Joseph Buquet, you monster?"

"I was under the impression the man's death was a suicide," Erik answered lightly, knowing it would annoy Shaya more. "Do you honestly think I'm stupid enough to kill a man and leave his body hanging above my stage?"

"If you were sending a warning! The man crossed you! You tried to kill him before, when he saw your real face, and again when Carlotta sent him after your little soprano!" Shaya went on and Erik tilted his head in interest.

"And how did you know about that?" Erik stepped towards Shaya. He knew he had to look especially horrifying, dripping and unmasked in the dark.

"He told me," Shaya replied, but he was holding something back.

"And then what did he do? How did Joseph Buquet end up with your little pistol in his possession?" Erik asked, advancing further and watching Shaya flinch. "I have it by the way, safe where it won't hurt me."

"He knocked me out," Shaya confessed. "Nearly killed me."

"You should be thanking me. The Opera is a safer place without Joseph Buquet in it and you know it. And I should be quite annoyed at you for arming that fiend."

"So you admit it."

"I admit nothing but that I defended myself," Erik hissed, leaning close so Shaya could see the same face he believed condemned Buquet. "If this is the great crime you have been waiting for me to commit, I must extend my sympathies for your disappointment."

Shaya glowered at him. "I can go to the police. I'll tell them everything."

"Really? Will you tell the police about the *ghost* that only you and Buquet saw? Will you tell them how Buquet beat you and stole your weapon? It sounds like you're the one with the motive to kill. A Muslim foreigner with a grudge against a God-fearing Frenchman."

Shaya seethed as he stared, and Erik knew he had him. As always, the Daroga was harmless.

"In fact, who is to say poor Joseph would have met the fate he did if he hadn't had your gun to aim in the wrong direction," Erik went on, singsong and self-satisfied. "His blood is on your hands, as much as mine, Daroga."

"Fuck you, Erik."

"So, we remain, as always, in our stalemate. Perhaps it is time for you to look for a new game somewhere else." Erik turned away.

"What about Christine Daaé?" Shaya snapped, as if it was the ace up his sleeve and Erik froze.

"What about her?" Erik asked over his shoulder.

"She had something to do with all of this, your little pet," Shaya spat, growing bold at Erik's discomfort. "She's made you a fool, you know. Ever since you've become obsessed with her you've been rash, sloppy, erratic. The managers. Carlotta. Now Buquet. Will she be next? What will you do to her when she truly learns exactly what you are and runs for her life?"

Erik was sure Shaya was not prepared for him to laugh, for the man looked truly horrified when the sound echoed over the lake's murky waters. "You have no idea, Daroga."

"What does that mean?" Shaya demanded.

Erik gave a low bow. "You were always a better spy than you were a detective, I invite you to use either skill to discover what Christine is to me, and I to her. She knows everything," he intoned as he rose and backed away. "Now go home to Darius before you catch a cold."

"I'll be watching you! And her!" Shaya yelled into the emptiness Erik left behind before he turned and rushed away. It would take him a long time to find the way to the daylight world without a light and without knowing the way, only his hate and rage to warm him.

Erik smiled to himself, amused by the idea that he was the one who had someone waiting for him in the dark. And indeed Christine rushed to him the moment he stepped inside, dragging him to the fire to inspect him.

"I told you I'd be fine," Erik said, amazed by her concern.

"You're soaked. These will need to be replaced," Christine countered, fussing over his bandages.

"I barely need them now, we can—"

"What you need is a damn bath. You smell like a swamp," Christine snapped and pulled him by his wrist to her room, much to Erik's shock and confusion. Said confusion remained as she led him to the bath chamber and began to fill the copper tub.

"What are you doing?"

"What does it look like? I'm drawing us a bath."

"Us?" It was remarkable how she could surprise him. He noted the way she avoided his eyes as she returned to strip off his soaked shirt, then the bandages that concealed the place where he had taken a knife for her without a second thought. Her fingers lingered over the wound.

"I was worried he would hurt you," Christine whispered.

"Shaya's not like that. He believes in justice and honor and other such dreams." That earned him a glare and he could see the tears threatening in Christine's eyes.

"What if it hadn't been him?" she asked in a near whisper.

What if it had been that boy come to save her, was what she meant. *What if it was your rival? Would you kill him?*

"You need to stop worrying about every possible disaster. You'll go mad that way," Erik told her gently, pushing away a dark lock of hair from her face.

"Should I be like you and never think of the future then?" Christine asked back with a huff as she unbuttoned his trousers and let them and the blanket around her fall to the floor.

Erik followed without resistance as she led him to the water. It felt entirely natural to sink into the bath with her behind him, her legs wrapped around him, as warm and welcoming as the water. He let her guide him, let her wet his hair and touch the scars along his back, soft and gentle. Erik had been touched before Christine, but never cared for, not like this. She soaped his hair and skin and massaged his shoulders and arms when she was done. Soon he was as limp and relaxed as he ever had in his life. Utterly defenseless and at her mercy.

"How are you possible, Christine Daaé?" Erik sighed in contentment. He deserved none of this. He deserved to waste away in solitude, not have an angel wash away his sins.

"Sometimes I can't believe that you're real either, that the angel I was sent is...so many things I never could have expected," Christine replied, pulling him back against her chest and wrapping her arms around him. "And sometimes it's the world up there that doesn't feel real. I guess that's why you came here. Why you don't think about the future. There's no tomorrow, down here. And no yesterday. There is only the night that never ends."

It made something ache in him, to hear the resigned sadness in her voice as she described the kingdom in which she now took refuge.

"Even down here you can't hide forever," Erik murmured, his head against her breast.

"But right now I can," she whispered back.

The water around them was as smooth as glass as the silence stretched into the shadows.

No cab would stop for Shaya, so he was left with the indignity of sloshing down the streets of Paris in the snow, feeling his soaked clothes freezing against his skin. He had been mad to challenge Erik in his home. But what else was he to do?

"Allah be merciful," Darius sighed when he saw his errant master shivering at the threshold. "What have you done now?"

"I went on the lake. I was shouting for him, but he didn't hear. Then the boat went over," Shaya replied as Darius helped him strip off his sodden jacket and vest and led him towards the fire.

"You smell like the sewer."

"And I look like a fool," Shaya grumbled as Darius wrapped him in a rough woolen blanket. "What else was I to do?"

"Perhaps *not* go face that creature alone?" Darius shot back.

"I would not put you in that danger," Shaya sighed. He had already ruined Darius' life enough. "Erik was right. I have no allies. No one to help. You're the only person I have left that cares if I live or die."

"Some days more than others," Darius muttered back.

"This all comes down to Christine Daaé, I know it," Shaya groaned. "I have to find out what he's done to her. She knows something but she can't know *everything*. If he's done to her what he did to him..." The memory of Ramin's face – his dead face in the little house he had run to with Erik – flashed into Shaya's mind and pain stabbed his heart.

"Do you honestly think any woman would willingly whore herself to that thing? Even for the career she has?"

Shaya shuddered, recalling the horrific sight of Erik unmasked at the edge of the lake. Shaya had barely been able to keep his eyes on the man and he had seen the abomination unmasked before. "No. There has to be some other explanation."

"If Daaé is the key, perhaps the time has come to recruit help."

"And where will I find such help?"

"You know, you always mock me for reading the society gossip in the papers," Darius remarked with a smirk.

"What does that have to do with Erik?"

"It has to do with Mademoiselle Daaé and that young, brave Vicomte who continues to pursue her. His infatuation is the talk of the town. Well, some quarters of it." Darius turned and somehow even his back was smug as he began preparing tea.

"You think he could be the key to saving her? And drawing Erik out?" Shaya muttered as he considered the strategy. Of course, the young man was still interested in Christine. And he had no idea the danger he put himself and all those he loved in by pursuing her.

"Erik and that woman are tangled up together. That boy could be the one to tear them apart if you use him correctly."

"He just needs the right guidance," Shaya whispered to himself with a smile. "And he could save us all."

Christine did not think she could call herself happy. It was wrong to be *happy* after what she had done and seen and learned after *Rigoletto*. But she was content at least, wrapped once more in her lover's strong arms and dark sheets, looking up at the carved branches of his curious bed. She felt distant from the pain of the world above, music filled her mind and soul as Erik hummed an old Irish tune, and her desire was sated. It was close enough to happiness, for now, and perhaps even that was more than she deserved.

It had been three days since he had brought her below. Three days of her angel seeking to bring her whatever joy, distraction, or pleasure he could conjure to lift her spirits. Erik had brought tears to her eyes when he played for her, from Bach's cello sonatas to Romani tunes on the flute and fiddle. He had composed for her too; and astounded her when he had asked for her help and critique of his work. They had played together, and it had been exquisite to share music with him in such a way.

He had read to her: poetry and books and plays from across the world and told her stories he knew by heart in exchange for the same from her. He probably knew every story she told or read to him from the old books she had carried with her since childhood, but it was still a pleasure to share them with him. They had played chess and laughed because Erik was terrible at it after years with no opponent. Erik had endeavored each day to make Christine smile and laugh, dispelling her melancholy as often as possible, as much as he had sought to do the same by bringing her pleasure whenever he could.

It made Christine feel like a madwoman to think of how only weeks ago she had feared his touch. Now she craved it in every way. Tonight he had laid her out on the bed while he stood, fucking into her with force that made her scream with each thrust. His cock finding places so deep within her as he held her by the hips that she feared she would crumble. But she hadn't. She had come for him, as he always made sure she did. She had wailed his name and lost herself, only to return to reality and find that once again he had withdrawn and watched his seed spurt over her belly. She could still feel it now, the place where he had marked her again.

"You look pensive," Erik said gently, bringing Christine back from the memory. "What are you thinking about?

Christine smirked rather than blush. "It's entirely unladylike."

"Now I must know."

"I was thinking about how you never come while you're inside me," Christine said casually, looking up in time to look at Erik's bare face. It was much easier – now that he had stopped wearing the mask around her almost entirely – to tell what he was feeling. Right now it was scandalized.

"I-I..." he began to stammer, and Christine was reminded of what a pleasure it was to fluster him.

"I did warn you."

Erik gave her a gentle scowl. "I thought it would be clear. I don't want to defile and ruin you like that."

"As if it's different for me to have your seed on my skin than inside me?" It was strange, the way he still treated her like some pristine, distant icon.

"I meant I wouldn't want to condemn you to carry a child with my cursed blood," Erik replied quietly.

"Oh. Yes. That," she muttered, hiding her embarrassed face against his chest again. "That does make sense. I guess." She wanted to say she didn't think he was cursed, not the way he believed himself to be, but it was a useless argument.

"It would be a disaster," Erik went on, and the idea of how a child would change her life – their lives – indeed did make her skin crawl with fear and anxiety so she nodded in agreement. "Your career would be ruined too."

"My career," she scoffed. "You know, the more I sing on that stage, the less enchanted I am by the idea of a great *career*."

"What do you mean?" She could feel him peering at her curiously, but she didn't want to meet his eyes for this confession.

"What is a career in opera, anyway? It's not as if I could sing across Europe or the world like Patti or Jenny Lind. I couldn't sing anywhere without you. And even here, it's all so empty, all that applause from people who wouldn't deign to smile at me in the street if we met. The joy I find in the music all comes from you."

"I thought it made you happy," Erik said softly, and Christine finally dared to look at him. "All the glory. You deserve it."

"Don't tell me that you enjoy sharing me with the world," Christine countered and Erik gave a nod of agreement. "I'm not saying I want to give up, just that for me the music is more than my career. It's you. And I do think you'd enjoy sharing me with a child even less."

"I do think you'd be a good mother, if that's worth anything," Erik said, and it did make her smile, even as it also made her sad. Once again, she laid her head against his heart, listening to its steady rhythm as visions of the past filled her head. A warm smile, a sunny field of yellow flowers. And a grave.

"It scares me, you know, not being a mother, but giving birth. It killed my own mother."

"I didn't know that," Erik said, soft and careful.

"I remember the day. It was the end of summer, when the world had started to turn orange and gold. It was so beautiful. I was playing outside and I remember thinking it would be so wonderful when I could play with my little brother or sister. They had names already picked. Nils if it was a boy, Aud if it was a girl. For my grandmother. And then I heard my mother screaming and...I knew something was wrong." Erik's arm tightened around her. "I wish I remembered her better. I wish I had taken the time to learn from her more. Before she was gone. Papa never talked about her, after that day. He never mentioned the little brother that died with her. We buried them in the same grave and left Sweden and everything that would remind him of what he'd lost behind. Everything but me."

"At least you still had him."

"I had part of him," Christine replied. "Part of him went into that grave too. He never talked about her, but he talked about love. How it was never worth it to love something you might lose. That's why he worked so hard to keep me close to him, even when I should have been growing up. He refused to lose me. And when I lost him..."

Christine closed her eyes on the tears that were suddenly there and closed her mouth to hold back the confession that she knew her father was right. It was stupid and useless to love, an invitation to pain and loss. She had contemplated that, and her father, often in the past few days. Especially after the nightmares where Buquet's dangling body bore Erik's face.

"Tell me a memory about your parents that brings you joy," Erik said, pulling her back from the abyss of grief once again. "Don't only think of the pain."

"We'd go to the woods, in the summer, when the lingonberries and blueberries were ripe everywhere. We'd eat them right there, and they were so sweet when they had been in the sun. I remember the mess I made, all over my pretty white dress, so Mama wiped her hands on Papa's shirt so we'd be even. We laughed so much."

"Do you like the woods?" Erik asked fondly, and Christine opened her eyes to look up to the dark arbor of carved branches above them.

"I do. And I have gathered that you do too, given your bed is a forest."

"I've always loved the wild places of the world," Erik replied, his voice a low rumble in his chest as Christine rested against it. "Ever since I can remember, I'd run off into the woods. When I was older, living with the Romani, I'd do the same. I'd spend days in the forests and mountains where I never saw another soul and I could take off my mask without fear. No one screamed or ran away from me there."

"You felt safe."

"I wanted to run to the woods when my mother died, but they stopped me," Erik confessed softly. "She loved green growing places too. I think she would have gone there."

"I ran to the sea, when Papa died," Christine whispered back.

"I miss the sea," Erik said to her surprise. "My little lake is not the same."

"What about the woods?" She asked, her eyes beginning to droop with sleep. "Is this enough or do you have woods to go to like you have your stars?"

"I..." Erik began but hesitated. Had she been more awake, it would have concerned her. "I go to the *Bois de Boulogne*," Erik told her after a long pause, and she found herself laughing softly.

"Do you watch the races at Longchamps?"

"I go at night, when all the respectable people have abandoned it and I can pretend it's a real forest, not a park in a city. It can be quite convincing in the moonlight. I can show you if you don't believe me."

"Later this week, you'll take me. I'll need the distraction after going back into the real world," Christine muttered and stifled a yawn.

"That's not the real world, remember?" Erik said, his voice lilting, hinting at a song in his mind. "This is the real world. Right here. It's the only one that matters." And then he began to sing, and nothing mattered to Christine but that.

S haya found it surprisingly easy to get into rehearsals, as if Erik had left the doors of the Opera unlocked and open to him. Indeed it was possible that he had. Even so, Shaya did his best to remain hidden and unseen. A life as a detective and a spy made it second nature to him.

The talk of the Opera today was unsurprisingly about related topics: Joseph Buquet, Christine Daaé, and how the Ghost was part of their stories. It was accepted that the Ghost had been involved with Buquet's demise, but the chatter was that Buquet had brought that revenge on himself. And that the Opera was better for it. All of this Shaya knew, but it was still interesting to hear how the story evolved.

"I heard Carlotta fainted when she heard," someone said in a hall as Shaya listened.

"I heard she was already mad and they're hauling her off to an asylum any day now," someone countered. Shaya shivered at that idea and moved on. What would Erik think of sending a woman to the madhouse, if indeed it was true?

"I heard Robert Rameau is going to propose to Daaé any day now!" went another conversation among the *petit rats* as they passed in the hall.

"I heard the Vicomte de Chagny already asked – and she refused him!" another said.

Shaya had been unsuccessful in tracking down the young Vicomte. It was not as if he could simply go to the manor in the *Faubourg Saint Germain* and present his card. What sort of conversation would they have in a polite parlor as he told the young man that the woman he loved had possibly fallen into the clutches of the most depraved and hideous man in Paris?

No, Shaya needed to know if he could trust the boy and his love for Daaé before acting and proceed carefully. A man like Raoul de Chagny would never resign to be led or advised. He had to think any rescue or strike was his own plan. Or that there was no choice in the matter.

Shaya found himself in the wings, hiding among ropes and curtains, his eyes upon the woman his reflections continued to return to. Christine Daaé was, as she had been for weeks, free and unharmed. Yes, there was something about her that was distracted, even melancholy perhaps, but it went away when she sang. Even Shaya could tell that Daaé's talent was remarkable, and perhaps only he could hear the influence of the master that had taught her.

As if summoned by the thought, Shaya saw the shadow out of the corner of his eye. Like a bird flitting through the thicket, it was hard to see but if Shaya looked carefully... Yes. There it was. A shadow above the stage, watching Daaé's rehearsal with the orchestra as eagerly as Shaya.

Shaya's heart surged with fear and hope as he watched Erik watch Christine. The Phantom's shadow moved slowly through the flies, but he grew ever closer to Daaé, the proverbial moth to the flame. By the time Daaé's portion was done, Erik was close enough that Shaya could make out the white of his mask. And he saw when the fiend descended behind a scenery flat and into a trap door down on the stage. A trap door that remained open.

Maybe he was distracted. Maybe listening to his pupil's incredible display had left him in some sort of haze. Why Erik had made the error mattered not, only that Shaya was there to exploit it. He followed like a shadow himself, keeping back and staying quiet as he tracked Erik through the warren of discarded sets, past a castle wall and a prop bed wreathed in silken flowers. And then to a wall made to look like an Indian marketplace, a set from *Le Roi de Lahore*, if Shaya was not mistaken. It was there Erik paused, and Shaya hid himself again, peering around a flat to watch as Erik knelt by the market scene...and pushed a panel so that it opened. Shaya held back his gasp of shock as Erik went through the wall and the panel closed behind him.

"Now I have you," Shaya whispered, unable to control his grin. Not only would Daaé be the key to destroying Erik somehow, but now Shaya knew exactly where to find him when it was time.

E rik leaned back against the smooth surface of the wall, thankful for the darkness. He could almost hear Shaya's thoughts as he scurried off to scribble notes in his little black book. If he wasn't prohibited from liquor by his faith, Erik was sure the man would be on his way to have a drink. Or maybe he'd do something else to celebrate. He'd never known the Daroga to take a lover or even enjoy sweets, but he had to have some pleasure in life. Life's pleasures were there to be enjoyed, were they not?

Erik smiled at the edge of his mask as he stood straight. It was odd to have it on again after so many days with the woman who insisted he didn't need it. And he believed her. At least, in their part of the house he believed her. He needed it here, in his secret forest, even in the pitch-black dark, he could feel the mirrors waiting with his reflection to remind him of what he was. He did feel a vague sense of guilt as he triggered the mechanism to leave the one room in his house he had never shown Christine. And never would.

As far as Christine knew, the door he had just stepped through was nothing more than a wall to the left of the organ. The same way the Daroga believed what he had discovered was a secret way into Erik's home, the path he would take when the time finally came to rescue the princess from the evil monster. They had no idea of the horrors Erik and the communards had built. And that he had kept and added to when he was driven back into the dark.

Erik drifted to the shelf of his music, trailing his fingers over Cecilia's keys and then up to the great red score that waited among his other compositions like an open wound. What would Shaya think of his *Don Juan Triumphant*? There was no reason Christine ever had to know about what was in there either. She had never asked about it. Hiding it was not a lie. Just like showing Shaya the second, secret path to his home was not a death sentence.

Erik turned away from the unfinished work, looking instead at the pile of music that had been accumulating on the piano over the last few days. Music he had made for and with Christine. That music of love and passion had been pouring out of him since she had kissed him, so much sweeter than his Don Juan's songs of vengeance and hate. There was no need for such darkness, not while she was his. The only reason anyone, be it Shaya or that terrible boy, would ever hear his masterpiece would be if they tried to take her away.

Raoul was at the Opera under protest. He had no desire to see *Rigoletto* again. He did not want to be reminded in any way of Christine's beauty, neither her face nor her voice. He did not want to think about how he had spent the week since her rejection, throwing himself into the whirlwind of pleasure offered by Paris. Or trying to. Philippe's efforts on that front had been uninspiring, as Raoul resented brothels and cabarets. He didn't want to *pay* to forget Christine. And so he'd shirked his brother and Antoine to find Vincenzo and their sailor friends in Montmartre.

The first night had been a celebration, ostensibly, of Raoul's official enrollment in the North Pole expedition. He'd drunk himself to delirium and let things be done to him that he had only ever allowed at sea. Or the ache in his ass the next morning told him he had; he couldn't quite remember. It wasn't real anyway. It didn't matter. Neither those revels, nor the debauchery of the nights following, had driven Christine from his mind. The same went for his dutiful attendance at church and family dinners. And that had been fine until he'd told Sabine and Philippe yesterday about his journey north, and they had berated and yelled at him for hours after.

Since then they had not let him out of their sight and dragged him to the Opera. Philippe wanted to remind Raoul Christine was a common opera harlot and that there were dozens of ripe fruits to be plucked from the *Salon du Dance*, or even the chorus if Raoul was set on it. Antoine was along, of course, to laugh and to endear himself to Sabine.

Raoul retreated from their box halfway through Christine's first rapturous aria. He could not bear to hear her sing a song of love, especially for a false, manipulative man who would ruin her. Did the woman not see the irony? How could she sing with such unbridled passion that it was almost obscene when she knew how she had broken Raoul's heart. Perhaps Philippe and Antoine were right: she was a heartless whore.

He grabbed a glass of champagne from a tray as he passed through the *Grand Foyer* to the Grand Salon. He felt small and stupid here, a normal, honest man just a stain among the endless gilding, mosaics, and murals of angels or heathen gods. He could not be bothered to tell the difference. He scowled out the window onto the balcony at the *Avenue de L'Opéra* beyond and downed his drink. It was only a matter of time before Philippe or Sabine came for him. Hopefully, he could dull his senses somewhat before then so he could make it through the following acts.

"Are you not enjoying Mademoiselle Daaé's performance, Monsieur le Vicomte?"

Raoul turned to the source of the voice, immediately offended and subsequently shocked, for he knew the man that dared to accost him. "You. You're the fellow who was pestering Christine before!" Raoul squinted at the foreigner. "I've heard some very interesting tales about you since then." Indeed, the man in the astrakhan hat had been a regular feature in the ghost stories Raoul had been inundated with on the night of Buquet's death.

"And I have heard many stories about you as well," the Persian replied. "Most of them regarding your relationship to the lovely Mademoiselle Daaé."

"Then you should know I'm done with her," Raoul spat. His mind jumped back to the humiliation of waiting in that church, his heart breaking over and over each time the doors opened and it was not Christine who entered.

"Because another man has staked his claim on her?" The Persian replied, undeterred, and Raoul looked over the man. There was something dignified about him, despite his swarthy looks.

"That's one way to put it," Raoul said slowly. "I asked her to choose me over him and she didn't. So it's over. Not that it ever really began."

"What if I were to tell you that she could not choose him over you, because she has no choice in the matter?" There was no lie in the Persian's eyes and Raoul's heart went cold at the words.

"What do you mean? Do you know who the man is who holds sway over her? This angel or genius of hers?" Raoul demanded, holding himself back from taking the foreigner by the collar and shaking him for an answer.

"I do. And I will tell you now that he is the most dangerous man in Paris. I dare not even tell you his name if you have not been successful in learning it yourself," The Persian answered gravely. "But I know he has your Christine in his control. Her actions are not her own, be assured."

"How can I believe you?" Raoul demanded.

"You are a smart man, Monsieur," the Persian replied. "Think on what you have seen and what you know. Consider the accidents and incidents you have witnessed at the Opera around Christine. The rumors. Even perhaps..." The man paused, as if he was sizing Raoul up.

"Go on," Raoul ordered, puffing his chest.

"Ghost stories."

Raoul wondered if someone had opened a window to let in the winter air, for goosebumps raised on his skin. "What do the ghost stories have to do with Christine and her angel?"

"Are angels so different from ghosts?" the Persian asked in return.

Raoul fought a shiver. "Very. Though I will not fault you for the mistake if you have not read the Bible."

"I have actually. And many part are included in the Quran," the Persian replied, ignoring Raoul's scowl. "But you are correct, sir, a human soul cannot become an angelic one. It is men who become ghosts."

"What are you getting at?" Raoul demanded, eyes narrowing.

The Persian gave a polite bow and turned away, then paused, speaking over his shoulder with the slightest smile. "You know, the holy books remind us that Lucifer was an angel too."

Raoul starred after the strange man as he disappeared back into the echoing halls of the Opera. He felt as though he was waking from a week's worth of nightmares. What if the man spoke true? What if all Raoul's most terrifying suspicions had just been confirmed?

Christine had not rejected him in favor of some unscrupulous genius who refused to show his face. Rather she had been *taken* from Raoul by a character far more dangerous. One who had something to do with the horrifying stories that haunted the Opera and the man Raoul had found dead.

As it had all night, the applause rang hollow in Christine's ears as she took her final bow. All that mattered was that she could feel Erik watching her. She could even imagine that she saw his shadow in box five, standing for the ovation. It gave her a thrill to match the excitement coursing through her veins.

It was controlled chaos backstage after the curtain fell for the final time. Everyone had their own agenda and mission. Some choristers were ready to leave immediately, while the stagehands and dressers still had a great deal of work to do. Christine moved with her own mission too, handing off the flowers she had been presented with and nodding with the bare minimum of politeness to everyone who complimented her on the performance. She was determined not to stop for anyone.

"Will I be accompanying you anywhere tonight?" Robert asked, emerging at her elbow.

Christine shook her head, not breaking her stride. Erik might already be on his way to her dressing room as. "No. I'm not going tonight. Nothing good ever comes from those parties."

"I will give your regrets," Robert murmured, and Christine did not look as he left her at his dressing room door. She hoped he would be able to steal some time with his own lover tonight. Moncharmin had looked typically exhausted when she had last seen him.

She kept walking, picking up her pace. She braced herself for the emptiness of the room. Julianne hadn't been there to dress her, just as she had been absent for the entire week. Christine hadn't spoken at all to the other dresser who had swung in to help. What was her name? Aurora? Raquel? It didn't matter. It hurt to know Julianne still believed Christine was a fool for being with her ghost. It smarted even more to know that her friend was probably right... Which made the sight of Julianne waiting for her in the dressing room all the more painful when Christine walked in.

"What are you doing here?" Christine asked. "I thought you'd given up on me."

"That was before I listened to you sing tonight," Julianne replied, something like contrition in her face. "He cannot be all bad, a man that makes you sing like that."

"He's not," Christine replied instantly. She looked at the mirror, trying to sense if Erik was there watching, but no familiar shiver prickled her skin.

"I'm still worried for you, after everything. You still haven't been—"

"Myself?" Christine finished for her, remembering back to their argument from before. "Julianne, I'm not even sure who that is anymore." She looked at the mirror again, this time truly taking in her reflection. Was she paler from weeks in the dark? Were the shadows under her eyes from restless nights darker now that she had seen such tragedy? Could someone tell by looking at her how eagerly she took a man with a face like death to her bed and how deeply she wished to have him again?

"You are a good, kind woman who sees the best in people," Julianne said, taking Christine's hand. "Even a foul-tempered flirt like me."

"I would never call you that."

"Jammes did," Julianne sighed. "She called me a great many things last week when I told her how worried I was for you. She's convinced now that you and I are having an affair. Or that I'm heartless. It changes."

"I'm so sorry," Christine murmured. Another life she'd left upended in her wake. "Maybe I am cursed."

"I couldn't even tell her that's impossible given that you're in love with a phantom," Julianne said with a sarcastic chuckle and Christine blanched.

"I'm not..." Christine whispered, panic rising as her eyes darted to her reflection.

Julianne furrowed her brow. "But he's your lover, isn't he?"

"That's different," Christine replied. She did not want that. She had just died for love as Gilda in a father's arms, remembering her own father's warning that love was nothing but pain. Julianne still looked dubious.

"But you aren't going home tonight, are you?" Julianne asked.

"I'm not going to Adèle's," Christine corrected as goose flesh rose on her skin.

"Do you need any help?"

"I'm fine," Christine said too quickly. It was simple enough to get out of Gilda's boyish disguise. Julianne said no more, casting a dark look at the mirror before retreating. Christine didn't hide behind the screen to undress, simply throwing a robe over her underthings, followed by the dark cloak Erik had bestowed on her.

"Aren't you going to dress?" Erik's voice sounded from behind the mirror and Christine found herself grinning, her mask of propriety and decency falling away.

"What's the point? I'll just have them off again when we're home, won't I?" she said softly, her cheeks heating even as the words left her lips and the mirror slid open. Erik smiled back at her from the dark. He had the mask on again, as always when he was above, but she could see the pride and desire in his eyes. "Were you pleased by the performance?"

He answered by pulling her to him and kissing her. It was always like drowning, the first time he touched her after they had been apart. She was pulled down by the undertow in a savage sea. But it didn't scare her. The mirror closed behind them, and the world on the other side ceased to exist.

14. A Trick of Moonlight

The Opera was closed, much to Shaya's dismay. He had hoped he would be able to slip in on an uncrowded day to see if he could find Erik's secret path once again, but alas, every door was locked. Therefore, he was sulking on the *Rue Scribe* in the pre-dawn light, wondering what else to do with himself. No one had ever told him, when he began to train for the Shah's secret police, that being a spy would involve so much standing around and waiting. He'd been waiting all week for some sign that Christine Daaé was a prisoner or if she willingly served Erik. She had sung like an angel as Gilda the night before then disappeared entirely, and Shaya was sure he knew where to. Perhaps he might see her emerge...

"Would you like a croissant?" Shaya jumped at least a foot in the air at the sound of Erik's voice. He spun to the alley where the fiend stood in shadow, smiling past the edge of his mask. He was indeed holding a package that smelled like fresh pastry. "They're fresh. I'm sure you could use one on a cold morning like this."

"Did you come out here just to accost me?" Shaya declared, righting his hat from where it had become askew.

"Well, you have been lingering about for a few days. But no, I came out to fetch breakfast for Christine. She had quite a performance last night and she's rather tired," Erik smirked.

Shaya rolled his eyes. "So you did take her again?"

"I never *took* her, Daroga, she comes and goes freely because she wants to. That is what I have been hoping you'd see, but it seems your skills have diminished over the years." Erik looked pleased with himself, which was almost as disconcerting as seeing him outside of the Opera in all his sinister glory. It made Shaya think.

"On the contrary, I see a woman you've manipulated, lied to, and rewarded with a career," Shaya said and watched Erik's eyes harden. "If she knows everything as you say – which I *doubt* – then she knows you are a killer, and she only returns to you out of fear."

"Is it really so hard to believe that she wants me for myself?" Erik paused, and Shaya braced himself. "As others have."

"Will you lead her to her death as well?" Shaya snapped back. It was gratifying to see Erik flinch. "You condemn her to suffering and damnation just by being near her, you fiend. Don't you know that?"

"Since I know you refuse to actually ask her, how can I prove to you that she is no prisoner?" If there was pain in Erik's entrancing voice, Shaya refused to acknowledge it.

"Do you think convincing me that Christine is willingly yours in some way will make me believe you didn't corrupt and trick *him*?" Shaya demanded with a hollow scoff. He could see, even with the mask, that Erik was agitated. Good. This girl made him a fool. Maybe now he would make another mistake.

"What if you were to see her alive and well and with me? Perhaps at the Masquerade in a few days—"

"Any place in the Opera is still under your control," Shaya replied. He had to be careful with his next move. "Let me see her away from your kingdom and then maybe I'll be convinced that she doesn't need to be saved."

"What about the Bois?" Erik offered and Shaya blinked. "It's a park on the west of the city? People who actually enjoy life go there so I'm not surprised it's escaped your attention. But I've been meaning to take her there for some air."

"When?" Shaya asked, trying to keep his composure. Let Erik think this was some sort of triumph.

"Tonight, if it stays clear," Erik said and it was so close to cheerful it made Shaya sick. "And no, I shan't be telling you when. I like the idea of you waiting in the stands at the racetrack, freezing and frustrated. I'll need to rent a cab for Christine and myself. I can't have my student catching cold. Though I do enjoy keeping her warm..."

Shaya let out a guffaw at Erik's implication. "Pick a lie, Erik. Either she knows your secrets, or she's your whore. No woman could be the latter if she learned the former."

"She'll show you otherwise, Daroga. Just wait," Erik said, all illusion of good humor gone. "But do not insult her in my hearing if you wish to continue breathing."

Erik retreated into the alley and before Shaya could follow, he was gone. It didn't matter. In his arrogance, blinded by his infatuation, Erik had once again made a deadly mistake. Now Shaya not only knew the secret path to the demon's lair, he knew where he would be vulnerable and when Christine might be saved. And Shaya knew who to enlist.

Erik took particular care to be quiet as he reentered the house on the lake. He didn't like leaving Christine there alone, even for a brief time. She didn't like it either, he knew that, but he hoped she would have either slept through it or would forgive him for the sake of breakfast. Luckily, he received no remonstration when he entered his bedchamber. She was still asleep among the dark sheets, her naked back like a slice of alabaster in the candlelight. How had a monster like him found his way into the light of one so beautiful? Shaya didn't believe it and, in all honesty, neither did Erik, half the time. Perhaps that's why it was so important to convince the Daroga of her safety.

He set to work, quietly doffing his cape and hat back in the parlor, thinking of the rashness of going out alone and the boldness of talking to Shaya. Maybe he was getting sloppy, as the Daroga said. Or maybe he was changing.

He set the kettle to boil. Coffee was on the menu this morning as well. He wanted to indulge her, as he had done for the whole week since she had fully given herself to him. She deserved it.

She deserves more than what you could ever give her.

Erik's shivered, feeling as if something had just walked into the parlor behind him. He was alone with his ghosts, their eyes and judgment upon him. He could boast and posture for the Daroga, but not them.

You've trapped her here in your prison, a fly in a spider's web as you drain the life from her. She's miserable. She's fading every day, losing her light bit by bit.

"That's not true," Erik said aloud as he turned to the empty room. "She's happy here. She wants to be with me," he whispered, even as doubt gnawed at his mind. How could she though? Was it dependence that kept her with him? Music? Lust?

It's certainly not love.

Erik grabbed the closest object and threw it. It was not until it hit the wall with a dull thud that he even knew it was a book. He was panting, he realized, and his skin was moist with a cold sweat as his heart raced. Why wouldn't it? He was trapped under the ground in a windowless house fit only for a monster and he had trapped the woman he loved here too. He didn't want to be like this or live like this; why would she?

"Erik?"

Christine's soft voice from his bedroom door brought him back from the brink of panic. She was a vision when he turned to her, with her dark hair cascading over her shoulders, her pale skin set off by the red velvet of her robe.

"I'm sorry, I didn't want to wake you before—" Erik gulped, looking at the half-filled tray by the kettle. "I got you breakfast."

"Are those croissants? Where did you get them?" Christine asked with a smile full of curiosity and kindness Erik knew he did not deserve.

"I went up to the bakery down the avenue. Or the back of it." He answered. It was the truth. She didn't need to know about his detour to pester Shaya.

"Did you pay?" Her expression was so dubious he had to chuckle.

"I left a few sous."

"And coffee?" Her suspicion changed to amazement.

"You don't need to sing this morning, I thought I might indulge your only vice," Erik answered. Christine shook her head as she moved to the fire to stoke it while Erik finished his preparations.

"I think you are quite aware that I have other vices," she muttered when Erik finally handed her a cup and they sat on the floor by the fire. "Here, you don't need this." Before Erik could protest, she lifted the mask from his face. The heat of the fire on his bare skin was shocking, as was the way she smiled at him when he was revealed.

"You are too good to me," Erik whispered.

"Well, I'm not the one who went out for breakfast, I would say you are too good to me," Christine countered. "Though I wish you would have told me. I don't like—"

"Being here alone, I know."

Christine frowned at him. "I don't like the idea of you risking your safety to indulge me."

It always made his heart flutter when she revealed that she worried for him, even though he did not understand how it was possible. "I was hardly in danger," he said gently. "I know how to defend myself and avoid being seen."

"Did you have it with you? Your lasso?" Christine's voice trembled as she asked it, and Erik no longer felt the heat of the fire.

"I did." It was not accusation in her eyes when she looked at him, but a sort of sad resignation. She had grown accustomed to the horrors of his face, it was true, but he had gone out of his way since his confessions to help her forget the true ugliness. The evil that Shaya saw so clearly and believed Christine would never truly see past. "It's a habit. I—"

"Can I see it?" She was calm when she asked, holding Erik's gaze. His guts twisted. "Show it to me, Erik," she commanded in the face of his hesitation, and he rose immediately to obey.

It was like offering a sacrifice, when he returned to her, kneeling before the fire and presenting her with the simple line of catgut. Christine took it without hesitation, her face unreadable as she examined the weapon that had taken so many lives. She took a deep breath as she grasped it, then looked Erik in the eye as she threw it into the fire.

"That part of your life is over," Christine declared as the Punjab lasso burned. And as it did, Erik breathed easier than he had in years. He didn't need the lasso to kill a man. He had the means buried beneath this house and hidden in his walls to kill more people than Christine could even comprehend... But he didn't need to. Or want to. He hadn't wanted to for a very long time. He wished he could tell her, but all of that was in the past anyway. Just like she said. There was no reason to disturb the delicate peace they had found.

"Thank you," Erik whispered, and Christine gave a nod, relief on her face.

"What other plans do you have for us today, if we aren't going to sing for a while? Shall I beat you at chess again? Or shall we finish those dreadful Poe stories you were reading me?" Christine asked, lightness in her voice as she took up one of the croissants Erik had brought her.

"I thought you liked them," Erik chuckled. "Though perhaps you have had enough of the macabre in your waking life. I was hoping to finally take you to the Bois tonight," Erik heard himself say and watched Christine smile. "It will be clear. I hope you will like it."

Raoul was not a scholar, and he had no shame in that. He'd done well enough in his studies with tutors and at school, of course, as was expected of him. But he much preferred *doing things* to reading about them in books or pouring over sums and histories. For that reason, he was developing quite a headache today in his attempt to become a scholar of Christine's story and how it was mixed up with this so-called Phantom. He had written down snippets and notes and set them out on the floor of his room. It looked utterly insane. Raoul assumed that whoever was knocking on his door would find him equally as mad.

"Go away!" Raoul shouted.

"Not a chance in hell, little brother," Philippe declared as he sauntered in. "My God, this is worse than Jérémy said."

"Who?"

"Your valet? Who you ran out this morning when he found you up to...whatever this is." Philippe stepped on a piece of paper detailing Raoul's first encounter with Christine at the New Year's gala. "What is going on?"

"I'm trying to get to the bottom of what has happened to Christine," Raoul protested, and Philippe heaved the most put-upon of sighs.

"I thought you were done with the little slut after she humiliated you. Or have you decided not to abandon your family and duties to traipse off to the North Pole?"

Raoul scowled. "I believe that she hasn't actually rejected me. She's being forced away from me against her will."

"Not that I don't believe it would take threats and extortion to make a woman turn down a Chagny." Philippe picked up another scrap and squinted at it. "But what's that got to do with – what have you written here – *Carlotta poisoned*?"

"What happened to the woman was unnatural. Everything that's happened around Christine to make her career possible is unnatural!" Raoul exploded. "Christine said to me she thought she had found the angel her father promised her! But he wasn't! He lied and it broke her heart!"

"What are you on about?"

"And I thought it was just a man – her good genius teacher that refuses to be seen – but what if he's more? What if he *is* this ghost?" Raoul was breathless to finally say it aloud.

"So your lady love is having trysts with a dead man?" Philippe laughed as he asked it. And why wouldn't he? It all sounded insane. "Shall we have a séance with that medium that Madame Soleil keeps on her staff now? You can tell him what for!"

"No, I'm saying—" Raoul caught his tongue. "I don't know what I'm saying."

"Yes, indeed," Philippe chuckled. "You know, Antoine told me that his Adèle told him Christine hasn't been seen at her flat more than one night in the past month. I don't think a ghost would keep her so *occupied*."

"He's keeping her prisoner!" Raoul shouted back, the new information threatening to split his aching skull. "And how can Valerius not be concerned about what sort of peril Christine could be in!"

"Peril?" Philippe laughed again. "She's not in peril! She's in some villain's bed!"

"Monsieur le Vicomte, a note for you." Raoul looked up at the footman standing at his door and blushed. The help didn't need to be present for this.

"It couldn't wait?" Raoul snapped, snatching the letter from the silver tray.

"The messenger gave the impression it was urgent. And Monsieur le Comte told me—"

"Never mind that," Philippe blustered as the footman left with a sidelong glance. "Who's writing to you? I was under the impression you'd only been associating with illiterates this past week."

Raoul stared at the note in his hand, reading and rereading the brief missive. "It says Christine has been seen taking the night air at the Bois, riding in a Brougham on the Longchamps raceway."

"That's oddly specific. Who would write you this?" Philippe grabbed the note from Raoul and looked it over. "It's not even signed."

"It says she may be there tonight! The fiend who has her will be with her, I know it!"

"You can't seriously be considering this! Raoul, this is a prank of some sort!" Philippe truly did look concerned, and Raoul wanted to reassure him, but how could he? How could he explain what he knew in his soul? He had to call this 'angel of music' to account.

"I'm going to find the truth, Philippe. I have to if I'm going to leave Paris with a clear conscience."

"Or you could not leave Paris at all and find a woman worthy of you who isn't a half-breed gypsy with the heart and morals of a courtesan. Have you considered that?"

Raoul answered by walking past his brother into the hall. It was nearly supper. He needed to get to the Bois immediately if he was to station himself somewhere with an advantageous position. Where was his good coat?

"When you get your heart broken again tonight, do know I'll spend all of tomorrow telling you 'I told you so' while you weep in my lap!" Philippe yelled from above as Raoul descended the stairs. He didn't care. He was full of hope for the first time in a week. He would not let it go.

The crisp night air of the *Bois de Boulogne* was like a balm against Christine's cheeks. She hadn't realized until she had opened the window of their brougham and breathed the free air, thick with the scent of living things and wet earth, that she had needed it this much. Erik's world was one of dreams and illusion, of music and magic, and she was glad to escape into it from the intrigue of the Opera and the hurt she had caused there. But there was a different kind of freedom in just the illusion of being away from the city and its walls of stone and harsh lights.

"Do you like it?" Erik asked from where he sat beside her, remaining concealed in the seat beside her from the full moon above.

"It's wonderful. Thank you for taking me," Christine sighed. "And for the transportation. I imagine you don't usually employ cabs."

"You would be correct," Erik said warmly. "But a proper lady deserves something more civilized than traipsing through the sewers for a cold walk in the woods."

"I don't know if I'm a proper lady, but I do appreciate the luxury," Christine replied. It had been a shock to find their waiting cab when Erik had led her up to the side of the Opera. She had no idea how he had managed it. So many things he did truly were like magic or miracles. Such as the way he had made her feel safe and healed in the recent days, even when the world was chaos and consequences around them. "I imagine it's even more beautiful in spring," Christine mused, imagining the trees heavy with pink and white blooms against a blue sky while children laughed in the distance.

"I'm not sure. I like it in the winter," Erik replied. "You can view the stars and moon better through the trees. Would you like to see?"

"You mean walk through a park at night with a strange man?" she replied with a playful smile. "I would like that very much."

Erik rapped on the side of the brougham, and the cab rumbled to a stop. With the utmost speed and grace, he sprang out, holding his hand for Christine like the perfect gentleman to help her down to the ground.

"You look beautiful in the moonlight." Christine was surprised he could still make her blush. He offered her his arm and she took it with a quiet chuckle. If the sun had been out, it would indeed be a completely normal outing.

"I've read that in New York City they've set aside a huge park in the center of the metropolis; to be a natural space forever, for the benefit of the whole city. It must be quite a thing to see," Erik mused as they walked, leaving the brougham and their driver behind.

"Indeed. Have you ever considered visiting America? Since you have been everywhere else?" Christine imagined Erik on a long sea voyage across the Atlantic. He would probably read the entire time and not mind at all being so close to so many people if he could stay shut away. It would be bearable for both of them.

"I have heard that there are still wild places there that are larger than the whole of France," Erik replied with a dreamy sigh. "Where men can get lost for months, fortunes can be made. New lives can be begun by anyone, or so their myth says. I'm not sure how true that is for someone who doesn't fit in. But it would be quite a thing to see. Alas."

"Alas?" Christine furrowed her brow and pulled at Erik's elbow so he looked at her.

"I don't think I will ever leave Paris again. Or the Opera," Erik said plainly. As if it was obvious. Christine didn't want that to be true. Since she had burned his deadly lasso, it felt like so much more was possible for them.

"Not even with the right companion?" Erik stopped in his tracks as she said it, and Christine bit her lip.

"I had never thought about it," Erik said softly, drawing Christine to him. Past the brim of his hat and the white mask, his golden eyes were wide and amazed. "It would be a long journey. Even with...company."

"That's why we practice," Christine replied hopefully. "More outings like this, to start."

"There is the masquerade in a few days." If Christine had not known him better, she would have sworn he sounded and looked shy. She found herself smiling.

"Are you asking me to accompany you, *Monsieur Le Fantôme*?"

Erik laughed – a beautiful, bubbling sound from deep in his throat – then stepped back and made a graceful bow, not letting go of her hand.

"Would you do me the honor of attending the masquerade with me, Mademoiselle Daaé?"

"On one condition," she parried back, heart fluttering as Erik rose and drew her to him.

"Yes?"

"You must promise to dance with me."

Erik's eyes widened behind the mask. "Dance?"

"Surely you have heard of dancing? It's all the rage nowadays. Or are such displays beneath the dignity of the infamous Opera Ghost?"

"I don't dance," Erik whispered, both firm and seductive in his tone, close enough now that he could kiss her.

"Yes, you do," Christine smiled, pressing herself close against him. "No one could make love the way you do and not be able to dance. No one could make such beautiful music and not move to it."

"How can I argue with such flattery?" Erik murmured and Christine grinned. "I promise to dance with you, but you must promise to teach me." He leaned in to kiss her, but Christine sprang away.

"Done. Let us begin," she said as she extended her hand before her. Erik took it, laughing softly as she guided his other hand to her waist and smiled up at him.

"Not to be critical of my teacher, but don't we need music?"

Christine stood on her toes, pressing her cheek against the mask, her heart leaping to feel her lover solid and warm against her. "When you are with me, there is always music," she whispered in his ear. "Now, dance with me, my angel."

Erik smiled wistfully at her as she set her hand on his shoulder. Christine began to sing; an Irish tune Erik had taught her in recent days that sang of summer sun, and fields of flowers. The English words were still new to her tongue, but she understood the dream behind them. "*Will yee go, lassie go?*"

"*And we'll all go together,*" Erik joined her, surprisingly tentative as she began to move, but he quickly caught the rhythm of the dance. Suddenly they had gone from moving awkwardly to dancing. They swirled in smooth circles as they sang together, graceful and trusting.

Christine was glad she was singing, that she could speak to him with music, instead of useless words. There was no need to think or worry, right now, as they spun and she stared up into his eyes. All that mattered was that, somehow, looking at him made her happy. Not just content. Truly happy. The emptiness that had nearly swallowed her whole days before was so completely gone it was hard to believe she had ever felt it. Instead, she was full to overflowing with something she could find no words for, only a song. A song that was entirely for him, as it always would be.

"I will build my love a bower, on yon high mountain green, and my love will be the fairest the summer sun has ever seen..."

She was dimly aware that they had stopped moving. Now Erik was simply holding her close in the shining night, as their voices grew quieter, then faded to silence. She held her breath, praying he would kiss her as she tilted her face to his. He would kiss her, and she could forget the words that were fighting their way past every defense she could mount. He was so close, and his eyes were so beautiful. If she was to kiss him or to speak the thought coalescing in her mind, she wanted it to be Erik before her in the moonlight, not a mask.

Carefully she lifted the mask from his face, lost in his eyes and the truth thundering in her heart.

"Erik, I—"

"Get away from her! Monster!" The cry shattered the night like a gunshot, and every dream with it. Christine would know Raoul's voice anywhere, but it terrified her more than anything to hear it now.

"No," Christine gasped, as she spun to see the face of the boy she had once loved, awash with horror in the moonlight as he stumbled from the woods. Erik's hand locked on her wrist, yanking her away.

"Run," Erik growled, even as Raoul stumbled towards them.

Christine followed without thinking and rushed headlong from the patch of moonlight into the trees, panic filling her as Erik dragged her to their carriage at breakneck speed. He had replaced his mask at least.

"Christine! Wait!" she heard Raoul yell over the sounds of them crashing through branches and shrubs bare of leaves, the snow crunching under their feet. He was going to catch up and he was going to demand to know what she had done! What had he seen? How had she been so stupid! This would destroy everything!

"Let her go, you fiend!" Raoul yelled, his voice closer now and Erik, to her horror, obeyed. His hand was suddenly gone from her wrist. Christine stumbled as she turned to see Raoul a distance behind her, his face desolate and panicked. But Erik was nowhere to be seen. "Christine! Who was that?" Raoul cried as Christine tripped backwards, crashing to the cold ground. Raoul advanced, eyes wild. "Was *that* your angel!?"

"Get away from her, fool."

Raoul had no time to react before Erik had him by the throat, a beast of pure shadow emerging from the trees with eyes of fire.

"No! Please!" Christine screamed, horror rushing through her veins. *She could not watch another man die.* "Not him!"

At the sound of her voice, Erik turned, the fire in his eyes still burning, but mixed now with unfathomable pain. With terrifying force, Erik lifted his rival and threw him so that he crashed into the trunk of the nearest tree. Raoul fell limp to the ground. Christine wanted to scream, but no sound came from her throat as she rushed towards the two men.

"He's alive!" Erik said, catching Christine. "I promise you, he's alive!"

Christine looked for herself, watching Raoul's shallow breathing as he lay unconscious on the muddy ground. The snap of a branch and the sound of heavy breathing somewhere in the dark made her heart seize again.

"We have to go. He may not have been alone," Erik commanded. Once again, Christine did not resist as Erik pulled her away into the night. They rushed to the brougham, and the driver startled from his seat as they clamored inside. "Back to the Opera! Now!"

Christine was worried she was going to be sick as the carriage rumbled away from the Bois and Erik glowered out the window beside her. Was he looking for pursuers? What had just happened?

They rode in silence through the city, traveling swiftly through the quiet streets. Christine tried to stem her panic and anxiety, tried to breathe, but it was useless. The delicate dream they had lived in was shattered once again.

The horses snuffled as she and Erik passed through the stable to the hidden door. Christine paused on the threshold as Erik lit his lantern, dizzy with the idea of descending to the dark with her ghost once again.

"Why was he there?" Christine asked, leaning on the cold wall. "How could he have known?"

"He was informed we would be there. By the Daroga." Erik's voice was clipped and cold, but it didn't stop Christine from looking at him in horror.

"How did Shaya know?" Erik did not look at her, and it gave Christine her answer. "You told him?"

"We need to get home," Erik said, taking her hand. She wanted to pull away, but she could do nothing but follow. "He wanted to be assured of your safety," Erik added as they descended a flight of stairs.

"Then he should have bloody talked to me!" Christine cried, rage rising to match her fear.

"It's too late now. Your little friend knows you're a monster's captive," Erik growled, and Christine shuddered.

"We don't know that," Christine breathed. They had reached the lake. She could tell by the smell and the heaviness of the moist air. It was so different from the freshness of the Bois. Why was she here? She rushed after Erik to his home, the place he had fled so many years ago when another noble had tried to take his life from him. "He might not even remember or understand what he saw."

"He'll remember, Christine," Erik cried as the door slammed behind them. "The fool loves you: he will remember. And he – he saw me." His voice broke as he said it. Christine spun in time to see him crumble to the floor, his hands upon the mask. "He knows a living corpse keeps you here. And now! Now they will both come. The Daroga and that boy. They will take you from me. I should have—"

"No!" Christine rushed to him, kneeling beside him on the ground. Erik recoiled as he looked up at her, his hair falling in disheveled locks, black against white, one mask over another. His eyes were as pathetic as she had ever seen them.

"You saved him." Erik said it like it was the worst accusation he could hurl at her, but Christine shook her head, fighting through her panic. "Even after he *saw*."

"Because I told you: that part of your life is over," she gritted out, trying to let him see how she was trembling. Was she mad, to pretend she had not just locked herself in a tomb with a killer?

"Then how? How can I keep him away?" Erik asked, each word more desperate than the last, as he grabbed Christine by the fabric of her cloak, knitting his hands into the dark material and pulling her to him. "Tell me *how*, Christine, and I will do it. I cannot lose you!"

"I'll make him forget!" Christine said with a force that shocked her as the words passed her lips. "I'll write to him. And you'll contact Shaya, and we'll tell them to come to the masquerade. I'll make him go away. And Shaya – he'll see I'm safe and free. And no one will be hurt. No one *needs* to be hurt. We'll all be safe!"

"How can you say that?" Erik demanded. Christine could see the tears in his eyes even behind the mask, and her heart broke. "How do you know?"

"Because I command it. You said you could never refuse a command from me." A strange sort of strength welled up in Christine as Erik blinked at her. "You said I could trust you. You are mine, aren't you?"

"I am," Erik replied breathlessly without hesitation.

"As I am yours. And so, they cannot take me from you as long as that is true." Christine rose, pulling Erik up with her before throwing her arms around him. "I promise I will make this right, Erik. Trust me."

Erik pulled back from her, doubt and danger still in his eyes. "Christine..."

"I am yours as you are mine," she repeated and lifted his mask away before she kissed him. He recoiled, but she followed him, lips locked to his until they were against the wall, and he had nowhere to run from her. "You are mine and you will not harm anyone, unless it is at my command," she said, low and dangerous, before she kissed him again.

He gave into the force of her lips, his mouth opening for her tongue to explore. The sound he let out, low and wild in his throat, made Christine shudder with need. She pressed herself against him, her hand slipping between their bodies to his groin.

"Christine," Erik sighed as she kissed at his neck and jaw, finding the places she knew rendered him pliant with pleasure. His cock stirred between them as she pressed close, rising as if at her command. "My Christine." Her name in his angel's voice made her knees grow weak.

"My angel," she sighed in reply as she sank to her knees in a blasphemous mockery of supplication. She nuzzled his warm member through the fabric, leaving all propriety and dignity behind. This was hers.

She held her breath as she undid his belt and the fastenings of his trousers, her hands trembling at the knowledge of what she was about to do. She freed his hardening member and steeled herself, listening to Erik's ragged breath before she licked his cock warily from base to tip.

Erik gave a gasp that dissolved into one long moan as Christine repeated the action. The taste of him was bitter, but not unpleasant, and she lapped curiously at his crown, wondering what he might do as she explored new textures with her tongue.

"What are you doing?" Erik asked, his voice choked and tremulous as Christine dared to look up at him through her lashes.

She gazed into the face of a killer, a horrible sight that would fill any sane person with disgust and fear. The terror of the Opera, who would kill a man without hesitation to keep his angel safe or to assure she remained his. Christine knew she was mad to think she could control him. She was a harlot of the highest order to prostrate herself before such a creature to keep his trust. But there was no other choice. There never had been.

"Let me show you how I am yours," she said before she took his cock into her mouth without another second of hesitation.

Christine recalled the bawdy lesson Robert had given her. She sucked then licked, then sucked again as Erik gave a broken cry like none she had ever heard from him before. It was an education, an experiment in what she could do to him and what he liked. She added her hands to her ministrations, gripping the length she could not take past her lips, as well as toying with his balls and base. He cried out again at that, thrusting his hips so that he drove deep past her tongue and into her throat. She gagged, but she was undeterred. She continued, breathing in the musky scent of him through her nose.

"Christine...gods above...I...Christine..." he babbled, and the music of his voice was spurred her on. She relaxed her jaw, taking as much of him as she could and then more, bit by bit, her lips tight around his girth. This time when he began to move, she was ready for him and bobbed her head in tandem. She closed her eyes, accustoming herself to the weight of him on her tongue, the heat of him and the alien taste.

Did he feel this powerful when he ministered to her like this? Did it send a rush of pleasure through him every time he provoked a new cry or twitch as he commanded her ecstasy? Even though she was on her knees, she knew he had never been so completely at her mercy. He was utterly and absolutely hers.

She felt the falter of his hips as the first s ign, t hen the tightening of his balls and the twitch of his cock as his breath grew strangled and shallow. She sucked hard in response as he fucked into her mouth once. Twice. A final time and suddenly he cried out, grabbing her hair and holding her in place as hot, bitter spend poured from him into Christine's waiting throat. She swallowed it down, remarking how at last, he had spilled his seed inside her.

She pulled back with his hands still in her hair, wiping her mouth in amazement at this new sin. Erik fell to his knees before her, breathless, collapsing against her shoulder and taking them both to the floor.

"Do you believe me now?" Christine asked, her voice husky as Erik panted against her breast.

"Yes," he whispered. "Promise me you'll make him disappear. I hate him. Make him disappear for me. Break his heart."

"I promise I will," Christine replied without qualm, and she was not shocked when Erik kissed her in return. Could he taste the proof of devotion and damnation on her tongue? "No more of that now," she commanded as Erik's lips parted from her. "He doesn't matter now. You're going to make me forget him, aren't you?" Erik nodded vehemently. "Make me forget him, my Erik, right now."

And as she knew he would, her broken angel obeyed, tearing at her clothes as he rushed to undress her. Soon she was bare for him, her nipples hard and her skin rough with gooseflesh in the cold of their hidden home. Erik kissed her everywhere, his mouth and hands like heaven upon her skin. He barely seemed to notice when she pushed him to his back and took her place above him. But he did groan in hungry bliss as she framed his face with her thighs and let him taste her dripping desire at last.

Christine sighed in relief and delight as Erik hid his awful face between her legs. He was hers, and she was his. The thought overcame her as she rutted her cunt against his eager mouth, his tongue undoing her. She forgot everything, every crime and every care, as he devoured and delved with lips and clever finger. She threw her head back, her soul lost entirely in ecstasy as she looked up to Erik's painted stars and came with a long, echoing scream.

Raoul woke with a cry from the nightmare, his hands at his neck. The world swam into focus around him as searing pain filled his head.

"Easy now! You're hurt!"

Raoul fell back onto his bed and squinted at Sabine. Why was it so *bright*? "Dear God, what time is it?" he groaned. It had been past midnight when...when he had seen her with a monster! "Christine! Where is—"

"I knew she had something to do with this!" Sabine crowed. She was seated by his bed and diffuse sunlight was coming in the windows.

"How did I get here?" Raoul demanded, trying once again to rise. "I have to go. I have to find her! She's in danger!"

"Call the Comte," Sabine said to a waiting servant as she rushed to her brother. "Raoul, it's past noon. The doctor said to let you sleep. And we don't—" His sister stifled a sob, covering her mouth. "We don't know *how* you got home! Someone rang at three in the morning and we found you on the steps! You were covered in mud and bleeding! And those bruises!"

Raoul reached for his throat as Sabine began to weep. It was tender from where the man in the mask had choked him. But before that, Raoul was sure he had worn a different mask.

"Oh thank heaven you're awake!" Philippe exclaimed as he burst into the room. "You certainly gave us a fright! What on earth happened? I should like to call the police!"

"They won't be able to do anything," Raoul muttered, thinking back to the night before. "How could they apprehend a ghost?"

"A what?" Sabine asked through her tears.

"How hard did you hit your head?" Philippe asked at the same time.

"It was the Opera Ghost," Raoul said, remaining calm as his siblings stared at him. "I know it sounds insane. But I swear to you last night I went to see if that letter was right, hoping I could find Christine." Raoul swallowed. He did not need to give them the whole tale. He would sound even more divorced from his senses if he were to confess to hearing the voices of angels wafting through the night. The man's voice had been exactly the one he had heard in Christine's dressing room. Then he'd found them and saved Christine from a monster about to claim her lips.

"The Bois is full of criminals, vagrants, and degenerates," Philippe cut in. "One of them must have attacked you."

"No. It was him. Christine's good genius. Her angel. I saw her with him," Raoul went on, remembering Christine in the man's

arms before she took off his mask. "He wore a mask. And under it...
I swear I saw..."

"That doesn't mean he's a ghost!" Philippe scoffed.

"No of course not, don't you understand!" Raoul cried,
springing from the bed despite the pain in his skull. "He *is* a man!
A human man! I don't know how he could put on such a charade,
but the Ghost is Christine's teacher, and he has her! He has her
captive!"

"I'm calling the doctor back in to give you something to calm
down," Philippe said slowly, patting Raoul on the arm. Sabine
heaved a fresh sob and ran from the room weeping. "Now look
what you've done!"

"I have to find her, Philippe! The fiend has her! He caught me
and did this to me!" Raoul pointed at his neck even as dizziness
overtook him and he fell back into his bed. He had been certain he
was about to die before Christine saved him.

"You're telling me some Phantom strangled you and nearly
broke your skull? You're lucky you're so hard-headed or you'd be
dead."

"Christine begged him not to," Raoul muttered. Everything
was jumbled and it hurt to try to remember. But when he closed
his eyes, he saw one image plainly. A masked face and eyes like a
demon's. "His eyes glowed."

"Now you do sound insane," Philippe sighed just as a servant
entered. "Go get me the laudanum for my brother. Then—what's
that?"

"A letter for Monsieur le Vicomte," the footman stuttered.
Raoul's heart jumped. "I was given instructions to only hand it to
him and to tell him it was from the Opera."

"Give it here!" Raoul grabbed the letter. The hand on the
address was delicate. It had to be from Christine. His head swam as
he tried to focus on the words on the ivory paper.

Raoul,

I pray this reaches you before you have done anything rash. Please believe me when I tell you I am in no danger. I can explain everything. Go to the masked ball at the Opera this Tuesday night. At twelve o'clock, stand near the door that leads to the rotunda. Wear a white domino and be carefully masked. As you love me, do not let yourself be recognized.

~ Christine

"Well, what does the little trollop have to say?" Philippe asked as Raoul read and re-read the note. He didn't understand.

"She says she's safe and..." He bit his lips and looked at his dubious brother. "And that she can explain."

"Well, that's encouraging," Philippe scoffed. "I hope it also says to leave her alone and never worry about this again for your own good!"

"What if she was forced to write this?" Raoul mused aloud. "What if she's with some madman? He could have killed Buquet. Everyone thinks it!"

"Who?" Philippe looked like he had a headache worse than Raoul's. And Raoul's was significant.

"The stagehand who died the other week. The one I found! All night I listened to stories about how he was on the wrong side of the Opera Ghost, how he'd seen the thing's face."

Raoul remembered the night before and the image of Christine with that man. Raoul had thought at first it was just a trick of the moonlight, the way his face had looked like a skull. That was the story the Buquet had spread that got him killed: the ghost looked dead under his mask. But how? Was it a second mask? Why would he go to such lengths?

"Raoul you need rest, you're raving," Philippe said, calmly stroking Raoul's arm and pushing him back into his bed. "You didn't see anything. It was a dream. It was all a dream."

"This isn't like when I was a child!" Raoul snarled, but the look in his brother's eyes made him doubt his senses.

"You were eighteen. Remember how you woke every night, convinced the house was on fire after Father died?" Philippe went on, soothing and infuriating. "Stories have a way of getting into your head, little brother."

"I didn't dream it!" Raoul cried again.

"Sir, I have it," a servant's voice came from the door. Raoul recognized the brown bottle the vale held.

"I don't need to be drugged! I need to go—" But Raoul didn't know what he needed to do.

"Take it. For me and so I can tell Sabine I'm looking after you." Raoul stared at his brother, hanging onto his petulance for one second longer, before nodding and downing the concoction. "Good boy. Now, rest some more."

Raoul fell back onto his pillows. The memories danced through his head. And they were memories, no matter what Philippe said. He had seen what he had seen; but what had he seen? What an absurd way to think about it. But he remembered that moment in the clearing, the full moon so bright above and a death's head revealed for a terrible instant before he had stopped them.

"Why would he have another mask?" Raoul muttered, surprising himself by speaking aloud. If Philippe heard, he didn't say anything. He had to learn the truth. And he would do anything to be there so Christine would tell him. At the masquerade. There he would finally learn the truth.

E rik had not needed to borrow César to get his message to Shaya, but it had saved him some time and had hastened his journey home. It was a surprise to find Jean Paul actually awake when he returned the gelding to his stable.

"Again!" Lachenal cried, rushing towards the white horse, and Erik could not help but smile as the groom lumbered into the stable only to come face to face (or face to mask) with a ghost. "Mary Mother of Christ!"

"Go away," Erik ordered, and Lachenal obeyed as quickly as his wobbly legs would carry him. Erik didn't have the will to give the man anything more for whatever new tale he'd spread today. He turned his attention to César, stroking the horse's white flank and appreciating how he nuzzled into Erik's hand. Animals were so much better than people. So much simpler and kinder. Well, most people.

"What did you do to Jean Paul?"

He looked up to see Christine framed by the afternoon's fading sunlight. His heart ached just to see her return to him once again. "I told him he wasn't needed." Christine looked dubious, as she should. "Is it done?"

"Yes. Yours?" Erik nodded. "You're still worried though, aren't you?"

"I don't trust people," Erik sighed. Christine raised an eyebrow. "Most people."

"It will be alright. I promise." Christine took his hands as she said it, and César whinnied in jealousy.

"I trust you," Erik whispered. If he said it enough times, it would be true. "Were you successful with your shopping?"

"I was. And no, you cannot see. I want it to be a surprise." Her tone was mocking, though gentle.

"Are you still put out that I won't tell you my costume?" Erik asked and found himself for the first time since that terrible boy had ruined their peace, grinning. "I promise you will recognize me."

"Well, we shall see if you can recognize me then too," Christine said defiantly.

"I would know you anywhere," Erik replied, reaching to touch her perfect face. How could someone like her even bear him? It didn't matter. He would not let her go. "I would find you anywhere, my angel."

15. Masquerade

Shaya adjusted the purple velvet cape over his shoulders as he pushed through the crowd in the *Place de L'Opéra*. He was not even inside and already the noise and chaos were astounding. He had heard stories about the Opera's legendary masked balls, where champagne flowed in fountains and only the requirement to remain in costume kept things from dissolving into an orgy that would rival the depravity of Rome. It was barely past eleven o'clock and things were just beginning.

"Invitation?" the satyr looming by the door asked. Shaya fumbled under his cape for the gilt-edged paper and presented it, still wondering if it was legitimate. He didn't trust anything from Erik, even a literal engraved invitation. "Go on in," the man rumbled, and Shaya obeyed.

If it had been a stream of revelers going in, Shaya now stepped into the sea and he was immediately drowning. Every soul in Paris had to have donned a new face to parade themselves into the glittering *Grand Foyer*, intent on one more night of debauchery before the dour Lenten season. The music of the little orchestra down below the *Grand Escalier* in the rotunda strained over the laughter and cries of excitement as dancers twirled and others peered from behind their disguises. The spectacle was astounding.

A reveler jostled Shaya from behind and Shaya spun to give a reprimand. The skull that confronted him made his heart jump before he realized it was nothing but another mask.

"Apologies," a deep voice spoke, and Shaya gave a nod as the man moved on. Shaya keenly felt the weight of his own black mask, the rough papier mâché already rubbing uncomfortably into his cheeks. He envied some of the attendees around him who were already swilling down champagne and wine to numb their senses and worries for a time.

Moving further into the Opera was like walking into an explosion of color and movement. In all honesty, it made Shaya's head spin. He was used to a quiet life, not a hundred strangers cavorting around him in masks that all looked like Erik. A few attendees had made even less effort at a real costume than Shaya, wearing only a mask to match their shining silk gowns or black, swallow-tailed coats. The rest had taken the ball as an opportunity to indulge their wildest fantasies.

Everywhere Shaya looked was a new color or character: fairies, bulls, devils, goddesses, cats, kings, ghouls, and heroes. There was laughter and gossip in every corner, amid the clink of glasses filled to overflowing. There were performers set throughout the crowd, jugglers and dancers and illusionists.

Though the crowd was a tempest of noise and motion, it was slow going for Shaya to get through. Not that he was in a great rush. Erik's ominous note in blood-red ink had commanded that Shaya wait in box twelve on the second tier and listen. There, allegedly, he would hear proof that Christine Daaé was in control of her own actions. Shaya of course intended to do much more than listen if he could.

He should have done more than listen the other night. He had been sure that it was the right course to show the young vicomte that Christine was in the clutches of another man, but he had not counted on the boy's rashness. Shame on Shaya for underestimating the stupidity of masculine youth. He had heard the distant sound of voices in the night and snuck quietly through the woods to catch

Erik and the girl, but he had not been fast enough. First, he had heard cries and then commotion. By the time he reached the scene, Raoul was unconscious with welts around his neck. And Erik was gone.

Shaya had dragged the boy to a carriage then home. He'd been impossible to wake, much to Shaya's dismay. He wanted to know what the young vicomte had seen and if he knew yet of the nature of his rival. Shaya could not lose this one ally so soon after discovering him. He had a deep suspicion that Erik's plan for the evening, whatever it was, involved the young hero.

Shaya made his way through the crowd, listening to conversations in snippets and noting all the small dramas and delights happening throughout the party. A monkey and a butterfly with dark skin quarreled in a corner, a devil and a jester danced for a brief moment before scurrying away for a tryst. A goldfish flirted with a dancer that had managed to be half-man and half-woman, and Shaya wondered which side of them was giving the fish pause. Finally, he perched himself in the gallery above the staircase, where he could watch the pageantry until it was time.

"Shouldn't we stop for a drink?" Antoine asked as they passed into the rotunda from the patron's entrance, and Raoul groaned.

"Or more than one!" Philippe chuckled in turn. Raoul spun towards the men who had insisted on following him to the masquerade, mocking him the whole carriage ride here about how he looked the part of a blushing, naïve virgin in his white domino and mask.

"Do you two think of anything other than drinking?"

"Sometimes we think about fucking," Antoine replied without losing a beat as Raoul rolled his eyes. "Ah, here we are!" Antoine grabbed two glasses from a silver tray as it passed and handed one to Philippe before he downed his own. The two older men made quite a contrast to one another. Philippe was dressed as a soldier, cutting a dashing form, while Antoine had donned a harlequin's mask to go with his top hat and opera cape. Raoul disliked how much he resembled the figure that had been with Christine.

"I'll leave you two to your exertions," Raoul grumbled. At least if they were drinking and carousing, they could not distract him while he looked for Christine.

"Do try to have some fun out there!" Antoine called, and Raoul thanked heaven that he was rid of the man for now as he launched himself into the churning crowd. He vaguely knew where it was that she had said to meet him so he had arrived early to find the appointed spot.

He pushed his way through the crowd, feeling like a pariah of grief and anger in this throng of jubilation. At least he didn't have to plaster on a false smile as his mask did the work for him. At last he came to the right place and sulked against the wall as a clock somewhere began to strike midnight. He hoped he was not late.

"This way."

Raoul jumped as a figure in a black domino took his hand and spoke with the voice of the woman he loved.

"Chris—"

"Hush!" she hissed, glaring over her shoulder as she pulled him through the crowd to who-knew-where. Was she taking him somewhere to be alone? Was this the moment when she would finally admit her feelings matched his and she wanted nothing to do with the villain who controlled her?

A hundred scenarios played out in his mind as they climbed the great staircase and headed to the boxes, but a cry of horror from behind them made Raoul turn. A commotion had gone up through the crowd and people were rushing to see whatever new spectacle had been unveiled.

"What on earth is everyone looking at?" Raoul asked aloud, as he craned his neck to see past the swarm that had gathered to overlook the grand double-horseshoe staircase below. Christine stopped dead in her tracks so abruptly that Raoul nearly crashed into her. He looked down and knew immediately what was causing the uproar. The sight made the blood in Raoul's veins turn to ice.

"Bloody hell," Christine whispered beside him.

Raoul wanted to look at her to see if there was fear or amazement in her eyes to mirror what was in her voice, but he could not look away from the figure below: Death himself, clad head to toe in scarlet.

It was a costume like nothing Raoul had ever seen. The specter wore a wide, plumed hat and a great red silk cape that flowed behind him like blood as he stalked up the *grand escalier*. But it was not the riot of red velvet and gold fringe that made the figure terrifying, it was his face. The mask was horrible, with a sunken hole for a nose and terrible deep-set eyes. The skin – Raoul had to remind himself it was not *real* skin – was taut over jagged, sharp cheekbones, and was marred by terrible scars, as if from long ago battles against the devil himself. But what was worse, so much worse, was that he knew in his soul he had seen this death's mask before. And very recently.

"Red Death, stalking abroad," Christine muttered, and Raoul shivered.

Below them, the figure – Red Death, as Christine had named him – came at last to the landing before the entrance to the auditorium and turned slowly, surveying the crowd with eyes that seemed to burn. The revelers grew silent as the deathly gaze passed over them one by one. Christine's hand tightened on Raoul's wrist as Red Death's eyes swept up to the galleries and took in each masked face staring at him with slow, defiant curiosity.

"We should go now..." Christine muttered, but it was too late: Red Death had found them.

"That's him, isn't it?" Raoul demanded, looking between Christine and the grim figure below. "Is that your—"

"Now," Christine ordered, grabbing Raoul and dragging him from the macabre sight.

Christine led Raoul up flights of stairs to the higher, cheaper boxes where he had never been before. It was deserted compared to the chaos below, and even so Christine looked over her shoulders in worry every tenth step. Was she afraid that Raoul's rival was following? Finally, she ushered them into a deserted box, pushing Raoul away while she peeked out the door.

"Is he there?" Raoul charged towards the door. "Let me see him! Let us end this like men!"

"For God's sake, I did not summon you here so you could have some sort of duel over me!" Christine growled, shoving Raoul back with a force that stunned him as she threw herself against the door to block the way.

"Then why have you brought us here?!" Raoul demanded.

"To make you see reason and to explain what you saw." Christine heaved a sigh as she said it. "I should have been clearer before, and I'm sorry to have led you on, but—"

"But you have chosen him?" Raoul finished for her with a scoff. "You are a great actress, Christine, but not good enough to make me believe that."

"It's the truth," Christine said, shoulders sagging in dejection.

"The truth? I will tell you the truth!" Raoul snapped, yanking off his mask. It was strange that Christine flinched as he did it. "Red Death out there is the man I saw you with trying to seduce you, the one who lied to you and said he was an angel! And such a deception came easily to him because he has adopted some fantastic fiction that he is a ghost! But a ghost could not do this!" He pulled down his collar to reveal the bruises Christine's paramour had left.

"I can explain," Christine protested.

"And it will all be more lies that fiend has forced you to tell! Because you are not the sort of girl who cavorts about at balls and goes for rides in the Bois with a man who wears a mask beneath his mask! You aren't a hussy who breaks men's hearts! You are not that cruel."

"You know nothing about me, Raoul de Chagny," Christine said calmly as she removed her mask. Raoul nearly gasped. She was a woman transformed, hardness in her eyes and resolve stiffening her jaw. The pure fire in her expression rendered her almost unrecognizable from the demure girl whose scarf he had saved a decade before. "And you know nothing about him."

"But—"

"No buts. No claims that you know my heart because of how I sing. I sing for him, don't you understand? Every note is for *him*." Christine looked away, regret edging on her defiance. "The girl you loved is gone. Let her go and *let me be*."

"She's not," Raoul protested, unmanly tears welling in his eyes as he rushed to Christine and took her in his arms, worry and remorse eclipsing his anger. "She's still there, but I can see her drowning. And it is he that seeks to pull you down to the depths."

"I'm not a scarf you can snatch from the sea," Christine whispered, closing her eyes and refusing to meet Raoul's gaze. "If you try to come after me, the tide will take us both."

"I can save you, my Christine," Raoul implored. He wanted nothing more than to be as bold as her duplicitous angel and kiss her, but her face hardened again before he could get too close, eyes finally meeting his.

"He is the one who saved me," Christine said slowly, pushing Raoul away. "I don't *need* to be saved again. I don't want to be. I am his, and you must accept that."

Raoul stumbled back, shaking his head in disbelief. "Christine."

"He knows me, Raoul, as you never will." There was something in her eyes and tone that made Raoul's stomach churn. She was admitting to his worst fears.

"I am beginning to," Raoul sneered, and Christine had the gall to look offended. As if a woman who had rejected him and all but confirmed herself to be the harlot everyone had told him she was had any right to modesty. "It must be so very romantic, to love a ghost who tears down your rivals and dances with you in the night! Christ in heaven, to think I wanted to cast my good name into the gutter with an opera *whore*!"

Christine closed her eyes as tears fell down her cheek. "At least you believe me now."

"You must love him terribly," Raoul spat back. "To let him ruin you so."

"I can't say," Christine stammered, but Raoul had no time for another equivocation or lie.

"You come here to send me away and you can't even admit you love him! Well, that's quite a thing!" Raoul wailed. "Good then! I don't think you *can* love, Christine. I should be glad to be rid of you."

Raoul shoved past her and this time she made no attempt to stop him. He stormed through the empty lobby and back down to the party below, where things had somehow grown even louder. He had a glass of champagne in his hand instantly and downed it in one gulp. Another followed, and another, but the liquor did nothing to ease his fury or shame.

She had humiliated him again! She had cast his heart aside like garbage *again*! How could she? How he hated the man who had changed her from the girl he knew and loved. How he wanted revenge. But what was the point? Would it bring Christine back to him? Why did he still want her after all of this?

He was a fool, such a fool, Raoul thought miserably as he drank and stumbled through the crushing crowd and tears fell behind his mask. The refrain of his failure and idiocy kept on in his head as he stumbled away, determined to find something, anything to stem the pain in his heart. He wanted somewhere to weep alone. Either that or a quiet place to plan his next move against the man who had ruined his dreams. A man whose name he still did not know.

Christine waited, gazing at the chandelier blazing over an empty auditorium as she slumped against the wall. She pushed the tears from her cheeks and listened for any sound from the neighboring box where Shaya had been told to wait. Perhaps he was waiting for her in the same way.

"Are you there, Monsieur Motlagh?" Christine asked aloud. In answer, she heard the click of a door opening, and a beat later the door of her box swung out to reveal the Persian staring at her as she rose to meet him. "Are you satisfied?"

"Not in the slightest," Shaya replied, and Christine sighed. "I heard a woman lying to a man to save his life."

"I wasn't lying!" Christine exclaimed. "Why will you not believe? Why have you stalked my steps for a week and never simply asked me if I am safe?"

"Because I cannot trust your words as long as you are under Erik's control."

"You have to believe that, don't you?" Christine asked, realization dawning. "As long as Erik is a monster who corrupts and controls, you can blame him for your brother's death and absolve Ramin of his part in it."

"Don't you dare say his name!" Shaya burst out.

"I am not him," she said firmly.

"No, you're not. *He* was a good, kind man. You're nothing but a naïve girl blinded by your ambition and your fantasies of – what was it? An angel of music? Erik is the opposite of an angel, and you know that." Shaya glowered at her, and Christine tried to remain calm, to remind herself that it was not her to whom he spoke, but to a ghost he had not forgiven for past sins.

"I know him," Christine replied.

"Which is why you could not say you love him," Shaya countered with a cruel sneer so like the one which had recently twisted Raoul's face.

"If you won't believe my words, then I will give you further proof that I do not fear Erik," Christine said slowly. "Watch. And then, please, leave us alone."

Christine did not wait for a reply. She flew from the box and back to the stairs, her black satin cape billowing behind her before she discarded it. She didn't need her disguise anymore. Erik had been brave enough to show his face to the world. Like everyone else at the masquerade below, she was ready to be who she truly was. The person only Erik saw. Tonight, she would be that woman before all of Paris.

The crowd continued to part like the sea before Moses as Erik stalked the masquerade, and it was difficult not to smile. Erik was admittedly unused to keeping his face this still, to maintain the illusion that what the onlookers gaped at was a mask. He listened as people whispered behind his back, reading the embroidered warning on his cloak. *I am Red Death stalking abroad! Do Not*

Touch Me! He believed Poe would be pleased with his homage, as he stared down at the nobility who had come to celebrate while the world suffered in winter and plagues outside.

He had come to the rotunda below the *Grand Escalier* where the patrons tended to gather. The orchestra faltered in their waltz and the dancers scattered away as Erik made his circuit of the room.

"And what if we do touch you?" a defiant voice asked from the crowd as Erik passed. He turned slowly to meet the eyes of a tall man with pale blond hair in a harlequin mask. Again, Erik had to force his expression not to change, for the cruelty in the man's ice-blue eyes reminded Erik powerfully of the last time he had exposed his face in public before the elite.

"Then my curse would fall upon you," Erik replied, his mouth perfectly still, and a murmur went up in the crowd. The blue-eyed man sneered.

"Prove it then. Curse me before I take off that mask," he said as he lunged at Erik. He was obviously drunk, for the movement was slow and inelegant, and Erik had more than enough time to react, catching the idiot's wrist in a grip like iron. The man cried out pathetically as Erik twisted his arm and laughed, his face still as stone.

"You asked. I shall oblige," Erik whispered, staring into those hateful eyes and squeezing hard enough to bruise. Even with a mask concealing his face, Erik could see how the lout was clearly terrified and it was delicious.

"Or perhaps—" Erik dropped the man's wrist at once, spinning to observe the woman who had addressed him. "You will show mercy."

She was dressed in black and silver, a diaphanous costume of silken veils over a tight bodice that was scandalously revealing. It reminded Erik strongly of the dancers' garb for the Walspurgisnacht scene of *Faust*, but this was no mere imp or witch.

This was their ruler, for a silver crown rested on her head above a face concealed by a mask of black lace.

"Who are you to command death?" Erik asked defiantly. The woman smirked and laughed, a deep, smoky sound that crackled like a dying fire.

"Even the underworld has a queen," she replied, and Erik used every ounce of control he had not to smile. Instead, he bowed and extended his hand as the crowd began to whisper around them.

"Would you do me the honor of a dance then, your majesty?" The crowd gasped as his Persephone took his hand and he swept her into his arms. "I keep my promises," Erik added in the softest whisper, using his ventriloquist's skill to speak only to Christine as their dance began. She smiled.

It broke the spell his face had cast over the crowd, that smile. Suddenly he was just a man, another reveler at the masquerade, dancing with the woman he loved. He tilted his head closer to hers and enjoyed the sparkle of the lights in her green-gold eyes as they moved across the floor.

"Did I fool you at all?" Christine asked.

"Perhaps for a moment," Erik replied, warm and quiet. "I was not expecting you to have such a trick up your sleeve."

"I learned from the best." Christine's eyes were playful behind her mask, and it made him quite annoyed he could not embrace her right now. But it was trying to kiss her after a dance that had gone so wrong before.

"Is it done?" he asked, and she looked away.

"Halfway. Raoul is taken care of. Shaya remains unconvinced, but I may just have changed that. Or I hope I have." She nodded to the crowd and Erik looked over her head as they spun, catching sight of a glowering figure by the fountain under the stairs. Even masked, he would know Shaya's disapproving frown anywhere.

"You are truly a wonder," Erik told her, as they spun across the floor and other couples joined. "I'll deal with him later. I want to enjoy this for now. I so rarely get to be...normal."

"Because you are extraordinary," Christine replied so easily, her eyes so warm and perfect it made the world melt away.

"You know what I mean. To walk among the living, just for one night, and not be chased away." Erik sighed through his nose, or what he had that passed for one. "It's not entirely terrible."

"I've found it to be overrated," Christine muttered sourly, but then smiled and leaned to Erik as the music finished, standing on tiptoe to whisper in his ear. "I'd rather be home. With you."

Erik glanced across the rotunda to see Shaya huff and stalk away. "And we will be. Let me attend to our friend. Wait for me."

"Be careful," Christine ordered, and Erik bowed to her again in acknowledgement. Shaya was gone when Erik turned, but it was no matter. Erik would find him. The crowd still parted before him as he walked through, but there was less fear in their eyes now. Another gift Christine had given him.

Shaya stalked back through the bacchanal to one place he knew for sure was silent and quiet: the boxes where he had listened to the Vicomte and Erik's whore. What a waste it had all been. Erik's control of the girl was more insidious than Shaya could have ever imagined. It was all so familiar it made Shaya want to retch.

Shaya stopped short of the box he had occupied before, removing his mask and casting it aside. He hated wearing the thing while Erik of all people paraded about with none on. The utter gall of that man – if he could even be called a man.

"Aren't you worried about being recognized, Daroga?" Shaya turned to see Erik looming behind him, his terrible face made even more horrifying by the smile upon it. "Oh wait, I'm your only friend who isn't paid to remain with you. What a shame."

"Aren't you worried someone will see your mask coming alive?"

"They're all drunk. Who knows what they think they see," Erik said with an infuriating shrug. "But I came to ask if you had seen enough from Christine to allay your suspicions."

"She confirmed she's a whore, if that's what you mean," Shaya sneered, thinking of the wanton way Daaé had displayed herself to dance with Red Death. "What did you promise her? What lies did you have to tell her for her to spread her legs for a monster like you?"

"Watch your tongue," Erik growled.

"Do you really fancy yourself her protector? After you've destroyed and degraded her?"

"I have warned you, Daroga, I will not let you insult the woman I love." Erik's tone was deadly as he advanced. Any other time Shaya would have cowered, but now he sneered.

"You are not capable of love."

"Oh I am," Erik replied. "I always have been. Despite what you want to believe. I love her, just as I loved—"

Erik stumbled back when Shaya struck him, perhaps more in shock than pain. Shaya's fist stung though, as he watched Erik rub his jaw. Maybe he'd done some damage. "Don't you dare say his name."

"That was below you," Erik muttered.

"She doesn't love you," Shaya hissed, and Erik winced like it was another blow. "I heard that boy ask her, not an hour ago. And your little slut could have so easily lied to him. But she didn't – because she cannot even bear the thought!" Did he see pain in Erik's twisted face? Good. He deserved that and more. "She will *never* love you."

"I know, Daroga," Erik murmured, his eyes downcast. "I'm not a fool. I know she'll never love me. But what she gives me when I'm with her...it's like love. Her pity, her trust, even her lust. It's close enough." Erik looked back up, his eyes shining and calm. "I love her enough for us both."

"It won't be enough to keep her with you," Shaya countered, sickened by the contrition in Erik's words. "One day, you'll lose her."

"I know that too," Erik replied with such sincerity it made Shaya tremble. "I know that something, someday, will take her from me. I will lose her to you, or that boy, or another opera's stage, or even death itself, whether it is in a few days or fifty years. No matter how much time I have with her, it will not be forever. And thus it will not be enough, because only forever will suffice. So, I swear to you, I will fight for every moment I can. I will face you, that boy, the world. At the end of her days, I will stride into Hades like a new Orpheus and defy death itself for one more second at her side. So do not try to take her from me, Daroga. Because you will regret it."

Even Shaya could not deny the conviction and ardor in Erik's eyes. The monster truly loved that foolish girl. And that filled Shaya with hope as much as dread.

"I won't take her, Erik," Shaya said slowly. "I don't need to. You say now that you don't care that she doesn't love you. But you will. Day by day, that knowledge will eat at your soul. That fear and doubt; it will consume you. And I'll be here, to watch it drive you mad." Shaya smiled grimly. "I will have the pleasure of finally seeing you be the one to lose what you love most. Oh, it will be glorious."

Erik stared at him, and for the first time since Persia, when Shaya had seen a broken man slumped over Ramin's body, Erik appeared an entirely pathetic creature.

"We shall see," Erik intoned quietly as he swept past Shaya and pulled open the door of a box. "Get out of my Opera," he ordered before he disappeared into the opening. Shaya did not follow. He didn't need to. He turned instead – just in time to see a figure in black rush away. Someone had been listening.

Did he pursue the fool? Shaya shook his head. He had no strength for it. He wanted to go home to Darius and sleep. He would need the rest before he sought out Raoul de Chagny once again. It would be a task to convince the boy that Christine was not a faithless whore. But people tended to believe what they wanted when it came to the objects of their love.

Erik believed Christine Daaé would be loyal to him. And Shaya would do everything in his power to prove him wrong. The girl was fickle and reckless, anyway. It would not be hard.

Christine raced to her dressing room from the boxes, her heart pounding as tears stung her eyes. Was there no extreme of emotion she wouldn't feel tonight? Fear, joy, anger, shame...and pity. Such terrible pity. It was the same pity that had consumed her on that morning that felt like ages ago, when she had first seen Erik crouched and broken in a corner after she had torn off his mask. She reached the dressing room door, happy to find she had forgotten to lock it.

She could still smell the stink of the party – the smoke and liquor and sweat – when she came into the quiet of her sanctuary and lit the oil lamp on her vanity with a shaking hand. She couldn't speak to the dead, so she had to write it down. She had to remember those words exactly before they faded from her mind. She had to remember how they made her feel, so she could be brave.

She grabbed pen and paper from the drawer and began to scrawl, her heart racing. *He said, 'no matter how much time I have with her, it will not be forever' and he was not afraid of that.* Her hands shook as she wrote and remembered different words that had etched themselves so deep in her heart that believing them had been as natural as breathing. *You told me 'whatever you love, you will lose. It's better not to love at all and avoid the pain.' You were wrong.* Shaya's voice was in her head too, telling Erik that she did not love him. And never would.

"Poor Erik," she whispered, her heart breaking all over again as she paused. The words on the page mocked her. *At the end of her days, I will stride into Hades, like a new Orpheus, and defy death itself for one more second at her side.* He had said that, even when moments before he had admitted that he knew she didn't... "My poor Erik," she sighed again, throwing down her pen and shutting her eyes.

And then, the music began. It always surprised her, even after so many months, how Erik's voice worked upon her soul like magic. He was singing from behind the mirror, plaintive and perfect, and what a song he had chosen. The wedding night song from *Roméo et Juliette.* Why had he chosen it, she wondered, even as the angelic notes stirred her heart. Did he think their story was doomed to be a tragedy? Did it matter if it was? Or was this to be a new wedding night, now that all the obstacles had been swept away?

She rose, tucking the paper into her bodice to keep those words close to her heart. She put out the light as Erik's voice rose, transforming Gounod's melody into something truly extraordinary.

"You're late, Erik," she teased. What was in his heart as he sang to her? Was the doubt there that Shaya had promised? All she could hear was love, but that meant there had to be pain.

"Fate links me to thee, forever and a day," Erik sang, and her pulse quickened at the words. It was true. Fate had brought her an angel, fate had entangled her story with the Opera Ghost's, and now there was no running from it, no matter how part of her wished she could. Her angel sang to her, passion and desire in each note that kindled need within her like a match to a bonfire.

She walked to the mirror without fear, seeing only the hope and joy on her face that had driven away the pain. She could do it. She could follow him back to where she belonged. Where she was meant to be.

"Fate links me to thee, forever and a day," he exalted as the mirror slid aside and revealed Red Death offering his hand. Christine took it without pause, ready to return to the underworld. She was bound there, to him. Perhaps she had been bound from the moment she set foot in the Opera. It was freeing, to not have a choice. To know she would always follow, not just because of the secrets Erik knew or the music that entranced her, but because of the truth in her heart.

"Fate links me to thee, forever and a day," she sang with him as they descended home.

R aoul's head still rang with the voice of an angel when he stumbled through the front door of the Chagny manor. The commotion in the foyer shook him from the fog he had been in since he'd watched Christine disappear into thin air. To his surprise Sorelli and Adèle were walking towards him, huffing with consternation.

"Oh good, another one!" Sorelli crowed. "And how drunk are you?"

"Looks like very," Adèle answered before Raoul could. "Let's hope you're sober enough to talk some sense into him, because I'm not going to bother."

"Talk sense into who?" Raoul stammered. He did not like coming into conversations where he had missed the beginning. "Is Philippe alright?"

"He's useless!" Sorelli cried in reply. "He cares more about talking that jackass off a cliff than attending to someone who left the party early for him!"

"Antoine isn't well," Adèle translated. "But he and your brother are your problem now. Adieu, sweet boy." Adèle took the sputtering dancer by the arms and led her out the door as Raoul rushed to the sitting room.

It was impossible that anyone had experienced a worse evening than Raoul had, but Antoine certainly looked it. He was sprawled on a couch, eyes closed and face pale. Philippe looked up from where he was slumped in a chair by his friend.

"What happened to him?" Raoul asked numbly.

"He says Red Death cursed him," Philippe sighed. "He's been raving. Saying the thing was a ghost." Antoine groaned at that but didn't open his eyes.

"He is a ghost," Raoul said simply. "The Phantom. The one who's haunted the Opera for so long and corrupted Christine. It was him."

"You were adamant yesterday that said phantom was a man," Philippe scoffed.

"That was before I saw what he did tonight. Before I heard him." Raoul's mind strayed back to that supernaturally beautiful voice filling Christine's dressing room, singing from the very walls.

"Bloody hell, was something in the water there tonight? Have you gone mad too?" Raoul didn't look at his brother. He knew the annoyed and dubious expression he'd be making. Instead, he stared at the fire as he remembered.

"Christine summoned me there to end things," Raoul began, his heart still stinging. "She told me how she had changed and how she chose him. The other. And I said cruel things and left her there. But the more I thought, the more I *knew* she had to have lied. She is being controlled, Philippe, by her fear of this man or her gratitude for her career. I was sure of it. So I went to her dressing room."

"You what?" Philippe balked. "Raoul, I must tell you that following young ladies into their private rooms and stalking their steps is not the way to win a lover. That should be obvious."

"I was drunk, delirious with heartbreak, and I found nothing. I heard her coming and hid. I was ashamed but, I have to admit, I also wanted to catch them or confront them if I could." Raoul would have blushed at the foolishness of that plan, had it not succeeded.

"You absolute idiot," Philippe sighed.

"But I did see!" Raoul cried, grabbing his brother by the lapels. "I saw her! She came into the room and wrote a letter and wept! She wept over *him* when she should have been weeping over me!"

"And how do you know that, little brother?" Philippe asked, carefully prying Raoul's hands off his coat.

"I heard her say his name!" Raoul protested, grabbing his head to shut out the echoes of what he had heard next. "And then he came! The walls – the mirror! Philippe, the mirror started singing. It was a voice like I've never heard in my life, except for the other night. It was the voice of—"

"An angel." Raoul turned to see that Antoine had revived. And his face was grim.

"Exactly," Raoul muttered. "And then I swear I saw Red Death there too, in the mirror before Christine disappeared from that room! I can't explain it!"

"Little brother, you were drunk," Philippe said soothingly. "Just like Antoine here. You both still are."

"What was the name?" Antoine asked, ignoring Philippe. Raoul had never seen the man so serious.

"Why does it matter?" Philippe sighed.

Antoine did not look away from Raoul, his eyes wild. "Was it Erik?"

The world began to spin again, like it had before Christine had vanished. "How in God's name did you know that?" Raoul whispered.

"I told you, Philippe! It's him! The one!" Antoine said, as if it made sense.

"What are you talking about?" Raoul demanded.

"When I saw Red Death, I swore I knew that face! I'd seen it before! And now you've confirmed it!" Antoine went on as he grabbed Raoul.

"You're raving! Both of you!" Philippe cried, throwing up his hands, but Raoul was intent on Antoine.

"You weren't there! Neither of you were there that night," Antoine continued, and Raoul's pulse began to race in horror. "And I've never told the whole story to you! What was the use? Our fathers were dead. Did it matter who started the fire?"

"You said it was the gypsies," Philippe muttered, and Raoul looked to his brother. He'd never told him even that much. "They were brought to entertain, but there was a thief among them that started the fire."

"Not a thief – their leader!" Antoine yelled. "I saw him! He was a magician! Raoul, that's how he made your Christine disappear! How he lives as a ghost! He was a magician with the voice of an angel and the face of death. A face I saw again tonight. A voice you heard. And his name was—"

"Erik," Raoul repeated, hating the sound. "She called him Erik."

"My father was the one who hired him, he knew him somehow," Antoine muttered, and he looked as if he was as sick as Raoul. "I looked for him in the fire and I heard him yelling a name. He was calling out to someone named Erik! I didn't know who it was. Until now."

"What are you saying?" Raoul asked. He wanted to hear it aloud. He wanted to know.

"I'm saying that the man who haunts the Opera and stole your Christine is the same man who killed my father," Antoine replied, slow and dire. "And yours."

"If this is true, then we have to find him and bring him to justice," Philippe interjected, but Raoul's eyes were locked on Antoine's. And the fire there ignited Raoul's own soul.

"No," Raoul declared, as steel stiffened his spine. "We have to kill him."

Erik was worried, he was brave enough to admit that. He was afraid that when he stopped singing it would end, all of it. So, he kept singing all the way home, holding onto Christine as he had the first night he had brought her to his realm. But this time when they entered his home, it was different. This time Christine flew to his arms and kissed him the instant he paused. It was such a gift, each time she gave him her lips, and Erik savored it as he embraced her.

"I missed you," Christine whispered as she pulled back, stroking his bare face with unfathomable tenderness. "Isn't that strange?"

"No," he sighed back. "Sometimes I miss you even when you're here. When I can't touch you, or see your smile, or know your heart." She surged up and kissed him again, ardent and insistent.

"Make love to me, please," Christine commanded, her cheek to his.

"As you command."

It was she who pushed off his hat and started to divest him of his cumbersome costume, her mouth eager and warm all the while. He helped as well as he could, but he was just as intent on unlacing her bodice and exposing her skin, tearing at the flimsy fabric when necessary. It was she who guided them, leading Erik to the couch by the fire rather than her bed. It was closer. They left a trail of clothes behind them, and he kissed Christine's breasts as she pushed him down and trapped him beneath her.

It was like the first time the dam of lust had broken between them, but now there were no bindings to keep him from holding her by the waist as he took her hard nipple between his lips. She cried out, throwing back her head, her dark hair cascading behind her.

"Erik," she whimpered his name, her fingers weaving into his long hair as she pushed him back. Her breath was ragged as she looked at him, her eyes intent. "Don't hide from me tonight."

Even with those words, he wanted to bury his ugliness against her breast and avoid her gaze, but she would not let him. She kept one hand on his cheek as the other dipped between them. He groaned in pleasure as she found his rigid cock and stroked, then gasped when she guided him into her waiting heat. He was ready to expire from pleasure already as her tightness engulfed him, slick and safe.

"Erik, I'm so sorry," Christine whispered as she kissed along his scars, and when she pulled back, he saw tears in her eyes. He wanted to ask what possible crime she had committed that she needed to apologize for, but he couldn't speak once she began to move her hips in a steady, urgent rhythm. He could only answer with his body, thrusting up into her, and she keened in response. "Erik, I heard. I heard you and Shaya. And he was wrong."

"What?" Erik gasped, confusion and panic driven back by the growing tension in his belly as Christine rode him, utterly in control, her beautiful eyes locked on his.

"Do you know what he heard Raoul say?" Erik winced at the name of his rival, but Christine kissed him in consolation, her hips gaining speed. She pulled back and her eyes were dark and dreamy. A flush spread across her breasts where they rubbed against him, soft and hot against his scars. "He said I must love you terribly."

"You don't have—"

She silenced him, a finger against his lips. Their pace was frantic now, and Erik could feel his pleasure rising to an intoxicating peak, but he had to hold back. But how could he when she was fucking him like this, her eyes so sincere?

"I tried to deny it. Because it scares me," Christine whispered, her body beginning to shudder and tighten. "It terrifies me: What I would do to keep you. What I have done. What I would let you do." Erik gasped in awe, every muscle tense as he listened in utter disbelief. "I would let you ruin me, my angel. I would let you destroy and defile me just to stay here in your arms. Don't you understand?"

"Christine..." he rasped, holding onto her as her body clenched around him.

"I love you, Erik."

He came at the sound of those impossible words, spilling into her as she joined him in the climax. They shook and sighed, riding the pulses of ecstasy, embracing and joined. She was still trembling as she kissed him, long and deep, before looking into his eyes once more.

"Say it again," he begged. He needed to know it had not been a dream, that the thing he wanted most and deserved the least was somehow, miraculously true.

"I love you. Terribly," Christine whispered, as Erik held her tight in the darkness.

Erik and Christine's story will continue in...
Angel's Fall.
Coming Spring, 2024

Acknowledgments

Thank you to all the friends, collaborators, readers, and supporters who have helped see this book into publication. I especially wish to thank Ana, for being by first beta and listening to my whining about every chapter, and Jordan for her assistance with editing. Additionally, I want to thank Andrea, Lisa, Miriel, Lynx, and Iryna for their constant support and inspiration. Angels, all of you.

This book and the entire Phantom Saga would not exist without the love, support, and inspiration of my wonderful family, especially my beloved wife, Heidi, who will always be my first reader, and my incredible daughter Tam, who can read these books when she turns fifty or so.

Until next time, be brave enough to love.

Don't miss out!

Visit the website below and you can sign up to receive emails whenever Jessica Mason publishes a new book. There's no charge and no obligation.

https://books2read.com/r/B-A-RZHV-EJLIC

BOOKS 2 READ

Connecting independent readers to independent writers.

Also by Jessica Mason

The Phantom Saga
Angel's Mask
Angel's Kiss

About the Author

Jessica Mason lives near Portland, Oregon with her wife, daughter, and corgi. She has studied opera, practiced law, and has worked as a fandom journalist and podcaster, among many varied careers. But first and foremost she has always been a storyteller. When she manages to stop writing, she enjoys gardening, travel, music, and witchcraft.

Find her on social media: @ByJessicaMason

About the Publisher

Murmuration Books is an independent publisher bringing readers, steamy, spellbinding, spooky, sensational stories. We are committed to diverse themes, new authors, and creative takes on old ideas.

For more, visit Murmurationbooks.com

Printed in Great Britain
by Amazon

31781002R00223